THE GRUMPY BOSS AGREEMENT

A BILLIONAIRE GRUMPY SUNSHINE OFFICE ROMANCE

VIVIAN WOOD

Edited by THERESA LEIGH

Cover Design By NAJLA QAMBER

Photography by WANDER AGUIAR

For the ladies that made my book better: Theresa, Patricia, and Angela. Thanks for treating my book with the love and care that it deserves.

THE SOUNDTRACK OF THE GRUMPY BOSS AGREEMENT

- Taylor Swift — Cruel Summer
- Boygenius — Emily I'm Sorry
- Cigarettes After Sex — Motion Picture Soundtrack
- TV On The Radio — Wolf Like Me
- Sufjan Stevens — Will Anybody Ever Love Me?
- Mike Posner feat Seeb — I Took A Pill In Ibiza (Remix)
- Camilla Cabello — Don't Go Yet
- Ariana, Miley, and Lana — Don't Call Me Angel
- Disclosure feat Sam Smith — Omen
- Father John Misty — Real Love Baby
- Cardi B feat Bad Bunny — I Like It
- Megan Thee Stallion feat Dua Lipa — Sweetest Pie
- Glass Animals — Heat Waves
- Mazzy Star — Fade Into You
- Taylor Swift — Vigilante Shit
- Arctic Monkeys — Baby I'm Yours
- Japanese Breakfast — Boyish

Check out the playlist on Spotify!

WANT SEE CAPE SIMON?

1. Sarah's horse stables
2. La Ville Coralle (Bennett-Taylor residence)
3. The Cape Winery
4. Cape Simon Lighthouse
5. Grandad's House
6. Lacey's Boutique
7. Movie Theater
8. Peterson's Grocery
9. South Shore Community Center
10. Cole's Beach House

Head to vivianwoodwrites.com/cape-simon-map to see a larger version.

COLE

How could my ex do this to me?

And where the hell do I go now?

I'm sitting on a stool at the bar in Gem's Diner, staring vacantly into the middle distance. Outside the window, clouds gather over the Cape Simon beach. The sky is bleached of color, and I can hear the distant rumble of thunder. A storm is coming. It's normal for the hot Georgia afternoon to turn into sideways rain for a few hours.

I'm sitting all the way at the end of the counter on a sparkly pink stool that has been in place since the Reagan administration. My dark wool suit jacket is thrown over the seat beside me, looking to all the world like a crumpled, discarded napkin.

As I absentmindedly trace the rim of my coffee cup, my thoughts are on my wedding. Or rather, on the event this morning that would have been my wedding if my fiancée, Holly, hadn't up and disappeared. She'd left me standing at the altar, with three hundred of our closest friends and family looking to me for answers.

She'd also left our son Charlie without a word of goodbye. What kind of mom does that?

A narcissist who was only with me for the money, that's who. That's the only answer I can come up with.

But there are no answers to be had today. I shove my hand through my dark hair and shift my coffee mug around.

"Hey there."

I look up, blinking, at the voice. It belongs to a pretty girl wearing a yellow and white waitress uniform. She's got a wild mass of curly, dark hair, and dark amber skin, and she clutches a tiny notepad. She scribbles something on the notepad and then smiles at me.

"Have you decided yet?"

I glance outside, trying to catch my brother Rhett's attention. I rap my knuckles against the window, and he turns, his cell phone pressed to his ear. He's wearing the same uniform that I wear. Black tux, bow tie stuffed in the pocket, top button of the shirt undone at the collar.

Rhett shakes his head and waves me off. Then he shouts into his phone, looking aggrieved. I shrug a shoulder and look back at the waitress.

"Is there anything that's fresh here? It's been a decade since I've been back to Cape Simon and I don't intend to start eating a bunch of frozen, deep-fried junk now."

The waitress flashes me a funny look.

"Everything is made fresh. We take a lot of pride in that." Her eyebrows rise and she gives me a curious look. "You're from the Cape?"

"Yep. I only came back to get married."

"Oh! Well, congrats!"

"Don't get too excited. The actual ceremony never took place," I tell her with a heavy dose of sardonic humor, as if I didn't just get stood up in front of hundreds of friends, family, and strangers. "The bride took off faster than a rabbit down a rain shaft." To punctuate my point, I let out a low whistle and quickly bounce two of my fingers along the table, miming a rabbit running away. "I'm pretty sure that this whole damn town is cursed."

Now the waitress just appears confused. "That happened today?"

I nod and sip my room-temperature coffee. "Do you see any other guys in tuxes sitting here?"

She gives me a pointed look. "No."

Outside, I spot a shiny red convertible pull up along the length of the building. A figure jumps out and stalks to the diner's front door, yanking it open. My stomach drops when I see who it is.

My brother Rex enters the restaurant with a steely expression. "There you are!" he calls as he strides over to me.

I spread my hands. "I don't need my two big brothers to babysit me. I'm perfectly fine on my own."

"Do me a favor? Stop whining. It's unbecoming." Rex gives the waitress a nod. "Hey, Pearl. I'm going to join my brother here for a bite."

The waitress's eyes go wide, and her cheeks are smudged with red. "Hi, Rex. Sure thing. Let me get you a menu. Or maybe a cup of coffee?"

"I'll have both. Thanks, sugar." Rex touches her arm.

She shudders with something like ecstasy and then hurries off. Rex tosses his dark hair, which is cut short on the sides and back of his head, but grown foppishly long in the front. He has ditched his tux shirt and jacket for his usual tight-fitting black track jacket and black joggers. His clothes casually emphasize the muscles in his arms, his trim physique, and his powerful build.

The most standout feature on Rex's body has to be his tattoos, though. Every single inch of bare skin on his arms and his neck is covered in colorful, scrawled artwork. Some are religious tattoos, some are funny, and some are thoughtful. There are at least two sets of song lyrics that I can see inked into his skin.

To me, most of his tattoos look like something an artistic school kid would doodle.

"Everybody is looking all over God's green earth for you," Rex says. "I thought you might head over here. I guess Rhett figured it out, too."

Rex looks out the window at Rhett, who is on the phone trying to cancel the rest of the wedding vendors that haven't set up already. Rhett catches his eye and nods, but turns back in the next instant.

"He getting you any money back?" Rex drawls.

"Nope. I'm on the hook for six figures." I fidget with the knife and fork already laid out on the table.

"That's absolute bullshit," he says, shaking his head. "I'm sorry about all of this, Cole. It's not what anybody wanted for you. Or for Charlie. God knows he's devastated."

I wince when Rex says my kid's name. I make a noncommittal noise and pray that he'll move on. Accepting apologies and being the object of someone else's pity has never been my thing.

Rex leans over and snags my untouched water glass, pulling it across the bar before drinking it down into a couple of gulps. I shoot him a glare.

"That's my water," I snap.

"She'll bring you another one." He shrugs.

I give him a considering look. "You couldn't have known that I would head here. I didn't even remember it existed until I walked in the door."

Rex rolls his eyes, scratching his stubbly chin. He cracks an easy grin. "It might have been the third place I tried."

I usually have a lot more patience for Rex's jokes. After all, aside from being my older brother, he is far and away my best client. But today, I have none of the goodwill or tolerance that handling Rex usually calls for.

I sigh. "What can I do for you, Rex?"

His answer is cut off by a woman and her young son rushing up to where we sit. The kid's voice is excited as he shouts, "You're Rex Bennett! You're my favorite baseball player!"

The woman blushes, crowding Rex's personal space. "Hi, Mr. Bennett. Would you sign my son's jersey?"

In the moment it takes him to look over at his fans, Rex switches gears from his normal ornery self to Mr. Popularity.

"Of course. Let's step over to the other side of the diner for just a minute. Give everybody else a little privacy." Rex's smile remains unbothered, and he winks at the boy. He stands up and moves the fans back with his sheer size alone. I see him accept a marker and jersey from the little boy as they walk away, asking, "What's your name, kid?"

I slump lower on my uncomfortable stool. Pearl stands behind the autograph seekers, juggling a cup of coffee, another glass of water, and a menu. I motion her over to me, accepting the items one by one and placing them on the bar in front of me.

She looks at Rex and I see the same emotions I've seen on every girl's face since before Rex went pro. A little awe, a lot of excitement, and no little bit of desire. I can't fault her for being star-struck. Even Holly thinks Rex is 'a perfect specimen.'

That thought irks me. I look down at my hands, trying not to clench them. Who cares what Holly thinks?

Holly dumped me this morning, in case I forgot.

"Can I bring you some food?" Pearl asks, tucking some hair behind her ear.

I want to pout, but I can't do it here.

"Can you bring me some wheat toast and…?" I think of Rex's fanatical diet and wrinkle my nose. "Two spinach salads and two plates of scrambled egg whites?"

"Sure thing. Would you like Rex's regular order? That's a five-egg white omelet with spinach and grilled deli turkey, a spinach salad with tomatoes and no dressing, and a cup of black coffee." Pearl gives me a shy smile.

Ugh. That does sound like what Rex would usually order. I sigh.

"Whatever he usually gets is fine. Bring a second order of the same for me."

She purses her lips. "How about some dessert to go with it? We have sweet potato pie, apple pie, and peach cobbler today. Made from scratch in-house by our chef, Diego."

"I don't really need a staff rundown." I sit back with a sigh. "Just bring the grown-up food, if you please."

"You've got it, hon." Her tone of voice says that she feels sorry for me, but I'm not too interested in that. She picks up the stack of laminated menus and sticks them under her arm, then pats my hand. "I'll be back with a warm-up on that coffee, shortly."

I snatch my hand back and glare at her. She's already turning away and misses my show of distaste. As she leaves, Rex makes his way back to his seat. He sits down with a sigh.

"You know, I always dreamed of being a famous baseball player. Now I am one, and I am totally sick of being recognized."

"Uh huh." I don't mention that he would probably die without the attention of his adoring fans. "Just don't go making any career-altering decisions without telling me. I am your agent, after all."

"I don't think you're on the clock right now. The fact that you're not three sheets to the wind right now is honestly pretty impressive." Rex waves me off. "Besides, I love baseball. I love being a pitcher. And I love my team. I'm definitely not making any moves. If the team ever talks about trading me, you'll be the first to know."

He grabs the full glass of water that Pearl dropped off and guzzles it down in the blink of an eye. I nod, trying not to glare at him for taking the second water without asking. Even my four-year-old son would know better than that.

I come up with, "You are my biggest client… and the biggest pain in the ass I've ever known."

Rex grins at me, his dark blue eyes sparkling. "You're damned right."

Just then, the restaurant door swings open. A bunch of high school girls enter, their gazes fixed on Rex. They start moving toward us.

"Fans incoming," I say, nodding toward the girls.

Rex turns, lets out a little groan, and starts to get up. "I'll head outside and sign autographs while we wait on food. Then we'll talk."

I stifle a snort. "Yeah. Sure."

Rex gives me a hard look, his eyes flashing. But in the next second, he's gone.

I nod and let my gaze drift back out the window. Rhett is still on the phone, which is fine by me. He has a certain voice that he uses when he's talking about sensitive topics, one I'm sure that they taught him in med school. His comforting-a-patient voice. I'm not sick and I've had just about all I can take of being a sensitive topic today.

I pull my wallet out of my pocket and take out the piece of ripped notebook paper that I'd tucked inside. Smoothing it out on the white Formica table before me, I blink at it.

The only message from the missing bride.

> Cole, I'm sorry. I can't marry you. I can't be Charlie's mother right now either. I'm going away for a while to find myself. Please take care of Charlie for me until I get back.
> Kisses, Holly

This piece of paper provides me with almost no answers. And yet, it tells me everything I need to know.

She doesn't want to marry me.

She doesn't want to be a mom to her four-year-old son.

Every time she said *I love you,* it was a lie.

What more did I really need to know?

I crumple the note and push it aside. Staring blankly out the window, I try to figure out just where I went wrong.

Was it pushing back on Holly's insane demands for a luxury wedding with seven hundred guests? Or maybe putting my foot down when she wanted to start her own line of purses even though she had almost no business sense?

It could have been the time I got angry that she came waltzing in from Paris Fashion Week with over fifty thousand dollars' worth of luggage from Louis Vuitton. Or the time that she went to her plastic surgeon for what I thought was a little Botox and came out with a completely different face and a new set of breast implants. On top of all that, I was expected to drop everything to help her while she recuperated as well.

If I really think about it, there are probably a dozen more incidents where Holly spent a lot of my fortune to make bad choices.

Pearl arrives at just the right moment with a coffee refill. She slides the steaming mug across the table and then lays down a slice of appetizing-looking peach cobbler. Before I can protest, she holds up a hand.

"The pie's on the house. We give it to all heartbroken men in tuxes who were just left at the altar," she jokes. "And I already served it to you, so there's no taking it back. It's yours now."

"Thanks," I say, somewhat surprised. Should I be hungry when I was just jilted at the altar? I honestly don't know.

She looks at me, lifting a brow. "Want me to bring you a scoop of vanilla to make your pie à la mode? It's on the house."

She obviously feels bad for me. I look down at my left hand, which should be wearing a wedding ring just now. I am sort of pathetic today.

"Stop feeling sorry for me," I demand. I grab my fork. "But ice cream does sound good."

She vanishes with a wink and returns with the scoop of ice cream on a side plate.

"Thanks," I grouse. "But again-."

She holds up her hands. "You've made yourself clear. I'm not going to baby you. Do let me know if I can get you anything else, though."

I think about asking her if she keeps any extra wives in the back, but I decide not to inflict my dark humor on her. Nobody needs that.

I dig into my cobbler first, savoring the sweet stickiness of the peaches and the pleasurable crunch of the crumbs and crust. Taking a bite of the ice cream, I notice the tangy creaminess of the icy treat.

A bell chimes softly as a young woman pushes the door open. With her bouncy, honey-blonde hair, bright yellow sundress, and sun-kissed skin, she looks like the embodiment of summer. She's on the tall side and has a slender frame. She raises her hand to greet Pearl. The two women are probably about the same age, just out of college.

Way too young for me to be noticing that the blonde is hot as hell. Not only have I only been single for all of two hours, but I'm also probably ten years older than this girl. But I find her unspeakably attractive. She seems so carefree as she takes the stool next to mine.

I imagine her as being the total opposite of Holly. Holly is always impeccable and elegant, with her dark hair pulled into a sleek bun, clad in a fluttery white silk shirt, and the latest wide-leg trousers that just came off the runway in Milan.

If my ex is polished and cosmopolitan, then this girl's beauty is the opposite. It's delicate and homegrown. She has broad cheeks set with high cheekbones. A delicate spray of freckles is dappled across the bridge of her nose and falls gently across both sides of her face. Her eyes are bright against the rosy glow of her cheeks. The sweet sweep of her butterscotch hair frames her heart-shaped face. Her button nose and expressive blush pink lips are so damn perfect that it honestly takes my breath away for a few moments.

She's *stunning*.

Our gazes meet briefly and her sparkling green eyes startle me. She arches a brow and smiles.

God, is she flirting with me? She smirks before looking down at her menu.

I swallow and straighten imperceptibly. A little shaft of sunlight pierces my near-impenetrable gloom.

2

———

SAVANNAH

"Hey, hon."

I look up from the Gem's menu to find a couple in their early sixties looming over me. The woman wears a long beige dress covered with tiny pink printed flowers. She clutches the arm of a man in faded jeans and a white T-shirt with the Atlanta Kings' crown logo on it. I squint, trying to place where I know them from.

"We went to Cullen Bridge Baptist Church with your momma," the woman says, her Georgia accent thicker than a bowl of grits. "Your mother was such a spirited woman. She was the best community advocate in the coastal South. She had a big voice and she used it to stick up for people who needed protecting. The entire state of Georgia misses her. We just wanted to say how much we loved her. We pray for her. And of course, you are in our prayers, too."

She leans forward and gently pats me on the shoulder. I force a smile to my lips.

"Thank you so much. It's nice to hear that she had such an impact."

The woman looks like I've just made her day. "You're welcome. You should come to services this Sunday! The congregation has been looking for someone to fill your mother's shoes."

I blush twenty-three shades of pink.

"That's so nice of you, but I'm afraid I attend another church," I lie. I don't attend church, but I certainly don't want to discuss my faith with a random woman.

"Our door is always open." She squeezes my shoulder and then steps back. "Have a blessed day."

"Y'all too," I say earnestly. "Happy Sunday."

They shuffle off and I lean my head back, exhaling. It's been three months since I lost my mother to pancreatic cancer and I've had countless blessings heaped upon me. I've come to dread it, but I can't bring myself to tell anyone that.

I hear my mother's voice in my head. *"Girls should be bright as sunshine and sweeter than honey."*

I let out a silent sigh, straightening. When I sit up, my gaze clashes with the handsome stranger sitting next to me. Had he just caught me internally raging about someone being nice to me?

Busted.

I can feel my face heat as embarrassment stains my cheeks red. I put my menu up in front of my face, but peek at him over the top.

He is incredibly tall, with a swimmer's physique. His short, dark hair is parted on the left side, and his finely chiseled features are to die for. His white button-up shirt and black dress pants tell me that he just left some kind of fancy party.

What parties call for black-tie attire during the day? A yachting regatta? Sabering a bottle of champagne to christen the opening of a vineyard?

Because this handsome stranger just radiates an aura of wealth, the way that *Charlie Brown*'s Linus gives off stink lines.

For some reason, he is still staring at me. And by God, his eyes are such a deep, sapphire blue that I want to strip down and take a swim in their depths.

Pearl surprises me by setting down a tall glass of unsweet-ened tea and a plate of lemon wedges before me. I jump, putting a hand to my heart.

"Oh my god." I set the menu to the side. "I'm so jumpy today!"

"Today? Try always." Pearl smirks at me. "Am I disturbing your thoughts?"

My gaze strays over to the hot stranger, who is now pretending to be engrossed in his phone.

"No," I waver.

She catches the direction of my curious gaze and smirks. She leans her head close to me and drops her voice to a whisper. "I'd steer clear of him if I were you. He makes Oscar the Grouch look like a ray of sunshine."

I quirk a brow at my friend. "I don't believe in grumpy people. Just people that have not been cheered up yet."

"You're crazy." Pearl shakes her head.

"I'm right. I'll prove it!"

"Don't do it on my account. And let me save you the trouble of fretting over this menu. You'll have the waffle of the day, which is blackberry, with a ton of whipped cream and powdered sugar on top. And you'll have a side of hash browns."

My lips lift. "You do know me well. Can you make those hash browns scattered, smothered, and covered?"

"Of course."

"Thanks, Pearl."

As Pearl flits off to another table, I sneak another sidelong glance at the handsome stranger. He is toying with his knife but after a second, he raises his eyes. Our gazes connect.

Something electric crackles between us. I shiver, and realize that goosebumps have risen on my arms.

What is it about this man that makes me stare at him so boldly?

He looks at me as though I've suddenly started juggling pineapples. He opens his mouth, perhaps to ask me what I'm doing. I offer him my hand with a little grin.

"I'm Savannah," I say. "I don't recognize you, so I thought I would introduce myself."

His eyes narrow and he glances at my hand. There is a palpable air of uncertainty for a second before he takes it, shaking it very hard for the briefest time possible.

"Cole." His eyes bore into mine. I expect him to elaborate, but he doesn't. He looks over his shoulder, though I'm not sure what he's checking for.

"Are you in from out of town?"

"No." He crosses his arms and tilts his head.

"Hmm. So, you're a local, but someone I don't recognize. What's your story?"

He frowns. "I'm back in town for the weekend."

"Oh? For what event?"

Cole thinks about that for a second, then shakes his head. "I don't want to talk about it. I want to be left alone to eat my meal in peace."

He's more resistant than I anticipated. I mull my next move. I have a whole arsenal of tactics to put a smile on someone's face. But which one to try next?" I smile and pin him with my gaze.

I suppress a grin and pull out my phone. Using it as a shield, I study the hunky man. He takes off his bowtie and unbuttons the top button of his shirt, revealing a little triangle of tanned skin at his neck. He grimaces and throws me a sneaky side glance.

What is his deal? I can't put together any scenario that makes sense.

Pearl reappears with several plates, dropping a magnificent-looking waffle in front of Cole. She puts down two plates of bland-looking eggs and two spinach salads in front of me. I open my mouth to ask Pearl if she accidentally gave my plate to Cole, but she is distracted.

"I'll be back in just a sec," Pearl says, looking at the doorway. Fifteen people are crowding into the restaurant, looking for seats.

I look down at the eggs, making a face. What a boring meal choice. Then I peek over at Cole's waffle. I'm willing to bet that delicious-looking waffle is actually mine.

He's staring at the syrupy, whipped cream-covered confection with something like horror. "What the hell is this?" he mutters.

"I believe you've got my order." I smile at him.

"Surely not," he growls. "This must be for a five-year-old."

"Nope. That's mine. Dessert for breakfast."

He looks disgusted and stands up, his height surprising me. I didn't realize he was so big. He picks up my waffle and slams it down in front of me with a thud. Then he grabs his plates and moves them over to his spot at the counter, looking as tense as a rattlesnake in a room full of rocking chairs.

"These are mine," he spits. He says it like he's accusing me of stealing from him.

"Okay," I say, raising my hands. "I never said that they weren't."

Pearl reappears with my hash browns and a pot of coffee. She plunks down my hash browns and refills his coffee cup. Cole has a huge mouthful of eggs at the moment, otherwise, I get the feeling that he would definitely correct Pearl's mistake.

But she is gone the next second.

Cole frowns and grabs a piece of toast, cramming it in his mouth. He eats like a starving man.

"Are you trying to get in your final meal before the rapture happens?" I joke. I decide to switch to the next tactic in my arsenal, which is gentle ribbing. Most guys eat it up with a spoon.

Cole glares at me, his mouth full. He doesn't say anything, which just makes me want to crack him open like an egg and learn what's inside his shell.

I grab the syrup from between us and pour a healthy dose of it onto my waffle. He wrinkles his nose, swallows, and gives me a side-eye. "Are you serious?"

I blush. "What? Can't a girl eat her sugary breakfast in peace?"

He snorts. "Do the rules of grown-up nutrition not apply to you?"

"Not at breakfast." I punctuate that by spearing a forkful of waffle and syrup and shoving it in my mouth. I close my eyes and enjoy the taste of a thousand angels singing. "Pure bliss."

He shakes his head. "That's disgusting."

"When's the last time you tried it?" I slide my plate toward him. "Take a bite."

He stops me by putting up a hand.

"No way. We don't even know each other."

"Sure we do." I lick my fork and set it down, then put out my hand. "I'm Savannah. And you're Cole."

"Very funny. You know what I mean."

"I will reiterate my offer. Do you want to taste the best thing on this side of the Mississippi River?"

He rolls his eyes and shakes his head.

"No thanks. You shouldn't be offering unless it comes with a syringe of insulin to counterbalance the sugar rush."

I wiggle my eyebrows and take another huge bite. Syrup drips down my lip and I catch it with my thumb. Cole seems to take this as a near-personal offense and frowns as he shovels some egg whites into his mouth.

"So, what are you all dressed up for?"

Cole flinches and stares at his food.

"You're awfully talkative, Savannah. Anybody ever tell you that?"

I'm irritating him, which is kind of funny to me. I shrug my shoulders.

"Lots of people. Grumpy people."

I lift my eyebrows and make it clear that I'm talking about him. He glares at me.

"I'm not grumpy."

"No, no. You're a bucket full of rainbows." I keep my tone light and teasing, which only seems to make him angrier.

"You're lucky that you're a pretty girl. Because if you were a guy–."

I cut him off. "You think I'm pretty?"

"Pretty annoying," he snaps back.

I can't suppress my grin. "You can't take back the compliment. And why would you even want to? The world has enough thunderclouds as it is."

Cole blinks at me. "You know what I really think?"

"I feel like you're going to tell me no matter what."

He points at me, his expression a glower.

"I think there are a lot of practical people like me trying to protect foolish people like you from all the bad things in the world, darlin'."

My smile turns into a smirk. "Oh, is that right?"

"Yeah. I bet that you see the world with rose-tinted glasses."

"I prefer to see the glass as half-full, if that's what you mean," I say. I cross my arms, growing slightly defensive.

Cole mirrors my posture, and I can't help but notice his muscular, sun-tanned forearms pop against his white shirt.

Say what you will about this stranger, but he is making me a little hot under the collar… in all the ways that matter.

"What's so wrong with having a little fun at breakfast?" I ask.

"Nothing, as long as you realize that you ate like five thousand percent of your recommended sodium and carbohydrate intake for breakfast."

I roll my eyes. "I'm happy to say that I don't even know what that means. I think you're just looking for something to be crabby about."

He leans in very close. "I bet you're a sheltered little brat who hasn't ever seen much of the real world."

My mouth opens and a sound of disbelief comes bursting from my throat.

"You're not even close to being right. You don't know me from Adam."

"I know your kind!" he hisses.

"You–."

My words are muffled as Cole slides his arm around me, jerks me to him, and covers my lips with his. My eyes go wide, and my body is completely rigid as he kisses me deeply, plundering my mouth.

Then, as suddenly as he kissed me, he pulls back and pushes me off.

"What the hell?" he mutters, glaring at me. He shoots to his feet, roots around in his wallet, and drops a hundred-dollar bill on the counter.

"I should be the one saying that," I say, frowning.

But Cole just storms past me, leaving his tuxedo jacket behind as he pushes out the door. I watch as he gets into a gray Mercedes and peels off, leaving the parking lot in a plume of gravel and dust.

What the hell? I touch my lips, still feeling the heat of Cole's kiss on my lips.

3

———

COLE

SIX MONTHS LATER

DRIVING UP THE WINDY COASTAL HIGHWAY THAT LEADS TO Cape Simon feels timeless. The top is down on my convertible. The sun spills over everything, saturating the early afternoon with color. The sky is robin's egg blue, dappled with wisps of white clouds. The cool wind whips around my head and yanks at my shirt.

I can't see the beach from the highway at this point, but I know from the crabgrass and the dark sandy soil that we are practically on top of it.

A deep breath of salt-laden air in my lungs reminds me that I'm still alive.

My phone vibrates. I check it and see that Holly is calling. Silencing it, I flip the phone over on my passenger seat.

She's calling to talk about taking custody of Charlie. And I am dodging her attempts at communicating.

Holly has continually iced me out for a solid six months. Ever since she pulled off a vanishing act while I was standing at the altar of our expensive wedding, I've been left to tend to Charlie alone. I'm not about to pick up Holly's calls now that she's suddenly decided that she's interested in being a mom again.

I look out over the road and push her from my thoughts. Life is simpler here. Purer, somehow, than living in the smog-ridden, traffic-congested heart of Atlanta could ever be.

I hit the edge of town and slow when I see the signs. *Cape Simon, Georgia. Est. 1598. Pop. 7460. Speed limit 30.*

I am home.

"Daddy?"

I look over my shoulder. My four-year-old son, Charlie, is just waking up, his mop of dark hair wild and his ocean-blue eyes sleepy. He is wearing his favorite T-shirt with a huge yellow truck emblazoned on it, and a pair of dark pajama pants. Not my ideal outfit by any means, but I wasn't willing to fight with him about it.

Not today when we're leaving the only home he's ever known, and not planning to return.

"Hey, kiddo. Did you have a good nap?"

He frowns at me. "I gotta potty."

"We're about ten minutes from seeing Big Daddy and Mimi. Can you make it?"

Charlie seems to turn that over in his head a few times. Then he shrugs again.

"Yeah."

He frowns like he has the weight of the world on his shoulders. He looks so similar to my Dad when he's disappointed. I smother a smile.

"Okay. If something changes, you let me know."

I focus on the road in front of me. The road splits, the right fork heading toward town, the left fork seemingly heading right down to the water. I take the right fork, coming up over a crest. Suddenly, the beach is right there, sand piled up in a long furrow on the other side of the freshly repaved black asphalt highway.

"Gonna see Mimi?" Charlie asks.

I slow down again and take the right turn into the long driveway that leads to the sprawling Italian-inspired estate where I grew up. From here, I can see the white marble mansion and the crushed pink stone turnaround before the house.

"Yep. Big Daddy and Mimi live at the beach. We're going to stay with them for a while, remember?"

I know the next question is coming, whether I want it to or not. I steel myself.

Charlie asks quietly, "Where's Mommy?"

My recent ex wouldn't stay here if it were the last place on earth. Not only is it too far from the city for her tastes, but she never got along well with my dad.

Besides, we aren't exactly on good terms now. Not after she threw a very public fit over my taking Charlie and dragged me on social media. Her actions were directly responsible for several athletes finding new representation.

So my ex can cool her heels in California for another six months. *Then* we'll talk.

Meanwhile, I still have to answer my son's question as tactfully as possible.

"It's just going to be you and me for a while—a fun father-son trip. We can build sandcastles and pet the horses and walk into town. Doesn't that sound good?"

I look back. Charlie's head is turned away toward the beach. He seems to study the sandy terrain and crashing waves for a moment. His blue eyes are so expressive. I often find myself wondering what Charlie's inner monologue is about.

"Okay," he finally says. But he doesn't sound sure about it at all.

Like father, like son. We make quite a pair.

I pull the convertible up in front of a massive, Italian granite mansion. Before I can even blink, my dad's lumbering form appears at the passenger side door.

"Y'all made it!" he crows. "There's my favorite grandson. Welcome to La Villa Coralle!"

My dad is a tall, broad-chested man with short salt-and-pepper hair and indigo eyes. He wears an untucked light blue button-up and a pair of jeans. My son Charlie lights up as soon as he lays eyes on him.

"Big Daddy!" he shouts, instantly reaching out to my father. My dad leans into the car and unbuckles him, swinging him high in the air. For a second, I'm sure my kid will plummet to the ground. I scrabble with my seatbelt, bracing for impact.

But my dad swings Charlie down without incident. My heart stutters back to life. Charlie squeals delightedly as my dad kisses him.

I get out of the car. My stepmom Sarah catches me by surprise because I didn't see her standing there.

She's as tiny as my father is big, with long blonde hair that's teased to high heaven and a neon orange oversized t-shirt thrown on over a pair of green patterned leggings. Little gold crosses hang from her delicate necklace and the matching bracelet on her wrist.

"Sam, you really shouldn't be throwing your grandson around like that," she tells my father. Her accent is thicker than molasses. The gentle way she scolds my father is like a mere mortal tiptoeing around the presence of a god.

"I'll be fine," my father says. He tickles Charlie's stomach. "Isn't that right?"

"Charlie has to use the little boys' room," I warn my dad.

"Is that right?" Dad says to Charlie. "Let's go inside real quick. Hurry! Hurry!"

Charlie laughs as my Dad chases him into the house.

Sarah beams at them and then turns to me. "Cole! It's so good to see you. Come here, give me some sugar, sugar."

She comes over to me, giving me one of her tight hugs. I force a smile and hug her briefly.

"It's nice to be here. Thanks for agreeing to put us both up."

"Are you kidding? I may not have given birth to you, but I've lived with you since you were knee-high to a cricket. You're always welcome in his house. It's your home!"

I repress a sigh and move around to the convertible's trunk.

"I was thirteen," I correct her gently. I grab a couple of my suitcases and move toward the house.

Sarah follows, grinning at me. "You were the most handsome seventh grader in the tri-state area. That's how I always think of all of you boys. Like you were the first day I moved in here, after your dear mother passed." She crossed herself. "God rest her soul."

I turn away so Sarah doesn't see my grimace.

There are no subjects that are off-limits in Sarah's book. It's just like her to bring up my life-altering break up with my fiancée *and* the death of my mother in the space of a couple of minutes. Sarah's probably never had a private thought that she didn't immediately announce in her whole life.

"Uh huh," I mumble. "Where should I put these bags?"

"Oh, just leave them there. Your dad can fuss with them when he gets a chance. You know how he is about making sure guests don't lift a finger while they're staying here."

My lips twitch. "I do. We might be here for a while, though. I hope y'all won't be too put out by having us around for a few weeks."

She leans in and whispers, "I think your daddy wants you to stay forever. He's getting lonely in his golden years."

My dad barrels out of the house with Charlie on his back. Charlie screeches a laugh. My heart squeezes at the sound.

"Okay, kiddo. Why don't you have Mimi show you the beach? Your dad and I will catch up to y'all in a few minutes."

Dad kneels down a bit stiffly and Charlie lets out a whoop. Sarah holds out a hand, grinning at Charlie. She looks at him like he is her pride and joy.

Obviously, I'm not the only one having that same thought.

Sarah leads Charlie off toward the beach.

"That son of yours shines a ray of light here, I'll tell you what," Dad says. "When you told us four years ago that you had knocked up your girlfriend and y'all weren't getting married, I was madder than a toothless fox in a hen house. That's certainly not the way I saw my first grandchild being born. But damn if that boy isn't worth his own weight in gold."

I wrinkle my nose but nod. "Yep. He's been so strong through Holly leaving. He still cries for her at night, though."

My father scowls and crosses his arms.

"Damn that woman. I still can't believe she up and cheated on you. And she left Charlie alone downstairs while she did it! Anything could have happened to that boy while she had her back turned and she wouldn't have been able to do boo about it. I tell you, I have never seen anything as shameful as that."

My heart thuds in my chest at his telling me my own story. "Yeah," is all I can say. "Holly seems to lack common sense."

How can I explain what my fiancée was thinking when she screwed around behind my back?

"Lacks common decency is more like it. If Charlie hadn't accidentally told on her, I think you two would be married and she would still be screwing around. It's a good thing he turned on the sink and accidentally caused the first floor of your house to flood."

A little acid indigestion burns my stomach and I run a hand over my chest.

"Holly got lucky. Charlie was young enough that he could've been seriously injured while she wasn't watching. I couldn't believe that I was foolish enough to leave them both while I flew all over trying to sign new clients. I just... it gives me nightmares."

My father crosses his arms and rocks back on his heels.

"And to think, you found out about all of this after she left you at the altar. She came awfully close to being Mrs. Bennett."

"It was only a matter of time before I figured it out. She hurt my pride when she disappeared, but she made the right call. We would be divorced if she had met me at the end of that aisle. If it weren't for Holly calling to talk to Charlie, I don't think I would have talked to her ever again."

As it stands, whenever I do talk to my ex, it's invariably about how she's *allowing* me to have custody of my kid. There is a very real threat underlying those words.

"I suppose I ought to be thankful that she's gone." Dad clears his throat. "We're always glad to have you back here, son. You're welcome anytime. And you can stay forever as far as I'm concerned."

I squint.

"Thanks, Dad." A high-pitched giggle sounds from far away. I take the chance to change the subject. "Well, Charlie hasn't been this happy in months. It's nice to hear him laugh."

My dad pats me on the shoulder.

"It's good to have all my chickens come home to roost for a while."

I shove my hands in the pockets of my khakis. "Just for a few weeks. Two months at the outside. I'm trying to launch a new branch of the agency in London."

My dad looks at me as if I've just admitted to being from outer space.

"London? There are not a lot of baseball and football players in England, son. I don't see how a sports agent can really make a living over there."

I roll my eyes. "Three words for you, Dad. Soccer and cricket."

He gives a startled laugh.

"Have you told Rex that you're leaving him yet?"

I wave him off. "No one is leaving anyone. I'll have to come back once or twice a month to make my rounds. And Charlie can come visit you."

My dad glares at me. He opens his mouth, presumably to rip my idea apart. But luckily, I hear an engine rev. Looking out at the driveway, I see a brand new bright red lifted pickup come roaring down the pink gravel road.

"There's Rex right now." A smile plays over my father's lips and he looks at me with something approaching pity. "You can explain to your eight-time all-star baseball player brother who let you sign him as a client when you were first starting out just what you mean. See what Rex has to say about your namby-pamby move to London."

"Cool it," I tell him. The back of my neck warms. My dad smirks at me and then trudges toward the pickup.

I follow, steeling myself to talk to Rex. He climbs down from the truck, a grin on his face. He wears black joggers, a red track jacket, a white t-shirt with the Atlanta Kings logo on it, and a pair of dark sneakers. Along with a shit-eating grin, it's his normal uniform. He runs up to me, grabbing me and hugging me hard. I hug him back, but I can't get my dad's words out of my head.

Is Rex going to throw a fit over my plan?

"Cole! It's about damn time that you came back home."

I slap him on the back and he moves on, hugging Dad.

"Old man," Rex jokes. "How's the shoulder feeling?"

"Good." Dad smiles. "Rex, I can't wait until Cole tells you about his plans."

"What plans?"

I shoot my dad a long look. "We can talk about it later."

A strange look crosses my brother's face, but he just shrugs. "Okay. Well, I came over to see if you felt like taking a ride into town with me. I have a plan too, and I think it's going to knock the shoes off your damn feet."

I clear my throat and smile. "All right. Let me just say goodbye to Charlie. He's been clingy ever since Holly vanished."

"Great. I'll drive. You can test out my brand new ride."

He wiggles his eyebrows. I frown. "You're the worst driver I've ever met, Rex. You are one speeding ticket away from having your license revoked."

"Those Atlanta judges have got their britches in a twist over nothing." My father cuts in, eager to defend Rex.

"Besides, the oldest ticket is about to hit the five-year mark and fall off your brother's record.

"See? Dad gets it. Besides, driving out here, you can go as fast as you want as long as you don't drive drunk." He waves my comment off. "You let me worry about my record. Go and say goodbye to Charlie. Then get in the truck and get ready to have your mind blown. I have big plans for us, little brother."

I roll my eyes but just sigh. "All right. Dad, why don't you walk me around the house to where Sarah and Charlie are? Leave Speed Racer here to get that huge truck started."

Rex grins and turns toward his truck. Dad walks me around the house, chatting excitedly about the upcoming Red Rice Revel.

But I'm a million miles away, wondering just what my brother has in store for me.

4

———

SAVANNAH

WHEN I GET OUT OF THE RUSTING HUNK OF JUNK I CALL A CAR, I straighten my blue and white polka-dotted dress and then shade my eyes against the early afternoon sun. It's cool enough that I snag my white sweater from the car before hurrying toward Gem's Diner. Pushing open a heavy door, I am immediately enveloped in the scent of fresh coffee and sizzling bacon.

I look around the diner, eyeing the pink and white checked linoleum floors, the hot pink booths, the chrome bar and order window, and the well-worn white tabletops. Gem's is open early and late and serves up fluffy hash browns, perfectly fried eggs, and enormous stacks of buttery pancakes. Add in the wail of 50s music from the old jukebox rising over the sound of hungry patrons chatting, and you get Gem's.

"Savannah!" Over in the corner, a pretty redhead is trying to get my attention. Lucy Taylor-Bennett is in the far corner, looking cute as a button and eager to see me.

There are ten other booths in the restaurant, but my eyes are glued on Lucy's table. Two dark-haired men are seated opposite her, both much too large to be squeezed into the booth together. I recognize the one with the buzz cut and motorcycle jacket as Rex Bennett. But the other person at the table is a curious mystery.

I thought that I knew everyone that is anyone in Cape Simon and the next town over from here. But as I slide into the booth and give Lucy a little side hug, I meet the rather blunt gaze of a stranger.

A really handsome stranger.

A really handsome stranger who kissed me six months ago and then vanished without a trace.

Cole.

"Savannah, this is my brother, Cole," Lucy explains. "And, of course, you know Rex."

I blink a few times, caught in Cole's dark blue gaze. His eyes don't give much away. Does he remember me?

Does he ever think about the searing heat of that kiss late at night when he's alone?

His dark hair is extremely curly and well-groomed. He's dressed kind of preppy, in a button-up and chinos. The sleeves of his shirt are wrinkled and pushed up, as though he ran out of patience with them. And his scent…. He smells like freshly shaved cedar and soap.

Yum, I think. If I had any idea that the Cole who'd kissed me like I'd never been kissed before was not a stranger, but was, in fact, my friend Lucy's big brother, I would have asked her about him months ago.

Cole clears his throat, swiping his hand across his mouth. Then he puts his hand out for me to shake.

"Nice to meet you," he says. He scowls while he says it. The timbre of his voice is low and his tone is flat, so I don't get the feeling that he's speaking the truth about it being nice to meet me. He's definitely still a grumpy storm cloud.

"Hi." I flush and have to look away, eager to shift my attention elsewhere. "Hi, Rex."

"Hey, Savannah." There is a semblance of a smirk on Rex's face. "Long time, no see."

I give him my megawatt smile. "I didn't realize that you both had another brother. I've met you, Rex. And I've met Rhett and River."

Lucy rolls her eyes. "There are actually five of them, believe it or not. Rhett, Rex, Cole, River, and Brooks. Plus, I have a big sister named Eden."

My jaw drops. "You have six siblings?! Your poor mom!"

All three of the Bennetts look at each other, and something dark passes between them. Tension builds. I must have stepped in something, but I haven't the faintest idea what.

I'm ready to drown in the awkwardness when Cole finally extends me a life preserver. "We're a blended family."

"Oh!" I jibber. Blood rushes to my cheeks, turning my face to what I'm guessing is the shade of a tomato. "I'm sorry, I honestly didn't mean any offense."

"It's all right," Rex says, amicably.

But the look on Cole's face says that he feels differently. His steely gaze stays locked on me, making me wish I could crawl under my seat and disappear. He steeples his fingers and gives a long-suffering sigh.

Thank god the waitress comes over at that very second, saving the day.

"Hey, y'all." Pearl bustles up to our table. She wears a pink and white waitress's uniform, and bright pink Converse. She side-eyes Rex, her lovely, mahogany-colored cheeks flushing a deep pink, and she fidgets with one of her long, dark, pigtailed braids. "Hey Sav. You want coffee, hon?"

"Herbal tea, please!" I reply smoothly. "And a pecan waffle, when you get a chance."

"Mmhm." She makes a quick note on the notepad she keeps in her apron pocket. "Coming right up."

I lean in closer to Pearl, eager to avoid Cole's blazing stare. I touch her wrist lightly. "Don't forget that you still owe me the details of your date with that guy we met at the bar."

Pearl blushes even harder and rolls her eyes. "He was a dud. So boring. I'll be sure to catch you up later." She looks around the table with a smile. "Coffee for anyone else?"

Cole shoves his empty mug out. Lucy scowls at him and puts her fingers over his forearm.

She smiles up at Pearl and says, "More coffee would be divine."

"You got it, guys." She turns around and grabs the coffee pot off of the counter. Quick as lightning, she refills the coffee and then zips off to talk to another table.

"Pearl is so impressive," I say. "She runs this restaurant with an efficiency that would make the Swiss jealous."

Rex and Cole turn to give her appraising looks, both raising a single eyebrow in eerily similar expressions. Lucy crinkles her nose and takes a sip of her coffee. "That was not an invitation to stare at her legs."

Cole snorts. "I wasn't staring at her legs. I was just wondering why I don't know any of your friends."

"You live in Atlanta. And you rarely drive the five hours back home to visit," Lucy protests. "Besides, how can you complain? You're literally meeting Sav right now."

My eyes connect with Cole's, and I blush so hard that I'm sure everyone in the history of ever knows that I'm hiding something.

"Uh huh," Cole says vaguely. "I meant more generally."

Rex puts his hand on the back of Cole's neck and arches his eyebrows at us. "Cole is staying here for a while. He's going to help me with my secret project. Isn't that right, Cole?"

Cole grips the edge of the table and grimaces. "You keep saying you have a project to work on. But that's all I know. I can't commit to something that is a big fat question mark."

"Sure, you can!" Rex pulls Cole into a half hug, half tackle, gritting his teeth while he smiles. "You're my sports agent. Your entire job revolves around getting me whatever I want. And this project? It's what I want."

Cole smacks his hand away with a look of irritation. "Just tell me what the project is."

"Nah. We'll have to go for a drive."

"I thought that's what we were doing!" Cole shoots him a glare.

"You guys can fight later," Lucy intervenes. "Right now, you're supposed to be hanging out with me, your sweetest, youngest sister. And I desperately want you to change the conversation."

Rex and Cole exchange glances. Rex shrugs. A lull in the conversation opens up. I can't help but notice that Cole is regarding me with that dark blue gaze of his. I wrap my arms around myself and smile at Lucy. I'm about to ask her about her college studies when Rex practically shouts over to me.

"Savannah, I heard your mom passed a few months ago. I wanted to say that I'm sorry. Your mom was an absolute spitfire. She used to come to my baseball games when I was in high school and razz the other team."

My mouth drops open. Rex remembers anything at all about my life?

Rex was, and still is, this town's hero. Him asking me a personal question is sort of like finding out that your favorite singer wrote a song about you.

"Who are we talking about?" Cole asks, wrinkling his brow.

"Sav's mother. She was a real character. She always had the loudest voice on the field, no matter where the field was." Rex prods Cole.

"I must have missed that somehow," Cole says, crossing his arms. He seems distracted, as if his mind is somewhere else entirely.

I smile brightly, dropping my gaze to the table.

"Thanks, Rex. I…." I search for the right words. How do I express my thanks, while at the same time discouraging anyone else from asking me about my dead mom? "I think she's at peace."

Lucy changes the subject, for which I am forever grateful. "Sav, I haven't seen you in so long! What have you been up to? Are you still working at the bridal shop?"

God, I am really put on the spot. I feel like these two very successful, very handsome men are staring at me, waiting expectantly for me to answer. It's difficult to maintain my bright, upbeat expression.

As my mother always said, girls *should be brighter than sunshine and cleaner than honey*. It's important to keep things light and upbeat so that people will look forward to talking to me again. So I put some extra effort into my attitude before I speak.

"I work a few hours a week there. But I'm on the hunt for something better, with more hours. I need to earn enough money to move out of my grandfather's house."

"Oh!" Lucy lights up. "Cole, weren't you just saying that your last assistant quit? Maybe you can use someone like Sav. She's got serious people skills."

Cole scowls at her. "I don't need any help."

"Oh!" I gawp at the people around me. "That's so nice, but I couldn't possibly impose. Really."

"You aren't imposing." Lucy gives me a stern look. "The last time I saw you, you told me you were scrimping and saving to move out of your grandfather's house. This would help you while you help Cole. And by help, I mean keep him from chewing out people that he's supposed to be nice to. It's a win-win situation as far as I can see."

She's right, I am trying to move out. Since I finished college a year ago, I've been staying at my grandfather's house, the house I grew up in. And ever since my mother's funeral, Grandad has been muttering about reverse mortgages and moving to senior living.

But right here, right now, with Cole and Rex staring me down? Yeah, not the ideal time to talk about my lack of funds.

"I'm saving enough money," I defend myself. "It just requires patience."

Cole grunts and Rex elbows him in the ribs.

"Yes, but you could work for my brother and save more. How much would you need?" Lucy starts, then stops. "Like ten thousand dollars?"

I gape at her, unable to speak. What in the heck would I do with that much money? I'm still stuck at a thousand dollars, and struggling to earn the next thousand.

Cole looks at Lucy quizzically. "Seriously?"

"You could pay Sav that much," Lucy says, emphatically. "Especially if she manages to keep you from biting everyone's heads off."

"You could stand to be more personable," Rex admonishes. He grins and leans forward. "That's actually a great idea. This project is going to be huge. You'll need at least one person, maybe more. And using someone local, that knows the Cape and the surrounding areas, will be essential."

"Are you really not going to tell me what the project is?" Cole wheedles.

Rex makes a face. "No. And I don't want to hear any griping about me being secretive. You told me last month that three of your all-star clients left you. So I know you have the time and energy for my project."

"You're being an asshole." Cole scoots out of the booth and reaches into his pocket for his wallet before dropping a hundred-dollar bill on the table. "I'm going back to my kid."

He has a kid? I tuck that fact away and force myself to focus.

"Good. Tomorrow morning is a better time to visit the site anyway," Rex responds, smirking. "You and Savannah."

Cole looks at me sharply.

"I don't really think–."

Rex stands up suddenly, fixing Cole with a hard stare. "Just show up tomorrow and listen. I'll text you the address in the morning." He pokes his finger into Cole's chest. "Don't come without Savannah. You'll have more success on this project if you have her to make nice with the locals."

He shoulders Cole aside and stalks out of the restaurant.

Pearl watches as Cole follows him. She turns to us, her brows raised.

"Is everything okay?"

Lucy waves her off. "My brothers are just butting heads. It happens literally all the time. We're staying though. Right?"

She looks at me and I nod. She wiggles her eyebrows and moves to the other side of the table.

"There. Now you have a little more space."

I run my tongue over my teeth, looking out the plate glass window to the parking lot. I have a lot of emotions churning around in my brain right now. But unbidden, my mother's voice filters through my head.

Go along to get along if you want to make and keep friends, Savannah.

Lucy is just trying to help. Plus, it's not like she's wrong. I do need money. I shut my mouth and give Lucy a bright smile.

"Thanks, Lucy."

Lucy beams at me. "Of course. If you decide you can't work for old Grumpy Guts, I'll understand. But I think you should give it a week."

A week? I gulp. Before I can say anything, my waffle arrives. I dig into the buttery, savory-sweet goodness, and let Lucy take the reins of the conversation.

But in the back of my head, two questions burn brightly.

How can I get out of working with Cole?

And what is this secret project that Rex is so excited about?

5

COLE

By the time I park my car in the gravel driveway and head into my parents' house, it's fair to say that I'm in a bad mood. As I bound up to the mansion, I try to focus on something that won't make me frown. But it's hard to know just what that could be.

I've only been back for a few hours, and Rex is already driving me crazy with his secretive demands. And as for Lucy and her friend Savannah... I love Lucy as much as anyone can love their little sister, but damn if she hasn't put me in a tough position. Employing Savannah, who is so gorgeous that I can't look at her without my tongue lolling out like a cartoon wolf, is going to be a problem with a capital P.

I shoulder open the heavy front door. Easing inside, I glance around. The house is the same as it has always been, all cool, wood floors and light, airy spaces in each room.

"Hello?" I call out.

I'm immediately greeted by the one sound that can always cheer me up.

"Daddy!" Charlie yells. He comes running in from the living room in his socks and slides a little on the hardwood floors.

I kneel down and catch him, hugging him. He feels solid and reminds me that there are definitely good reasons that I brought him home to visit my parents.

Because I know, without a doubt, that my parents love Charlie. And Charlie could use some extra people in his corner now.

"Hey, kiddo. What have you been up to?"

Charlie gives me the biggest grin. He shoves a sand dollar into my hands. "Look!"

Turning the graying sand dollar this way and that, I smile. "What do you call this?"

"Sandy!" Charlie yells.

"A sand dollar?" I prompt.

He nods vigorously. "Yeah."

"Did Mimi show you the ocean?"

"I saw crabs!" Charlie pinches his fingers together and moves his arms in imitation of a crab.

"Did you get pinched? If you get too close, they'll get ya." I pretend that my hand is a crab's claw and tickle his side.

He giggles. "That's silly."

I stand up and shake my head. Sarah appears, holding a pack of crayons in one hand.

"We also checked out the swing set, didn't we? We put the swing set in the side yard just for you, buddy." She ruffles Charlie's already-disheveled hair. Then she winks at me. "Hopefully Charlie will get some cousins to play with eventually. If your brothers and sisters ever manage to fool people into marrying them."

I know she's only teasing, but I am still quite annoyed. "Rex probably has a few kids that he doesn't know about," I say, not trying to be helpful. "He's your best shot at having a pile of grandkids."

She smiles a little bit ruefully and shrugs. "We'll see. Have you eaten?"

"Yes ma'am. I ate at Gem's Diner."

Charlie runs past her into La Villa Coralle's main living room. Endless fluffy white couches beckon you to sit on them in this room, but that's before you catch a look at the sea through the sliding glass doors that lead out onto the expansive marble patio.

I see that Charlie has made himself at home here, pushing back several pieces of the sectional couch to make room for a spread of half a dozen coloring books and ten different packs of crayons. He lies down on the hardwood and returns to coloring, so intent that the world might not as well even exist.

"Charlie, are you hungry?" I ask.

"Yeah." He doesn't even look up from his coloring book.

I smile and look at Sarah. "I brought lunch stuff. I'll go grab him one of the pre-packaged meals and throw it in the microwave."

Sarah stops me with a gesture. "I want to make him a fresh meal. He looks like he could stand to put on a little weight."

"That's really not necessary." I turn and head toward the kitchen.

"Cole Alexander Bennett, you stop right there."

I freeze and look back at her. She has her hip cocked and her arms folded across her chest. She pins me with a glare.

"My house, my kitchen, my rules. I'm asserting my grandmotherly rights. If I say I want to feed your child, you just say thank you, ma'am."

I'm speechless for a moment. "Uhh… yes, ma'am. Thank you."

Defiance gleams in Sarah's eyes, and she gives my arm a squeeze as she passes me. "Good man."

She vanishes toward the kitchen. I wander back toward my son and sit down on the hard floor beside him. He is now drawing on a stack of loose-leaf paper, and I reach over to wiggle a few of the drawings he's already made out from the pile.

The first one is familiar. A two-story house of brick with a large green grass circle that I take to be the yard. I hold it up for him to see.

"Is this our house in Atlanta?"

Charlie scrunches his face up and nods, not taking his eyes off his work. I look at it again.

"Nice details. I like that you made the shutters blue like they are in real life."

He purses his lips but does not respond.

I flip through the others. One is a fantastical scene featuring some stick figures with swords climbing a mountain. Another has a stick figure petting a ton of dogs. But it's the third one that I can't stop staring at.

It's me, him, and his mom all holding hands. I can tell it's Holly because she has red hair twisted up in a clip. And I'm wearing what looks like the world's largest button-up shirt. Charlie drew himself in the middle, his dark hair a scribble of crayon that doesn't look too far from reality, honestly.

But in the picture, his mom is scratched out with a green crayon in a hasty scrawl. He used the same green crayon to draw a slashing bold line through his and his mom's hands.

I hold up the drawing. "Is this us?"

Charlie sighs and looks up, tossing his dark hair. "Yeah."

I try to use my gentlest tone for my next question. "Why is your mom all scratched out in this picture?"

His lower lip protrudes. "Mommy's gone."

He shrugs and looks back down, his brow furrowed.

I nod slowly. It's true enough. We've only seen Holly a whopping three times since she left me high and dry on the day of our wedding.

She's 'finding herself' in Atlanta, whatever the hell that means. My free hand gathers into a tight fist. I swallow around a knot of tangled feelings.

I need to be here for Charlie, but I want to scream every time Holly's name comes up. I take a measured breath.

"You know, kiddo. You can talk to me if you ever miss your mom. You can talk to me about anything."

"Okay…" He looks up at me, shoving his hair out of his face. "Stay here."

His words are a plea that level me. They hit my chest and run straight through to my heart, piercing me cleanly. I feel like Charlie has removed my skin and now he can see my heart pumping, my lungs inflating, my stomach gurgling.

It's *painful* to have a kid. You feel like you want to wrap them in a hug and protect them from the world. But you can't protect them from everything. And it is doubly agonizing to realize that you have failed them.

"I'm not going anywhere." My heart constricts painfully. "Not on your life, kiddo."

Charlie frowns down at his crayon drawing. "Mommy left."

"Hey. Can you look at me for a minute?" I tap the paper before us. Charlie looks up, tossing his too-long hair. I pull him into my arms and give him a tight hug. "Your Mom still loves you. We both know that *you* didn't do *anything* wrong. And I will always love the stuffing out of you, no matter what. Do you know that?"

"But Mommy—" His eyes shine with unshed tears. "I want Mom."

I grit my teeth and look at my son, who is obviously hurting deeply. For making him feel this way.

"Your mom is just a phone call away. I'm sure she would love for you to call her. You just let me know when. Okay?"

Charlie hugs me tightly. "Can Mommy come here?"

God. Please don't let her come to Cape Simon.

"Sure. In the meantime, you and I will hang out here. We'll have so much fun visiting Mimi and Big Daddy that you'll never want to leave."

He is quiet for several seconds. "Mommy lies."

That gets me right where it hurts. I suck in a breath and rock side to side with him. I can't think of what to say to that.

Charlie's lip quivers. "I miss her."

"I miss her too."

Sometimes, I qualify my statement in my head. *I miss the person I thought she was.*

"You do?"

"Yup. You know what I do when I'm feeling lonely?"

He shakes his head. I give him a soft smile.

"I talk to somebody else that I love. And now that we're here visiting Mimi and Big Daddy, that list is way bigger. I could talk to Big Daddy. Or Mimi. Or Uncle Rex."

"Who's that?" he asks.

"Uncle Rex is my brother. That's why I wanted to bring you here. So you could get to know all of my brothers and sisters better now that you are old enough to remember them. It's good to be surrounded by family."

Charlie nods, taking it in. "Uncle Rex is nice?"

"Trust me, he's going to be one of your favorite people. He knows everything there is to know about sports."

His eyes light up. "Like karate?"

"Yup. Jiu-jitsu, baseball, swimming, hockey, running marathons… he does it all."

"What's a marathon?"

The front door creaks open and I raise my eyes to the doorway.

"It's a really long race."

Lucy pops her head in. "What's a really long race?"

"A marathon," I say with a smile.

"Aunt Lucy!!" Charlie yells. He bounces up like a tennis ball and flings himself at her. She has to rush a couple of feet to catch him before he hits the wall. She spends a lot of time at college in Atlanta and we see a lot of her, especially since Holly left. He clings to her like a barnacle, and I can tell that she's one of Charlie's favorite people.

"Hey, Bubba," Lucy says, grinning. "How's my most wonderful nephew?"

Charlie grins from ear to ear. "Good."

She hugs him gently. I hear the staticky buzz of the intercom click on. Sarah's voice comes through the intercom, presumably from the kitchen.

"Charlie, honey. I made you mac and cheese," she purrs. "Come into the kitchen to eat."

Charlie wiggles out of Lucy's arms and runs off toward the kitchen. I start picking up the crayons that Charlie left scattered all over the floor.

"So?" Lucy prompts. "Are you going to yell at me?"

I favor her with a hard smile. "For what?"

"You know what." She grins and comes over to help me put the coloring books in order. "I know I might have overstepped a little by suggesting Savannah work for you. But you haven't been to her grandfather's house. She has to get her own place."

Suddenly, my brain is full of Savannah's perfect curves, and long lashes swept over gorgeous hazel eyes. I stand up and stack the crayon boxes on top of the coloring books.

"I'm sure she does." I jerk my head toward the patio. "Want to sit outside?"

"Sure."

She follows me out through the sliding glass door, and I sit down on the white, cast-iron patio set. From here, I have a view of the beach that's pretty damn glorious. This was always my favorite view of the beach as a kid.

My great grandparents were smart when they chose this location for their home.

Lucy pulls up a seat across from me, her eyes on the white-tufted waves. The quiet roar and smooth hiss of the ocean lull me the way only sounds of my childhood can.

"Sav is going to be a great help," Lucy says. She pulls her hands into the long sleeves of her fleece and squints. "She's literally the nicest person I know, too."

I roll my eyes. "Nobody said that she wasn't."

I feel her eyes on me, studying me.

"You know what I think? I think you could use some kindness in your life, Cole. I hate to speak ill of her, because she's not here to defend herself, but Holly was a selfish, snotty brat. She was vain and conceited before she gave birth to Charlie, and it's only gotten worse since then."

I'm stunned. I look at Lucy, easily the nicest of my siblings, with something like bafflement.

"What? How long have you felt that way?"

Lucy sighs. "Always. And I'm not the only one. Sarah hates her. Dad thinks she's totally stuck up. I can't imagine that the rest of the family feels much differently. And the way she just ran off like that! None of us wanted to see you marry her, but no one thought she would be that cruel."

"How did I not know this?" I lean forward in my chair and shove a hand through my thick mop of hair. "This is quite a secret, Lulu."

She wrinkles her nose. "There's no call for childhood nicknames. It's not exactly a closely held secret."

"Why didn't anyone ever talk to me about it?"

"I think Dad and Rex tried. You were off in LaLa Land. There was no way to reach you, especially once Holly announced that she was pregnant."

I grunt. "I swear this is the first I've of it."

Lucy purses her lips. "You're a Bennett man. Y'all were born more stubborn than a bunch of pissed off mules."

"Says the girl who didn't shower for almost two months when she was twelve. Rex calls that Pigsty Summer, 'cause you were against any kind of bathing or cleaning up after yourself. You only broke because Walker Harrison told you that you stank."

She goes bright pink, and gives me an outraged look. "I was protesting the oil pipeline coming down the coast!"

I smirk at her. "You were doing it to get a rise out of Sarah."

She scrunches her face up. "That too. Mom hated that summer."

"Yep."

After a minute, Lucy asks quietly, "Do you miss her?"

I give her a long look. "Who, Holly?"

She nods. I smile sadly.

"Yeah. It's been six months since she officially took off. But I just can't believe she's gone." I fish in my pants pocket, pull out Holly's huge diamond ring, and lay it down on the metal table with a clang. "She sent me a long letter with this enclosed."

Lucy picks up the ring and looks at it speculatively. "It's absolutely hideous. I can't believe that she picked this out."

I smirk and take the ring back.

"Not only that, but she designed it herself."

"Of course she did. Because she's a selfish b–"

My sharp glance causes Lucy to swallow her words. "She is!"

"It's too little, too late now." Putting the ring back in my pocket, I sigh. "I hate knowing that my entire family hated Holly and nobody said anything. It would've been nice if one of y'all had slapped me with a big sign that said 'Don't Marry Her!'"

"I'll remember that next time that you propose to a big jerk." Her eyes sparkle. "So, have you dipped your toes in the dating pool yet?"

"Hell no," I blurt out. "I'm in a one-year time out from all that foolishness. I'm in sexile."

"Ewww, what?" Lucy asks.

"Exiled from the opposite sex," I supply. "Sexiled."

"So you're not interested in being set up? Because you know my mom is just salivating over the idea."

"I told this to Sarah already. I'm not interested. The same goes for anybody asking about my dating status. I am not open for business."

"Noted." She wiggles her brows. "Mom baked a bunch of applesauce-ginger-molasses cookies for your arrival and hid them somewhere. Wanna go find them and pig out?"

I roll my eyes and stand up. "Not interested. But my son might be. Let's go find him. I'm sure he'll help us discover Sarah's hidden treasure."

"Arr, matey," Lucy quips. I offer her a hand up and she takes it. Then she shouts, "Last one there is a rotten egg!"

My heart is a bit lighter as I race after her.

6

───────

SAVANNAH

It's almost four in the morning when I give up on trying to sleep. I get up and pull on a pair of sweatpants, and one of Mom's favorite Susie King Taylor High School sweat-shirts. I stop to smell it as I pull it on. I finally had to wash it last month, so it doesn't carry her scent anymore. But I still love wearing it.

It's like wearing a big hug from Mom. And more days than not, that's exactly what I need.

When I slip downstairs into our kitchen, I'm not the least bit surprised to find that my grandad is awake. He's wearing a pair of blue flannel pants, a simple white cotton T-shirt, and a black-and-red plaid robe. His white hair is still damp from the shower. He rubs his lower back, an old ache from years of stooping over the edge of the boat to pull in traps full of crabs and shrimp.

He's sitting at the small kitchen table with a cup of coffee and several photo albums spread out in front of him. When he hears my footsteps, he stiffens and starts closing the albums. He peers over his shoulder at me.

"What are you doing up, Sweet Pea?"

I head over to the stove and set the kettle on to boil. "I couldn't sleep. I'm pretty sure that sleep disturbances run in the family."

Grandad snorts. "Whatever it is that you and I got, your sister sure doesn't have it. Birdie would sleep all day if you let her."

I smile. "That's absolutely true. When I went past her room, she and Dex were sound asleep. Snoring like two little bears during the winter."

"That sounds like them. Don't know where they got the ability." My grandfather closes the last album and starts to stack them up.

I pull a mug down from the dark-stained cabinet and drop an herbal teabag in it.

"I didn't mean to disturb you or anything. You can go back to looking at photos."

Grandad sips his coffee. "No such thing as disturbing a person who's so bored he's countin' the ceiling tiles."

I walk over to the table and point to the albums. "May I?"

Grandad's eyes blaze amber as he regards me. He purses his lips and pushes the stack of photo albums across the table. The tea kettle whistles and I pour steaming water in my mug.

Then I sit down at the now-crowded kitchen table and pull an album close. Opening it, I see a weathered Polaroid that's warped with age. I brush my fingers over the image of my young, red-headed grandfather and my gorgeous blonde grandmother. They are no more than twenty or so in the photo, and they are kissing while proudly holding up their matching wedding bands.

"Aww. You were both so beautiful."

Grandad gives me a soft smile.

"It's a trick of the eye. Your grandmother was so dang pretty, she just lit up everything around her." He smiles down at her picture and smooths a fingertip over her image. "You take after her. Your mom and your sister take after my side of the family."

I point to the next photo, which is a family portrait taken when my sister and I were kids. Grandad and Grandma stand in the back, dressed in their Sunday best. My mom is seated before them, her hair a vibrant red, her big-boned structure impossible to make out in her boxy gray sweater. She has a red-headed little girl in a navy dress on her lap and a bald baby wrapped in a cream blanket in her arms.

I remember how desperately I wanted a navy dress just like Birdie's when I was a little girl. Birdie refused to let me have the dress as a hand-me-down and wore it long after it was too tight and too short for her. Even back then, I just wanted to fit in with my sister. To this day, I still think she's pretty much the coolest person who's ever walked this earth.

Tapping the photo with a fingertip, I ask, "Where is Dad in this photo?"

"You can bet your britches that he was out in the trawler, bringing in fish. He always said he made the most money working on Sundays when everybody else was at church."

I wrinkle my nose. "I can't really remember him."

"Your dad didn't like to sit for photos too much. But he sure did love the ever-loving stuffing out of you and your sister."

I nod. My dad passed away from cancer when I was only two. Growing up without him was difficult. Once my father has passed and my mom moved our little family into her childhood home, my grandad sort of filled my dad's shoes.

I flip the page and see an image that twists my heart. My mom standing with her arms around my grandma's waist, grinning widely. My grandmother smiles at my mom and brushes back a lock of her auburn hair. The captured moment is so tender that it makes my eyes well up with tears. Though I've seen these albums countless times, the images still fill my chest with longing.

My grandad sees me get emotional and puts his hand over mine.

"Is this too much for you?"

I shake my head, wiping a tear away.

"No."

"It would be understandable if you didn't want to look at these albums. Your mom only passed away a few months ago."

I look up at him with a sad smile. "It's been almost seven months. But you lost her too. And you lost grandma seven years ago…"

I trail off, thinking that my grandfather probably knows better than I do the people in his life that he has lost. But Grandad just gives me a vague smile.

"I think we're overdue for a visit to the cemetery," he says. "It's been a while since we laid fresh flowers on the graves."

"Oh, that's a good idea. Maybe we can go sometime next week?"

"That sounds like a date, Sweet Pea."

He gets up to refill his coffee, keeping a hand on his lower back. I look down and flip to another page.

My mother stands behind a podium, her mouth open, her finger pointing. She looks youthful and her enthusiasm is obvious with just a glance. An audience sits before her, enraptured and hanging on her every word. Beside the photo, I see a caption scrawled in my grandmother's handwriting. "Adelaide + the Coastal Auto Workers' Union. 1992."

Scattered around the page are similar photos of my mother at work. There's one of her taken at the Sisters of Mercy hospital, where she's reading to an ailing little girl. In another, she's picketing in front of a school, facing down a bunch of frowning men in suits. In another, she's linking arms with others to form a human chain.

I turn the page to find a whole spread dedicated to her biggest accomplishment.

'Community Center Saved By Working Woman' the headline from The Island Daily reads. I smile at the article from ten years ago. It features a photo of my mother with her fist in the air, mid-yell, with thirty more people of every race and religion right behind her.

Grandad looks over my shoulder and cracks a grin. "Your mother sure was a firecracker."

"No doubt about it." I sigh wistfully. "I wish I had a tiny bit of her stubbornness. She was always happiest when she was the squeaky wheel."

My grandfather sits down again with a groan.

"Your mother was just plain loud as hell. She was born that way. Came out screaming and never did stop. I loved her to the moon and back, but it did cause some friction here at home now and again."

I snort. "Mom was never really interested in blending in or going with the flow. She demanded more from all of us."

"She was proud of you and your sister, though."

"She had a funny way of showing it sometimes."

"Hmm," he murmurs noncommittally. Your mom was a lot of things. But she wasn't really good at talking about her feelings."

I screw up my face. That was the understatement of the years —time for a topic change.

"I think I have a real job. One that will help me move out. You can finally have your own space!"

Grandad flinches. "I'm sorry to do this to you girls. I know that you've always called this house home. I just…." His mouth works and he looks down at the table. "I got an offer from a buyer a couple of weeks ago. And I think I'm going to say yes. Not because I want to… but because I have to."

I stare at him, trying to make sense of his words.

"What? Why?"

"Your mom's funeral wasn't cheap. I didn't have a lot of money before that, but that was the final blow."

"I don't understand!" I reach across the table and grip his hand. "Why didn't you tell me before now?"

"You all were losing your mother. By the time I realized how deep the hole I'd dug myself was, it was too late." Grandad grimaces.

"Grandad, I– I'm so sorry!" My eyes fill with tears. "You lost your daughter, and now you're going to lose your house?"

He's about to answer me when a voice cuts through our conversation like a sharp knife through dollar-store margarine.

"Aunt Sav!" Dexter's holler comes from upstairs. "Aunt Sav, are you up?"

I glance at the clock on the wall as I rise. It's only 4:30. Rushing to the staircase, I stage whisper. "Yes! Shh. Grandad and I are in the kitchen."

Dex's head of messy blond hair appears first, then his goofy grin, then the rest of his small body. He thumps down the stairs as silently as a marching band.

"Dex, quietly!" I whisper. Only then does he tiptoe on the last few steps. When he gets down to me, I look at his sleepy face and his superhero pajamas. Leaning down, I put my hands on my knees.

"What are you doing awake?" I ask in the softest voice I can conjure.

He does not pick up on that at all.

"I'm awake because Mom kicked me!" he almost shouts.

I pull him into the kitchen, where Grandad is already stirring hot cocoa in a saucepan over low heat. Grandad silently raises his hand and Dex charges at him, putting his entire five-year-old body into a forceful high-five.

"Easy, easy!" I chide my nephew. "Come sit at the table. Tell me why you weren't sleeping in your own bed."

"Aunt Saaaaaav." He plops down in one of the chairs and rolls his eyes. "My bed is teeny tiny. It belongs to a wimp."

I screw my face up. The rooms in our house are small and the ceilings are low. When the adults put their heads together last year to talk about how to make space for everyone, a lofted twin bed built over a double-sized mattress had seemed perfect. It let Birdie keep her adult mattress while allowing Dex his own space.

I sigh. "Your bed in your mom's room is not doing the trick anymore, huh?"

"No." His voice turns whiny. "I want my own room."

I smile and pat his knee. "You will get my room as soon as I move out. It just requires patience."

I swallow after this promise, wondering if it's really fair to make it now that I know he won't be staying here long with the house on the market.

Dex looks at me with a critical expression that he definitely got from his dad, Sean. He was an absolutely wild Irish hunk that Birdie met while reporting from Kabul. Birdie came home heartbroken and pregnant with Sean's child... but without Sean.

Dex currently has the same knitted brows as the ones seen on Sean in the picture of him that Birdie keeps on the refrigerator. It's the only one she has. "You told me to be patient a thousand million years ago. I've been patient!"

He yells the last bit and Grandad shushes him. He brings over a steaming mug of cocoa as he does it.

"Here. Put this in your face and be quiet. Your mom needs to sleep."

"Sorry," Dex says. "I'm trying."

"And I am trying to move so you can have my room. It's just taking some time."

Dex huffs and blows on his cocoa. "Thanks, Grandad," he says begrudgingly. He slides his gaze to me. "What is the hold up?"

"Dex!" Grandad says, the pitch of his voice rising. "Apologize right now."

"I said that bad." Dexter frowns. "Sorry."

I grin at him. "It's okay. I'm just saving up money. It's a painstaking process."

Grandad sits down and glares at me. "You don't have to move out if you don't want to. You know my feelings on the matter. Dex can deal with the living arrangements for a bit longer."

"No, I can't," Dex mutters into his mug.

"Go in the living room and watch some TV," my grandad says. "Keep the volume turned way down."

Lighting up at the suggestion, Dex jumps up and takes his mug along with him. My grandad shakes his head as soon as Dex is gone.

"That boy is a handful. It's too bad that his daddy is MIA. Dex needs a firm hand."

I smirk. "He needs to be told no once in a while. Birdie's too afraid of stepping on his toesie-woesies."

"Look. You and I both know that Dex will be heartbroken when he learns about the sale." Grandad sighs and turns to me. "But you take your time moving out. Or stay, if you want. I won't have you driven out of my house by that kid, no matter how much I love him."

I stand up, hugging Grandad fiercely. When I pull back, I see tears in his eyes. He blinks and coughs to cover his sudden emotional turn.

I kiss his hand. "When I move, I'm not going far. You hear me? I can promise you that."

He clears his throat. "Don't do anything on my account."

"You're stubborn and silly at the same time." I wrinkle my nose. "Now how do you feel about taking in some of the finest early morning cartoons?"

"Dex isn't watching early morning cartoons on television. He's doing a YouTube."

"I think you mean watching a video on YouTube." I screw up my face. "Ugh, I hate that my entire childhood has been erased in the name of the internet."

"Don't even get me started." Grandad shakes his head, motioning for me to go first. "After you, I reckon."

I skip into the living room and throw myself down onto the ancient, jade-colored couch beside Dexter. He smiles and moves over to make room without breaking his eye contact with the iPad in his lap. I grab the remote to the television and turn on screen sharing so that we can watch it with Dex.

Grandad hobbles into the room and eases down to sit on the other side of me. I sit back with a smile, surrounded by two of my favorite human beings.

But internally, my mind is awhirl.

Grandad has to sell the house eventually. Unless…

Can I somehow save it?

In my mind's eye, I see Cole. He's the man with the plan… and the money. If I'm able to work with him, maybe I can somehow springboard that into a plan that will save this beloved house.

But will crabby Cole actually be swayed by my sunshine and charm? Will we be able to work together? And why on earth is he such a grump?

More importantly, does Cole remember our kiss?

7

———

COLE

I PULL BACK THE SLEEVE OF MY GRAY FLEECE TO CHECK MY watch. It's five minutes to nine in the morning, and a biting chill is in the air as I climb out of my car.

I've parked right on the edge of a dirt road that runs on for about another twenty feet before it trails off into rocks and weeds. I slam the door shut, and I turn myself in a slow circle, taking in the green-gray, wetland grasses that go on for miles in every direction. I can still see the tip of the Cape Simon lighthouse from here, but I can easily blot it out by holding up one finger.

Why am I standing in this huge empty field by myself?

"Fucking Rex," I mutter. "Of all the things you've talked me into, Mr. Superstar, this has got to be one of the most idiotic." I throw my hands up, gesturing at the empty air around me. I raise my arm to the sky and shout, "I'm talking to my goddamn self!"

Before I can belabor the point, I hear a long, grumbling cough. It sounds like whatever made it is heading toward me.

I whirl and see a little speck on the road ahead, getting slowly but steadily bigger. Eventually, I can make out a very old sedan. It limps in my direction, revealing rust-colored side panels, a single lit headlamp, broken windshield wipers that occasionally attempt to wipe, and a spiderweb of cracks across the windshield. When the car coughs and sputters to a stop about a hundred yards down the road, I'm honestly surprised. The fact that it made it that far is impressive, in a way.

I swallow. I'm nervous, I realize. I can't suppress the excitement that runs through me like a chill. I'm shocked that Savannah agreed to show up today.

She has no real reason to other than morbid curiosity, I feel.

The driver's door opens with a great creak and an attractive blonde head appears. Savannah slams the car door, but it doesn't want to close. I watch with amusement as she tries to close it once, twice, three more times.

She's put together, in a short pink dress with a Peter Pan collar, a huge white purse slung over her shoulder, and black heels. The fact that her car does not match her look makes a rumbling chuckle burst forth from my chest.

She eventually gives up on the door, and turns to walk toward me with a determined flip of her tumbled blonde locks. A bright pink, lipsticked smile is pasted on her face.

Does Savannah always have to smile? She doesn't look like she feels happy right now, but the smile still remains on her face. It gives her a serial killer vibe.

I don't love it.

"Hi!" she says, her forced cheer evident. "Sorry I'm not earlier. I had to borrow my mom's old car. And as you can probably tell, it's not really in racing shape."

Why does Savannah always seem like she's forcing herself to put on a brave face? Is it because the idea of working for me scares her so much?

Also, why the hell is she so goddamned sexy when she smiles?

I cross my arms, cocking a brow.

"You borrowed that car? With the intention of doing what?"

Her raggedy car is such a piece of junk. Having an employee in my service who drives such a clunker might reflect badly on me.

She blushes but doesn't look back.

"No buses come out this way. I checked. I had to choose between not showing up, and borrowing that old heap of junk."

"So you decided to ride out here in this pathetic excuse for a car?"

I scowl in the direction of the car. Even as I loathe the car, I'm still charmed by her determination to get here. I cast an eye over the rust bucket.

That thing is not safe for someone delicate like Savannah to drive. It looks like a prop out of a Rob Zombie film. It seems primed to explode at any second!

"Why did I drive the car here?" She stops three feet in front of me and tosses her head, leveling a challenging stare in my direction. "It seemed rude not to show up."

I smirk. "I wouldn't have taken it personally."

"Hilarious." She crosses her arms, making the hemline of her skirt rise a scant inch. "Should we talk about the elephant in the room?"

My gaze drops to her toned legs against my will, making me frown.

"And what is that?" I ask. Even though I know exactly what elephant she means.

I've only fantasized about that kiss a thousand times over the last six months. That it happened on the worst day of my life only added to my fantasies. Since I've been in my self-imposed sexile, the memory of her warm mouth on mine, the weight of her body as it pressed against my own… you could say that our kiss has been a regular feature of my late-night imaginings.

Especially when I start dreaming about what I would've done next. Pulled her panties down, put my hand up her skirt, and watched her eyes open in surprise when I touched her–.

"Hello?" Savannah waves a hand in front of my face.

I blink and my eyes focus. "What?"

"You asked what the elephant in the room is. And my response is…." She hesitates, and a little line of worry forms between her eyebrows. "The first time I saw you, you kissed me! Shouldn't we talk about that?"

Yes, please.

But actually, no. The kiss was just the act of a desperately sad man on the darkest day of his life. It means nothing to me.

My stomach flip-flops nervously. I screw up my face. "No. I don't think there's anything to talk about. I was having a tough day."

Sav licks her lips nervously.

"Your fiancée left you."

I grit my teeth. "Yes. Like I said, it was a tough day."

"And did you two… um… patch things up?"

I would rather dig a tunnel straight through the earth and come out the other side than have this conversation.

"No."

"Oh." She looks nonplussed. "Okay."

"Listen, do me a favor? Don't go around telling everyone about my moment of weakness. Especially Rex and Lucy."

Savannah looks amused. "I don't think that will be a problem. Generally speaking, I don't tell people how hot I find their siblings. It's a weird thing to say."

My heart skips a beat. Did Savannah just admit that she finds me sexy?

"Savannah–."

"Everyone that knows me at all calls me Sav," she interrupts.

I give her a hard look. "Savannah, I know my meddling little sister might want you here, but I don't. If Rex hadn't insisted on it, you wouldn't be. If I have my way, this little project will only take a few days. And then you and I will probably never see each other again."

A muscle pulses in Savannah's jaw. Then she smiles widely, as if she's talking to a little kid.

"I can sense that you're bummed out about being here in Cape Simon. Let's just try to stay positive and not bicker with each other. We'll see what the project is and go from there. What do you think?"

I grimace and stick out my hand to her.

"Shake on it."

Savannah puts her palm against mine, making way too much direct eye contact as she shakes my hand.

"It's an agreement," she says softly. The roar of a diesel engine in the distance cuts off whatever Savannah was going to say next. I step back, putting space between the two of us. But even so, I can smell her perfume: honey, vanilla, and a little cinnamon.

Savannah smells like what I imagine heaven must smell like.

She turns and brushes the stray hair out of her face, then squints at the approaching dust cloud.

"Is that your brother?" she wonders.

"Must be. He drives the same vehicle as a Mad Max villain."

She looks at me with surprise, her lips curving up. But she doesn't say anything else as she watches Rex drive his enormous, lifted truck toward us. I shove my hands into my pockets and eye her while Rex screeches to a halt and jumps out of his truck.

Mostly I'm wondering if Savannah will react to Rex like most girls from around here. It's like he's a salt lick and they're a bunch of deer creeping closer, hoping to taste him. I have yet to meet a woman who didn't find my brother charming.

Including Holly, sad to say. She hung on his every word, laughed hysterically at every joke out of his mouth, and basically all but rubbed her whole body against him. All in a useless attempt to get Rex to pay attention to her.

Thankfully, Holly's desperation always had the opposite effect. The harder she tried, the more disdain my brother seemed to treat her with. His repulsion was actually one of my favorite things about my relationship with Rex.

My brother runs up to us, wearing his black motorcycle jacket and black jeans. He wears a dark snapback hat with the Atlanta Kings' logo splashed across it.

I expect Savannah to blush and begin to flirt with Rex as soon as he reaches us. But she just fidgets with the hem of her skirt. Her face is oddly blank, devoid of emotions. She seems more nervous than anything.

"Well?" Rex asks, throwing his arms wide and looking around. "What do you think?"

Savannah looks left and right. I follow suit and then shrug. "What are we looking at, Rex?"

"This is the land I want to buy." A grin explodes over his face.

"To build... a house?" Savannah guesses.

"He has a house," I grit out.

"I have three houses," Rex corrects me. "Four if you include the townhouse in Toronto."

"So what are you going to do with this land?"

"I'm going to build the biggest baseball training camp complex of all time." He grins at me, holding his arms out and backing away.

I squint, blood rushing to my head.

"What?" I shake my head, trying to make sense of his words. "What's wrong with the training camp the Kings use in Jacksonville?"

"That camp is old." Rex swats that idea away. "The buildings are refurbished from an old school. The grass is trash. It's too damned hot, even in the fall and spring. I want a totally new complex. Something that the Kings can use, but also all kinds of other sports teams, too. Four fields, great local grass, brand new pitch machines, specialized classrooms, a clinic for players to do rehab." He finishes his list with a cool smile. "My camp will have everything. I've got all the ideas. I just need you to close the deal with the financiers, and maybe River to help with buying the land itself. I've laid all the groundwork! I've already got seven potential teams lined up. They are tired of having to fly halfway across the country just to get to a decent camp."

As Rex talks, a knot forms in my chest. I shake my head.

"What you're talking about sounds like it's going to cost a lot of money. Like billions, with a B. And it's not just a casual project either. It's going to take at least until the summer to get through all the red tape and corporate bullshit. That's assuming that this land isn't the protected habitat of the wild sea slug or some garbage like that."

Savannah looks concerned, but she just bites her lip. Rex doesn't even look at her, though. He's focused on me.

"Look, Cole. Between you and me, I don't know how many years I've got left playing pro ball. Maybe a year, maybe five, maybe ten. I could tear my ACL tomorrow and be benched for the rest of my life. Right?"

"Of course. But I've seen players last for much longer than that. You're only thirty-three."

Rex glances at Savannah and shrugs. He smiles at Savannah. Something in my chest tightens.

He says, "That's not really the point I'm trying to make. At some point, I'll have to retire. I want to have something to fall back on."

"That's pretty smart of you," Savannah says, nodding slowly. "It's good to think a few steps ahead of your current position in life."

Every word that comes out of her mouth praising Rex's idea makes me curse my brother's charisma. I know his game all too well. But Savannah?

She is totally innocent.

I cut her a hard glance. "Sure. But–"

Rex holds up a hand to silence me.

"Cole. You're my agent. And I'm probably your biggest client. Right?"

I set my jaw, but nod. "Yeah."

"You're like having a tiger in my corner. But when I stop playing, you'll lose all of the income that I bring in." He waves to the land around us. "If we take the time to build something now, with our eyes on the future, that won't happen. Essentially, you would trade a few months of work on this project for a lifetime of repayment. I'll be the general manager of this place whenever I retire. And you will be a stakeholder that earns large dividends." Rex lifts his hands and looks around us. "All you have to do is to relax and say yes."

Honestly? This is not the first time that Rex's retirement has come to mind. I have noticed Rex miss a few pitches over the last year. He's been winded a little more easily. But I just chalked that up to age.

No one can play ball like a twenty-year-old when they are closer to forty. Still… Rex is suddenly bringing it up like it's no big deal.

And that makes me *worried.*

"Are you saying that you're ready to retire?" I squint at my older brother. "Did your team's medical examination turn something up?"

Rex rolls his eyes and waves me off. "Nothing like that."

"You're talking about a ton of work. Building a training camp is a huge project."

Rex sighs. "I mean, if you feel like you can't do it, I'll find someone else. But if they are an agent, they will probably want me to sign with them."

Great. He's using his position to control me. I clench my teeth.

"I didn't say that. It's just a lot to think about. Like, where would the athletes that stayed here eat? Where would they sleep? You've seen the training camps in Jacksonville and Tucson. They all have cities close by so that their athletes can go out to eat and…." My gaze slides to Savannah. I don't want to say the next part in front of her, but I have to. "You said that Tucson is great because it has so many bars to drink at and good-looking women to cycle through."

If Savannah is scandalized, she doesn't show it. She chuckles a little to herself and looks at the ground.

"You're absolutely right. I was thinking that we would build a brand-new hotel, and maybe facilitate local restauranteurs opening a few new bars and restaurants."

My eyebrows shoot up in alarm. "In the Cove? I don't think those tight asses at the city planning commission would even consider approving that. Plus, what do you know about running restaurants and hotels, Rex?""

"That's not the point," Rex dismisses me. "And anyway, I was thinking about building in South Shore. The entire downtown area is in serious decline. It's just begging for a renaissance. The land prices are infinitely cheaper, too. I think the community would be appreciative."

Savannah barks out a laugh, then claps her hands over her mouth. Rex frowns at her.

"What?"

She fidgets. "I live in South Shore. I love the downtown area. Sure, it could use a few new restaurants and coffee shops. But you should really get the opinion of the community before you just decide to 'improve it.'"

Rex looks stunned. "Are you saying that they would say no to money? Because that is crazy talk."

She shakes her head slowly. "Not exactly. But I don't think you can just decide for a whole group of people. You need other opinions to make a balanced, fair decision."

I pretend to rub my mouth to cover my smirk. That's about the nicest way I've ever heard anyone tell a person that they are a selfish asshole.

"Savannah–" Rex says.

I stop him. "Wait, wait. Maybe Savannah has a point. If we go ahead with this project – and that's a big if – we should check and see that everything we're considering is actually doable."

Rex crosses his arms and gives me a pointed look.

"Everything is for sale. Especially South Shore. They should be thanking me for bringing a lot of jobs and tax money into their dead little town. Seriously."

He turns away. Savannah pulls a face for a second before she manages to control her features, but I catch it. She was disgusted by him.

A woman that isn't reduced to a pile of mush by Mr. Baseball? What do you know?

"Rex." I pull his attention back to me. "I'll check out this piece of land for you. And I'll start putting out feelers in downtown South Shore. Give me a week to see if the idea is even possible. Then we can talk in more detail."

Rex narrows his eyes at me.

"The only answer I want is yes. I hate to be the problem child...." He purses his lips. "Actually, I don't care if I am being a brat. This is what I want. I am trusting you to get it for me."

"Okay, but–." I start.

Rex holds his hand up. "One second."

He runs back to his truck, retrieves a thin file folder, and runs back to me. He shoves it in my hands.

Opening it, I find an employment contract. Rex has been busy, because my name and Savannah's name are inked on the document already. He's filled in the payment amounts for me, too.

I glare at him. "You were a busy beaver."

"You need her for this project. She can play nice when you are engaged in your grunting and growling. And Lucy asked me to make sure that you pay her well. You really don't have any options here."

No, I really don't. Rex offers me a pen, and I scrawl my signature across the dotted line. I motion to Savannah and give her the contract to sign.

The entire time, I glare at her instead of cussing out the cocky athlete that I really want to yell at.

Savannah silently hands the pen and contract back to Rex. He gestures between us.

"I want to see you two shake on the agreement."

Savannah flushes scarlet and honestly looks like she'd rather disappear. But I hold my hand out stiffly. She takes my hand, her fingers warm against mine as we shake. Our eyes catch.

The slide of her skin against mine. Her grip on me is firm, which is surprising given how crimson her cheeks are. I want to pull her in, touch her cheek, and tilt her head back until her full lips are just in the right position for me to kiss them.

But I can't. I need to snap out of it! I squeeze her hand a little too hard before letting go. Savannah keeps staring at me, her eyes wide and her breathing a little too fast.

"Wonderful!" Rex starts to walk back toward his truck, keeping the contract with him. "I think you two are a match made in heaven."

I swallow the words that want to leap from my mouth because they are foul.

Rex gets to his truck, stops, and then checks out Savannah's car.

"Savannah, darlin, do you need a ride?"

"No!" she shouts, then bites her lip. "My car will drive home just fine."

"Kay." He gets in his truck, turns on country music that's loud enough to burst your eardrums, and takes off.

After he's gone, I look at Savannah. She smiles and shrugs.

"Guess it's just you and me," she says softly.

I snort and check my watch. "I have to go."

"Oh?" she says, raising a brow.

"Yep." I can tell she wants to ask, but I don't give her a drop of information.

Pausing, I purse my lips. It's obvious enough to me that I like Savannah. But getting involved with her is a bad idea for more reasons than I can count.

Savannah is now my employee. She's beautiful, but if she knows my sister, she's young. And I am supposed to be in a one-year-long period of not dating anyone.

That's all *before* I carry out my plan to uproot Charlie and start our lives over in London. No girl like Savannah will want any part of that.

Savannah seems like a forever type of girl.

I jerk my chin at the car. "You really think you can drive that thing?"

She straightens her spine and her eyes twinkle with defiance. "You bet I can."

"Can you work tomorrow?"

She nods. "Absolutely. I'll be there with bells on."

"Hm," I grunt. I ask for her phone number and put it in my phone, then head for my car. "Later."

I climb in and start the car, watching Savannah for a second. She sighs and turns toward her vehicle, but she is dragging her feet. It goes against everything in my body to just leave somebody in a situation where they might not be able to get home.

But half a minute later, she's still only halfway to the damn car. I roll my window down and lean out the window.

"Get in the damned car!"

Savannah flashes me a surprised look and scurries to the car. She tries to start it once, the starter whirring. Then silence. I pull my car up to hers.

Savannah tries again, cranking the engine. The screeching mechanical sound is rough on my ears.

"Savannah—" I call out.

She ignores me and cranks it a third time. To my surprise, after ten seconds of coughing and screeching, the engine turns over. The car roars to life.

Savannah gives me a thumbs up and pulls off. I just shake my head.

All the time, I am wondering how the hell I'm supposed to pull off this project for Rex. And with pretty Savannah standing too close the whole time... I'm sure it's a recipe for disaster.

I'm too attracted to Savannah for us to work together. I'll always be on tenterhooks, thinking that something may happen. How can I not be with someone as beautiful and charming as Savannah?

I want to do more than kiss her. I want to bang Savannah like a bass drum. And the emotional train wreck that I am, that would be a mess. She doesn't deserve to be drawn into my world of hurt and confusion.

Sighing, I shake my head as I pull my car onto the dirt path.

8

———

SAVANNAH

WHAT AM I SUPPOSED TO WEAR ON THE FIRST DAY OF WORK for a hot boss with a grumpy outlook? I look at myself in the mirror, critically. This lacy pink dress paired with cream-colored tights and glittery gold pumps looks great. But does it say 'I'm here for serious work?'

My phone chimes in distinctive tones. Two long ones, three short ones.

That's the Cupid's Arrow notification. I pick it up and navigate to the bright pink and red icon. *You have two arrows waiting in your quiver,* the app tells me.

I have been so busy for the last few days that I managed to forget that Cupid's Arrow even existed.

I quickly swipe through both of the would-be suitor's profiles. One man holds a fish proudly as he grins at the camera. Underneath the photo is the caption, *Working as a fisherman fills my days. Will you fill my nights?*

Blech! He is definitely not the type I'm fishing for. I quickly swipe left to let the app know that I'm not interested in him.

The second man is also a bust. While he's more conventionally attractive, he's wearing a dark suit and looking at the camera with a somber expression. But the kicker is the caption.

Traditional women only! Must be a virgin. Fatties, hookers, pick-me girls, and hoes need not apply.

"Gross. Also, hookers and hoes are basically the same thing, I think." I send him to the trash where he belongs. No judgmental assholes in my quiver, thank you.

My ideal man is one who walks down the beach, shirtless and shoeless, strumming a guitar. He'll have long blond locks, an impressive eight-pack, and he'll pick flowers to tuck behind my ears. Romantic words will be coupled with chivalrous gestures.

But most of all, he will be as positive and sunny as me. That's the part I find really hot.

Closing the app, I toss my phone on my bed. I pick up a different dress from the bed and consider it. There is a knock at the door, followed almost immediately by my big sister shoving it open. Her honey-blonde hair is curled into tight ringlets, her short black dress has white collar and cuff accents, and the heavy swoop of black eyeliner makes her green eyes look enormous.

"Savvie...," she starts, then stops. "You're dressed cute. Are you going somewhere?"

"Just to a new job," I say. I glance at her with suspicion. "Why?"

She flaps her hand at me. "Nothing. I was going to ask you to watch Dexter for a little while. But I can just take him to work with me."

Dexter comes running into my room at full tilt, full of so much energy that some of it comes out of his mouth in a scream.

"Aunt Sav!" He barrels into my knees and then peers up at me. "Did you know that dinosaur fossils have been found on all seven conti-."He looks at my sister. "How do you say it?"

"Continents," she supplies.

"Yeah. Did you know that Aunt Sav?"

I kneel down, grab his hands, and twirl him around. "Nope. That's super cool. I had no idea."

Birdie ruffles her son's hair. "Can you go grab your dinosaur shoes? We have to go in a minute."

I check the time on my phone, then panic.

"Oh my god. I'm going to be late!"

Birdie smirks and follows her son out of my room. "Later!"

After a frantic minute spent grabbing all the things I need, I'm finally ready. I burst out of my tiny bedroom with a breakfast bar wedged between my teeth. It's my first day of working with Cole and I'm already late.

I can only imagine the disappointment and anger in his eyes. I swallow and then fling myself down the stairs and into the front hall.

"Stop right there!"

I freeze, then turn to see my grandfather frowning down at me from a stepladder. He wears ratty canvas pants and a stained T-shirt. His 'workin' clothes,' he calls them.

"Hey, Grandpa." I slink back to give him a hug and a kiss on the cheek. He steps down and embraces me before starting his interrogation.

My grandad eyes me up and down. "Put on a sweater and a coat today, baby girl. And are you sure you want to wear those high-heeled death traps?"

He nods at my feet and I give him the trace of a smile.

"I'm sure. But I will definitely take your advice about bundling up. Okay?"

Giving him another quick hug, I walk to the hallway closet. Putting on a white, woolly duster, and my heavy gray-and-white checked coat, I turn to my grandfather.

"Warm enough?"

He grunts. "Take a scarf, baby."

I grab a gray scarf and throw it on as I step out the front door. "Bye!"

I'm halfway to my mom's car by the time I notice Grandad standing in the doorway, his whiskey-colored eyes watchful. I wave and get into the car.

He's always so worried about me. It's a little stifling. Between Grandad, my sister Birdie, and my nephew Dexter, my home is never still and certainly not quiet. Just like this closely packed South Shore neighborhood, it's always teeming with life. I wave to several neighbors who pass by me on their way to catch the 7:45 bus into the Cape.

After several minutes spent trying to get the engine to turn over, I finally manage to get the car going.

"Yes!" I cheer, pulling the car out and heading toward downtown South Shore.

I drive through a few neighborhoods. Some are full of dilapidated houses; some are full of dated but well-kept properties like Grandad's house.

I turn into downtown, which is more like an area full of small businesses. I pass restaurants, a hair salon, and a bank. A couple of old, two-story buildings are at the far end. These house the library, the town hall, and the post office.

I turn the corner and the street becomes a pier. I hurriedly park between the bookstore and the SaltLife Inn, then climb out.

A lone figure stands at the far end of the pier, away from the businesses. Without even seeing his face, I know it's Cole. The way he stands – hands shoved in the pockets of his black overcoat, looking out at the gray sky overlooking the dark gray sea – the image of him projected against the sky is very stark and makes me feel lonely.

Is Cole lonely? I wonder.

I call out to him and he whirls, his jaw set. When I click-clack my way over to him, his lip curls.

"You're late!"

I pull a face. "I got caught up."

Cole surprises me by grabbing me by the hand and pulling me close to his body. Not touching, but right at the edge of it.

"Your time is not more valuable than mine, I assure you." Under the weight of his full, direct glare, I feel like a cell under a microscope. His fingers press into my wrist. "You can't be late again, Savannah."

I blink, gulp, and nod. "I'm so sorry. It won't happen again."

"It had better not." He looks as though he wants to say more, but he doesn't. He just pushes me away with a gentle shove. "You are supposed to be showing me around this…area."

The way he says 'area' makes it sound like a curse word. I suck in a breath, and give him a cheerful smile.

"Of course. If you want, we can walk a few blocks down and then circle back around."

Cole puffs out his cheeks and holds up a hand. "You're the expert. Lead the way."

I tuck the ends of my scarf into my coat. "Right. Well…let's start on the right side."

Each click of my heels sounds like a muffled gunshot on the warped wood of the pier. I hurry toward the first building on the far-right side.

"Here you see the only boutique in South Shore. Along with Savage Pizza, and a hair salon."

"Savage Pizza sounds familiar." Cole shoves his hands in his pockets and scrunches his face up. "I never really spent a lot of time around here. My family is-."

He searches for the right word. I flash him a cheeky smile.

"Rich?" I suggest.

"A rich person would never say they are rich," he fires back. "I was going to say well-off and discriminating."

"I always wondered where Lucy got the money for her rent. She and I lived in the same block of apartments my senior year of college."

He ducks his head and nods.

"She's low-key about coming from money. She doesn't feel like her privilege defines her. My dad pounded that into all of our heads."

I nod, thinking that jives with everything I know about Lucy. I point across the street as we walk.

"That's Shoreline Cinema. It's ancient, but it's still in business. And next to that is the pet grooming place–."

He stops, looks around, and seems confused.

"I thought you said there were restaurants, plural."

Cole takes off at a jog, briskly moving off the wooden pier. and down the street. A car surprises him by turning into the main street and honks angrily when he just flashes them an odd look.

"Hey!" Running in these heels is killer on my feet, but I sprint over to Cole and haul him onto the sidewalk anyway. The car honks two short beeps and drives off.

I'm a little bit winded, and it takes me a second to realize that he and I are awfully close now.

Cole's eyes dip down to my lips. He smooths his hands down the front of his dark overcoat and swipes his tongue across his lips.

Is he thinking about kissing me again?

Then he seems to remember himself and turns away with a scowl. "Let's get this tour over with, Savannah."

I smirk and fall into step beside him.

"What's the matter, Cole? Got a hot date planned?"

He snorts. "No. Definitely not. I'm sexiled."

I tilt my head. "Come again?"

"Sexiled. It means no sex, dating, or worrying about any member of the fairer sex for a period of time. I've sentenced myself to a year."

His words take me by surprise. "Why on earth would you do that to yourself?"

"Because I don't know what the hell happened to my marriage. But I know that I'm a good dad and a hard worker. So, I am giving myself permission to focus on only those two things right now." Cole glances at me coolly.

"Oh," I say, nodding as if I understand. I don't, but appearances are important right now. "I'm sure you know best."

He gives me a long look and then clears his throat. Turning around, he points to the only three-story building in the whole downtown area.

"What is that?"

"That's the community center. We are going to get there at the end of the tour."

He puts his hand on my arm to stop me.

"Humor me. Let's go look at it now."

He takes off again, zigzagging to cross the road. I have to really book it to keep up with his long strides. I'm on the tall side for a woman, but Cole has mile-long legs.

When I get to the concrete entrance of the community center, I'm a tad out of breath.

Cole is looking straight up at the building. There is kudzu on a full third of the façade, and a huge, dark water stain on the left side of the building. All in all, the place doesn't seem terribly impressive from the outside. Couple that with the fact that if you put a ball on the floor, it will surely roll toward the beach. It's fair to say that the community center has its problems.

"I don't even know what to look at first," Cole says, squinting. "This place seems like it's ready to fall over with the first strong wind."

"It's very sturdy." I feel weirdly protective about the community center, like I am the only one that will stick up for it now that my mom is gone. "It's lived through every hurricane that made landfall here since the Nixon administration."

Cole pokes out his cheek with his tongue.

"Okay...," he says slowly. "Let's look inside."

Without waiting for a word from me, he goes into the slight alcove and pulls on the doors. They won't budge, even though Cole rattles the door handle.

"Damn." He steps back, looking up again. "This place would be perfect."

"They don't open until eleven. You can't just swan into the community center and start doing renovations!" I protest, my voice rising. I'm trying not to connect it to my personal feelings, but I can't help it.

My mother loved the South Shore community, and she adored the community center. If she were the one standing in my place, she would shout at Cole until he went away.

But she can't help me now. And shouting at people isn't really my thing.

I clear my throat. "They teach ESL classes here. There is a pottery studio, a great theater, and even a tiny pool to teach babies to swim. There are cooking classes every spring, and rhumba classes in the winter. All summer long, there are driver's education classes taught by community volunteers. This community is a closely-knit one. And this building is one of the bindings."

It all comes rushing out in a great gust of excitement. Once more, I feel breathless, and my cheeks warm.

Cole, for his part, doesn't even have the decency to look vaguely impressed by my speech.

"All of that wholesome community building can be done anywhere." His lips thin. "I'm going to mark this down as a strong contender for our hotel site."

"You can't just–."

He holds up a hand. I stop talking, not at all used to his abruptness.

"You've said your piece. You have provided context for the building. Now let's move on."

Cole starts moving toward the next building, a run down, single-story gymnasium.

"What is this building?"

I sigh and tell him the story of how it was a thriving gym into the 1980s, and then it slowly became a ghost town.

"They closed their doors in… 2012, maybe?" I say. "You could definitely buy that!"

He shoots me a sour look. "That isn't nearly large enough."

I jerk my chin down the street. "It might be enough if you also bought the Peterson's grocery store that's next door to it."

"Maybe." Cole glances back at the community center with a pout on his face. "Let's keep looking."

I walk him around the entire downtown, circling back to the community center. Then I walk out onto the pier again, heading to a bench near the railing. My feet ache and I need to rub the right arch of my foot.

I sit down and pop my shoe off to rub my complaining foot. Cole follows at a leisurely amble, looking at me with a smirk.

"What?"

"Those shoes are ridiculous. They may make your legs look nice, but they seem like more trouble than they are worth."

My mouth opens, but no words come out. Did Cole just tell me my legs look nice?

Cole sits next to me and looks at the beach. "So, what do you actually do for fun around here?"

That was not the question I expected him to ask. I put my heel back on and huddle down in my coat. Grandad was right about the weather. Then again, he usually is.

"Are you asking what there is to do here, in general? Or are you asking what I do?"

He looks thoughtful. "What you do, I guess."

"Well. There's a lot of University of Georgia tailgating this time of year. I also love the bowling alley that's in Cullen Bridge. My friends hang out at Savage Pizza a lot. Annnd…." I shrug. "Other than doing town events, I mostly just get on dating apps and try to scroll for Mr. Right." I give him a meaningful glance. "That's what you should do, by the way."

Cole looks offended. "I should get on dating apps?" He pulls a face. "No way."

I gently lean in, teasing him.

"No? Come on. Your sexile must be almost over."

"Wrong. I've got six more months." Cole rolls his eyes.

"God. You're really going to try to go a year without having sex with anybody?"

What I don't say is that I am now picturing myself naked, mouth open, astride his cock. Blowing his mind, and simultaneously having my freaking brains boinked out.

It's a satisfying thought.

"That's the plan," he says. "Better than trying to find Mrs. Right by playing a mobile game."

I smack Cole's arm, laughing.

"You're so stupid."

"Hey, I'm just being honest," he says.

I scoot closer to him on the bench, leering at him. "You think the perfect woman will just magically divine that you're single? How can you expect that of Mrs. Right?"

Cole smirks, then seems to realize just how close we are. He looks between us. There is a moment – just a moment – where I don't know what he's about to do.

My breath catches.

His eyes land on my mouth. For several breaths, he seems to think about something.

Would it be too forward of me to kiss Cole?

Then he gives himself a shake and pushes up to a stand, then strides away from me.

Uh oh.

"Cole?" I start as if to follow him.

He doesn't even look back at me. He just waves a hand in my direction.

"Wait for my text!"

I watch as he hops in his silver Mercedes and pulls off with a screech.

What the hell just happened? Did I push his buttons?

Or did I potentially just ruin my job?

Shaking with more than from just the cold air, I head to my mom's car.

9

COLE

It's unseasonably nice outside. Though it is overcast, temperatures are in the lower fifties. And I've let River drag me and Charlie down to downtown Cape Simon for some sort of festival. Charlie is raring to get out of the car and be set loose.

"Slow down," River warns me, sticking a hand into the front seat to get my attention.

I glance at him in the rearview mirror. I see his worried gray eyes, and his short, dark, slicked-back hair. He wears a black motorcycle jacket, and black jeans, and looks like Cool Hand Luke riding in the backseat of my Mercedes.

"I'm perfectly capable of seeing that there is traffic coming up." I swat at his hand and make a face. "Stay in the back seat."

Charlie bursts into a fit of giggles. "Daddy, you're being a silly-billy."

River relaxes. Glancing in the rearview mirror, I see him turn to Charlie and tickle him savagely.

"I'll show you silly-billy," River says, his tone gleeful.

"Daddy! Daddy, help!" Charlie shrieks, dying of laughter. "Aaaah! Uncle River!!"

I smile and ease us into a line of cars that are waiting to turn right into the downtown area of Cape Simon. As soon as I make the turn, I see that other cars are parked on either side of the road. Pulling off to the right, I park in the only free spot near some scrub brush.

"Okay, boys. We're going to have to hoof it a few blocks."

I climb out of the car and my passengers do the same. River stretches and then makes sure Charlie takes his hand.

"The town started throwing the Red Rice Revel a few years ago. Since then, the festival has exploded," my brother tells us both.

As if to punctuate his point, a gaggle of kids walk by. Each one of them is wearing a white Red Rice Revel T-shirt with an orange-red cartoon mascot on the front. It's a single grain of red rice that's grinning and giving a thumbs up. I think it's ridiculous. But Charlie will probably want one.

We start to walk the few blocks to downtown. More and more people pack in around us. I take Charlie's hand protectively, and gape at the growing throng.

"This has to be half of Savannah! And some people from Charleston, too," I say.

"Yep." River wiggles his eyebrows at me. "People love red rice, I guess."

We step into the packed main street area. People are clustered at booths that are stationed up and down the street from here, and down the three blocks that lead to the lighthouse. A huge banner hanging from the lighthouse reads 'Red Rice Revel.' There are matching red and black flags hanging from every lamp post, and street sign, and strung in zigzags between the two sides of the street.

It's louder here. I squeeze Charlie's hand and look down. He grins at me, his deep blue eyes set off by his yellow parka.

"Cool!" he exclaims. "Lotsa people!"

River starts pulling Charlie toward the closest stand, which has a line of people waiting patiently. Under a small tent, two older Black women serve up scoops of red rice into paper bowls.

"That smells amazing," River says. "Charlie, do you smell that?"

My son turns his nose up to scent the air.

"Smells weird."

"You mean the spices, I think. Red rice isn't really spicy, but it does have spices in it. It has little bits of sausage and bell peppers and celery." We come to a stop behind the line of people.

"Shouldn't we look around first and then decide where to eat?" I squint at Charlie and River.

"No!" Charlie cries. "I'm hungry!"

River flaps a hand at me. "We'll all share one scoop. It'll be fine. Don't be such a tight ass."

Charlie looks at River, a grin on his face. "That's a bad word."

I roll my eyes. "Yes, he did, kiddo."

I'm jostled by someone right behind me. Ire pushes at my chest and I whirl, ready to tell them to back off.

But then I look down into Savannah's startled face.

"So sorry!" she blurts out, stepping back and turning beet red. She's wearing the same gray overcoat as yesterday, with black tights and high heels with gray cats printed all over them.

I clear my throat. "Savannah. What are you doing here?"

A familiar-looking young blonde woman, in bright pink tights and a pair of shiny black loafers, appears by Savannah's side. She looks like a much curvier Savannah. She has a blond-haired little boy in tow. The little boy has his arms crossed and his tired irritation is evident in his expression. As a parent myself, I recognize a kid who's worn out from having too much fun and looks almost comically cranky.

"Hey. Do you have the car keys?" the blonde asks Savannah. "I want to drop Dex at home to spend some quiet time with Grandad."

Savannah digs in the pocket over her coat, producing several keys along with a pink rabbit's foot keychain. She hands them over and then touches the blonde's shoulder.

"Birdie, this is Cole. Cole, meet my sister Birdie."

"Hi." Birdie gives me a quick smile and then notices River behind me. "Oh, hey. Long time, no see, River."

River gives her a nod. "Sup, Birdie. How are things at the newspaper?"

Birdie gives him a tight smile. "They're fine. Staff reductions and layoffs are rampant, as per usual. I'm just glad that I have my second job as a backup plan."

"In addition to being a reporter for *The Island Daily*, Birdie is also a waitress at Savage Pizza," River explains to me.

River knows everybody. He considers it a kind of currency, I think.

I just nod. I'm too busy trying to read Savannah's pleasantly blank expression to give much thought to my manners.

"I'm Charlie!" crows my son.

"Oh yeah." The back of my neck heats. "This is my son, Charlie."

Charlie hugs my legs and I bend down to pick him up. Savannah smiles at Charlie.

"That's such a cool name. Charlie and the Chocolate Factory, Charlie Brown, Charlie's Angels. There are so many good Charlies in the world."

His expression is very serious. "I like Char Chaps."

"He means Charlie Chaplin," I explain. "Right, kiddo?"

Charlie nods vigorously.

"I love Charlie Chaplin!" she says. "My Grandad loves him too. You two would probably get along. You'll have to come to a movie night at the South Shore community center sometime. They show all the great films. Plus, they have all-you-can-eat popcorn."

"Daddy?" Charlie looks up at me. "Can we go?"

Savannah winks at me, which makes me feel a little "Yep. I'm making a mental note."

She jerks her head toward the line. "Y'all are hungry for some red rice, huh?"

Charlie gives a joyous shout. "Yes!"

He grins up at her. She smiles right back, completely on his wavelength. Watching them talk defrosts the cold inner core I work so hard to maintain ever so slightly. It feels distinctly uncomfortable.

"Let me see if Dex wants to wait for some rice." Savannah kneels, moving her head toward Dexter. She murmurs something to him. Dexter shakes his head, looking bashful.

"Okay." Savannah kisses Dexter on the cheek and stands up. "I think he wants to go home."

"He's had quite an exciting morning," Birdie says, ruffling her son's hair. "I'm going home to put him to bed and bring Grandad some long-grain rice. I'll be back in a little while."

"Sure thing." Savannah smiles as she watches her sister pick Dexter up and work her way through the crowd.

Savannah turns and her eyes land on my face. Our gazes catch. I can feel the back of my neck begin to heat as the moment stretches out like a lazy cat in the sunshine. My stomach does a few somersaults.

Her lips twitch. She jerks her head toward the lighthouse, one eyebrow rising. I think she's asking me if I want to go talk. And I'm dumb enough to feel my heart rate increasing at the mere suggestion.

Of course I want to go. I nod. I'm rewarded with a grin from Savannah.

God, she's gorgeous.

The line in front of us moves, and River and Charlie eagerly move up with it. I step out of line and gesture to River.

"I'm going to walk down and check out the other booths. Meet at the lighthouse in fifteen?"

"I'm going to eat all your rice!" my son shouts.

"I double dog dare you," I fire back.

"Go ahead. We're good." River takes Charlie's hand, smirking at me.

I don't like his condescending expression, but now is not the time to argue with my brother in public. Turning, I jerk my head toward the lighthouse.

"You want to walk?" I ask, offering her my elbow.

Savannah looks a little surprised, her mouth forming an O for a second. But then she grins and links arms with me as naturally as if we were the best of friends.

"Lead the way!"

Swallowing and clenching my jaw, I start to walk. Savannah looks up at me, a secretive little smile on her face.

First, she's great with Charlie. Then she's extremely friendly to me. What's next, she's nice to my parents and my Dad falls in love with her?

This girl is hitting me in all the soft spots. I'm doing everything in my power to stay stern with her, but it's a bit like expecting an inflatable man to withstand a hurricane.

Savannah purses her lips. "It's beautiful out here today. That's all. I don't understand how you could ever move away from here."

I give her a measured glance.

"My job demands it. And my ex is from Atlanta." I clear my throat. "She wanted the big mansion in the fancy part of town. I let her pick, and we ended up settling in Buckhead."

"Buckhead?" She whistles. "Nice neighborhood if you can afford it."

I look at her with humor in my eyes. "I could afford it."

Savannah touches my arm and points to a small tent selling jars of jelly and bars of soap. She heads there without another word and leaves me to follow. I do, watching her pick up a soap and smell it.

She wrinkles her nose and puts it down.

"I guess you probably had to give up that house when your fiancée left." Savannah says it so softly that I almost miss it.

"No. Charlie and I have been living in a short-term rental home in Sandy Springs for six months. But the lease was up there. So I packed Charlie up and came here while I figure out what our next move should be."

Savannah picks up another bar of soap and gives it a delicate sniff. She offers it to me, but I just frown and shake my head.

"That's really nice of you."

"Not really. We were together for eight years. In my mind, that's too long to just kick someone out after you break up." I shrug awkwardly and pick up an orange-speckled jar of hot pepper jelly. It's Dad's favorite condiment, but I'm not really buying it because Dad will love it.

I'm buying it to have something to do while I sneak side glances at bubbly, brilliant Savannah.

She's so freaking beautiful today,

"That's actually really sweet." She slides me a grin. "Are you feeling feverish or something?"

"Ha ha ha." I hold up the jelly to the young man working the stand, offering him a fifty. He gives me a dour look but scrounges around for change anyway. I slide the jelly into my coat pocket.

Savannah moves on, looking around at the other tent. "So, what's next?"

"You mean which tent?"

"No, silly." She smacks me very gently on the arm. "I mean for you and Charlie. Are y'all going to settle here?"

"Nah. I'm planning on going to London. I have an appointment to get us new passports in a few days."

Savannah looks at me like I'm a talking dog. "What's that now?"

I gesture with a hand, sweeping it over the horizon.

"It'd be a great career move for me. And we could start over fresh."

She makes a face. Frustrated by her reaction, I say, "What? You have a problem with London?"

"No. It's just really far away from here."

I give her a funny look. "That's the point."

Savannah sticks out her tongue at me and bursts into a tuneless singsong. "I would think that coming from a big family, that's the type of environment you would want Charlie to grow up in."

I blink. "What's with the singing?"

She shrugs and smiles. "I don't want you to take it as criticism, so I deliver it in the form of a song."

"You know what I just realized? You are really strange."

"That's fair." She tilts her head back and sings. "Don't you want Charlie to have a great childhood like you had?"

Her song gives me pause. I hadn't quite thought of my move in those terms. But I shake my head.

"Why wouldn't he have a great childhood in London? Also, you're making some assumptions. I didn't have it that great growing up."

She squints. "But you were rich."

"Yeah, I was privileged. But that doesn't really have much to do with anything. Besides, Charlie's the only grandkid, so I think he would get lonely if we stayed here. If we go to England, we can do our own thing. Charlie would be thrilled. He loves people with funny accents. And English wizards, too."

She doesn't laugh.

"You're going to move somewhere because your four-year-old son loves funny accents?" She arches a brow at me.

"No, but it helps." I point to a tent selling books, intending to move there next, but Savannah waves it off.

"Those are all gardening books."

"How do you know that?"

She gives me a knowing smirk. "Because that's Imogen Wright's tent. She's a widow who inherited no money, and five thousand copies of her deceased husband's gardening book. She's been renting out booths at every single event, trying to get rid of her enormous inventory."

I chuckle. "What, you don't feel moved to help her?"

Savannah grows quiet and shakes her head.

"She's not a very nice person."

Then she moves off, cutting around a few older couples and heading toward the lighthouse. I follow, wondering if I'd touched a sensitive spot, or if Savannah is just really eager to see the lighthouse.

She reaches the lighthouse and goes around the broad base, and I follow her. We are off the beaten track for the Red Rice Revel. Here, I can really see the ocean over the grassy lip of the cliff. It's midday, but the sea spray is like icy needles where it touches my bare skin. Savannah turns her face towards it, seeming to enjoy it as we pass close to the ocean. Then we move away from the cliff, and Savannah finds a bench miraculously free of salted mist.

"Want to sit?" she asks.

I shrug, taking a seat. When Savannah sits down next to me, I move down a bit to give us both some room.

She looks at me, her face not giving away her thoughts.

"What?" I snap.

She gives me a playful expression. "I have some news that you're not going to like."

I roll my eyes. "Why do I get the feeling that you're going to tell me anyway?"

She laughs and pulls out her phone. She taps a few buttons and then turns the screen to me. On it is a photo of her and me. It was taken a couple of days ago when we sat on the bench on the South Shore pier. In it, Savannah is looking up at me like she is expecting a kiss.

And me? I'm glowering down at her, but my expression seems more… hungry.

I'm looking at Savannah like I'm a man who hasn't eaten in a week, and she's a ten-course meal.

Underneath the photo is the caption, *Look who we found. Aren't they cute together?*

Oh. My. God. The very idea that Savannah and I are hooking up makes my toes curl. I'm part humiliated, part infuriated, part embarrassed at being caught out. Because in that moment… I *did* want to fuck Savannah. But I don't need the entire world to know all my dirty laundry!

I snatch the phone out of Savannah's hand, incensed. "Delete this right this second!!"

She gives me a funny look. "It's not my photo, Cole. It's a photo posted to Insta from CSAT."

I scowl at her as she takes her phone back.

"What's a CSAT?"

"Cape Simon Around Town. It's an anonymous Insta account for local gossip."

"We have to get it taken down! It's *embarrassing!*" I say, aggrieved. That gives me pause. "How do we do that?"

"It's anonymous," Savannah repeats. "No one knows who's behind CSAT. Although I personally think it's someone with a grudge against hookups. Maybe someone religious or something?"

"We are not a hookup," I growl.

She pins me with a hard gaze. "I think I know very well what we are and are not, Cole. I was there, remember?"

Oh, I remember all too well. The little sigh that escaped her lips, the one I wanted to coax into a moan... nothing would sound as sweet as Savannah feeling pleasure—

"Cole?" she prompts, bringing me back to reality.

God, I really am the worst. Just a complete wretched beast.

I clench my teeth. "I can't believe you aren't going to do anything about it. It's libel!"

"Easy, tiger. There's nothing to do but let the gossip die down. CSAT has been around for a while now. It'll pick something else to focus on soon."

I stare at her for a few seconds. My gaze slips down to her lips.

God, get it together, Cole. You can't just run around kissing your assistant. Your much younger assistant, during the year of your sexile. You are planning to move away in a month, for god's sake. Are those not plenty of reasons why I have to remain professional when Savannah is around?

I grunt and slide away from her, brushing at my coat like she might be contagious somehow.

"Look, you're very pretty, all right? There's no sense in denying that. And I'm obviously very handsome. Maybe that's why rumors are starting about us working together."

Savannah crosses her legs and bobs her foot.

Her silent amusement makes me cringe internally. But now that I've started explaining all the reasons why I don't want to get intimate with her, I have to finish.

I don't want to be accused of leading her on.

"Look, I'm just saying that you're cute. But you are way too young for me. I'm thirty-one. That's practically an old man. And I'm your boss, let's not forget that. I'm in sexile at the moment. And last but not least. I'm moving soon. In a couple of weeks or maybe a month. I'm not really suitable for anybody at the moment."

Savannah smirks. "Did I do something to indicate to you that I'm interested?"

I swallow. "No, but–."

She cuts me off. "Maybe we need to have a firmer agreement. We will be professional and polite, so that when you leave there will be no…." She searches for the right word. "Regrets."

"That was my assumption." I frown. "I don't know about being polite, though."

Do I regret my earlier decision to keep things between us strictly professional? Maybe. Yes. But I understand why it's necessary. For Savannah as much as for me.

Savannah shifts, and her knee slides out from her oversized jacket a little more. I have the urge to look at her legs, but I keep my eyes on her face.

"I may insist on a slight adjustment to the terms," she says. Her eyes glint, and she gives me the strangest smile.

Is she flirting with me? Or challenging me to test my boundaries?

"Savannah–."

A child's shout rings out across the grassy clearing. "Daddy! Where are you?"

I thank my lucky stars that my kid arrived in time. I don't know what I was going to say.

"Charlie!" I call out. "I'm right here."

Savannah and I both stand up. In the next second, Charlie appears, materializing out of the crowd. River is right behind him, looking back and forth between me and Savannah with a smirk. I kneel down to Charlie.

"Hey, kiddo. Did you find anything interesting?"

Charlie is completely wound up.

"A parrot! I pet it! It's soft."

"That's pretty cool!" Savannah cuts in. "I might go look for the parrot."

"Yeah!" Charlie bellows. "You should pet it."

Savannah laughs and nods. "Will do."

She turns and vanishes behind the lighthouse. Charlie keeps babbling about the parrot, and I do my best to listen. But I can't really give him my full attention.

There are too many things racing around in my head. The sizzle of attraction still lingers in the air. But behind it are feelings of hope and uncertainty.

Is this… a crush? Do I have a crush on Savannah? Oh *god*.

"See?" Charlie pulls at my hand.

"What are we looking at?" I ask.

"Daddy, you're silly," Charlie says. He rolls his eyes and beams up at me.

Racing ahead a few steps, he points at a lady selling balloons and makes a beeline for her.

"Oh man. You're in so much trouble," River whispers to me.

"What? Why?" I ask irritably.

"Because you think you're being sly about Savannah. But you are not, my friend."

I put a hand up. "I don't want to talk about her. Okay? Let's just focus on Charlie."

"Sure thing, chief."

But River won't stop smirking at me out of the corner of his eye. I'm starting to realize that maybe my… let's call it appreciation of Savannah's charm and good looks is not exactly going unnoticed.

Not by River. And not by Savannah, either.

Even if I routinely think about how satisfying it would be to kiss her again, I still need to figure out the words to tell my insanely hot assistant that I'm not interested in her… and convince myself as well.

10

<hr>

SAVANNAH

I GRIN AS I LOOK AROUND THE CIRCLE OF KIDS. TWENTY KIDS sit cross-legged on the stage floor at the community center, taking turns introducing themselves to each other, and to me. Two teen girls sit with us, happily volunteering at the community center for high school credit. Jess and Meg don't seem bothered by losing the early hours of the day. I am beyond thrilled that they would choose to spend their Saturday morning doing this.

A little boy says, "I'm Adam. My favorite animal is the tiger."

The girl sitting next to him says, "I'm Amelia. My favorite animal is… wait, are birds an animal?"

"They are," I affirm.

"Okay. Well, my favorite animal is a stork. A bunch live in a lake near my house."

"Wow," I say. "That's great! Charlie, would you like to share last?"

Charlie pouts his lips out and squirms.

"I'm Charlie. I like puppies."

"Puppies are a great animal." I clap my hands together. "Okay. The next game is a memory game. I'll get you started. My uncle Ted went to the store and brought back a…?" I mime thinking about it. "Banana! So, my sentence is, my Uncle Ted went to the store and brought back a banana'. Now Dex here" I gesture to Dex, who is the next in the circle, "will repeat what I said, but add an item. Go ahead, Dex."

He clears his throat and frowns. "My Uncle Ted went to the store."

"And brought back a?" I supply.

"Right. And brought back a banana."

"And what else?"

"Oh, yeah. My Uncle Ted went to the store and brought back a banana and a paperclip!"

"Amazing! Now the next person repeats that sentence and adds an item." I look at the next girl in the circle. "Do you want to give it a try?"

For the next couple of minutes, I listen as we go around the circle. The kids can make it to eight items, but when they try for nine, they burst into giggles. I grin and look around the stage, spotting Lucy sitting in the front row of the auditorium. I get up, urging the kids to continue while in the capable hands of Jess and Meg and jump down to meet her.

"Do you have the scripts?" I ask in a hushed tone.

Lucy grabs the stack of photocopies from the ratty red velvet seat beside her and walks them over to me.

"Thanks! And thanks for bringing Charlie."

"Are you kidding? The kid was born to be on a stage. Putting on a version of *The Wizard of Oz* is a great idea."

My smile grows and I wink at her.

"Don't tell anyone, but I spent a couple of sleepless nights trying to think of how I could prove the community center's worth to your brother Cole. It had to be something good."

That cracks Lucy up. "You are a diabolical genius."

"That's me. An absolute assassin when it comes to protecting the people and places I love," I joke. "Hold on, I'll be right back."

I clamber back on the stage and clap my hands to get everyone's attention.

"Okay. Does everybody know what part they are playing?"

A chorus of yeses arise, followed by the sound of pages turning. Dexter frowns as he sits on his hands.

"I got Toto." He looks up at me. "Is that a good part?"

"Every part is a good part. Everybody gets to speak and act equally."

A girl raises her hand. "I'm The Wizard. But the Wizard is a boy."

"Only in the movie. In this play, the Wizard of Oz is whoever we want to play the role."

She looks thoughtful. Another kid starts to shout a question, but I raise both my hands.

"Meg here will help you all do a line reading of the play. If you can read, read along, and participate. But for those who can't read, Meg will let you know what your lines are when the time comes. Okay? If you aren't satisfied afterward, you can switch roles with each other."

Meg tosses her raven head of hair and smiles at the group.

"Who's Dorothy?" she prompts.

A little girl raises her hand. "Me!"

"Well, then you have the first line, Sarah Ann."

"Oh! Okay." She flips to the right page and starts reading, her words slow as she sounds some of the larger ones out. "I don't like living in T-- …Tex-- …Texas, Auntie Em."

I leave them to it and head back to the auditorium. Lucy is now seated by a young woman I don't know. The stranger has dark hair and gray eyes and is wearing a dark wool coat over a shimmery gold romper. Her makeup is dark and dramatic, but beautifully applied. She smiles at me as I approach.

When Lucy makes eye contact with me, she sits up and makes introductions.

"Savannah, this is my sister Eden. Eden, Savannah. She's working as Cole's temporary assistant."

Eden guffaws. "Poor you! Cole is the bossiest man I know. And that includes my father, who made his fortune buying up small companies, firing the staff, and leveraging the remaining assets. Dad's a cuddly teddy bear compared to Cole. Dad has a more pleasing demeanor, at least."

Lucy elbows her. "Be nice."

"I'm just trying to tell the woman that I totally get her point of view." Eden sighs dramatically and collapses back into her seat.

"She didn't complain about Cole yet. Let Savannah say her piece." Lucy puts her hand on Eden's arm.

"He's not that bad to work for so far." I smile at her. "But if I need to vent, I know where to go."

"That's right." Eden looks pleased. "I do love me some gossip."

I turn my head, looking at the kids on stage. Charlie is grinning so wide his face might split while he says a line fed to him by Meg.

"I'm a Munchin!" he shouts. "I'm--."

Meg feeds him the next bit. "A member of the Lollipop guild."

Charlie tilts his head back and shouts. "Lopilops!!"

I try my best to smother a snicker. "He's a born actor. I knew it from the moment I met him last weekend. The kid's a star."

Charlie shoots to his feet and proceeds to dance, starting and stopping while he makes animal sounds. The whole auditorium fills with whoops of laughter.

"I don't think I've seen Charlie so happy since his mom left," Lucy comments.

"Like I said before, thanks for bringing him. It only took about two minutes of knowing Charlie to predict that he would love being on stage."

Eden tilts her head at me. "You put this all together for Charlie?"

"Well… I'm in charge of watching Dex this week when Birdie is busy working shifts at Savage Pizza. So, I thought that Dex would like it. I wanted to showcase the community center for Cole, to show that it's worth saving. And then I thought of how much Charlie would love the stage… that pretty much settled me on doing the play."

Lucy leans over to me and whispers in my ear. "This is a great idea. Good job."

I start to reply when I hear the creaky old door hinges whine as someone strides through them. My stomach falls when I see that not only is it Cole, but he looks furious.

And right now? He's directing that anger at me.

Lucy curses softly when she sees her brother. She starts to get up, but I wave her down.

"It's okay. Can you watch the stage for me? I'll just be a minute."

Eden turns her head, takes in her brother, and blanches. She sinks down an inch in her seat.

"Crap. He looks mad," she whispers.

I rush toward Cole, who is wearing a pair of dark Dockers under his black overcoat. If he were part of the cast, his expression would make him a shoo-in for the Wicked Witch of the West.

I bring a finger to my lips before he can say anything, then point back out the door he just came through.

"Shhh. Let's talk in the hallway."

Cole gives me a particularly nasty and forbidding look, then sniffs. He turns around and stomps out of the auditorium. Lucy follows me.

I follow more slowly, worrying my lip with my teeth. Cole is in the hallway, scowling at the hole in the wall where a painting used to hang. He looks from the obviously damaged wall to me.

"What is my kid doing here, Savannah? Why did you make my sister bring him?"

Lucy puts up her hands. "Hey, now. Savannah didn't have to force me. I brought Charlie here because it sounded fun."

I suck in a breath, and smile brightly. "And as you can see, Charlie's having the time of his life. He's finding out early that he loves the stage."

"If you are expecting me to say thanks for including him, you can forget it. There's a reason why I want him to play outside instead of playing pretend. His mom is an actress. Or she was. She had a recurring role on a daytime soap opera."

"I'm afraid I'm not seeing the problem." I have to work to maintain my smile.

"His mom loves the attention. But she's also vain, and vapid, and she failed all her school classes that didn't revolve around acting. I want Charlie to grow up knowing how to balance an equation, read more than gossip websites, and name all the planets in the solar system. His mom can't do any of that. I want him to thrive even when the spotlight isn't on him."

"You can act and still do all those things, Cole. But to be fair, I didn't know that there was an actor in the family." I scrunch up my face. "Somehow, I don't think you'll let him get away with that kind of behavior. And the kid clearly loves playing pretend, Cole."

His jaw clenches. "You don't make decisions for my family."

"I'm not trying to. Not one, but two of your sisters are sitting in the auditorium right now. I just sent out a mass text and invited them to come."

That's not the entire truth, per se. But it's all Cole really needs to know.

He pushes out his cheek with his tongue and looks exasperated. "When we get to the car, I will have a word with them. Be sure of that."

I smile at the threat in his tone. Somehow, I don't think that either of his sisters will be fazed.

He continues to glower at me, but his gaze wanders down to the little bit of skin I'm showing at my cleavage. He yanks his gaze away, but it's too late.

I saw Cole looking.

Apparently, the two hours I spent picking out this short dress with pink hearts in anticipation of this moment was time well spent.

Not that I'm into Cole. Not at *all*.

But it's nice to be appreciated, nonetheless. Tossing my hair, I toy with a strand and give him a flirtatious smile.

"I don't suppose you saw the CSAT post about the two of us this morning?"

Whoever CSAT is, they managed to get a great picture of me and Cole at the Red Rice Revel. I'm standing by the jelly booth, clutching Cole's arm and looking at him with a seemingly adoring gaze. It's so *dumb* that someone thinks by shipping us like we're anime characters, they will convince us that we want each other.

Because we do *not*.

Cole clenches his teeth. "No, I haven't seen the post. And I don't want you to show me, either."

I shrug innocently. "Sure."

"Listen, about us working together–."

I cut him off. "I've had a thought about that. I know that you like this building's footprint for the hotel. But I was thinking that I could put together a packet of alternate sites. There are a few that you haven't even laid eyes on yet."

This gets his attention. "Oh?"

"Mhm. If you haven't at least looked at all the locations, how will you know that you've chosen the best one?"

I'm trying to appeal to the practical side of Cole Bennett.

And unsurprisingly, it works.

He nods slowly, then agrees.

"All right. I'll look at all the properties first." He gives me a hard stare. "But if I don't like what I see, you'll have to sit back and let me make inquiries about buying this property."

I lift a shoulder and give Cole a coy smile.

"We'll see."

A second later, I hear a rumbling sound come from over my head. I look up and my eyes widen. Cole shouts and yanks me out of the way just before a section of ceiling tiles crash to the floor. Years of built-up debris and dust rain down from the massive hole, then a pipe bursts, drenching every-thing below it in dirty, rust-colored water.

My breath hitches. My eyes go wide. Suddenly, I realize that I'm nearly face to face with Cole, who holds me tightly against his solid torso with his strong arms. He is very warm, and I get a huge whiff of his naturally clean, male scent.

The temptation to lean closer, press my nose against his neck, and breathe in more of that scent almost overwhelms me. I manage to keep my wits about me, but only just.

The noise subsides as the water slows to a trickle. Cole looks down at me as though he's just now realizing that I am in his arms.

His throat works and he looks directly at my lips.

Lips that know exactly how well he kisses.

I lean in.

I want him to kiss me, I think. *No, I need him to.*

But then Cole gives himself a shake and lifts my body up and away from his. He sets me down and takes a step back, clearing his throat.

"Your ceiling seems to be leaking." His eyes leave me and assess the dirty mess on the floor. "Do you have a mop?"

I'm too busy gaping at the hole in the ceiling. "Oh my god. Oh my god, how could this happen?"

"Easily. Years of neglect can do that."

Without thinking, I reach out and push his shoulder, reprimanding him. "This place is sacred. Have some respect. No one was negligent, okay?"

"So you didn't know about plumbing issues?"

I hesitate, licking my upper lip. In truth, I'd been warning the community center board that we should get some people out and do routine maintenance to the structure of this building for several years now. But this is the first time that anything has gone so terribly wrong.

"Ummm…"

"I take it from your lack of response that you knew."

"I didn't say that!"

"You didn't have to. Now where do you keep the mops?"

"Oh! Probably." My cheeks have got to be the shade of Mars right now. "I'll go look for one."

"Look for a way to turn off the leak while you're at it," he suggests.

"Uh huh." I glance at the broken tile and hurry off toward the nearest closet, hoping to find a mop.

But inside my head, I am reliving the fireworks that I felt when Cole kissed me in the diner. Not just once, but over and over again in my memory. Pow! Pow!

I want to feel that again. For real this time. And I know that only one person can make me feel that way.

Christ. I have a serious crush on Cole! And I think he likes me too.

The question is… do I want him to admit that? Or am I just interested in having him bend me over a park bench?

This situation with Cole has got me wondering what exactly I have to do to make him make a move… and what move I want him to make.

11

SAVANNAH

WHEN COLE PULLS HIS CAR UP TO THE CURB IN DOWNTOWN
South Shore, I am already waiting on the sidewalk because I
refuse to be late. I would rather sit in the freezing cold than
get dressed down by Cole again. It's gloomy today, and
thunder cracks in the distance as I juggle my oversized purse,
a box of the best crullers around, and the two lattes I
snagged. I'm early, and I brought out the big guns to appease
my boss.

Cole emerges from his car with a dark umbrella. He looks
dapper as always, wearing a pair of dark dress slacks under
his usual overcoat. He hurries over to where I stand huddled
under the awning of South Shore's only set of unoccupied
offices.

"Jesus. Let me take something. You look like you're about to
topple over." Cole snags the lattes from me.

I give him my brightest smile. "Thanks."

He peers up at the two-story, chipped brick facade of the
building in front of us. I can almost read his mind.

Is this really where Savannah intends for us to work?

"It's the only place I could find on such short notice. Let's check it out before making a decision."

Cole's lips thin as he opens the plated glass door. Inside, we are presented with two dark wood doors and a set of stairs. The door to my left is already open a crack; I phoned Ms. Brown last night and she said it would be ready for us.

"This place smells like mildew," Cole comments.

I shoulder the left door open all the way and ignore his complaint. The office is a one-room affair. The walls are painted a dingy beige-gray. Several tall windows line the wall, with ancient window shades pulled down. A small powder room is off to the right. To my surprise, the office is already furnished with two old, but massive, teak desks, and a long brown leather couch. The dark wood floors have been redone fairly recently.

Everything seems well-worn but cared for.

"This is actually pretty cute." I turn to see him lingering in the doorway, as though stepping into the office was some kind of commitment. "If it helps, it's very cheap."

Cole perks up at that. "Really?"

He walks in and sets the lattes down on one of the two big desks. I smirk and put the box of crullers and my purse down on the other.

"You know, one of those lattes is for you," I point out.

"Thanks." Cole wrinkles his nose. "I'll drink it. But I prefer an Americano with just a hint of almond milk."

"Noted. When I become a barista, I'll remember that."

He cuts me a look. "You're so funny."

"I try. Now, about the office. Why don't we take it for a month? Then we can decide between renting a nicer space if we need it for another month."

He mulls this while sipping his latte. I take mine and drink a little as he looks around the office, presumably weighing the pros and cons of renting it.

I open the box of crullers and present it to Cole. "Have one. They'll help you think."

"You can't be serious." He makes a face like I just offered him a box of spoiled oysters. "Donuts? No. I'm a grown up."

"Suit yourself." I take a huge bite of my sugary breakfast treat and survey the office.

Being stuck in an office with a grump is easier with the windows open. I bustle around, hoping he'll take note of the way I'm making things easier and stay.

Mostly I'm wondering... is Cole really planning on leaving? And why the frick does that bother me so much?

Cole seems to be lost in a daydream in his own right. It makes me feel a little better. But I notice the white cup in his hand drifting down toward his lap. "You're about to spill your coffee on that very expensive pair of pants if you're not careful."

"Oh. Err... Thanks," Cole says. He sets the coffee down and starts rolling up the sleeves of his blue button-up shirt. I can't help but watch him as he exposes his strong, tanned forearms.

Is that supposed to be so distractingly sexy?

Cole doesn't seem to notice that he's making me flustered. He takes the first office chair and wheels it over to his chosen desk, then sinks down in it with a sigh.

I wheel the second office chair around, turning my back to Cole. I reach over to the chair to grab my coffee cup.

When I turn my head, I see Cole looking right at my ass.

I straighten and turn around. When I glance at him again, he is pretending to be very busy with the papers in front of him.

I smirk. He thinks he got away with sneaking glances at me, but I saw him looking. It's nice to know that he appreciates the dark blue, body-con dress I'm wearing over white tights.

"Knock knock?"

Both of us startle when River pokes his head into the office. He sets down an enormous pile of rolled blueprints on Cole's desk.

"Hey." River embraces Cole. "Nice digs. It's a little sparse in here, though."

Cole shrugs. "Suits me just fine. Did you get all the blueprints I asked for?"

"Yep. Every single building that is on the list of potential building sites." River swings his gaze to me. "Hey, Sav. You look nice."

"Thanks!" I favor him with a sunny smile. "How did you get the blueprints?"

"River is the CEO of Bennett-Taylor Realty. Knowing how to access blueprints is most of his job." Cole slaps his brother on the shoulder.

River pulls a face. "It comes in handy at times like these. But listen, I have a client meeting over in Pineville in an hour. Let's keep this meeting short and sweet."

"Okay. Where should we start?" Cole casts an eye over the blueprints.

"You want to write this down?" River suggests.

Cole smiles pointedly and raises his hands helplessly. "That's why I employ an assistant, isn't it?"

I wave my cell phone at both of them. "I'm keeping notes. Go ahead, River."

River leans against my desk.

"Okay. The first thing you are going to need is a plan. That way, when you present to the City Council, you can answer their questions. Assume that your baseball camp is successful, and you're at maximum capacity. How many athletes will that be? How many staff? Where will the staff live? Where will the guests stay? How will they get to and from the camp? What will they eat when they are at the camp? What about the rest of the time? Where will the guests park? Where will they be accommodated?"

"Those are all good questions," Cole says with a sigh.

"When the planning commission meets, you want to wow them by showing them you have thought of every detail. Plan for emergencies. Plan for hurricanes. Show them that you have put in the work. They will reward you by giving you permits. The permits are your gold stars."

"Gold stars...," I say as I type. "Got it."

River looks at his watch. "Do y'all have any other questions?"

"About a million," Cole says. "But not enough to keep you here. Thanks for making the time."

"You got it. Remember, preparation and planning are half of the battle. The rest is finishing up all the shit the contractors forget to do."

At that, River hustles out of the office, closing the door behind him. I walk over to the blueprints and lift a few, checking them out.

"They are interesting."

Cole's lip twitches. "This entire project is a giant pain in the ass. Rex isn't wrong to plan for the future, but he has terrible timing."

"Well, you did come back to Cape Simon. You're clearly in a period of transition. Maybe he was just taking advantage of the opportunity."

"He is taking advantage all right. And now he has dumped this huge project in my lap." He shakes his head. "I'm going to do it, but it's going to be a slog."

"Let me try to paint this in a different light." I sit on the edge of the desk. "You are going to be working on the main part of a huge project that will earn you a lot of profit in a few years. Not just that, but you're going to be an active part in revitalizing this community. The money that you put into building a hotel and funding local restaurants will be life-changing for the residents of South Shore."

Cole narrows his eyes. I'm sure he's about to pick apart my words, but he surprises me.

"You're saying that the work we are doing could be considered charity? For tax purposes, I mean."

"That's…not exactly where I was going with that."

He gives me a sly smile.

"I think you're onto something there, Savannah. I thought that this project would help Cape Simon out, but…."

"Cape Simon doesn't need any help. It's one of the wealthiest towns in the state. South Shore is hungry for your money."

Cole looks thoughtful. "I guess you're right."

I lean back, accidentally toppling the pile of blueprints. They roll and fall off the desk, unraveling haphazardly as they fall.

"Oh shoot."

I bend down and start rolling up the first blueprint I lay my hands on. Cole comes over and does the same.

We both pick up the same blueprint. He tugs on his end. I stand up, tugging back.

Cole smirks and pulls the blueprint his way, eyeing me defiantly. His yank makes me lose my balance and rips the blueprint. I let go but stumble, trying not to step on any of the rolled-up blueprints. He reaches out to steady me, and I step in his direction, balancing myself up on his arms.

When I straighten, we are practically nose to nose.

Cole's indigo gaze ensnares me. My hands clutch at his shoulders. His scent tickles my nose as I suck in a breath. An expression ripples across his handsome face. If I didn't know better, I would say it was hunger.

His eyes travel down to my lips. I swipe my tongue across them, my breath shuddering to a halt.

Is Cole about to kiss me?

His eyes sink halfway closed and he moves toward me, his hand snaking up to tangle in my hair. My lips part, and my eyes flutter closed. I can feel his breath fanning over my lips, hot and sweet.

My heartbeat thuds loudly in my ears. I can't breathe.

Is this the moment when he finally kisses me? Or am I going to be let down again?

Just when I am certain he's going to pull away, Cole brushes his lips over mine. The touch is teasing, a prelude before he covers my mouth with his.

His kiss is searing, possessive, demanding. It's better than fireworks. Going off in my brain, better than I remembered. His lips shape mine and draw a tiny mewl from my lungs. I can't breathe, but it doesn't matter as I open my mouth to him and let his tongue plunder mine. His fingers in my hair curl to hold me still so that his lips can work against mine.

I push up on my tiptoes, needing more of his heat. My fingers find their way into his silky, dark hair, and all my senses zing at the same time.

I've wanted this ever since he first kissed me all those months ago.

Hell, I dreamed about this. And now Cole is bending me backward and gripping my hair while he kisses me like a starving man falls on a crust of bread.

"What in the sweet Lord Jesus's name am I walking into?" an outraged female voice cries out.

Polarized magnets couldn't fly apart as fast as Cole and I separate. I run my hands down my dress and look to the door, where the landlady is standing.

Five feet tall, seventy-five years old, and exactly the color of a piece of knotted mahogany, Mrs. Glory Brown scowls at us. Wearing a stylish gray, belted tweed coat, and a plastic rain bonnet to keep her hair from getting wet, the owner of the building looks at Cole and me like she just walked in on something altogether scandalous.

"Is this what y'all plan on renting this office for? Because I don't rent my space to people who are gonna disrespect it like that," she scolds us.

I jump in to smooth things out. "Of course not. We just dropped–."

Mrs. Brown stops my words with a hand.

"I don't want to hear excuses, Miss Guthrie. I am just saying what I saw, nothing more than that."

Cole clears his throat, clearly flustered.

"Are you the proprietor?"

She sniffs. "Glory Brown. I own this block of offices."

"This is Pearl's aunt," I supply, making Cole aware of the relationship.

"Great aunt," Mrs. Brown says, lifting her chin proudly. "You all know my little grandniece. I do suppose she's around y'alls age, now."

"Yes, ma'am. Pearl and I went to the same college, Mrs. Brown. Different years, but we are both Agnes Glen girls."

Mrs. Brown manages to look down her nose at me, which is a feat since she's so petite.

"I see. Pearl went on full scholarship, you know."

I nod emphatically. "She's incredibly gifted."

"I know it." She sniffs and looks at Cole. "You're one of the Bennetts?"

"Yes ma'am." He clasps his hand before him and musters a somber expression.

"I'm on the Sisters of Mercy hospital board with your mother, I believe."

"Sarah." Cole gives her a cool smile. "She's my stepmother, but yes. She does great work over there."

Mrs. Brown stares him down for a solid thirty seconds. He keeps the same placid expression on his face. She eventually sniffs.

"All right. Since I know your mother, I'll take you on as a tenant. I will need you to sign a lease, of course. Month-to-month. I'll need a deposit from you. The deposit is nonrefundable because I will use it to pay a cleaner when you leave. Understand?"

"Of course." He inclines his head.

"And you." Mrs. Brown points her finger at me. "I expect that you will conduct yourself better on my property. You hear? You're an Agnes Glen girl, so I know that you know how to behave yourself better than what I just witnessed."

I open my mouth, but no defense seems to leap to mind. I just make a strangled gasping sound.

"Mrs. Brown," Cole says sternly. "Leave Savannah alone. What you saw wasn't her fault. It was my doing. Savannah is nothing if not the perfect picture of propriety. I won't hear you disparaging her."

She looks outraged. "A girl has to take the burden of respectability on herself, Mr. Bennett. And a gentleman ought to know how to conduct himself. It's a dog-eat-dog world out there. Young women need to look out for themselves. Stop letting these raggedy-ass men get between you and what you want in life."

My hand flies to my chest and humiliation burns through my veins.

"Yes, ma'am. Thank you," I reply meekly.

"Thank you, Mrs. Brown." Cole interrupts, putting out his hand. "I'll take the contract if you have it. And the keys."

Mrs. Brown huffs and opens her purse. She stacks a manila folder and a set of keys on top of the desk, deliberately leaving his outstretched hand empty.

"The deposit is fifteen hundred dollars." She looks between Cole and me, frowning. "I'll see myself out."

With that, she turns on her heel and marches out of our office, closing the door with a firm click.

I put a hand to my heart, exhaling a long, steadying breath.

Cole squints out the window. "She's a busybody."

Then he turns, hands the keys to me, and opens the manila file folder she handed him. He sits down at his desk and starts reading, looking completely unbothered. As if we weren't just caught red-handed with our hands in the cookie jar.

I envy his ability to simply not think about what we could have gotten up to had the landlady not interrupted.

I watch Mrs. Brown out the window and wonder about what she said.

Do I need to watch my reputation more closely around Cole?

Moreover, would it be a terrible thing for me to wonder when I can kiss him again?

12

COLE

"So? What do you think of the property?" Beatrice Wilson asks. "Isn't this place an absolute dream?"

I squint at the house, trying to ignore Beatrice. She's a very sprightly sixty-five-year-old real estate agent who has lived next door to La Villa Coralle for as long as I can remember. She tugs on her crisp white pantsuit and looks at me imploringly.

"It's spacious," Rex says. He lopes up from behind me with the property flyer in his hand. "Does it really have his-and-hers, wet-and-dry saunas?"

"Yes! They are outside. Let's head toward the beach."

"Rex." My voice is testy. "This house is way too big for a bachelor."

Rex shrugs. "What is too big, really? Maybe you and Charlie could crash here with me while we work on the training camp."

I check my wristwatch, trying to hide my complete annoyance. "That's three bedrooms. This place has ten. It has the same footprint as our parents' house. You can buy this place, but you're going to pay a fortune in property taxes and insurance."

"It's paying for luxury," Bea interrupts. "Can you really put a price tag on that?"

I give Bea a hard stare. "This place has been on the market for years. I assume that's because the owners won't accept less than some magic number they have in mind. That means it has almost no resale value."

Rex casually leans over and punches me in the arm. "You're always such a downer."

"I thought that was why you brought me here!" I exclaim. "I'm your brother. But more importantly, I'm your agent. I have a pretty good idea of your net worth, Rex."

"I brought you here because you were the only person in our family who wasn't busy today."

"I think you brought me because you like to have someone tell you that you shouldn't do something. You live for the negative reaction. If this is going to be like when you were house shopping in Atlanta all over again, I can just go home."

Rex slides his glance over to Bea. "Cole was very against me buying my last home. But I think I thrived there."

"Your last home was a deconsecrated abbey. It was an insane purchase."

Rex hikes his thumb over his shoulder at me, still talking to Bea.

"He's not a very creative thinker. But I still like to hear his opinion. You know?"

"You have this whole narrative that I'm the grumpy brother," I protest. "But I think I'm the only sensible one. All the rest of you wear the biggest pairs of rose-colored glasses ever."

"Mr. Opinionated over here," Rex says.

"You're being a dick."

He splays his hands and grins at Bea.

"We've been arguing about this exact thing since we were kids." He finally turns to face me. "Remember when Sarah moved in and you kept throwing a fit? You were unbearable even back then. Sarah was moving in with River and Brooks, and you wouldn't let the movers in through the front door. I think Dad had to ground you to get you to stop."

My eye twitches. "It was a lot more nuanced than that and you know it. We had just lost Mom. The whole family was in mourning! And then Dad just moves a strange woman and her kids in without even talking to us about it."

"That's not exactly how it happened." Rex's grin drops away. "Dad had to pick you up and physically move you to stop you from blocking the doors. I seem to remember that you also got in trouble for throwing a fit when Sarah tried to rearrange the knick-knacks in the living room."

"Gentlemen, I–," Bea tries to cut in.

"She took our mom's portrait down and replaced it with a photo of the family dog. Of course I was upset."

Rex flaps a hand. "Sarah didn't mean for anybody to get upset. She was just trying to make the house comfortable for her family."

"I wasn't the only one who didn't take it well. I was just the one who got in trouble for smashing the damn dog photo to pieces."

Rex gives me a cold smile. "You are being emotional about it even now. How is anybody supposed to talk about the past when you are lurking around like a thundercloud, ready to rain on anyone's parade?"

I clench my jaw. "I haven't changed since we were kids? Tell me more about it, Mr. Baseball Hero. Tell me why you relentlessly pursued your dream of going professional, even when you had to give up your hometown and everyone you knew and loved. If I haven't changed, you sure haven't either."

He gives a stunned little laugh. "That's not what we are talking about, Cole. Jesus. I didn't mean to get you started."

"Well, you did."

We stare at each other for a long time. Eventually, Rex caves with a sigh.

"Whatever. Can we continue with the house tour, or are there more past issues you want to rehash in front of Bea?"

I cock a brow. "I'm taking your cues, brother. Doing what you want to do. I am nothing if not loyal to a fault."

His eyes flash and he favors me with a tight smile. "It's one of your many redeeming qualities."

Bea clears her throat. "Are you interested in seeing more?"

"Hell yeah," my brother answers. He elbows me hard in the stomach. "Let's go."

Bea smiles and herds us out of the room.

"Why don't we check out the saunas? There are also two hot tubs and a cold plunge."

Rex rubs his hands together. "Nice!"

"I'll wait for you in the car." I peel off from them and stride toward the front door.

My brother is normally pretty damn demanding, and no little bit infuriating, but today he is killing me. At least he acknowledged that he brought me along to be the squeaky wheel.

I sit with the engine running for almost twenty minutes before Rex jogs up to the passenger side. He opens the door and hops in, his eyes sparkling.

"So?" I prompt.

Rex holds up a set of keys and jangles them.

"I'm buying it."

"Of course you are." I roll my eyes. "Put your damn seatbelt on so we can go get a drink."

13

SAVANNAH

WHEN COLE PULLS HIS SILVER MERCEDES UP OUTSIDE MY house, I peek out the front door. He honks the car's horn at me, and I clatter down the front steps to cross the broken sidewalk in the yard. I have an umbrella, but it does little to protect me; it's raining hard, almost hurricane-like. Sheets of rain pelt me from the side. The wind blows the trees in great gusts as I fling open the passenger door and fold my umbrella.

When I climb inside Cole's car, shaking the raindrops from my light blue trench coat, Cole arches a brow as he looks at me.

"We're going to be late."

He flicks on a button in the console and pulls away from the curb while I'm still putting on my seat belt. The seat grows warm almost instantly.

"You're in a mood, I see." I lick my lips and flip down the visor to try to fix my hair. I had bouncy waves before I stepped outside, but the weather has made me look like a half-drowned Chihuahua, I am sad to discover.

Cole glances over at me coolly when I grunt and flip the visor back up. "You're not as cheerful as I expected."

I force a smile to my lips. He's right. Just because he's as dark as the storm clouds overhead doesn't mean I should mirror his mood.

"Where are we going?" I ask.

"I actually have clients other than Rex. One of them is a football player who lives in Three Oaks. I need to drive over to get his signature on his new contract. I need you to come along to be a witness. That way, if this meathead decides that he doesn't want to pay his agency fees at the end of this year, I can say that he did, in fact, sign the contract. He tried to pull a lot of shenanigans the last time he signed with me."

"So why not just tell him to kick rocks?" I ask.

Cole smirks. "Because he's going to earn ten to fifteen million dollars this year. Depending on whether he's traded to Tampa Bay or Dallas."

My jaw drops. "For that much money, he'd better be the Michael Jordan of football."

"Some of the higher paid QBs make thirty million dollars a year."

I smack his arm. I can't help myself.

"That's bull and you know it."

"It's completely true." He side-eyes me. "What, did you just learn that you're in the wrong profession?"

"I think I'm in the wrong tax bracket to even consider such a thing."

"Speaking of which…." He jerks his head toward the dashboard. "Your first paycheck is in the glove box. I just gave you cash."

I grin and pull out the envelope, then rip it open. Cole looks on as I count out twenty-five hundred dollar bills.

"Oh no. You gave me too much." I take four of the bills and offer the rest to him. "I've only worked for you for a week."

He groans but doesn't take the money.

"I only plan on needing you for a month. Lucy blurted out twenty thousand dollars as your rate. Twenty thousand divided by four weeks is twenty-five hundred dollars. That's what I paid you."

I stare at the bills, trying to process what he's telling me. "You gave me this much on purpose??"

"Well, I don't know that I would've given you so much. But according to Rex and Lucy, I need to quit being such as tight-ass with money."

I'm stunned. I shake my head, unsure what to say. What is there to say to your boss, that you've made out with twice, to convey your total and utter gratitude for your paycheck?

I unbuckle my seat belt, throw my arms around Cole's neck, and give him a tight hug. "Thank you. You really don't know how much this means to me."

"God, okay. Okay!" He leans away and makes a face. "Christ. Put your damn seatbelt back on."

I squeeze him tighter for a beat, then I move back to fasten my seatbelt once again. Cole is looking at me warily, as though I'm a rabid dog wandering around his yard.

My phone chimes. Three times long, two times short. I pull out my phone and see that I have a new match.

Is this the day that my long-haired, hippie prince finds me? Sure, my prince's timing could be better. I'm involved in a flirty, sometimes make out, sometimes brood relationship with Cole. But if Prince Charming is right around the corner…

Apparently not, because Cole clears his throat. "I think we should get some things straight."

Slipping my phone into my coat pocket, I fold the bills up and tuck them away in a zippered pocket of my purse.

"About what?"

"About the… uh… mistake I made the last time I saw you." He looks straight ahead, his hands gripping the steering wheel as this topic is going to drown him and it's his life preserver.

I decide not to throw him another lifeline. "I'm going to need something more than that." I feign confusion. "What mistake?"

Cole's lips thin as he looks over at me. "The kiss. It shouldn't have happened. I'm sorry if it made you think I was somehow coming on to you. I wasn't. It was just, you know, a fluke. It won't happen again."

"Oh!" I blink and try to absorb this.

Cole kissed me, and now he's telling me that it won't happen again? My heart sinks an inch.

I paste the sunniest smile on my face. "Seriously? It was no problem. It was like you said. Just a fluke. I mean, pssh, whatever."

"I'm your boss. You're my assistant. We shouldn't be mixing business with pleasure." He winces. "Not that I really got a lot of pleasure from the kiss. Really, it was just a non-event."

"You're not what I'm looking for. Sorry, but you're not." Words come tumbling out of my mouth. "My dream man is like… the opposite of you. He's a surfer. He has long blond hair, perfect abs, and he serenades me all the time on the guitar. We go for long, barefoot walks on the beach together. He smiles all the time. He never talks about things that would upset me."

Cole snorts. "He sounds about as deep as a rain puddle."

"Maybe that's what I'm looking for," I fire back.

"Maybe that's who you think you want. I can't ever see that working out, though."

I glare at him. "It doesn't matter what you think."

He cocks a brow, challenging me. "I'm not interested in you either. And even if I were, I'm still in the last six months of sexile. And I'm way, way too old for you. Not that you need a bunch of reasons why we can't… explore each other."

I spread my hands. "And you're moving to London soon."

"Right!" He swallows. "Yep, can't forget about that."

"Totally."

He pulls off the main road and onto a dirt road, frowning. "So, we're on the same page?"

"Same paragraph, same line, same word. We are in lockstep."

He peers at me, the relief flooding his features giving me a flash of guilt for feeling a little crestfallen. I don't know if I believe Cole, frankly. But what else am I supposed to do but agree?

"Okay. That's good to know."

I stare at my phone screen forlornly, trying to process the whole mess that Cole just dumped into my lap. We bump down an unpaved country road. The silence stretches between us, filling up the car, seeming stifling. I don't know how to break it, though.

We're both stuck in a bubble of our own thoughts, it seems. Cole clears his throat and attempts to make conversation first.

"Listen. I brought you here to smooth the way for me in getting this guy to sign another contract. When I found out Holly was a cheater after our would-be wedding, she dragged me on social media. There was a lot of fallout; I lost several important clients in the aftermath. So it is really important that I keep every single client I still have. Even ones like this jackass that we are about to go see."

I'm dying to ask him a million questions about Holly and their public blowout. But that's the moment the car slows down.

We pull up in front of a busted-up, brown double-wide. There are five cars parked in the yard, but only one of them – a fancy low-slung coupe – seems to be in working condition. Toys are scattered across the scraggly lawn and a three-year-old sits under the trailer's ripped awning next to a pile of multi-colored toy blocks. He doesn't appear to be wearing anything but a swim diaper even though it's raining buckets and as cold out here as a polar bear's toenails.

When Cole cuts the engine, the front door of the trailer swings open and a scantily clad young woman comes out to snatch the kid up. She glares at us and vanishes inside. I open my car door just in time to hear her shout.

"Boyd! That lawyer is back for you! Boyyyyd!"

Cole looks at me, shrugs, then climbs out of his car. He doesn't fuss with an umbrella-like I do, so he strides right up the three crooked front steps to the door. I follow behind, throwing my umbrella up.

The storm has only grown in intensity since Cole picked me up.

A guy, who I can only assume is Boyd, steps out of the trailer. Approximately the size and shape of a Mac truck, Boyd sports jaw-length dirty blond hair, a white muscle tee, and a baggy pair of black athletic shorts. He looks suspiciously between Cole and me.

"What are y'all doing here?"

"Just came out to get your signature on your contract." Cole steps under the awning and offers his hand to Boyd. Boyd manages to make the normally intimidatingly large Cole look dainty as he shakes the proffered hand.

Boyd looks at me with interest in his eyes. "You gonna introduce your lady friend?"

"Miss Guthrie is just here to help us with the signatures. Miss Guthrie?" Cole looks at me, arching a brow. "Will you fetch the papers from the car?"

I have no idea what Cole is talking about, but Boyd is staring at me with such intensity that it makes me squirm.

"Sure!" I say with a smile, eager to have this over with. "I'll grab them, Mr. Bennett."

I open the door and see that Cole has left the contracts on his seat. Reaching in and grabbing them is the work of a few seconds. I stuff them inside my trench coat for the walk up to the door just as the young woman carries the toddler back out of the house. They are both bundled up in what look like matching blue snowsuits. The woman gives me a nasty glare as she stomps down the steps toward the sports car.

Boyd rolls his eyes and jerks his head toward the house. "Let's get out of the rain."

He grabs the door and holds it open, making eye contact with me. I swallow and hurry toward it, glancing at Cole. Cole's eyes are fixed on Boyd, watching him like someone would eye a caged tiger.

I shiver against the gust of wind and rain that chases me inside the house. When I step inside, I admit that I'm shocked by what I see.

Sleek black couches, a huge TV, and everywhere I look are piles and piles of brand-name shopping bags, their contents spilling half out of them. Designer gowns, high-tech toys, and expensive watches lie in puddles around the living room. A marble statue of two cherubs in flight sits in the corner. A copy of *Everything You Need To Know About Investing In Tech Startups* sits on the end of the couch.

Whoa. I guess I expected to see an extension of the white trash lifestyle displayed in the front yard, not a mixture of nouveau riche and wise investment strategies.

Boyd follows my bewildered gaze to the book on the couch. He grunts, "That's Belinda's. She's the keeper of the purse strings around here. I just catch footballs."

He leans down, scoops a football from amidst the toys and priceless items on the floor, and heaves himself onto the couch. Then he pats the spot beside him.

"Why don't you come sit beside me, Miss Lady?"

Cole cuts in. "We're just here for your signature, as you requested. You said you don't trust the messenger service I used last time."

"I don't. Damn idiots clipped my Chevy Camaro out there. It might not run, but it's still a gem." Boyd flips the football in the air and eyes me speculatively.

Cole holds out his hand to me. I open my trench coat and hand him the contract. He smiles at me and then takes it over to Boyd.

"Here you go. All the terms are what you agreed to when you were last in my offices in Atlanta."

Boyd sucks his teeth. "How can I be expected to remember what we said? How do I know that you didn't change any of the terms?"

"Your lawyer already signed it. You got sick suddenly and had to leave. I'm sure you remember." Cole smiles wanly and shuffles the pages for Boyd. "Sign right here so I can start making deals on your behalf. I can't talk to anyone for you until I get this signed. Your team already sent an offer over to my office last week. I'm curious as the devil, but I can't open the letter until you sign this contract."

"Maybe I won't sign this year," Boyd says. "Maybe I'll represent myself."

Cole's smile turns icy. He leans down, putting his hands on his knees. "You could."

"Maybe I will!" Boyd crows. He glances at me. "What do you think, sugar? I could take you out with all that money I saved. I'd treat you real nice."

It takes everything I have not to shudder in disgust. "You're sweet, but I'm taken."

"Shoot, so'm I. You just saw my old lady."

"She said she's not interested," Cole interjects. "Don't make her say it again."

Boyd stares at me hungrily for several seconds.

"All right. I'll sign. Get me a pen."

Cole frowns and pats his pockets. "I don't have one. Miss Guthrie, could you run and get one out of the car?"

"I think you should do the runnin'," Boyd says. "Miss Lady should come sit on the couch with me. I can keep her company while you're gone."

I swallow and edge toward the door. There is no way in hell I'm going to stay here alone.

But Cole doesn't even let me get that far. He sneers at Boyd and raises his voice.

"You know what, Boyd? You're fired. You're no longer a Bennett Agency client."

Boyd rises to his feet, his eyes narrowing.

"You can't fire me. I'm Boyd Jackson!"

Cole grabs my arm, steps in front of me, and backs me toward the door. "You have been a pain in the ass every single day since I signed you," he tells Boyd. "I was willing to deal with it until you acted like some asshole caveman in front of my assistant. Here's a tip. You don't hit on people that are just here to do their jobs, Boyd. And representing you? It isn't worth the hassle."

Boyd uses his immense physical heft to swing a fist at Cole's face just as Cole is turning his attention to me. Boyd cold cocks him, hitting him squarely in the right eye. The sound of Boyd's fist connecting with Cole's face is a sickening smack.

Cole is totally unprepared for the blow. He sways, his hands coming up in a defensive posture.

"What the fuck, Boyd?" he practically screams.

Boyd swaggers forward, bottom teeth bared, ready to fight. "You can't fire me, you fucking city-slicker piece of shit!"

For a second, I'm afraid that Cole is going to try to hit Boyd. I grab at the back of Cole's coat.

"Cole, please!"

Cole doesn't look at me, but he doesn't move forward, either. Boyd hisses and lunges toward us. Cole pushes me out the door just as Boyd roars and rushes him. There is a scuffle and a few thumps as fists are thrown. I cringe and run toward the car, trying to think of who I can call.

Lucy? Rex? The police?

"Asshole!" Boyd hollers.

Cole ducks out of the double-wide and bolts for the car. I climb in and open his door, my heart pounding. Cole scrambles inside just as I hear the last thing that you want to hear while fleeing a redneck's property: the sound of a racking shotgun.

Cole floors the car just as Boyd shoots, the pellets spraying the back window and shattering it.

Cole whips into reverse and we jolt down the dirt lane. I scramble for my seatbelt and can't control my runaway heartbeat.

But Cole?

Cole is grinning.

He turns the car around and throws it in gear, racing away from Boyd's house.

My heart is pounding. Cole just told me how he can't afford to lose any more clients. Then Cole dumped Boyd because he was an asshole to me.

I swallow. I feel vindicated, but also a little bit scared of Cole. Seeing him blow up like that was a totally new, and frankly scary, experience.

In the back of my mind though, I must admit that it was also titillating.

Cole stood up for me… But what did it mean?

And more importantly, what do I want it to mean?

14

COLE

Stepping outside the La Villa Coralle onto the patio, I squint into the bright sunlight. It's a rare sunny winter day and my family is taking full advantage. They all move like ants swarming the beach below, all dutiful and industrious. Call our family anything you want, but you can't call us lazy.

I bend down to pick up a piece of driftwood and wince as the blood pounds in my face. Bringing my hand up, I gently touch the edges of my monstrous black eye. Two days later and it still looks absolutely terrible.

And the questions I've gotten from my family are so incredulous as to be almost funny.

Almost.

Down on the beach, Lucy arranges a circle of folding beach chairs under an awning. Rex and River are digging out posts for the volleyball net. Dad and Eden are filling a giant sandy hole with charcoal briquettes for a low and slow seafood roast.

Sarah stops beside me, her arms full of rolled towels.

"What do you need, Cole?" she asks.

I pull a face. What do I need? So many things. But none of them are things that she can provide. I sigh deeply.

"Nothing." I heft the ice chest off the ground and start down the path to the beach. Sarah follows. I give her a tight smile over my shoulder. "I hope it's okay that I invited my assistant here."

"As long as you two don't spend the entire time working." Sarah shrugs. "I guess you've been in the city for too many years to remember that we hold a bonfire anytime the Lord blesses us with a winter day like today. It's so gorgeous out here."

Sarah is making a subtle reference to me moving away, and insinuating that I don't remember my childhood in the Cape. My first instinct is to tell her that this has been my home longer than she has been here. But that would only start a fight. I would look like a bully.

My grip on the cooler tightens, but I force my face to relax. Instead of reacting to her words, I just say, "It is pretty outside."

"Cole!" Walker, Rex and Rhett's best friend, shouts my name. "Come help me dig this pit for the food to cook in! It's almost done."

I give Sarah a hard smile. "I'm off to help."

She nods and walks over to Lucy. I plunk the heavy ice chest down by a chair and walk over to the area that Walker has cleared of debris. Walker is a frequent house guest at La Villa Coralle, being in charge of the legal department for my father's company. At the moment, he's rolled up the sleeves of his button-up and the cuffs of his blue Dockers, and is dragging a large piece of driftwood into the middle of the circle. He looks over at Charlie, grinning at him.

"Doing okay over there?"

My son is making a circle of grapefruit-sized rocks around the perimeter of the three-quarters-finished pit. He raises a rock with the seriousness of an undertaker. "Almost done."

"Can you start digging while I grab some more driftwood?" Walker asks me.

"Sure." I walk to the middle, grab a shovel, and start digging. In the back of my mind, I wonder where Savannah is with the blueprints I asked her to pick up from the office before coming here.

Did that piece of rusting metal she insists on calling a car finally clank to a halt for the last time? I'm about to stop and check my phone when I hear Lucy's voice.

"Sav! Sav, over here!"

I turn and see Savannah clutching an oversized white sun hat to her head. I'm glad to see that she chose blue jeans, pink canvas shoes, and a very warm-looking bright pink parka to wear today. I admit, I was afraid she would show up in her normal heels and short dress. Don't get me wrong. I like Savannah in any clothing. But if I'm honest, I prefer to see her dressed more comfortably and laid back, like she is right now. There's something sexy about picking substance over style. A lesson that Holly could have used, for sure.

Savannah has an oversized black canvas tote over her shoulder with several rolls of blueprints sticking out.

"Hey!" She hurries over to Lucy, giving her a quick squeeze. "Wow, I didn't realize that y'all were gonna go all out."

Lucy grins. "Blame my mom. She freaking loves the beach during the winter."

My dad stands up and walks over to the girls. He thrusts his hand out. "Hi there. I'm Sam Bennett."

Savannah beams from ear to ear. She puts her tote bag down and shakes his hand.

"I've heard so much about you. It's nice to match a face to the stories Cole tells me. And this house is just…" She whistles. "Like, wow. I love the hydrangeas that you have out front. Those really take a lot of hard work to maintain. They look gorgeous."

My dad lights up. "Thank you, young lady. The house is my pride and joy, after my grandson of course. You should make sure that one of the kids gives you a tour later."

Savannah smiles and turns, scanning the beach. Somehow, she hasn't noticed me yet. And a petty little voice inside my head is practically screaming for her attention. It fucking stings that she hasn't looked my way yet. I want her eyes on me, and only me, right this second.

I stand up, stick the tip of my shovel into the sand, and wave at her. Savannah spots me, blinks several times, and her eyes widen. I glance down at my rolled-up sleeves and bare feet. Ah, she's not used to seeing me dressed so casually.

Surely, it's that and not the fact that she might find me attractive. Sure, she kissed me back… but a large part of me wonders if she's hungry for more. Me? I'm a starving man. But I can't figure her out.

Savannah comes over, lugging her tote. She grins at me as she comes to a stop. Then she bends and curtsies.

"Sire, I hath brought thou the maps thou hath ask-eth for."

I arch a brow at her.

"Savannah!" Charlie calls. He runs straight over to her, plowing into her hard enough to send them both tumbling to the ground.

I jump into the fray and help Savannah up. She flips her blonde tresses back with a hand and grins at Charlie. "It's nice to see you too, Charlie."

I frown at my son. "You shouldn't knock people over, kiddo. Tell Savannah that you're sorry."

I help him up and he brushes his hair out of his eyes sheepishly. "Sorry. I got excited."

Savannah bends down to pick up her hat from the ground and winks at him. "I feel that way all the time. It's always nice to see people that I know."

"I love acting!" he blurts out. "I love the L--." He pauses and his brows lower. "Loll-i-pop."

"You make a great Munchkin, kiddo," Savannah says.

I tousle Charlie's hair. "Go ask Walker if he needs any help."

"Okay!" Charlie takes off, sprinting flat out toward my dad.

"Where does his energy come from?" Savannah shakes her head. "My nephew Dexter is like that. I would kill for a tenth of that kind of energy."

"I know. It's annoying that it's a natural resource that seems to dry up when you get past childhood."

She nods then looks up at the sun. "Do you want to look at these blueprints now?"

I shade my eyes and glance around the beach. "I don't know. Can you stay for a while, or…?"

"You can have me for as long as you want me," she says. Our eyes connect and she blushes. "Today, I mean. I'm not busy."

"Right." I squint, refusing to feel awkward. "I'll just get my family set up and hang out with them a bit. Then we can sneak off and study the blueprints."

She swallows. Our eyes meet once again, sticking for a few seconds too long. I can't help but notice her worrying her lip. The curve of her full bottom lip draws my attention.

The sense memory of Savannah in my arms as her lips work against mine is almost paralyzing.

…and then I realize that I've been staring at her mouth for what seems like an age. Jesus.

Shaking my head, I clear my throat. Savannah looks at me like she isn't quite sure what to say.

"Hey!" Walker comes over with another stack of driftwood. He tosses it down in the clearing and brushes his hands off. "I think this is a good start." He notices Savannah and gives her a friendly smile. "Hi, I'm Walker."

Savannah's smiles. "I know who you are. You're almost as well known in Cape Simon as Rex. You raised a lot of money for Lighthouse Hospital by running a marathon."

"That's me," Walker admits. "To be fair, Rhett and Rex were running it with me."

I scowl as they shake hands. Walker is tall, handsome, and has a great head of dark blond hair, I can see why any woman with eyes would fall head over heels for him. He's a lawyer, he's in shape, there's always a smile on his face, and he looks like he just hopped off a runway.

In essence, Walker is Savannah's *type*. If he were shoeless on the beach, I would legitimately be worried right now.

Every girl I liked in high school lusted after Walker. I'll always see him as a threat, no matter how nice he is. And because I have *certain feelings* about Savannah, I can't help my kneejerk reaction. Walker and Savannah are still smiling at each other when I cut in.

"Savannah, let's head back to the house now." I clap my hands and look around. "Everyone else is still busy."

Savannah narrows her eyes at me. "Didn't you say that you wanted to help your family get settled?"

I laugh and place a hand on her arm. What am I doing? I shouldn't be touching her so casually.

"I changed my mind. Will you come with me?"

Walker looks at both of us as if trying to puzzle out what is going on. Savannah gives him an apologetic glance.

"Excuse me. I'll be back."

Physically shepherding Savannah by putting my hands on her upper arms and gently beginning to push her, I usher her toward the path leading to the patio. I feel like a madman, but I can't help but put myself between her and Walker. I just can't trust him not to make her swoon.

"Wait!" She puts her hand on my arm, stopping me in my tracks. She runs back for the tote bag holding the blueprints, then speed walks back. She is eyeing me with a mixture of worry and curiosity.

Fair enough. I behaved oddly. I just have to get her away from Walker.

"Come on. We can go into the dining room. It should be completely empty."

I lead her up the patio, into the living room, and through the dining room. I spin around and watch Savannah as she looks around with wide eyes.

"Wow. Your parents really are loaded, huh?"

"I guess so." I shrug and step into the dining room. Frowning, I glance around. "My Dad runs a number of companies. Sarah's just... there."

Savannah squints. "Who is Sarah again?"

"My stepmother."

"Oh! Well, I'm sure she does her part." She squints around at the mess. "Let's find another room to look at the blueprints in. Unless you've changed your mind about wanting to work now that I'm not meeting your handsome friends."

She sneaks a grin at me. I feel my neck heat and a denial is the first thing out of my mouth.

"I don't know what you're talking about," I say pointedly. "Let's go to the study."

She laughs lightly as she follows me toward the study. "Your sudden change of heart had nothing whatsoever to do with the way you scowled at Walker? He was just being friendly."

I huff. "It was perfectly innocent. And I know what his version of friendly means, okay? I went to high school with the guy. Women can't seem to help themselves around him."

"I see. And you think that by shaking his hand, I will realize that I'm deeply in love with him?"

Pushing open the study door, I glare at her. I point at the couch. "Of course not. I didn't mean that at all."

Savannah walks past me, a little smirk on her face. It's extremely annoying and I want to shut her up.

She looks around, then takes a seat on the couch, setting her tote bag down. I take the other end of the couch, pushing my hand through my hair.

Savannah sizes me up. "So. What did you mean?"

I scowl at her.

"About Walker?"

"Yep." She sits back and crosses her long, shapely legs.

"I didn't mean anything. I just know the way Walker gets around cute women."

Her eyebrows rise. "You think I'm cute?"

Could this conversation get any more embarrassing? What do I tell her?

No, you're horrible to look at, please leave?

Her eyes pin me in place, and I roll my eyes.

"You are exactly the kind of girl that would catch Walker's eye. Okay? I'm not going to lie about your… qualities."

"My qualities?" Savannah gives me a playful smile. "Please, continue to paint yourself further and further into a corner. It amuses me."

"Very funny." I can feel the tips of my ears growing red. "Give me that bag."

She pushes the tote over to me and I pull out the first blueprint.

"This is…." I unroll it. "Ah, the first draft of the potential sports complex. Nice."

Savannah scoots closer, her jeans-clad thigh brushing mine. I swallow heavily and try to focus.

What was I saying?

She reaches over me to touch the far side of the drawing. "Is this the…?"

She brushes my knee and pulls her hand back, turning red. "Sorry. I–."

That's when I realize just how close we are. I glance at her face and I'm caught in her hazel gaze. From this close, I can see now that her eyes are actually the color of cognac with flecks of deep green. Have her eyes always been that exact shade of hazel?

Before I can speak, Savannah puts a couple of inches between us. "Sorry. That's my fault."

Shoving a hand through my hair again, I shake my head. "It's fine."

Tension sizzles between us as I grab another blueprint and unroll it. Secretly, I'm wondering what kind of idiot I am to think that bringing Savannah somewhere more private was a good idea.

I'm supposed to be in sexile, not lusting after desirable women in my dad's study. What is this, tenth grade of high school? *Pull it together, already.*

I grunt as I try to straighten out the blueprint, which seems determined to retain its curled shape. Savannah scoots close again, and tries to smooth out a corner. The thick curtain of her blonde hair tickles my nose, and I am suddenly in a field of delicious smelling wild roses. She flips her soft hair over her shoulder, and smiles at me, nervous as a newborn foal.

I would have to be a much stronger man than I am to resist her allure.

Grabbing her shoulders, I cover the seam of her lips with my own. It's a gesture of frustration born out of futility. But I swear, when my hands slide down to dig into her waist, it's the only inevitable conclusion.

I need to taste her lips, to cup her jaw, to tease her mouth open, and snake my tongue inside.

She responds with the tiniest moan, and by slipping her hands around my neck. I feel like my kiss is what she's wanted for so long.

What we have both wanted. The first two kisses were fiery. But this kiss? It's *explosive.*

Savannah shifts toward me, and I pull her body on top of mine. She straddles my lap, desperately pressing her body against me. I'm hard and ready, rocking my hips against her, a soft growl coming from somewhere low in my chest.

I'm hungry, but kissing Savannah makes me hungrier than before. I'm damn near *starving* and kissing her is only making me realize the depth of my greed. My hands travel down to cup her ass while I plunder her mouth. God, her weight on top of me feels good.

But I need *more*.

I bury my face in her hair, smelling her delicate rose scent, and thrust my hips up against the seam of her denim-clad thighs. I know what I'm doing is wrong… but it feels–.

"Hey, can–?"

River opens the door, gets a peek at what Savannah and I are doing, and then practically jumps backward out of the study.

"Whoa. Sorry."

Savannah and I scramble to opposite ends of the couch. If I could stand up without showing off my raging erection, I would hightail it out of the room in an instant.

"I'll be out in a minute," I say in a strangled voice.

River plays it cool. "Sure. Sorry again. Uh… yeah. Come find me. But, uh, take your time."

I grimace. "Totally. Be right there."

If my brother hadn't just interrupted us, would we have just had sex on the couch? Looking at Savannah's red face, I think I know the answer. She stands up, straightening her clothes.

"I should go."

"No!" I say, unintentionally raising my voice.

Savannah looks at me with wide eyes. "Is everything okay?"

"Yes. Yes, sorry. I just meant… I invited you here for the day. I don't want you to feel like you have to leave. This was… this was my fault." I clear my throat, finally deciding to take a chance and stand up. "I should go find my brother. But you should… you shouldn't leave. Stay for the food."

"Sure." Savannah ducks her head. She literally could not be any redder. "For the food, And… for Lucy."

I edge out of the room. "Great."

"Great!" She gives me a thumbs up. "Fantastic."

I turn and get the hell out of the study, my steps carrying me toward the front door. I open it, slip through to the outside, and then lean down with my hands on my knees.

"What the hell was that?" I whisper to myself.

My head throbs. Worse than that, my cock is still half-stiff.

What is this woman doing to me?

15

SAVANNAH

The day of the Bennetts' beach party was the last time the sun shone in the Cape. Today is another in a long string of blustery, cloudy days. I am trying not to be miserable, but it's pretty hard when Lucy brandishes her latest find at me.

"Eww." Lucy uses a long, wood pole with a spike attached to pick up what appears to be a half-melted diaper from the beach. She stuffs it in her bag and shivers comically. "Gross."

"Yep. Humans are disgusting. That's what I'm finding out today."

"They really are. I am so done with people. I literally just deleted all my dating apps last night."

Lucy glances at me. "You did?"

"Yup. Because humanity sucks." I spear a piece of trash and add it to my overflowing bag.

"No other reason?"

I shrug and smile at her. "What other reason could there be?"

Lucy stays mum, but I'm sure I catch her pulling a face.

The wind whips around me, snatching at every piece of clothing and trying to tear the trash bag from my hands. It's not storming out, but this icy wind is threatening to freeze me solid. I hitch my neon-yellow safety vest against my dark parka, and wiggle the elastic band of my right work glove. It's really itchy. Everything is bothering me today more than it should.

I push out a sigh and grab my trash bag.

"What's up, buttercup?" Lucy asks. She uses her trash picker to snag a few pieces of newspaper. "I thought you were all pumped for this year's South Shore beach clean-up day."

I wrinkle my nose. "I was. I mean, I am. Everything is just getting on my nerves today for some reason. Like my parka is too baggy. My gloves are itchy. And we keep finding fricking diapers on the beach. I mean, who throws their diapers away in the ocean?"

"Heathens would be my guess." She slides a thoughtful gaze my way. "And I'm not used to hearing complaints from you. Are you by chance about to have your time of the month?"

"No." I flush and shake my head. "I think I'm just having an off day."

Lucy cocks a brow at me and points her stick in my direction. "This wouldn't have anything to do with my big brother, would it?"

"Which one?" I stab an empty cigarette pack hard. "You have so many to choose from."

She stops and pins me with a hard gaze.

"Are we pretending that you don't spend a lot of time with Cole?"

"Ah, yes. Mr. Doom and Gloom himself." I glance at her with a smirk, then look up and down the beach. There are clusters of people in yellow vests, with trash bags and picker sticks, in both directions.

"Do you want to take a break for a few minutes? I'm about frozen though."

"Ugh, I thought you would never ask." She grins at me. "The volunteer tent has cocoa."

"I would kill for a heated blanket right now." I blow on my hands and cover my nose. "Let's go get warm."

Lucy grins and links arms with me. I laugh as we both try to wrangle our trash bags with our picker poles as we head up the beach.

"So? Are you going to dish?" she asks.

"About…?"

"Cole! What happened? He's been an unbearable grump for the last few days since you left our house. And I never got the whole story about how he ended up with a black eye, either."

"Do we have to talk about Cole?" I stick out my tongue and make a gagging sound.

In my head, though, I'm remembering exactly how it felt to kiss Cole in the den several days ago. A rush of heat shudders down my spine.

"You're blushing!" Lucy giggles. "Tell me, or I will be forced to impale you with my interrogation stick."

She wiggles her trash picker at me. I roll my eyes.

I'm so cold that I huddle closer to her as we walk. "There's not that much to tell. Cole got that black eye from one of his clients." I hesitate. "His client was being extremely rude to me, and Cole wasn't interested in taking his crap anymore. Cole did stand up for me, but it was just because he felt like the client was disrespecting his whole company."

Lucy bleats a bark of laughter.

"That's not it! Cole is notorious for not caring how clients treat him. He gets screamed at for a living. Plus, his ex, Holly, was always getting in his face for every little thing. He's weirdly immune to it. So, I'm calling BS on your theory."

My eyes widen. The mention of Cole's ex makes me deeply curious. But of course, I can't ask Lucy. That would be prying.

"That's pretty much the whole story."

We climb the crest of grassy sand that leads us off of the beach. Lucy pouts.

"You're being evasive. Something happened when you came to visit the house. You two disappeared for a long time. And when you came back, you couldn't even look at each other." She elbows me in the ribs, which honestly hurts.

"Ow!" I protest. "God, okay! Cole kissed me. Are you happy?"

"What?!" She stops, drops her trash bag and picker, and claps her gloved hands over her mouth. "How? When? Did you kiss him back?"

I flush and pick up her trash bag. "No comment."

"Oh my god!" Lucy picks up the pole, and rushes to catch up to me.

The volunteer tent is within sight; I can see a plume of steam rising from its white plastic roof. If I can just get there, I can neatly avoid having this conversation with Lucy.

"I can't believe you are dating my brother," she says, sounding awestruck. "How are Rhett and Rex still single, and Cole's now on his second serious relationship?"

"Whoa, whoa." I stop, pinning Lucy with my gaze. "Cole and I aren't dating. We are not in a relationship either. He's my boss, Lucy. And…."

Lucy grabs my hand, a grin plastered over her face. "And?"

"And I'm not interested. Even if I was, he's too old for me. He's fresh out of a marriage. And besides that, he's planning to move abroad! We basically have nothing in common other than, you know, a kiss."

I'm lying. I know it. Lucy probably knows it. But it feels too dangerous to just openly admit that I want to bang her brother.

No, actually. It's not the sex that I'm trying to cover up. It's how Cole makes me feel.

Like I can do anything.

Like I'm the most wanted person in the room.

Like he actually sees me. No one sees me, not really. But Cole… he makes me feel like a person worth listening to. That's some heady yet scary stuff.

I huff, hauling my bag up to the tent.

"Wait!" she cries.

But I can feel the tears gathering in my eyes. Tears that have no business being there.

I am not interested in Cole. I am *NOT*.

"I am super done with this conversation," I rasp. I'm desperate to escape Lucy's questions. "I need a break."

Lifting the tent's flap, I barrel right into a surprised-looking Cole. He manages to steady himself while holding onto me.

Because of course I would literally run into the very subject I was trying to flee.

Cole looks as put-together as ever. He even smells nice. I, on the other hand, probably smell just like the trash bag I'm holding. It's not good.

Our gazes catch and hold like Velcro. It's impossible not to be mesmerized by those azure eyes. A crinkle of humor flits across his face as he looks down at my outfit.

"Neon yellow suits you."

If I kept a journal, my entry today would start with: *Dear Diary, today I made Cole smile.*

I put that expression on his face. I made his eyes crinkle. It feels monumental.

I swallow, and notice Lucy nudging her way into the tent behind us. It takes everything inside me to step out of Cole's grasp and put some distance between us.

He notices. I swear, a tiny wrinkle of worry forms between his brows. And then he sees Lucy and moves back, clearing his throat.

"Looking for something warm to drink?" He jerks his head over to the corner. " Coffee, tea, and hot chocolate are over by the snack table. Here, let me take your trash bags."

He grabs both black plastic bags and ducks outside. Lucy raises her eyebrows.

"Something is going on with him." She whispers it so that no one else can hear, but I shake my head.

"Go get something hot to drink."

She just smirks and walks over to the table. It's piled precariously high with every kind of baked good imaginable. When I turn, Cole pops his head back in the tent. He looks at me and jerks his head outside.

"Come on."

Curious, I slip outside the tent. We haven't spoken at all in the two days since we kissed. And now that I'm presented with the chance, I feel butterflies low in my abdomen just from seeing him.

Honestly? It's so cliché that I could *die*.

"Should we… talk?" I call out to Cole as I hurry to keep up with him.

"Not here," he mutters. "Get in the car."

Cole is already walking toward a gleaming white Range Rover. He opens the passenger's side door and stands there, looking impatient. My eyes widen.

Have I earned this gentlemanly treatment all the sudden?

"Are you coming or not?" he calls, his voice testy.

I have no idea what he's talking about, but I hurry to get in the passenger side of the SUV. Cole shuts my door, sprints around to climb in his side, cranks the heat, and pulls out before I can even get my seatbelt on.

"Where are we going? And whose car is this?"

His lips curl up just slightly.

"We're on a food run to the grocery store in the Cape. Apparently, whoever got the food neglected to get anything gluten free. So I volunteered to go get something." He presses his lips together. "And this is my dad's SUV. I borrowed it to be able to haul stuff today."

"Ah." I chew my bottom lip. There are about fifty things I want to say to Cole. Ten of them are things I probably *need* to say. But somehow none of them seem called for.

So I stare out the window at the bleary gray landscape instead.

"What, no cheerful quips today?" Cole prompts.

I hear my mom's voice in the back of my head. *Girls should be cleaner than sunshine and sweeter than honey.*

Funny, I don't feel particularly sweet today. And I'm covered in grime. I wonder if Mom ever made allowances for beach clean-up day? Since I'm not clean, do I have to be sweet? Because I sure don't feel it. But I can fake it.

I turn to Cole, forcing a smile to my lips. "What do you think we should talk about, Cole?"

"Well... I should apologize for this weekend. I was out of line." He looks straight ahead. "I kissed you. You didn't ask me to. I just... couldn't help myself. I want us to have a good working relationship, you know?"

I give him a little side eye. He deserves a little ribbing.

"And yet you keep kissing me. Why do you think that is?"

He drums his fingertips on the steering wheel. "I don't know. I can't seem to stop myself. It's embarrassing, frankly. I think it's a physical need. Not... not anything emotional or complex."

Cole's words bruise me. He's really going to downplay this by blaming his body? I can't even process that. I'm over here, wanting Cole to want me back. And he's just downplaying and dismissing our make out by blaming his hormones?

Yuck.

I huff. "So you were just kissing me because you were horny? That isn't very flattering."

"Sorry. I shouldn't...." He tightens his hands on the wheel, and shakes his head. "I'm just saying, I will do better. I'll behave like a gentleman. Not some oversexed teenager. I swear."

He bangs the wheel for emphasis, startling me.

"It's not completely your fault. I kissed you back. I might have been... flirtatious. Not because you're you. Just because I'm a flirt by nature." Is that true? I don't know, but it seems like the thing to say. "I'm just saying that it isn't personal. Like you said."

"So I'm just a warm body to you? Is that what you're saying?"

"No! You're a beautiful girl who is nice to me. And I'm being weak. That's the root cause of all of this. It's my fault, like I said."

"That's a cop out and you know it."

"You're making this harder than it needs to be." Cole licks his top lip.

I smile, but it feels as fake as a three-dollar bill. "Let's just iron this out, then. There will be no more kissing. There will be no longing glances. And no hand holding."

"Exactly! I think we're on the same page. I mean, it's not that you're a bad kisser. I just… I should be focused on my work."

"And Charlie," I add.

He nods. "And Charlie."

"You know, I deleted all my apps yesterday. But now that you've made things between us clear as crystal, I should get back in the saddle. I am downloading Cupid's Arrow right now." I pull out my phone and wave it around. "My sister says I need to find someone and settle down."

That's a lie. Birdie has never said anything of the sort. In fact, I think my sister might be permanently sowing her wild oats, as they say. As much as she can as a single mom, anyway.

Cole pulls up outside the grocery store. I blink, having completely forgotten our mission.

"So, we're good?" Cole asks.

"Yeah, of course. Why wouldn't we be?"

His eyes narrow to slits, piercing me through. For several seconds I wait, my breath catching.

Then I think, *this isn't normal. What would I normally do?*

Easy. I'd be happy that I made a grumpy man smile, and I'd stop wanting anything more than that.

16

COLE

"No. Absolutely not."

I gesture at the landscape surrounding the decommissioned school. Savannah stands in front of the building, hugging her long, gray coat closer to her body.

"You haven't even looked at the school yet. You asked for something with a sizeable footprint." She waves her hands at the school. "This is perfect!"

I cross my arms and glare at her.

"The community center had the advantage of being placed right on the shoreline. This place is in the middle of nowhere. I can't even make out the outline of South Shore from this distance."

I shade my eyes and look at the wetlands around me. On my far right, some sparse woods spring up. To my left is a bumpy gravel road. And directly ahead of me are miles of wetlands that end with beach somewhere in the distance.

"You're not imagining the possibilities." Savannah shivers. "God, it's so freaking cold!"

"Get in the car." I jerk my thumb toward my Mercedes. "We can argue in there as well as anywhere. At least it has heated seats."

"Oh, ha ha. You're so witty."

But Savannah still hurries toward my car. We get in and I turn the heat up all the way. I also engage the heated seats, as promised. She stuffs her hands into her pockets and gives me the stink eye.

"Why do we have to look at lots that already have buildings on them again?" she asks.

I sit back with a loud sigh.

"Because that way we know that an environmental study has already been done. We're in the middle of the wetlands. A lot of protected pieces of land are dedicated to species around here."

She wrinkles her nose. "What about the new training camp? It's a huge stretch of untouched wetlands. You'd have to get a study done on that land anyway."

I smirk at her, catching and holding her gaze. She blinks, breathing hard, then flushes and looks away.

God help me, but I like that I can force a that kind of reaction from her. It reminds me that I am still very much a man.

"Actually, a site study was done on that land a few years back. Some billionaire from Macon was thinking of building a football stadium there, for reasons unknown. He didn't, obviously. But as long as the survey stakes are still in place, we're good to go."

"I guess figuring out where the hotel should go is the last thorn in your side." She appears pensive.

"The only thorn in my side is you complaining about my intention to take over the community center."

Savannah grabs my wrist, yanking on it to ensure she has my attention.

It works.

"The town of South Shore will let you do almost anything you ask because you have money. They might even green light tearing down the community center. But it's against their own interests. Do you understand what I'm saying?"

I twist my wrist and then grab hers instead, giving me the upper hand.

"That's capitalism. Can you blame the planning committee for being willing to take my money?"

She tugs her wrist from my grip and pins me in place with beseeching eyes.

"Money may blind the committee. But it won't hold computer literacy classes or chess tournaments. It won't put on children's plays or host Geechee cooking classes. The community center costs more to run than it can ever fundraise. But it is the one place that doesn't ask if you're rich or poor, what kind of family you come from, if you're young and able-bodied, or old and still active."

It's frustrating to see how much Savannah cares about the crummy old building. I take a breath, waiting a few beats to gain my composure before speaking.

"Why the hell are you so passionate about that place? It's like you are personally invested in it. I don't get it."

Her cheeks flush the same shade of pink as Sarah's roses at La Villa Coralle.

"Because my sister and I used to hang out there a lot as kids. We never had money, but the volunteers at the community center never gave us a moment of grief over it. And besides, sticking up for the community center is exactly what my mom would do."

Her words startle me. I never put much thought into her lack of funds. I just accepted her not having money as a temporary situation and went on with my life. I guess that makes me a bit self-involved.

What do I say to Savannah's status? I wanted for nothing as a child.

"I didn't know," I finally say. I find that I can't quite meet her eyes.

She shrugs and looks away out the window.

"You asked. I struggled in the same way that everybody in South Shore struggled. I know the temptation that money will bring."

There's nothing that I can say to that. It's true, obviously.

"The thing is, Sav, we are not here to protect the community from itself. We're here to line up the best accommodations for our project. I'm sorry, but I think we're going to have to move on the community center." I try to word the next bit delicately. "I will try to offer the planning committee a little more money to build the community center *if* they accept us funneling the cash toward a new center. But… I don't expect them to accept any amount that I'm offering."

She clenches her fists, looking straight ahead. Her throat works and her eyes blink rapidly.

I was in a serious relationship for long enough to know full well when a woman is fighting off tears.

The fact that I made her this upset doesn't sit well with me. Should I... try to embrace her?

She's upset about something bigger than me.

"You have to... you have to let me keep trying," she hiccups. "Let me search on the other side of Cape Simon, up by Jackson."

"You can look until the end of time, honey. But as soon as I present this plan to the South Shore planning committee, I expect them to accept my offer."

Savannah looks at me with an oddly blank expression. "Don't call me honey while you're spitting in my oatmeal, Cole."

Her eyes spark with vehemence. I'm shocked, to be honest, and intrigued by her display of an emotion other than the false cheer I've seen so many times. I knew that Savannah had more complex feelings under her perky, sunny exterior. I just haven't seen them before.

It's hot. Not that I would ever tell her that in a million years.

Forcing myself to remain diplomatic, I put the car in drive. "Let's head back to the office."

She looks away. I feel like a teenager who's just made his first ever girlfriend madder than a wet cat.

The drive back is a silent one. Savannah doesn't look angry. In fact, she doesn't look like she has any particular feelings about the event at all.

That probably isn't a good sign.

When we return to downtown South Shore, she gets out of the car as soon as I throw it in park.

"If you don't need me, I have plans tonight that I'd love to go home and get ready for."

I give her a strained smile. "What plans?"

"A date."

I make a strangled, winded sound. "Who's the lucky guy?"

She tosses her hair impatiently. "Someone I connected with on an app."

"Ugh. The dating apps. Right." I squint into the distance.

"Yep." She smooths her hands down the front of her jacket. "So? Can I go or not?"

The back of my neck heats. "Sure. Yeah, whatever. Have a great date."

"Thanks. I will." She closes the car door and practically sprints to the ancient junker she drives.

I stare after her for several seconds.

That could've gone better. I'm just not sure how.

Something tickles the back of my brain when I run over the conversation again in my head.

I kissed Savannah. No… I've kissed her several times. And I apologized for my actions. But her answer was not exactly the eager acceptance I was looking for. I wish Savannah was still here.

I wish I could try apologizing again.

Fuck, I wish I could kiss her and feel the rush of excitement when she kisses me back. I crave that, for whatever reason.

I crave her.

I don't have any right to get possessive over my personal assistant. But the idea of Savannah out on a date with another guy gives me an uneasy sensation at the pit of my stomach. The fact that she's gone for a date with someone else... that she might get excited when someone else kisses her...

It's tearing me up inside. Can I really be so immature?

Just because I'm back in my hometown does not mean I can start acting like a lovesick teenage boy again.

I frown as I climb out of my car and walk toward the office building. It's cold as hell outside, and I pull my jacket closer, my mind still on Savannah. The main question is whether Savannah told me about her date to make me jealous.

Would she do that? And why was it working?

Just as I reach the door to my office, my brother River claps me on the shoulder.

"Hey!" He looks at me, a little puzzled when I startle. "I was calling your name from down the block. Are you okay?"

"Yeah. Just distracted." I catch my breath as I embrace him, then unlock the office door.

He follows me in with a grin, and flops down on the couch. River has always been like this. He's at home anywhere. It's a mild annoyance.

"Oh? Is it building permits on your mind?" He grins and leans back. "Or maybe that sexy secretary of yours?"

"She's a personal assistant, not a secretary. And I was wondering about how we are going to build this training camp in three years."

It's a lie and it sounds phony coming out of my mouth. My brother looks at me and narrows his eyes.

But then he shrugs and lets it go.

"Where is the lovely Savannah?" River asks.

"She went home early." I turn around and grab a bottle of water, smiling ruefully. "I think I might have pissed her off."

"Here is a God's honest question. How in the hell do you get these great women entangled in your web? Do you exude some kind of big dick energy or something?"

I pull a face. "You're ridiculous."

River considers me. "No, seriously. First you had that girl in college. Kate? Kat?"

I cross my arms. "Kara."

"Right, right. She was a volleyball-playing goddess, if I recall correctly. Then you snagged Holly. She was insane, but also unbelievably hot. She bought into your whole caveman thing so much that she had your baby."

"Very funny."

"No, really. Now you've got this sexy little blonde ingenue working for you. And it's obvious she wants to get in your pants. You snap and snarl, but Savannah still seems enchanted." He spreads his hands. "Please explain."

I drop down into my desk chair. "Did you come here just to rag on me?"

"It's just a question."

I pick up a pen from my desk and start to drum it against the surface. "I have work to do, River."

He looks at me for several beats before relenting. "Fine. Keep it all bottled up inside. I actually came to bring you the forms that the South Shore planning committee sent to my office by accident."

I push out an angry breath. I do snap and snarl at Savannah. Because I don't want her to like me as much as I like her.

But then I hurt her. And I don't want that either.

Maybe I should…. Not be a dick?

Sighing, I push my hand through my hair and try to figure out how to be better the next time I see Savannah.

17

SAVANNAH

With a deep inhale, I knock on the door of the Bennetts' mansion. I hold my breath as I wait. This place, this mansion really, is huge and absolutely gorgeous. White marble, inlaid dark wood accents, ceilings that are easily twenty feet tall. It's my second time here and I am not even a bit less anxious than I was on my first visit.

Clutching a number of briefs and contracts to my chest, I exhale and start to knock again. But before my knuckles make contact with the dark wood of the door, it swings open.

Cole's stepmother, Sarah, opens the door. She looks me over approvingly, which gives me a jolt of surprise.

"Savannah! It's so nice to see you again. Come in."

She steps back and ushers me through the entry hall, and into the lush living room. She runs her hands over her hair and long gray jacket.

"Sorry that I'm such a mess. I was out at the stables. We just brought a new mare into our stables recently and I've been getting acquainted with her."

"Stables?" I ask.

"Oh yes. They're just a few minutes' walk away from the house. Sam had them built for me as a wedding present."

"Wow, I had no idea that there were stables so close." That explains her beige leggings and knee-high, dark leather boots. "I have to admit that I don't know the first thing about horses."

"You should ask Cole to take you for a ride on the beach. Cole acts like he doesn't like horses, but the truth is that he learned to ride when he was younger. Cole gets along with about every horse he meets."

Cole on a horse? The idea strikes me as odd.

"I'll have to ask him about that," I say noncommittally. "Alas, I'm here today to work."

Sarah gives me a knowing smile, and glances at the papers I'm clutching. "I'm guessing those are for Cole?"

"Yes ma'am."

"Let me show you to his wing of the house."

Is this house so large that all of the Bennett kids have their own wing? It looks big from the outside, but this tour is really eye opening as to just *how* big. Looking at the well-appointed hallways, the sleek beige and white decor, and occasional cozy sitting areas that Sarah leads me past, I am inclined to believe it.

"Is it just y'all here? Or do you have a staff? I imagine that cleaning a house this size would be an unbelievable burden," I wonder aloud.

"We have cleaning and kitchen staff." Sarah winks at me. "We just don't have them answer the door or put on airs. There's no need for that. Nobody in our house is too important to answer the front door when somebody knocks."

Sarah finally comes to the end of a long, airy corridor and knocks on a door. There is a muffled solicitation from inside the room.

She pops her head in and stage whispers, "Savannah is here."

"Thanks, Sarah."

Sarah moves out of the way, squeezing my arm as she heads back toward the living room. "Nice to see you."

"You too!" I call after her.

Cole surprises me by meeting me at the door. He holds up a finger to his lips and steps back. To my surprise, I see that he's in a kid's bedroom.

There are dinosaurs painted on all the walls, and a neat bookcase full of brightly colored books and a few toys. Cole quietly pads over to the twin bed, where a pale and flushed Charlie sleeps. He lifts a baby monitor from beside Charlie and then pulls the blankets up around his son. He backs me out of the room and closes the door softly, then points to another door that's across the hall.

The door opens into a bright, light office. The desk and rolling chairs are white and clear plexiglass. There is a thick shag carpet, a neat little cow-printed loveseat, and the walls have romantic sconce lighting. The windows have soft sheer curtains gathered with white satin bows.

There is no way that Cole decorated this room.

Cole walks in and stretches. Gone are his button up and khakis. Instead he's wearing dark plaid pajama pants, and a simple white T-shirt.

This is the first time that I've seen Cole without his dress clothes. I feel like I'm getting a peek behind his defenses.

If I'm honest, this rumpled, undone version of Cole is really frigging hot. Not that he needs to know that.

"Thanks for running out here. Charlie is sick and refuses to let anybody else play nursemaid for him."

The idea of Cole dressed up as a nurse makes me smile. "It's no problem. Is he okay?"

"Yeah, he just has a stomach bug. I've been up with him since the middle of the night, but I can't do much of anything other than take care of him."

I nod, looking around the room. "Maybe you should've just taken the day off. I wouldn't have minded."

"I don't want to be in Cape Simon for that long. So whether Charlie is sick or not, I have to work."

"How very practical of you." I offer Cole the papers I'm holding but he waves me down.

"Have a seat." He points to the loveseat. and drags one of the rolling chairs around to face it. "Did you bring the leasing terms and the property flyers for all the places that we are looking at?"

"Yup." I sit down on the rather uncomfortable cowhide loveseat and edge forward, handing him a manila folder. "The rest of the files should be–."

The baby monitor crackles to life. Charlie plaintively whines, "Daddy?"

Cole shoots to his feet, dropping the file on the chair. He is across the hall in a flash. I follow quietly to find him kneeling at Charlie's bedside.

"I'm right here, kiddo." Cole smooths his hand over Charlie's forehead and brushes back his dark hair as the little boy clutches at his t-shirt. "What do you need?"

"Can I have a juice?"

"Of course. Let me go grab it from the kitchen."

"No go," Charlie protests.

Cole looks up at me beseechingly.

"Can you stay here just for a minute?" he whispers. "I've been mixing apple juice with electrolyte solution. I just have to run and grab it from the fridge."

"Of course." I step fully into the room.

"Miss Savannah's gonna stay with you while I get you some juice, is that okay bud?"

I move closer and sit on the end of Charlie's bed.

"Hey there. I heard you're not feeling well. Can I stay in here with you for a minute?" I ask softly.

Charlie thinks about it, his blue eyes trained on me. Then he lets his dad go with a nod.

Cole stands up and leaves the room at a sprint.

Charlie scrunches up his face, looking ready to cry.

"Do you know what my mom used to do for me when I was sick?" I ask to distract him.

Charlie squirms and shakes his head.

I get off the bed and slide to the floor beside him. "Do you mind if I touch your forehead?"

He looks at me for a long second, then lies back and shakes his head again. I touch Charlie's forehead with a finger, smoothing each eyebrow slowly.

"Close your eyes," I suggest.

His eyes drift shut. I continue touching his face with a fingertip, tracing gentle strokes down his nose and across his cheeks. I hum a little, the tune of 'Baby Mine' coming to me.

My mom used to hum that song when she stroked my face whenever I couldn't sleep or felt sick.

A wave of sadness rolls over me. It's been a while since I've missed Mom so sharply that it feels like I have trouble even breathing.

Charlie's breathing deepens as I continue my humming and stroking. I hear Cole's bare feet coming down the hallway and turn my face to look at him.

He arches a brow at me as he elbows his way into the room, but I don't stop humming or touching Charlie's face. Cole comes closer and sits a red plastic cup down on the nightstand.

He assesses the situation for a moment, then moves back to the doorway and leans against the jamb. I can feel his eagle-eyed stare on my body as I comfort his son.

We stay like that for a few minutes. When I finally stop touching Charlie, he's asleep. Slipping off my heels, I get up as soundlessly as possible and creep toward the door.

Once we're back in the office, Cole sits on the loveseat with a huge sigh. I take the seat next to him, placing my heels on the floor beside the couch.

"Thank you." Cole's voice rumbles from his chest. He sounds exhausted. "How did you know what to do?"

I smile at him and cock my head.

"It's what my mom used to do for me when I was a kid."

"Ah." He nods and rubs the bridge of his nose with a hand. "It looked like the sinus massage that Sarah does for him. Minus the humming part, I guess."

I cast an eye over his stooped shoulders.

"Everybody likes to be stroked sometimes. You know, I can try some massage on you." I blush, shaking my head. "Err not that I'm trying to mother you, or anything."

He gives me an odd look. "No, thanks." He lets out another huge sigh. "It's just hard being the main parent for Charlie."

I nod. "I get that."

"When we lived in Atlanta, Charlie was involved in a bunch of activities. Not to mention that we had a full-time nanny to run him from one place to another. And there was Holly, of course. Although I feel her contribution to raising Charlie was…." He waves it away. "Minimal at best."

Trying not to show my intense nosiness about Cole's ex, I change the subject slightly.

"What happened to Charlie's nanny?"

"She has her own family in Marietta. She couldn't move all the way over here for a job that would end in a couple of months."

"That makes sense. It's kind of a shame that he is down here for such a short time, though. My nephew Dex is involved with learning Mandarin, plays t-ball, and goes to a weekend science camp. All of them are fully paid for by the school since there is only one elementary school halfway between South Shore and Cape Simon."

"Mandarin? That's pretty impressive. When I was a kid, it was just Spanish or French. And only in high school, I think."

I shift and resettle, my knee pressing against his thigh. Cole doesn't move away.

"Is that why you're moving? Because you miss the city?"

"Well, yeah. I used to live in Atlanta when I went to college there."

"But you decided to settle here? That seems crazy."

"I miss being able to walk right out the door and get dinner. Or go to the movies. Or... basically do anything interesting. Cape Simon may be fancy, but downtown Atlanta it is not."

I roll my eyes.

"The Cape is nice. And besides, it's where my grandad, my sister, and my nephew are. I'd be crazy to leave all of that just for better dinner options."

Cole shoots me a smile. "I guess when you put it that way. But don't you have the itch to live in the city?"

I shake my head emphatically. "I got a taste. I really don't miss it."

"You know, before Charlie was born, I planned to move to somewhere far away. Hong Kong, or Brisbane, or Dubai. I wanted to get away."

"From what?"

Cole glances away into the distance.

"Things around home were kind of tense."

"Meaning what?"

"My mom died when I was a kid. Ten months later, my dad showed up with Sarah. And Sarah brought her kids. Suddenly our family of five became a family of ten." He flicks his fingers. "They all moved in here with no problem. There was plenty of room. And I eventually grew to love my step-siblings. But it was tough, watching Sarah replace my mom. Heartbreaking."

On impulse, I put my hand over Cole's knee and murmur a sound of sympathy.

Cole looks at me and shrugs. "It's fine. What are you gonna do? I had no say in the matter anyway."

"Still, that sounds like a pretty bleak year."

He snorts. "I never really fit in to the big family portrait. By the time I was seventeen, I started making plans to go to college in Atlanta. That's where I met Holly. And the rest, as they say, is history."

I want so badly to poke around in his relationship history that I'm about to burst. But I don't say a thing about it. Instead, I say, "I'm sorry that you feel like you didn't fit in."

"Ah." Cole waves his hand dismissively. "It was a really long time ago."

"No amount of time seems long enough to mourn. Granted, I haven't hit the one-year mark yet. But I lost my mom last year. Some days, I'm sure that I'm going to drown in a sea of sorrow."

Cole presses his lips together and nods. "I'm so sorry you lost your mom."

I shrug my shoulders. "Everyone has losses. That's life."

"Still." Cole squints. "My mom died of breast cancer."

"Cancer absolutely sucks." I scrunch my face up. "My mom died from a glioblastoma, specifically. It's a really aggressive form of brain cancer."

"Holy shit. Isn't that what John McCain died of?"

"I don't know. All I know is that cancer can suck rocks."

Cole takes my hand and gives it a squeeze.

"I'm sorry."

Forcing a smile to my lips, I shake my head.

"It's fine."

"It's not fine. I–."

Charlie pops his head in and gives us a sad frown. "Daddy, can I come sit in your lap?"

Cole gives me the briefest of smiles, and then claps both of his hands against his thighs. "Come on. There's plenty of room."

Charlie scrambles up, and Cole settles his arms around his son. Cole hands Charlie a sippy cup full of juice and Charlie takes a noisy swig. Charlie's bare feet end up between my thigh and Cole's knee. I cover the tops of his feet with my hands playfully.

"Aren't your feet cold?" I ask.

Charlie nods, as grave as the day is long. I pull a throw off the floor to put over them. He reaches down and pulls it up over his body with a shiver.

Cole kisses the top of Charlie's head. Charlie snuggles into his chest. Cole looks at me helplessly.

"I don't see myself getting too much work done right now."

I smile as I look at the father and son scene. It's pretty darn sweet.

"I think maybe you need to take life a little more slowly while you're here in Cape Simon. No one else is working at a breakneck pace. Why should you be the only one?"

Cole narrows his eyes.

"It's what I'm used to."

"Well, my suggestion would be to unwind just a teensy bit. It'll do you good. Charlie doesn't have to grow up watching his workaholic father put in eighty hours a week his whole life. Imagine that."

I wink. Cole's cheeks turn an interesting shade of red.

"It's not my fault things down here are as slow as molasses in January."

I raise my hands in surrender. "Just go with the flow. That's all I'm saying."

His dramatic sigh is almost comical. "We'll see."

"I suppose so." I wrap Charlie's feet up and rest them on my lap. "What do you suggest we do now?"

"Can you tell me a story?" Charlie asks. His eyes are closed, but he is obviously still listening.

"Sure, kiddo." Cole clears his throat.

"No, I want Savannah to tell me a story. I like hearing her talk. It's like bells ringing."

"What?" I ask, laughing. "That's a really nice thing to say, Charlie."

"Charlie, Savannah probably has places to be."

This is exactly where I want to be. I can't imagine anyone else I would rather be spending time with right now.

"I'm all yours. I've got nothing but time," I assure them both.

Light shines in Cole's eyes. He adjusts Charlie in his lap, and sprawls an arm against the back of the loveseat. His fingers trail against my shoulder.

"Well. I guess a story would be good, then."

"What story should I tell?" I ask the sleepy little boy.

"I don't know. Something new," Charlie murmurs.

I think for a second. "Have you ever heard the story of The Little Prince? It's my nephew's favorite. I've got it on my phone."

Charlie shakes his head.

"Then that's the one I'll tell." I get my phone out of the pocket of my dress and hold it aloft. "You're going to love this book, Charlie. Get comfy and I'll start."

I glance at Cole. He's looking at me, the corners of his lips lifted in an enigmatic smile. He runs his fingers through Charlie's silky hair and puts up not one more word of protest.

Biting my lip, I begin to read. The book of princes, planets, roses, and sheep is sweet but short. By the time I read the last lines, both Charlie and Cole have closed their eyes to catch some much-needed sleep.

Turning my phone off, I let it fall to my lap, greedily devouring the sight of father and son slumbering tranquilly.

18

———

COLE

I HUNCH OVER THE MOTOR OF THE AIRBOAT, MUTTERING curses under my breath. "Why won't this godforsaken engine start?"

I pull the cord again, only to be treated to the sound of it winding back.

Savannah sighs and shifts her weight impatiently. I can just picture her standing in her white swamp boots, hip cocked, looking at me with disdain.

The way her perfect ass is encased in those tight blue jeans is making matters worse.

Thinking about her ass makes me hot and tense. My neck heats and I rip at the cord again.

Nothing.

"Did you engage the safety latch first?" Sav suggests.

Refusing to look over my shoulder, I glare down at the motor. Underneath the steering column, a small red box is outlined against the boat's white hull. Beside it is the bold red word "START". Inside the red lines of the box is a small throw switch. I throw it a few times as if testing the switch, and pull the cord again.

The engine starts with a sputtering roar.

God, I hate that she was right.

Keeping a low center of gravity, I turn in my seat right next to the boat's navigation. "The latch wasn't connecting or something. I fixed it."

Sav sits down on the only other seat and smirks at me. "I see that."

"I was raised here on the water, the same as anyone," I tell her.

Savannah rolls her eyes and clutches her big white sun hat. "Uh huh. Are we going to go or what?"

"We're going," I say, still salty. I guide the boat away from the dock and out on the marshy water. "Have you got the map and the coordinates of the last survey flag?"

"Right here." She pats the black backpack that sits at her feet. "It's wild to me that this is the only way to reach the survey flag. I would think that the people who did the original survey would have made roads that went to all four corners of the proposed football stadium."

"The surveyors probably didn't have the permits to make any permanent markings on the land. They just planted their boundary corners as high up as they could. The high metal posts were the only reason we were able to find the first three corners."

She nods, shading her eyes as she looks into the bright sunlight.

The sluggish water trails in the opposite direction as we head up the tributary. My eyes are on the shining black mirror that stretches before us, constantly scanning the surface for signs of underwater obstructions.

But if I'm honest, it's difficult to think about anything other than her ass. The way she smiled at me and took my offered hand when I helped her into the boat isn't far behind that, though.

My head is swimming with thoughts of Savannah.

"Do you have the geotag marker thingamabob?" she asks.

I realize that I've been staring at her for a couple of minutes. I blink, give myself a shake, and nod.

"Yep. It's in my backpack."

Thunder suddenly crackles overhead. I look up for the first time since we left the dock, and I'm surprised to see that the sky has darkened considerably. Overcast skies have turned into a blanket of darkness spread across the sky.

"I hope it doesn't rain on us."

Sav pokes out her bottom lip thoughtfully and then shrugs. "We'll be fine. I brought an emergency shelter."

I grunt. "For a little rain?"

She eyes me but doesn't respond to my question. Instead, she changes the subject.

"How's Charlie feeling today?"

A gator blinks at us from twenty feet away. I jerk and steer the boat to the other side of the waterway, avoiding him like the plague. One of the first things I learned living out here was that you don't mess with gators if you don't have to.

"Charlie's fine. Actually, he woke me up this morning by jumping on my bed and telling me about a shell he found on the beach. He's back in action as if he was never sick in the first place. It's almost miraculous."

Savannah favors me with a grin.

"Oh, that's great. Kids are so resilient."

A great arc of lightning sizzles through the sky. I look up as the thunder sounds only seconds later.

"Should we go back?" she asks. "We can try again later."

Frowning, I jerk my chin toward her backpack. "Check how far away we are."

She pulls out a gadget that looks like an old brick phone and powers it on. Turning to point it in the direction we are headed, she scrunches up her face. Then she pulls out the matching map.

"According to these, we're about ten minutes from a dock with a boat house. And it's about a twenty-minute hike inland to get to the marker."

"I don't think we should turn around yet. It might not even rain." I study the sky, feeling a gnawing sensation growing inside my chest. "We'll face these conditions anytime we come out here. If we can just get to the dock, we can hang out in the boat house until the storm passes. You know how storms are down here. They never last long."

Something in her face tightens. But she nods and folds up the map.

"I would suggest that we go faster. There should be a toggle to control the speed to the right side of the tiller."

Savannah is right. I turn the knob and the engine grows louder. The boat skips forward.

"Whoa!" Sav laughs, clinging to her hat with one hand and gripping the hand hold with the other.

"What do you know?" I mutter. I stare straight ahead, scanning the water frantically. An alligator slides through the water, eager to get out of the way of the boat.

That's a bonus to going this fast, I guess.

Lightning flashes again. The first drops of rain splash the surface of the stream almost casually. The spray is icy, making my hands sting with cold.

The fine mist quickly grows into a rapid pitter-patter across the water's surface. Sav scrunches up her face and turns her body so that she isn't getting the full brunt of the water in her eyes.

"This sucks!" she yells.

"Sorry." I point ahead to a dark shape that appears on the bank a little way ahead. "I think that's the boat house."

She turns to look and shades her eyes. "Yeah. We'll be fine." But she doesn't sound too sure.

A gator appears much too close to the boat, its eyes and nostrils the only thing that I can see. Before I can tense up and maybe shout at it, Savannah dips her fingers into a pocket in her parka. She produces several marshmallows and throws them out over the water. The gator is distracted and our boat jets by. When I turn my head, I see one of the marshmallows has disappeared as if by magic.

"What the hell?" I shout.

She laughs at my expression. "I came prepared."

I shake my head in disbelief, aiming the tiller toward the dock. At the last moment, I remember to turn the boat's speed down by flicking the dial and then I nose the boat gently against the dock.

Sav hops off like she's been working the docks for a thousand years. I cut the engine and turn to find her offering me a hand out of the boat.

The sky opens up just then. The wind whips rain at me horizontally and I yelp as it hits my face, driving into my skin like needles.

I grudgingly accept Savannah's hand. She pulls me up, and I tie the boat down to the dock in two places. When I'm done, I see that Sav has already opened the rickety boat house's door and is holding it open for me.

I grab my backpack and dash after her. Inside amounts to not much more than an ancient wood floor, four battered plywood walls, and a door that only keeps out part of the wind and rain pounding outside.

I wedge the door closed with a simple wooden latch.

Then it's just Sav and me, in the gloom.

She rustles around in the darkness for a moment, then turns on a lightweight lantern. My eyes take a second to adjust, but when they do, I see that the little shed is only four feet by four feet. There is nothing else to see but a bunch of bent, rusted nails lying in one corner.

"Damn." I wipe my face on my sleeve. "How the hell did we end up here?"

Sav takes off her sun hat and looks me up and down. "You are a mess."

"Me? What about you?" I touch her hair, which hangs, limp and dripping, past her shoulders.

She grins and shrugs. "I'll be okay. Plus…." She pulls a couple of those metallic emergency heating blankets from her backpack and spreads one on the floor. "I come bearing gifts."

I'm surprised that Savannah had the foresight to bring the blankets. Where do you even get those things?

God, the fact that she is so much more multi-dimensional than I even realized rocks me back on my heels. Who *is* this girl?

She sits down on the blanket. I look at her, cocking my head.

"You're content to just wait out the storm?"

Sav sighs impatiently.

"You should be too. This is the weather in the coastal south this time of year. It doesn't rain much, but when it does, it rains like it's the end of the freaking world."

She gives me a tight-lipped, haughty smile. I grumble as I sit down beside her.

"I grew up here, the same as you did."

Sav unfurls the second reflective blanket, offering me part. She pulls part of it around her shoulders and raises an eyebrow in challenge.

Huffing, I scoot closer to her and pull the other part around me so that we are pressed closely together underneath.

"Maybe years living in the city ruined you." She nudges me in the ribs with her elbow.

I pin her with my gaze. I'm intimately aware of all the places where our thighs and arms touch.

But the part that kills me is Sav. She is gazing at me with humor and defiance sparkling in her eyes. I can smell her sweet scent wafting from her damp hair. I can feel the heat rolling off her body.

I have to say something soon… or kiss her upturned mouth. And while I desperately want to feel Sav's lips against mine again, it's not really fair to either of us.

I can't start something that I have no intention of finishing.

I open my mouth, unsure what I'm going to say. What comes out is, "Do you see yourself growing old here?"

Her brows knit. "Yeah. It's where my family has been since time immemorial."

"If you don't mind me asking, why haven't you settled down?"

A blush rises to Savannah's cheeks and she looks away. "I don't know. I haven't met the right person, I guess."

"And who's this magical person that you are waiting for?"

She clears her throat. "Well…"

"No wait! Let me tell you. He is super hot, of course. He likes walking barefoot and shirtless on the beach, strumming his guitar. He'll have like… flowing hair that I you can run your fingers through."

Sav huffs. "You're so superficial. My dream guy will have way more depth than just good looks."

I let out a bleat of laughter. "Is that right?"

She gives me a tiny glare. "My perfect guy will have good energy. Like how I'm all positive vibes and sunshine? He'll reflect that back to me. Nothing will ever be hard. It'll always just be… perfect and easy."

As Sav talks, my brows start rising.

"Wow. I know why you haven't met this guy yet."

She swallows tightly. "Oh? Why is that?"

"Because that dude does not exist. Anyone who claims to be that magical and reflects positive vibes back to you… or whatever it is you said… they're trying to pull one over on you."

Sav balls up her mouth. "He exists. I'm sure of it."

I can't help but grin at the self-assurance in her tone.

"You don't really believe that."

"I do!"

"That's crazy! Take it from me. I'm older and wiser. I've lived in the real world."

She rolls her eyes. "You're not that much older than me."

"Ten years!"

Sav pokes me in the center of my chest. "More like eight."

I catch her hand. She grins and tries to wiggle out of my grip. As I show her how easily I can dominate her, I give her a huge smirk. She leans back in her attempts to evade my hand. But I follow, essentially bowling her over in my enthusiasm to win.

We end up pressed together against the side of the boat house, nose to nose, both of us grinning like fools. She sucks in a huge breath and my own slightly heavy breathing catches.

I'm honestly not sure who makes the first move. She opens her mouth. I brush my lips over hers. In the cramped space of the boat house, my heartbeat sounds like the frantic galloping of wild horses.

Sav's fingers rake through my wet hair. My lips work against hers, teasing her mouth until she opens for me, as timid as a schoolgirl. We both sigh and our tongues meet. My tongue snakes against hers. My hands grip her waist.

What is it about this girl that drives me so wild? It's her smile, her sass, her unshakable optimism that I can't help but admire even as I complain.

A second later, my hand slips under her shirt to feel the smooth, bare skin of her lower back. Sav's lips leave mine to kiss a blazing trail down my neck. It lights a fire inside me, making me hungry for more.

I lift her onto my lap and she straddles me. My hands find her ass and I grip it tightly. There is a ragged groan, and I realize a moment later that the sound came from me. Like a man possessed, I bury my nose in the crook of her neck, kissing down until I run into her parka.

"Get this off," I growl.

Her hands are already tugging at the zipper. She sheds it, leaving her in only a lacy white camisole. The daintiness of her top makes me crazy. I want to shred it with my teeth.

But I settle for running my hands up her sides and shaping her perky tits. I kiss her collarbone and drag my tongue over the lace neckline of her top. She bucks her hips against me suggestively and throws her head back.

As Sav's hands knead the muscles of my shoulders, I kiss her breasts through the silky camisole. Her nipples are hard, their tips pointed. I close my mouth over one and she squeaks in excitement.

Her hand travels down between our bodies to my zipper. My heart races and my mind hurries to catch up. I want her to touch me anywhere, but at the same time, I'm a little taken aback at how forward Sav is.

Damn, she must really think I'm hot. Knowing that Sav thinks I'm a catch fills me with a strange kind of pride. It's a feeling I've been lacking ever since I was left at the altar.

I try to take back the power by dragging my teeth across her damp, fabric-covered nipple and pushing her hand away. She freezes, thinking that I'm rejecting her.

But when I start plucking at the zipper of her pants, Sav goes wild. She pulls my face up to hers and gives me a demanding kiss, working her hips against mine, rubbing up against my clothed cock in a way that makes me almost see stars.

Unzipping her fly and slipping a hand around to feel her bare ass is a revelation to me. She bites her lip and grabs my other hand, pressing my fingers over her breast.

I've never seen a girl so enthusiastic in my entire life, and damn if it isn't making my cock so hard that it actually aches.

When I slide my hand down in between Sav's thighs, she's clearly not just wet from the rain. Her panties have a clear wet spot on the front just from kissing.

What will Sav be like if I get her worked up? Will she taste just like sweet honey if I tease her clit, and fuck her hot pussy with my tongue?

"God, yes." Sav flexes her thighs and presses against my fingers. Though there is still a silky scrap of fabric between me and the golden heat that lies between her thighs, I'm so close to her pussy. I shudder with anticipation.

I can just imagine the sounds she's going to make. How sweet my fucking name will be when she calls it out.

Suddenly, I feel a nail poking up through the floor. My eyes snap open.

Sav is gorgeous, glowing, her head thrown back in ecstasy, her eyes closed tightly, her mouth open. Her expression is one of rapture.

If I could take a picture to remember that look, I would. I want to remember it. Savor it.

But I can't ignore the fact that we're in a shed in the middle of nowhere. Sav may be on cloud nine, but I'm all too aware of how rough this place is. There are nails coming out of the floor. There are holes in the wall. This entire place is all but made of dirt.

And Savannah? Savannah deserves to be kissed. She deserves to be luxuriously spread out on million-count thread sheets in the priciest damn hotel in the world. She definitely deserves more than a quick fuck in a dirty shack from a guy who can't promise her even one entire night.

Savannah opens her eyes a bit. She notices that I've gone still.

"Cole?"

"Yeah." I drag a hand over my face. "I'm sorry. This isn't right."

She stiffens and hops off my lap. Her cheeks and chest turn bright red as she tries to right her clothes. "I'm sorry. I guess I got carried away."

I shake my head and run my fingers through my hair. "Don't apologize. Just… look around. It's not exactly the most romantic setting."

Sav grabs her parka and zips it up. She won't look at me.

"We just… you know, we're both so tense. We just need to blow off steam. Er…"

"Look at me." I grab her by the shoulders and give her a tiny shake. "You? You're great. I'm the problem. You are the dictionary definition of perfect."

Her throat works and she ducks her head. "Thanks."

I drop my hands, feeling like the biggest moron on the planet. "Yep. No problem."

We stare at opposite walls as silence stretches between us. I'm trying to remember the reason why I stopped us.

Am I really that dumb? Who knows if I'll ever get the chance to touch Savannah again?

She clears her throat and lifts the latch on the door. It's still raining, but the insane storm that reminded me of a hurricane has now died off to a drizzle.

"Care to chance it?" Sav asks.

Inhaling deeply, I nod. "It seems calmer."

She packs the lantern and foil blankets into her backpack, then we step outside. The sky has lightened up again

The boat catches my eye. It makes me curious.

"Hey. Why do you know so much about boats?"

She laughs a little, looking at me like I've gone bonkers.

"My grandfather is a fisherman. He owns his own company and his own boat."

"Wait. What?" I try to imagine Savannah on a fishing boat, but my imagination isn't that good.

She nods. "I grew up mending nets and going out trawling in the early morning and late evening. I am legitimately living the Salt Life."

That earns an eye roll from me.

"I didn't know that about you."

She squints at me. Then she drops her backpack and hat on the ground, takes a step away from me, and does a standing back handspring.

My jaw drops.

"What the hell?!"

This girl surprises me every single day that I know her. God, she's so perfect. She's a goddess. And I'm just a loser who doesn't even deserve to grovel at her feet. I honestly can't decide right now if I'm more disgusted with myself or more admiring of Savannah.

Sav stands up straight and flips her blonde hair over her shoulder. Then she shrugs and smirks at me.

"I guess there's a lot about me you don't know."

She jogs back and scoops up her backpack and hat. Sliding the backpack on, she jerks her head away from the water. "Now can we find this marker already so we can get the hell on with our lives?"

I gape at her for two more seconds. She rolls her eyes again and then heads toward the marker.

I'm left trailing after her, wondering what hidden depths she has that I might never know.

19

———

SAVANNAH

I AM LEANING OVER MEG'S SHOULDER AS THE TEENAGE volunteer points to a sketch of a set she's completed.

"We just need a bunch of colored construction paper to build the back wall. And then we can cut pieces of construction paper out and glue them to a chair to make the Wicked Witch's bicycle."

Halfway through her proposal, I notice Charlie running down the center aisle. Straightening up, I tell Meg, "That sounds great. Can you make sure you email these to me?"

Charlie runs straight to me, stopping just before he hits me. I grin and crouch down.

"Hey! Can you go over to where the other kids are practicing? They should be running over their lines."

"Okay!" Charlie says, sprinting away toward the stage, eager to join the circle of kids sitting cross-legged there. He struggles to climb on the stage and I hold my breath. Jess notices him and scoots over to give him a hand up.

Once Charlie scrambles on stage, he races to the first gap in the circle and drops to the floor. Smiling at his antics, I shake my head.

"That kid has too much energy."

Cole comes up behind me, holding Charlie's coat. He tosses it on the seat beside himself and looks at his son.

"Charlie's been wound up since dawn. It's too bad he doesn't take naps anymore."

I can feel myself smile.

"We're glad you guys made it, even if you're not exactly on time."

"Yeah." His eyes turn to me, probing. "Listen, I know we talked about it, but I just want to say, about the other day…"

My face flames as I remember just what he's talking about. My lips and nipples tingle with the memory of his sweet tongue.

I'm intimately aware of what a bad idea it was. I really should know better.

I shake my head vehemently. "Nope. No need to talk about it again."

One of Cole's eyebrows arches. "Oh?"

Embarrassed, I cough a little.

"We've been over this. I know all the reasons you're going to list off. You're my boss, you're still in sexile, you're bound for London. We can't let our hormones tell us how to act. That's the gist of what you're about to say, isn't it?"

Cole smirks. The expression is cold though. His eyes lack the usual sparkle that makes my legs quiver.

"That's about it."

"Then we're in agreement. No need to argue the matter further. Don't get me wrong. Making out with you was the hottest thing to happen to me in a long time. But it was a bad idea nonetheless."

His brows descend and he looks at me as if he is wondering whether he can actually trust me or not. "I see."

"Good!" I put on my most saccharine smile. "In other news, I hope you're feeling handy today. While the kids rehearse, the adults have the pleasure of building the sets. Come on."

I lead him around the seats to the side door. The backstage area already has a couple of men and a handful of women discussing how best to divide up the work.

"Hey everyone! I brought another set of hands." I walk into the middle of the loosely gathered circle of bodies, sizing everyone up. "Hannah and Sara, you're artistic. Can you start constructing the papier-mâché animals? Jared, you and Cole are probably the strongest ones here. Can you two use hammers and drills to help build the big boat? Artie and Beatrice, you are both detail-oriented. Can you help fill in the frame of the boat with some painted construction paper once they're done?"

I rattle off a couple more assignments and then look at my sister, who is the last one to get an assignment. "Birdie, you and I are the jacks of all trades. We can start making some of the props if you want."

Cole arches a brow. "You actually remember all of these people's names and their strengths as people? How is it possible that you know all of this and care enough to name each person's strong suit?"

I give an exasperated sigh. "I just do. It's not magic, Cole."

He shrugs, his expression impressed, and moves off toward Jared. There is a low buzz of conversation as people find their partners and figure out exactly what needs to be done. Birdie gives me a sheepish grin.

"I'm glad you announced the job assignments. I was staring at this and trying to make head or tails of it." She picks up the list of props to be made and squints at it. "I know that I'm dyslexic, but these are seriously in an alien language or something."

I laugh. "If I say build me a giant, construction paper hammer, you already have an idea of what to build. Right?"

"Well, yeah. I can picture it in my mind." She taps her forehead. "It's just reading the words that I'm terrible at."

"That's why I wanted you in my group. I have no original ideas, but I can read the items aloud and follow your instructions. That's why we're the dream team."

Birdie looks at me with a sly smile.

"You're really good at that."

"What?"

"Knowing where other people's strengths lie. Pairing up teams. Or maybe I'm talking about how you gave sneaky compliments to everyone here."

"I'm just saying what is perfectly evident to anyone with eyes." Picking up a pile of construction paper, I hand it over to her. "The first things we'll need are a hammer and a watering can."

She sits down with construction paper, scissors, and glue sticks. I check on everyone else and answer a few questions.

When I get to Cole and Jared, the warmth in Cole's eyes has returned.

"Everything going to plan?" I ask. Cole is holding a drill but not working.

If that is a nod to me and he's actually listening instead of working himself to death, I consider that a major win.

"Perfectly," says Jared. "I'm already loving this shape."

"I think we've got this." Cole gives me a small smile and holds up a cordless drill. He puts the drill to a piece of lumber and then drills a screw into it.

I grin at him, my heart skipping a beat. Then I realize what a dope I probably look like and drag myself back over to Birdie.

As I expected, Birdie is already done making the hammer out of construction paper.

"Holy cow. That was fast!" Taking the hammer from her, I turn it this way and that. "This is a serious hammer. Look at the craftsmanship."

Birdie rolls her eyes. "You're so silly."

"Even silly clocks are right twice a day." I wink at my sister.

Across the room, I see Cole climbing up a ladder to screw a joist into the skeletal scaffolding that Jared holds in place. My eye snags on him and sticks there for a moment too long.

He has shucked his dark sweater, trading it for the tight gray T-shirt and dark jeans that do wonderful things for his thighs. He laughs at something Jared suggests, a bright flash that is gone too soon.

Maybe Cole doesn't realize that his smile makes him a hundred times hotter than his usual scowl.

Not that his scowl is that bad. I'm coming to find it calls to me. Challenges me in a way that I can't explain.

I rub my fingers over my mouth to disguise a grin.

When I look back at Birdie, she is staring right at me with the biggest smirk. She leans forward, whispering, "Busted."

My lips thin and I look down at the hammer in my hands. "I don't know what you are talking about."

"Yeah, right. I saw your face. You totally have the hots for Mr.…. what did you call him? Mr. Doom and Gloom?"

Why oh why did I tell Birdie that nickname? I don't want to snap at her, but neither do I have a witty comeback that springs to mind. Smiling is my only real defense mechanism. So I do that as I tick reasons why I'm not into Cole off on my fingers.

"You're dreaming. I mean, look at him. He's way richer than me. He's almost ten years older than me. He's grumpy as the day is long. And if that weren't enough, he's not in town to stay."

My sister reaches out and gently grabs my fingers. Her eyes burn into mine.

"I've known you for your whole life, Savannah. Don't up and start lying to me now."

At that moment, Cole turns his head and looks at me. I'm drowning in a sudden sea of navy blue. I gulp and blink rapidly.

He looks away and I'm left feeling like I just got punched in the stomach. All the breath whooshes out of my lungs.

Birdie's lips twitch as she turns her head and catches him turning away.

"Oh, I see. You aren't just pining after Cole. He's into you too. It makes sense. He is such a grump, you're all…." She spreads her fingers wide. "Sunshine-y. I could see it happening, to be honest."

"Shhhh. Keep your voice down."

"You shh." Birdie sticks her tongue out at me. "Don't be mad at me. You're the one with a big fat crush."

I feel my face and neck turning red. I'm about to say something unkind to my sister if I don't remove myself as soon as possible.

"I'm going to do another lap." I put the hammer down on my seat.

She gives me an evil little smile.

"Say hi to loverboy for me, Savvie."

I whirl away. It takes everything in me not to stomp off.

Girls should be cleaner than sunshine and sweeter than honey. I remember my mom saying that to both my sister and me.

So did my sister just skip out on listening? Because Birdie is not being sweeter than honey by rubbing my face in what I already know.

I circle the room, cooling off. Helping here and there where I can. A bit of glue, a quick swab of paint.

Thank god I am fully composed when I circle around to check on Cole again. He's trying to drill holes in a long, skinny length of wood. Where Jared is, I'm not sure.

"Need any help?" I ask in a soft voice.

He looks down at me.

"Yeah. Can you hold this still?"

I step on the wood piece. It creaks slightly.

"This doesn't seem stable. Maybe we should look for another piece of wood."

Cole shoots me a look. He knows I'm right though. "There aren't any here. I've checked."

"Let's go to the wood store room. I bet there are a dozen pieces of wood that will suit your purpose."

"What the hell is a wood store room?"

I shrug "That's what I've been calling the place with all the wood. We got a huge donation last year, and we had to store it someplace." I start walking backward, unable to keep myself from holding Cole's gaze. I am so intent on keeping my eyes from dipping to his lips that I pay no attention to where I'm walking.

I run smack into the wooden frame that Cole and Jared have been building. A large crack sounds and I automatically put my hand out to grab the rough wood.

"Ouch!" Pain lances my fingers and I pull my hand away. Flipping my palm over, I see several huge splinters sticking out of my hand and fingers. "Owww ow ow!"

Cole bolts to my side, taking my hand in his and examining it with careful fingers.

"Where is your first aid kit?" he asks.

I think about it for a second. "Maybe in the office at the end of the hall? Ow, it really hurts!"

"Okay. You're coming with me. You'd better hope I can get these splinters out with tweezers. Otherwise, we're going straight to the hospital."

He opens the door for me, puts his hand on my lower back, and gives me a little push.

All the hairs on my arms and neck rise.

Cole can give me goosebumps just by touching my lower back. It's a shame that I know what else his touch can do to me.

I grunt as he pulls me into the hall. "I'd rather not go to the hospital for something so minor. I'm not made of money."

"Pray that I can remove the splinters, then. Now which way is the office?"

It takes us about two minutes to reach the only office that is still used on this floor. Cole barges ahead, flipping the light switch on. It illuminates an old metal desk, a filing cabinet, a busted office chair, and an ancient bookshelf. Cole looks around and pinpoints the red and white plastic case emblazoned with the words FIRST AID.

He points to the desk. "Sit down, Sav."

This catches me off guard. Since when has Mr. Doom and Gloom called me Sav?

I plunk myself down on the chair as Cole pulls out tweezers, alcohol swabs, Neosporin, and Band-Aids out of the kit.

Clearing his throat, Cole comes around the desk to sit on the edge. He beckons.

"All right. Give it here."

I put my palm out, trying not to look too closely at the damage. Cole tugs me closer and the chair moves until I am sitting between his knees. He touches my wrist and glances up at me with some surprise.

"Are you nervous?"

What a dumb question. Am I nervous to have the man I almost banged in a boathouse touching me and tending my wounds?

Yes. Without a doubt.

I swallow thickly and gaze up at him.

"No...," I lie.

Cole grabs the tweezers.

"Don't worry. I have a system."

"What's that?"

"I ask you questions."

"What kind of questions?"

His fingers circle the back of my hand. His eyes are fixed on me.

"If you would've just said 'Yes, Cole,' this whole thing would probably be over."

"Are you saying I'm difficult?" I try to smile, but my hand throbs. "I'm only answering if you answer them too."

Cole traces his finger over the back of my injured hand again, circling just where the thumb and forefinger meet. "When you were a kid, what did you want to be when you grew up?"

His fingers trail around the same spot.

"A ballerina."

All at once, Cole pinches the back of my hand and plucks out one of my splinters. I start to protest, then stop.

"Hey, that kinda works. My hand doesn't hurt more than it already did."

Cole smiles softly. "It's a neat little trick. Sarah taught me to do it when I was a kid."

"Just because it worked doesn't mean you're off the hook. Answer the question. What did you want to be when you were a kid?"

He grins. "A doctor. But I soon found out that I can't stand hospitals. So that dream died a quick death."

"I see." I give him a lopsided smile. "You're doing a great job of doctoring right now."

"Thanks," he murmurs. He opens my palm again. His free hand begins tracing circles around my kneecap.

I feel like I've swallowed my tongue.

"Where do you want to be in two years, Savannah?"

My brows shoot up. My brain starts working overtime. "Oh! I guess... I mean, I want to always stay close to the South

Shore. But I'd like to work somewhere that makes a difference. Or go back to school for social work? I'm not–."

Lightning fast, Cole pinches my knee. I'm too startled to feel the splinter sliding out of my hand.

"Really sure," I finish.

"You're doing well, Sav. One more big one."

I wrinkle my nose. "Ah. Well... fair is fair. Answer the question."

He looks uncomfortable for a second. "I am in talks to move to London. You already know that. I actually had a phone call today with an agency that wants to talk about making me a full partner in exchange for bringing along my client list. So... that was interesting."

My breathing falters as my heart stumbles.

"Oh!" is all I can come up with. "That's... nice."

His gaze narrows. "Sav...."

"Can we do the last one please?" I lay my palm flat against his lap. "That way we can get back to what we were doing."

He lifts a brow at the same time as he starts tracing gentle circles on my thigh. I stare at his hand for a minute, trying to control my racing heartbeat.

Cole leans close and his warm breath tickles my face. "Is there a small part of you that liked riding my lap, Savannah?"

My eyes go wide. He smirks, pinches my thigh, and then moves the tweezers in a blur.

"Ow!" I cry, although it didn't actually hurt.

"Shh." He puts the tweezers down, and rips open one of the alcohol wipes. I feel the sting as he carefully swipes at my palm.

When he begins to attack my wound with antiseptic ointment, I square my jaw.

"That question wasn't fair," I say.

A huff of breath that could be a laugh passes his lips. "It wasn't really meant to be."

I scoot my chair closer to him, resting my arms on his open thighs. I can feel the pulse ticking faintly under my jaw. "No? Why ask then?"

He licks his lips. "To provoke you."

I ease my hands onto the top of his thighs.

"Yeah? What if I told you I did like what we did together? What if I told you that I went home and screamed your name into a pillow while I touched myself?"

Cole's eyes darken. He drags in a breath.

"Savannah." He runs a single finger along my jawline, making me shiver. "Such a responsive little thing. I wonder if you're like that with everyone… or just me?"

Biting my lip, I smile. "Just you."

For a long moment, I think he's going to kiss me. We're going to sweep the papers off this desk and tear each other's clothes off in a moment of heated ecstasy.

Cole grips my hands. From the possessive look in his eyes, I'm sure he's every bit as impatient as I am.

But then he pushes me away.

I'm still in the broken chair so it moves back easily. He stands up and adjusts the bulge pressing at the front of his jeans.

"Let's get back. The others will probably come looking for us soon."

Oh, right. I'm supposed to be leading his kid in a play. That's why we are all here.

I had completely forgotten.

20

COLE

"You would demolish the community center and pay for it to be reestablished somewhere else. Is that what I'm hearing?"

Mrs. Glory Brown takes off her bright red reading glasses. She's wearing a frilly white blouse, and a pair of red dress pants. Of two other women and one man that make up the South Shore Planning Commission, she is clearly the leader.

The commission sits at a pair of long folding tables; Mrs. Brown sits in the middle. I am left standing in front of them, in the role of petitioner.

Mrs. Brown looks at me with a frown, clearly expecting an answer. She makes me nervous for some reason. I'm not accustomed to people making me jittery.

I clear my throat and offer Glory a thin smile. "That's the gist of my offer. I want to build a hotel in the footprint of the community center. I will also pay to have several restaurants and cafes opened. It will be a renaissance for South Shore."

She gives me a long look, and fiddles with her glasses. "You still haven't addressed where you think the community center should go."

Clenching my teeth, I smile. "With the money I'm offering, South Shore can build a new community center in any place that you feel like. Or you can put the money into another revitalization project. You will have every option available at your fingertips."

Mrs. Brown rocks back in her seat. She turns to look at the committee members on both sides. Some kind of wordless communication flows between them, but I'll be damned if I can guess at what it means.

I pull back my sleeve to check my watch. This meeting is running long. I have a million things to do today and sitting here is just not one of them.

Mrs. Brown catches me doing it and harrumphs. She slides the proposition back across the table to me.

"You haven't put in the legwork on your application. It's half-put-together and lazily thought out. I'm surprised. I thought you were working with Savannah Guthrie. Savannah is usually much more community-minded than this."

She taps the proposal. I feel my neck heat. Grabbing the proposal, I incline my head.

"If I come back with a proposed new site for the community center, you'll sign off on it?"

"We'll see." Mrs. Brown gives me a catlike smile. "I would recommend that you get it back to us within a few weeks. In March, we recess until early June."

My fingers dig into the papers. It's a struggle to retain my composure. I nod stiffly.

"Thank you."

"Mm-hmm. You're very welcome, Mr. Bennett."

The guy to her right calls out. "Proposition 1422. A new parking lot off Highway 42."

I turn, hiding my grimace.

"Now this I like," I hear Glory announce behind me. "Can we bring in the petitioner?"

I hurry out of the room and into the lobby of the courthouse. Sav is there, a clingy peach silk dress layered over thick white tights and beneath a navy cardigan. Her gray checked coat lies on the seat beside her, and she appears to be engrossed in something on her phone.

I stalk up to her with a growl. "Let's go."

Sav shoots to her feet. "How did it go?"

"Not well." I storm past her and out of the building. A blast of chilly air hits me as I walk through the doorway and I look up.

It's a clear blue-gray morning. The sunny weather only makes me feel angrier. I'm pissed off at the committee's decision. But I'm even more irate that I'm being forced to hunt for a hotel site essentially by myself.

It's only a brisk walk across the street to our rented office. Slamming my way inside, I ball the proposal up in my hands, then drop it in the trashcan as I stomp by it on the way to the couch.

Savannah scuttles in after me, her high heels clacking loudly against the floor. She shuts the office door and walks over to her desk, shedding her coat.

"So what happened?" She takes a seat in her office chair and crosses her legs.

I glare at her tanned, toned legs that were revealed when she sat down. They make me twice as incensed than the sunny weather.

"The committee called the proposal unfinished and lazy." The words are bitter on my tongue.

"Oh!" Sav puts a hand over her mouth. But she doesn't look exactly shocked. "I'm sorry that it went badly."

"Yeah, well." I sit back with an exasperated sigh. "Mrs. Brown explicitly said that she was surprised to see my proposal because she assumed that you would know better. Apparently, I was supposed to include a list of buildings that could house the community center. That's not my job!"

"I told you the committee wanted to see that," she says faintly.

"Mrs. Brown basically implied that I hadn't listened to you." I pin her with a look. "I don't need to hear it from you."

Sav holds up her hands innocently.

"I didn't say anything."

"You were thinking it, though."

"You read minds now?"

I scowl and open my mouth to fire back a retort. But there is a knock at the office door.

Savannah straightens. "Come in!"

The door creaks open and River pokes his head in. "Knock knock."

"Hi!" Sav brightens. "You're just in time. Your brother was about to yell at me some more."

"Will you quit that?" I say, exasperated. "We really need to pin down the definition of yell."

River walks in, dressed head to toe in black. He points at me as he walks over to the couch.

"Easy. The lady is trying to tell you that you're pushing her boundaries."

Sav's cheeks stain with red and she presses her lips together. "It's fine."

River sits down. "It's basic decency."

I cross my arms, feeling a little ganged up upon. "Here's an idea. Why don't you both go straight to hell?"

Sav's eyes widen. She stands up, looking miffed.

"I should go."

"What?" I ask, a little taken aback. "No, Sav. Come on."

She smiles brightly, but her eyes show nothing but hurt. "I have to leave early to pick up Dex. My sister is in Garland overnight, chasing a story. So I'm in charge."

"It's only one o'clock!" I protest.

"Well, you'll just have to dock my pay then." Sav grabs her coat and hustles to the door. "I'll see you later."

She walks out the door without another word.

"It was nice to see you!" River calls out. If Sav hears him, she doesn't respond.

The office door swings shut behind her and I shake my head.

"That girl is going to be the death of me."

River snorts. "I give her two weeks, max."

"Before what?"

"Before she gets sick of being told to go to hell!" He shakes his head in disbelief. "You seriously have to quit taking your moods out on her. What has she ever done to deserve it?"

His question gives me pause. "Nothing. I don't talk to her differently than I do everyone else."

He leans over and stabs a finger into my chest.

"No one likes to be talked down to, Cole. I can promise you that. Take my advice. Be nice to people that you want to keep around."

WHEN SAV'S CAR COMES WHEEZING AROUND THE CORNER TWO hours later, I am parked outside of her house, waiting for her. She pulls up and Dexter flings his door open. He's halfway across the broken concrete path that leads to the house by the time I climb out of my car.

Sav gets out, her arms full of Dex's backpack and coat. She isn't even looking my way and doesn't notice me until I touch her elbow.

"Sav."

She startles and drops the backpack on the ground. Then her heel catches on a strap and she trips.

I grab her by the back of her coat, holding her up until she can get her footing again.

Sav blinks a few times, and her cheeks go pink.

"Thanks… but what are you doing here?"

She politely plucks her coat from my hand and picks up the backpack. Her red plaid scarf falls to the ground and I retrieve it. Her mouth pulls to the side.

"Can you drape that around my neck?"

I stuff her scarf under my arm and jerk my head toward the house.

"Why don't I carry it for you?"

She harrumphs. "If that suits your needs. It doesn't tell me why you're here, though."

"Yeah, about that." I screw up my face. "My brother laid into me over not treating you nicely. I thought I was just being businesslike… but in retrospect, I can see how you might have taken offense."

Sav pushes her cheek out with the tip of her tongue. "Uh huh."

"Yeah."

"And you're here because…?" she prompts.

"To… uh… say that I don't really want you to go to hell?"

Sav shakes her head and groans. "I'm going inside."

"Wait!"

"If you're not going to apologize, I don't know why you're here," she calls over her shoulder.

I'm stunned. "But I am trying to apologize!"

She stops on the stoop.

"It's funny. Usually, when someone apologizes, they start by saying they're sorry. But I definitely didn't hear those two words come out of your mouth."

"That's what you're upset about?"

Annoyance flashes over her face. "My list of complaints about your behavior is much lengthier. But that would be a good place to start."

"Wait, you have complaints?"

Sav sets the backpack and coat down. She turns around and for a second, I think she's about to throttle me. She forces a smile and a bright singsong tone.

"Yes, Cole. Even I have my limits. Now, either apologize or go home!" she warbles.

For the second time in as many minutes, I'm shocked. I've never heard her express any kind of complaint about anything. And now that she says something is upsetting her, she can only say it in song?

"You're crazy," I say, a laugh leaving me.

Her face goes blank. "Goodbye, Cole."

She turns to go inside but I step forward and catch her hand.

"Don't go. I didn't mean that the way it sounded. I'm sorry."

Sav pauses but doesn't turn back to look at me. "For what?"

"For… for… what I just said. And for talking to you the way I did when we were at the office earlier." I feel like I'm grasping at straws here.

"Thank you." She pushes the hair from her face, wearing a tiny smile. "You could have just texted, you know."

But then I wouldn't get a chance to see her. And I have to see her.

I might be a *little* obsessed with Savannah Guthrie.

"This needed to be done face to face. I am the first to admit that I sometimes speak without thinking. It can distort matters between me and the people I care about. And I don't want things between you and me to be all twisted up."

Her eyes fasten intently on mine. A small smile rides her lips.

"No?"

I shake my head. Some emotion seems to stick in my craw and it makes swallowing difficult.

"No. I want things to be honest and simple between us."

Sav arches a brow. "Really?"

"Yes."

She reaches out and plucks a speck of lint from my collar. Her eyes gauge me. She's measuring me, somehow. Against what metric, I'm not sure.

"Honest and simple sounds pretty good to me."

"That should be the basis for all business relationships."

I'm not expecting the look of hurt that passes over her face.

"Is that what we have? A business relationship?"

I don't quite understand where I went wrong. "Well… yeah."

She sighs, extracts her hand from mine, and scoops up Dex's backpack.

"I have to go make sure that Dex isn't burning the house down. I'll be in the office tomorrow morning."

Something in my chest feels tight.

"Okay." I step around her and open the front door. Catching her gaze as she steps through the doorway, I offer her a smile. "See you tomorrow, then."

Sav gives me a soft smile. "Okay. Bye, Cole."

It's weird how the sound of my name on her lips makes my stomach flip-flop. She shoulders the door closed behind herself. I head back to my car, a frown on my face.

More than anything, I wish that Sav hadn't closed the door. I stuff my hands in my pockets, feeling empty inside. I head to my car, thinking of an alternate reality where Sav let me in, instead of keeping me out in the icy cold.

21

SAVANNAH

I SIP MY PINT OF CIDER AND NERVOUSLY SCAN THE CROWD AT Savage Pizza. The area where I'm seated is desolate. Luckily, the kitchen and dining room are separated by a clear glass wall, and the big pizza oven is constantly going. I have something interesting to watch as the kitchen staff stretches dough on pans and adds the toppings for each pie. The bell over the door rings every minute or so as someone enters or exits.

I picked this table because it faces the door. When my date walks through it, I will spot him right away.

I take another gulp of sweet cider and try to keep myself calm. I check Cupid's Arrow on my phone and look at Daniel's profile again.

His photos show me exactly what I want in a buff, blond guy. The first photo is of him posing shirtless with a huge surfboard on his back. Then there is a picture of him sautéing a pan of something; this makes me think he is a chef.

But it's the last photo that really gets me.

In it, he's sitting on the beach, strumming a guitar. His eyes are closed as he sings and the wind blows his hair gently.

He is, in a word, *perfection*.

"Savannah?"

I look up and find Daniel standing right before me. I missed him walking in, somehow! He's wearing an ocean blue fleece vest, khaki shorts, and a pair of flip-flops. I startle and flip my phone over.

"Daniel!" I stand up to greet him. "It's nice to finally meet in person."

"Finally?" he says, a little puzzled. "We just matched an hour ago."

"Right!" I clutch my cider, forcing myself to give him a beatific smile. "Sorry, I'm a little nervous."

He waves his hand. "Don't be. We're all just humans, you know? Feeling each other's vibes. We're all just checking for another soul on the same frequency."

"Ha ha! Yeah. Definitely."

Daniel slouches into his seat and looks around the dining room. "It's dead in here, huh?"

"It's early on a Thursday night, so most people are just picking up to-go orders."

"You think? Seems weird. Why wouldn't people be out partying?"

His tossed-off question gives me pause.

"Well, the sun is still up. Most people aren't in party mode yet. And tomorrow is Friday. I think people have work in the morning."

He scrunches up his face like this is the first time he's ever considered the matter. "Could be."

The waitress comes by the table and Daniel orders a rum and coke. Then he stretches out like he owns the place.

"It's like… super nice in here. I've never been here before."

"I was just going to ask if you're from South Shore. But from your comment, I take it you're not."

"I don't claim any one place as my home. I like to think I'm a citizen of the world."

We get a fresh round of drinks and I smile at Daniel.

"Where do you live, though?"

He jerks his thumb over his shoulder. "I take my home with me wherever I go. I've got a pretty sweet van that's got a mattress in the back. Or I stay with friends when they offer. I live a really environmentally friendly, ethically clean lifestyle. Just me, my van, my guitar, and the beach. Hashtag Salt Life, you know?"

My eyebrows rise. "So you're just passing through South Shore?"

He gives me a wide grin. "I got a flat tire near here a few days ago. So I've just been waiting for a sign from the universe telling me where to go next."

I clear my throat. "What kind of a sign?"

"Like if someone gives me a new tire for my van, I'll know that I should move on. Or like last year. I had a dream about giant turtles. So I went up the coast to Shelbyville, because that's where the universe wanted me to go."

I squint. "I don't understand the connection between your dream and the city."

"Shelbyville. Shell. Giant turtle." He takes a long drink of his rum and coke. "You have to really listen to the vibrations that the universe puts out there. Maybe you don't get it."

I give him a stiff smile. "Maybe not. But you think that you could be in South Shore for a while?"

Daniel shrugs. "We'll see. Maybe later you'll invite me to stay for a few days or a few weeks." He grins. "In exchange, I can teach you some guitar basics. Or maybe you like massages? I give good massages."

I am pretty sure my cheeks are scarlet by the time the waitress drops by again. "Y'all interested in some food?"

"God, I'm starving." Daniel plucks a menu from the table and purses his lips. "I want an extra large. All the meats, all the veggies. I need an order of breadsticks. And let's see…." He flips the menu over. "Maybe add a slice of carrot cake, too."

My eyes widen. The waitress looks unsurprised and just jots his order down,

"I don't really eat a ton of meat. So I'll just have a slice of your vegetarian pie of the day and a small side salad."

"Got it. Will it be one check or separate?"

Daniel seems ready for this question. "We'll be on one check, thanks."

I lift my brows. "Thanks?"

After she leaves, Daniel talks about surfing. He tells me a long, meandering story about losing his guitar on the beach. The story doesn't seem to have a conclusion so much as Daniel just gets distracted and doesn't finish it.

Somehow, I'm okay with that.

I find myself comparing Daniel to Cole. Yes, Daniel does tick a number of boxes. He's blond, he has long hair, and he dresses very casually. Not like Mr. Doom and Gloom, who is nearly always in khakis or dress pants. Daniel is shorter than Cole, but Cole towers over most people except his brothers. And then there's the energy… I've been insisting to everyone who will listen that my perfect match will reflect my energy back to me.

Unlike Cole, who always has to have something smarmy to say back to me. It's *infuriating*.

Daniel is the man I've been dreaming of. He is flawless and should make me feel… something.

So why does Daniel leave me feeling a whole bunch of nothing? And why do I keep thinking of Cole rolling his eyes and groaning with every new story that Daniel tells?

It's upsetting. I toy with a fork and stay quiet. It's not a worry for Daniel, who fills the silence with an easy stream of chatter. I find myself wondering if I'm even necessary for this conversation.

Our food comes. I watch him add a mound of Parmesan to his pizza without tasting it first.

This guy is a little strange, I'll admit.

"So where are you from originally?" I ask. "You never did say."

"Here and there." He inhales two pieces of pizza and half the breadsticks.

"And what do you do for a living? I saw that you have a photo of you cooking on your Cupid's Arrow profile. When you settle in somewhere for a while, do you cook?"

He lets out a long laugh. "Professionally? No way. Do you know how little a cook makes?"

"No."

"Well, it's not enough." He holds up his hand to get the waitresses attention and orders another drink.

"So what do you do?" I press.

Daniel smiles at me. "This and that. I was trying to be a prosurfer, but all the boarding competitions are totally clogged with sell outs that have brand names behind them. It's super cutthroat."

"Uh huh." I take a bite of my pizza, eyeing him as he scarfs down two more slices. "So do you have family money or something?"

"Psh. Naw." He lays waste to another piece of pizza. "Trust fund babies are kinda scuzzy. They are all like, 'I'm a nepo baby, I need daddy get me a job, wahhhh'. I prefer my life to be more holistic and positive."

"So… you're saying that you don't have a steady job?"

"Listen, babe. I'm too busy digging on the sweet bounty of Mother Earth to be tied down like that."

"…right. So… what are you passionate about? I'm guessing you favor environmental charities?"

Daniel nods. He starts telling me a very long story about saving a beached whale. He stops every few sentences to expound on another topic, leaving whatever he was talking about in the dust. I pick at my pizza and eat the olives off my salad.

Daniel meanwhile finishes an astounding three quarters of the pizza, all of the breadsticks, and half of the cake. Once the pizza has gone cold, he nudges it toward me.

"Are you sure you don't want some?"

I shake my head. "No, thanks. Wait, what happened with the whale?"

"Oh." He pulls a sad face. "It went on to the next life."

I'm taken aback. "Why did you tell me a ten-minute story about it, then?"

"Babe, c'mon. It was a good story! It just didn't end like I wanted, so I didn't tell that part. I'm trying to keep things on the level, here."

I squint at him for several seconds. "Daniel...."

"You ready for a massage?" He smiles at me coolly and then stands up. "Pay the tab and we'll go out to my van. We can be more free there. Au naturel, if you want. I'll need a box for my leftovers, though."

"Pay the tab?" I sputter. "Are you serious?"

Daniel looks at me like I just said I'm from the moon. "Yeah, babe. Why do you think I asked for one check?"

My cheeks heat. "I am not paying for your meal. This was a first date. And not a very good one, I must admit."

"Psh. Just wait until I get you naked and massage you. Most chicks love that. You're so wound up. I can tell that you need to let off some steam, so to speak."

It takes everything inside of me not to scream at this man. I smile, but step away from the table.

"I'm paying for my meal. You pay for yourself. I don't think we are compatible, so I don't see any reason to prolong the date."

Like lightning, Daniel grabs me and pulls me into his arms. "Don't go, babe. You'll miss out on this."

He tries to kiss me, but I turn my face away.

"Get OFF of me!"

I manage to shake Daniel off and he stands there, gawping at me like I'm the first girl who's ever told him no.

"Are you serious?" he says.

"Yes!"

"You're seriously harshing my mellow, sister. You need to get right with the universe," he says, stabbing an accusatory finger in my direction.

The waitress sidles over, looking between us. "You all right, hon? You need anything?"

"I'm fine–," I start.

"No!" Daniel cuts me off. "She's paying!"

He halfway-sprints out the door as the waitress and I stare after him, open-mouthed.

"Well, I never," the woman says.

Shame fills me. "That is the worst date I think I've ever had."

"Is there anything I can do to make you feel better? A slice of cake on the house maybe?"

I shake my head, pulling out my rarely-used credit card. "Thanks, but I think I'll just cover the bill."

The waitress takes my card and leaves to run it. She comes back with the check presenter. I open it and my eyes bug out.

"Two hundred and seventy-two dollars??"

"Ah. Yeah, most of that's from before you came in. Your friend was sitting at the bar since opening, chowing down and drinking top shelf liquor. I'm guessing from the look on your face that you didn't know about that?"

"No," I wheeze. "I can't believe it!"

She nods. "We see a few of that type come in a year. A handsome beach bum with a first date he uses as a sugar mama. It's a tale as old as time, really. I'm sorry that you crossed paths with one of them."

"I shouldn't have agreed to the date so quickly. I just… I'm trying to get my mind off of someone else, you know?"

The waitress pats my shoulder. "Are you sure I can't get you a piece of cake to go?"

Tears fill my eyes and I shake my head. I quickly sign the bill, leave a good tip, and then hurry out of the restaurant before I break down into tears.

When I get outside to my car, I climb in and rub my hands together. Turning the key in the ignition, I wait for the engine to turn over.

No luck the first try… or the second….

By the fifth try, I am fully sobbing.

What am I going to do? Grandad is at home, but he's got his hands full with Dex. It's freezing outside as I call Lucy. Then Pearl. No answer from either.

Seriously?

I blow on my hands and try to make a decision. It looks either I'm going to bother Grandad… or make the one phone call I really don't want to make.

Sighing, I call the number, holding my breath.

2 2

COLE

I spot Sav leaning against that rusting hunk of metal she calls a car when I'm pulling up to the curb. Soft rain falls to the ground and she shudders against the weather. For some reason, she isn't wearing a real coat.

I hop out of my vehicle and hurry to her. Night has fallen over the South Shore sky like a blanket of sparkling stars has been carelessly tossed over the whole town. Sav spots me and her expression brightens. She smiles at me.

"Cole! You came!"

My heart squeezes. I feel like I've just been kicked in the chest. I don't know how long I've been waiting to hear those words from her lips.

"Of course I came." I take off my coat and put it around her shoulders. It's huge on her; she looks like a kid wearing my coat. "Why didn't you stay in the car?" My hands button up the jacket while she's wearing it, but I know that it's just an excuse to touch her.

"Thanks for the warmth. It's just as cold in the car as it is out here."

"Why didn't you go wait inside somewhere?"

Her cheeks turn the color of strawberries in the summertime. "Because…."

She mumbles something under her breath.

I lean down, putting my ear close to her lips. "What?"

"Auuugh!" She releases a frustrated sound. "I went on a really bad date, and I don't want to go back in the restaurant and relive any part of the experience. It was traumatic."

My stomach drops. I swallow.

"A date, huh?"

Sav squints at me. "Yeah. It was horrible. The worst date I've been on in the last year for sure."

Looking off down the street, I try to gather my thoughts. I want to know way more about this date. But Sav is still standing here, shivering.

"Isn't there a shop around here for ladies' clothes? Or am I misremembering that?"

She looks behind her toward her car. Probably thinking of whether she should call for a tow or not.

"Don't worry about the car," I tell her. I'll have someone come pick it up and take it to a repair shop."

Sav bites her lower lip and frowns. "It may just need some rest before I try the starter again."

Whipping out my phone, I shrug. "I'm texting the local towing company right now."

"Are you sure?" She screws up her face. "Can you ask them to take it to the cheapest repair shop possible?"

I fix her with a glare. "No, I can't. Just sit back and let me take care of it, okay?"

Sav lets out a long sigh. "Okay. I trust you."

Her words stick with me as I send a series of texts. Then I slip the phone in my pocket.

"Now where is that shop?"

Sav looks at me like I'm crazy. "I can take you there. But it's closing in like half an hour."

"They'll stay open for me. I plan to drop some serious money."

"I guess my car can wait." She twists her mouth to the side. "Who are you buying things for?"

Shaking my head, I push her toward the rest of the shops.

"You are the only woman here right now that's freezing because she doesn't have a coat."

"Wait, you're going to buy a coat for me? I don't need a coat. I have two at home."

"You are wearing mine right now. So I think I would beg to differ that you don't need a coat."

I catch her arm and link it with my own. She sputters and starts to unbutton my coat. I still her hands and march her forward.

"Just relax. I'm buying you a coat. It has already been decided."

"But–"

"Shh."

We walk up to Lacey's Boutique. There is a big storefront display in the window featuring several mannequins in stylish dresses, heavy wool jackets, and matching wool hats. I wave Sav through the door first, then step inside. The door chimes as I look around. There are well-dressed mannequins sprinkled between hanging racks of clothing, and tables full of folded sweaters and jeans. To the far right, an older woman looks up from the sales desk.

"Hello!" she calls. "Welcome. We are closing in a few minutes, but please do browse around."

Sav arches a brow at me. Waving her toward the first mannequin, I approach the sales desk. The clerk looks up, her expression distracted. I pull my wallet out and slide a hundred-dollar bill across the counter.

"This is for your time. I'd appreciate it if you were able to stay open a little late so my friend can browse."

The woman sucks in a breath and takes the bill. She starts to come around the sales desk.

"Your wife is a lucky lady. Can I help y'all find anything in particular?"

"Wife??" For some reason, the woman's mistake makes me laugh. "She's not my wife."

"Oh! I'm sorry. Girlfriend, then."

The sales clerk smiles warmly at me, and I suddenly realize it doesn't really matter what she thinks my relationship with Sav is.

"Sure, whatever."

Turning to see if Sav needs help, I spot her flipping through a rack of coats.

"I think we've got it. We'll let you know if we need anything else."

The saleswoman nods and smiles. "Of course. I'll be right here."

Cutting through the tables and racks, I head toward Sav. She pulls a long black coat off a rack, and examines the material by rubbing it between two fingers.

"This will do. It seems sturdy and practical," She murmurs. "And it's on sale."

"Put it back. You're not paying for it, so don't worry about whether it is on sale."

I flip through the coats, and pull out one that I consider impractical. It's a baby pink number, and as I inspect it, I realize that it's more of a cape than a coat. It's made of wool, and lined with incredibly soft cashmere. It feels luxurious.

"How about this one?" I offer it to Sav. "I've seen you wear pink before and this looks nice set against your hair."

Savannah flushes just shade darker than the coat. "I do like pink."

She takes the cape, then takes off my coat and hands it back to me. With a flourish, she tries on the cape, sinking her hands deep into the invisible pockets.

"Oh my god. This is so warm and cozy." She scrunches up her face. "I'm not going to look at the price tag, but I feel like you picked the most expensive coat possible."

"It's just a coat! It's not like I'm offering to buy you an all-expenses paid trip around the world. Relax."

Sav pins me with a look. "I could buy a nice coat at the thrift store for a fraction of the cost, and then spend the rest on things I actually need."

I look her up and down. "You could. But you would be missing out. That coat looks pretty on you."

She looks away, biting her lower lip. "Thanks, Cole."

"All right." I gesture at the coat. "You're getting it. Want to look at hats? Gloves? Or maybe there is a pair of jeans that catches your eye?"

She laughs. "No. No way."

"Are you sure? We could make this an actual shopping spree if you want. I'm feeling generous."

Sav grins and rolls her eyes. "Absolutely sure. This is way above and beyond anything a boss has ever given me."

"Suit yourself."

I start moving toward the cash register. When I glance back over my shoulder, I see Savannah slow down in front of mannequin wearing a gorgeous deep blue cocktail dress. She reaches out, delicately touching the mannequin's sleeve. I wheel around. "Want to try that on?"

Sav drops her hand as if I'd caught her doing something naughty. She shakes her head.

"I was just admiring it."

I turn to the sales clerk. "Will you get her that dress in her size? And throw in a pair of shoes that match."

"Cole!" Sav scolds. "I'm serious. Stop."

"Did I give you the impression that I was kidding?" I point to the velvet-draped changing room a dozen feet away. "Get your ass in there and try the dress on."

"But—"

I stop her with a hand and look down at her with a question in my eyes. "Would it help if I said please? For me?"

Sav squints at me, her lips twitching. But she can't do much in the face of me asking her nicely to do something. She shakes her head and follows the clerk over to the changing room. She disappears for a couple of minutes and I hear rustling fabric and some quiet curses from Sav's lips. But then she flings back the velvet curtain and presents herself.

"Ta-da," she says dryly.

My jaw hits the floor. I look at the dress, a strapless satin number in brilliant Egyptian blue that hits her mid-thigh. The dress has a sweetheart neckline, shows plenty of Sav's cleavage, and clings to her hips like it's kept there by static alone. Her legs are flawless and toned. She looks as radiant as a fucking gemstone.

I can't control the tsunami of lust and longing that sweeps over me. Just like that, I'm hard as a rock but my entire chest also *aches*.

What is this overwhelming feeling? When she does a quick turn and shows the dress off, the feelings seem to double somehow.

"Well?" She walks toward me, arching a brow. "What do you think?"

"I would tell you not to bother ever wearing anything else. But then other people would get to see you wearing that dress. And... I think I don't want other people to look at you like I'm looking at you right now."

"What way is that?" She cocks a brow and wanders closer.

I reach out and grab her wrist, hauling her closer. I know I'm leering at her, but *hot damn*. She's so fucking beautiful right now that I'm about to lose control and start ripping her clothes off right here and now. Leaning close, I whisper in her ear as I run my fingers across her collarbone.

"Like you're the sweet, innocent pray and I'm the big, bad wolf that's going to hunt you down and eat you alive," I rasp.

Sav's eyebrows jump up and heat fills her face. "Cole!" she admonishes.

"What?"

She steps backward, clearing her throat. "I knew this was a terrible idea. I am supposed to be your assistant. Nothing more. Remember?"

"I know it all too well. But what if I want to make an exception?"

"That isn't a good idea."

"It's my money. Let me spend it how I want to."

She shakes her head, her expression unreadable, and ventures back toward the changing room.

"I'm not letting you do this."

"You're only making me want to buy you more things. You realize that, right?"

I'm kind of enjoying watching her squirm at the idea of me spending money on her. When I was with my ex, she would pout and throw fits if I didn't lavish her with monetary gifts. But Savannah seems to be thrown off-kilter by me opening my wallet and insisting on paying.

It's charming.

Savannah reappears, holding up the dress on a hanger. She tries to hand the dress back to the clerk.

"This is nice, but I'm not getting it."

"Yes, you are. Stop making a fuss." Smirking, I tell the clerk, "You know, if you could add some accessories to that dress, that would be great."

"Cole!" Sav protests. "Now you're just being stubborn."

"Keep protesting. I'm happy to ask her to add more to the pile."

"Don't be an ass."

I hold up a credit card. "Just ring it up and let us get out of your hair."

The clerk's eyes sparkle and she hurries to bag the items up. Sav just shakes her head when the clerk passes me two shopping bags. I swipe my card, don my coat again, and then hustle Sav out the door.

"That was completely unnecessary," Sav tells me as soon as we are out of earshot. "I'm perfectly capable of buying my own dresses."

Looking at the sales receipt, I grin.

"I don't know about that. Look at how expensive you are."

She snatches the sales receipt from my hand and gasps. "What? Those shoes cost almost a thousand dollars? And there's apparently a handbag in here that cost more than my Grandad's monthly mortgage!" Her eyes widen. "This cape was a thousand dollars? No. Absolutely not. I'm taking it back."

She turns around to find that the door that we just stepped out of is locked. The clerk has shut off all the lights inside the store, too.

"Whoa. That was quick," Sav mutters. "If she thinks she can stop me from returning this coat, she is wrong."

While Sav is talking, I notice the sales tag still dangling from her elbow. I rip it off and make a show of stuffing it into my pocket.

"Just say thank you, and enjoy the damned coat," I demand.

Sav swallows and looks toward me. She waves the receipt.

"Thank you. But this is too much."

"We'll call it a business expense. I have a cocktail party tomorrow night that I have to attend. You needed a new dress to be my plus one."

"Your plus one? Isn't that kind of... like being your date?"

"No. You'll be attending as my personal assistant and taking notes on any business I talk while we're there."

She squints at me with suspicious eyes.

"Are you sure?"

"I'm always sure."

She huffs. "What about my car?"

"I'll let you know what the mechanic says. Until we hear back, I can be your chauffeur."

Sav frowns. "What? Why?"

"Why what?"

"Why are you suddenly being so nice?"

My mouth opens, but I don't know what to say. Why *am* I being so nice to Sav?

I shrug a shoulder.

"I'm in a good mood. I would take advantage while you can."

Sav studies me with that vibrant hazel gaze of hers. She purses her lips.

My eyes are drawn down to the fullness of the curve of her perfectly pink bottom lip.

It feels good to dress her in the way she deserves. And after hearing about her date, it's a strange way of claiming her. Marking her as off-limits, ever so subtly, to anyone who might get the wrong idea about who she belongs to. Even if she isn't supposed to belong to me, it's nice to pretend that she does.

23

SAVANNAH

The cab that I ordered drops me off at a dock, leaving me to stare up at the huge black yacht parked just steps from where I stand. The yacht has four decks and looks to be about fifty feet long. It's festooned out with gently twinkling lights, and I can hear a woman's laughter coming from the upper decks.

Cole didn't say anything about his party being on a ship. But as I'm trying to figure out what to do, a group of four people walk by me, laughing and having a good time. They head toward the yacht's stairs and I trail behind them.

I follow the revelers up the stairs and into the main cabin. A curtain of warmth hits me as I enter. Jazz music plays and there is a buzz of banter as I bite my lower lip and try to decide where to go.

Cole didn't tell me anything except to wear my new dress. I'm grateful now that he bought it for me, because as I look around at the well-to-do attendees in their tuxes and fancy dresses, I know I wouldn't have had anything even close to appropriate to wear. At least now I don't stick out like a sore thumb.

A couple pushes in the door behind me and I almost have to jump out of their way. People in fancy clothes are packed in this cabin and drinks are clearly flowing. Looking at the intoxicated flush on the face of the woman standing next to me, I wonder just how long it's been since the first drink was poured. She makes me think it's been a while.

"Savannah!" Cole calls.

I turn my head and watch him fight his way out of the dense crowd of people. "Jesus. Let's go upstairs."

He leads me to a flight of stairs, and we climb them. When we emerge into the next floor, the party has thinned significantly. Here I can see couples dancing, and small groups talking. White-uniformed staff circle the party, offering champagne and hors d'oeuvres from sparkling silver trays. The atmosphere up here is way less stuffy that it was downstairs.

Cole smiles at me, his eyes sparkling. "Hi."

"Hi back. This is not what I was expecting when you said you wanted me to attend a cocktail party."

"It's not what I expected either. But let's take our coats off, have a drink, and circulate for a minute before we give up."

Cole slides his hand around my waist and my breath catches. Yesterday he insisted on buying me things. And today he's acting sort of like... well, like we're on a date. What I'm supposed to make of this, I don't know.

We hand our coats to a passing waiter. Cole looks me up and down. I flap a hand at him, but I can't stop a grin from spreading across my face.

He offers me his hand. When I take it, he turns me around, whistling. "You look… I don't have the right word. Ravishing is the closest one I can think of."

"Cole…" I feel butterflies in my stomach at his words. It's as if the world melts away and it's just the two of us, smiling softly and standing close together.

"Wine, sir?" A waiter with a small silver tray offers.

Cole snags us both glasses of wine while I follow the window along the wall. Toward the back of the room, there is a small nook with a huge painting and a loveseat directly underneath it.

I head back and see Cole looking around for me. Tugging at the hem of my dress, I trot forward, surprising him with my hand on the back of his dark sweater.

Cole's look of surprise and anxiety vanishes the second he turns his head and sees me. He looks me up and down; I watch his gaze snag on my neckline near my hint of cleavage.

"That dress was worth every penny." Cole hands my glass of wine to me. "You've been turning heads since you took your coat off."

"Turning heads?" I scrunch my face up in confusion. "I don't know about that."

"I do. I saw it."

I sip my wine to hide my blush. "If you say so. I am dressed more provocatively than I usually do. This dress looked tamer on the mannequin last night than it does on me."

He smirks. "Mannequins don't have perky tits or asses that just won't quit. I think if more mannequins looked like you do in that dress, stores wouldn't be able to keep the shelves stocked."

Perky tits? An ass that just won't quit? Those are things I would have expected to hear from Cole's brother Rex, maybe. Coming from the same guy that told me he wanted an 'honest business relationship', it's more confusing than anything.

"Stop it." I laugh politely and smack his arm. "You're awful. You are buttering me up for something, but I don't know what."

He licks his lower lip and gives me a smoldering smile. "No butter. I'm just telling it like it is. You're an extremely attractive woman."

I grin and roll my eyes. "Yeah, yeah. I don't want to hear it, Mr. Sexile. All of that attraction and chemistry is nothing but pent-up sexual energy."

That makes him laugh. "Perhaps."

"Let's get the meet and greet portion of this event over with so we can relax," I suggest. Linking my arm in Cole's, I turn to face the crowd. "Who do you need to meet?"

At that moment, I feel like yacht pulling away from the dock. Everyone in the room suddenly leans toward the dock. Several people yelp. I grab Cole's hand as he steadies himself.

"Are we going somewhere?" he asks. "What the hell? We are supposed to stay at the dock! I don't mind being on the water, but... how are we going to leave?"

Peering out the window, I purse my lips.

"I'm pretty sure this is officially a booze cruise. The yacht is probably going to do a couple big laps."

"Ah, hell. I forgot that booze cruises were a thing."

"Oh the tradition is very much alive and well in the Cape."

He looks amused. "I came here on River's advice because he said that he would introduce me to all of the realtors and council people and architects he knows. But I haven't seen him all night."

"Hmm. Okay. Should we split up?"

He considers that. "I think I should run downstairs and look for him. You stay here and set up camp."

I give him a mock salute. "Aye aye, captain."

Cole smiles at me oddly. "You know what? You're a weirdo. I think I'm just starting to get that about you."

"Hi, I'm Savannah." I grin and twirl, presenting myself to him. "Pleasure to make your acquaintance."

He shakes his head. "Okay. I'll be right back. Then you can tell me some more weird stories."

Taking off with a skip, I hear Cole laughing as he turns away. I take a few seconds to down my glass of wine, then snag another from a passing staff member.

Remembering how short this dress is, I take care as I sit down on the couch. My eyes rove the party. There are a lot of attractive young women here and a few nervous-looking older men. Now that I am looking for them, I notice a complete lack of middle-aged women.

That is... odd.

A man in his late fifties stands at the bar in the corner, mopping sweat from his face with a handkerchief. He's well dressed in an expensive suit, but the pale gray pinstripe pattern does little to hide his considerable stomach. He has bulging eyes and a thin moustache.

And he seems to be staring right at me.

I smile politely and look away, sipping my wine. No sooner have I turned my head, than I notice his considerable bulk moving in my direction.

Uh oh. I'm dressed like a girl looking for a good time and sitting alone at a party. Classic mistake. But if I get up and move, Cole might not be able to find me again.

Before I can decide what to do, the man sits down beside me.

"What are you doing over here all by your lonesome?" He smiles at me and his teeth are eerily yellow, like he has a mouth full of banana flavored Runts candy. His voice is high and wobbly, but his accent makes me think of the well-to-do tobacco families up in Virginia. He leans closer and I smell a whiff of rank, stale cigars.

It takes everything in me not to gag. Trying to breathe through my mouth, I force a smile to my lips. Because of the man's age, my mom's voice plays in my head.

Girls should be cleaner than sunshine and sweeter than honey.

"I'm just waiting on my date. He ran downstairs for a minute."

"I'm Richard." He grins at me. I swear, his expression is as warm and comforting as a great white shark. He reaches over and runs the back of his finger down my arm. "I haven't seen you at these gatherings before. You must be new. What's your name?"

Alarm bells are sounding in my brain. But a lifetime of Southern politeness simply won't let me run screaming from this situation.

"I don't think I'm supposed to be here," I blurt out. "I should go find my friend."

I set my wine glass down on the floor and try to get up as quickly as possible. But Richard catches me by the wrist and yanks me back down.

"I'm not done talking to you yet." His grip on me digs into my flesh until it hurts.

"You're hurting me!" I whisper, tugging at my wrist. "Let go!"

My struggles seem to only make Richard more interested in me. He moves closer, his free hand grabbing my bare knee. His lips touch my shoulder and I jump out of my skin.

"Stop touching me!" I whisper. "I'll make a scene if I have to."

I won't. I know that about myself. But I'm hoping like hell that Richard can't hear the lie in my voice.

He releases my wrist and touches my cheek.

"Oh, I like you. Where has Vanessa been hiding you?"

"I don't know any Vanessa!" I insist, pushing him hands away. "Please, you're making a mistake."

"Savannah!"

I look up toward where Cole bellows my name. His eyes are wide as he spots me. "Shit."

"Cole!" I've never been so glad to see him as I am right now. My heart hammers so loud in my chest that I think it might dent my ribs.

Richard pauses, seeming confused. "What—"

Cole makes it to me in three impressive bounds. He grabs me by the wrist and yanks me bodily out of my seat. I go willingly into Cole's arms, clinging to him.

He feels safe and secure. He puts an arm around my waist and pulls me tight against him. He smells like a hint of exotic aftershave and I throw my arms around his neck.

"Now, wait a second," Richard growls.

"She's not with the rest of the girls," Cole growls. "She's on the boat by mistake."

Richard looks astonished. I am confused too, but I'm too busy burying my face against Cole's solid chest to protest.

"Wait, she… oh, my. It was my mistake, honey." Richard addresses me, but I'm too busy trying to hide in the folds of Cole's sweater to respond.

"Get out of here," Cole says. "Go find someone else."

"Is she—?" Richard starts.

Cole tenses and snarls, "I said to leave her alone, damn it!"

I scrunch my whole face up and close my eyes. Cole touches my hair and back for several moments, then speaks quietly.

"We're going to go to the top floor. We won't be bothered up there." He pushes me back a little and looks deep in my eyes. "Come on. I'll explain everything upstairs."

I suck in a breath and nod. Clinging to Cole's hand, I let him lead me up the stairwell. At the top is a closed door with a suited guard standing outside it.

"Name?" the guard asks.

"I want this whole floor. Whatever it costs." Cole pulls a credit card out of his pocket and hands it over. "Let us in. You can run my card once we are settled."

The guard licks his lips. For a moment, I hold my breath. Is he going to say no?

But then the guard takes the credit card and swings the door open. Cole leads me into a smaller, more intimate space. The walls are made of tinted glass everywhere I look. The room is set up as a lavish bedroom with a small bar. A sitting area is set up by the back of the boat and I can see some people smoking on the rear deck below.

"Is there a setting on these windows to give us more privacy?" Cole asks the guard.

The guard shrugs. "I'm hired help, man."

"Okay. Thanks." Cole shuts the door on the guard and turns to me.

"What the hell just happened?" I ask. "I feel like I'm taking crazy pills here."

Cole comes over, takes me by the hand, and leads me to the bed. "Sit down. You want another glass of wine?"

I sit. I can tell from my unsteady legs that I'm still trembling.

"If you will hurry up and tell me the deal, I'll feel a lot better."

He blows out a breath. "We got on the wrong boat."

"What?"

Yeah." He nods and heads over to the bar. He starts pouring two glasses of wine. "The realtors' shindig is on a dock three slips down from ours. We are on a boat for dominant sugar daddies to meet new submissive sugar babies. Everyone else on this boat is here because they want to be."

There are no words to describe how baffled I am. I make a choking, sputtering noise.

Cole comes over and sits beside me. He offers me wine and I drink half the glass down.

"I'm sorry that you ended up here," he admits. "I gave you the same bad directions that I had. It could've gone really sideways."

"Are you kidding? What if I ended up here but you didn't? I could've easily missed you. Then I would have been all alone." I gulp in oxygen. "You saved me."

Cole takes my free hand and squeezes it.

"From danger that I indirectly put you in. But the important thing is that you're okay. I mean… I didn't actually ask. Are you okay?"

I close my eyes and exhale. When I reopen my eyes, I am calmer.

"I think so. That guy was…." I shudder. "He was touching me and he wouldn't listen when I told him to stop."

"I'm so sorry." Cole pushes his hand through his hair. I catch his hand and feel it shake.

"What's going on?" I ask, looking at his hand.

He laughs a little but it falls flat.

"I blame it on the surge of adrenaline I got when I ran upstairs and… and saw you pinned against the couch. My vision went red and I lost almost a whole minute there. I scared him off, I'm guessing."

My heart gives a painful squeeze.

"You did."

He looks at me, his dark blue eyes intent on mine. "All I could think was that that ugly old geezer had his hands on you. And you are mine. I would do anything to protect what's mine."

Under Cole's direct gaze, I melt at his words. Because I am *his*. No matter what anyone says.

Setting my wine glass down, I take his from his hand and set it on the ground as well. Then I turn to him, my eyes burning into his, and cup his jaw. His eyes drop to my lips. I press my lips against his.

Kissing Cole is like putting a fork into a toaster. Except instead of getting blown back, pure electricity pours into my soul and coats my entire body. Every nerve ending is alive. Every hair rise and prickles.

I've never been so utterly alive as I am when Cole opens his mouth against mine.

Eventually I pull back, my breathing ragged. He looks at me with a hunger that is unquenchable and unmistakable. I put my fingers to his lips.

"I hate to be the one to say it. But this yacht is probably crawling with CSAT readers looking to snap a pic and send it in to get it posted. If we are trying to keep out of the public eye, we shouldn't get caught making out here like a pair of horny teenagers."

A muscle tics in Cole's jaw but he coughs into his hand and looks away. "You're right. You're always right, damn it."

I grab his hand and pin him with a look. "We could… go somewhere more private. Later, I mean. If we ever get off this yacht from hell."

He scans my face. "I think I've wanted to hear you say that since we first met."

I flush bright pink but offer him a shy smile. "What, that we're on a yacht from hell?"

"No, the first part where you propositioned me, you absolute goon. Who do you think I fantasize about every night when I'm alone in bed?"

I gulp. "Me?"

It comes out as an undignified squeak. But he just smirks.

"Yeah you. You and I have gotten up to some dirty things in my mind."

Oh. My. God!

"What about our honest business relationship."

"Screw it. Who gives a damn? You're right here and that's all I need."

I lean down and grab my wine glass. After a second, he does the same. I clink my glass against his.

"To the very, very near future."

2 4

SAVANNAH

THE PARTY'S DIM LIGHTS FADE BEHIND US AS WE STEP OFF THE yacht's stairs onto the dock. The cool night air brushes against my skin. Cole wraps his arm around me tightly and takes his phone out, tapping on the screen. "I'll call us a taxi, Savannah. I know somewhere that we can go for the night."

"Thanks," I say, feeling my cheeks flush from the alcohol. I'm grateful he offered, because I don't want to be this tipsy around my family. They'd never let me live it down.

"Your family's not gonna mind you staying with me?" Cole asks, raising an eyebrow.

"Trust me, they've seen worse," I laugh, thinking of all the embarrassing moments I've had in front of them. My mind wanders, imagining how nice it would be to spend the night with Cole instead.

The taxi arrives, and we climb into the backseat. As we settle in, Cole's hand lands on my knee, sending a shiver up my spine. His fingers trace the edge of my sapphire satin dress, and he looks at me with a mischievous grin. "You know, this dress is quite short, isn't it?"

"Isn't that the point of a party dress?" I retort playfully, trying to ignore the heat radiating from his touch.

"True," he says, chuckling. "But I think everyone at the party was having a hard time keeping their eyes off you. Can't say I blame them, though."

"Is that so?" I tease, leaning closer to him. Our faces are inches apart, and I can feel his breath on my lips. "Maybe it wasn't just the dress."

Cole's eyes linger on mine for a moment before glancing away with a smile. "Maybe not."

As our conversation continues, I can't help but marvel at the contrast between his practical, logical nature and the flirtatious, carefree side he's showing me now. I wonder if this is the real Cole, or just a temporary escape from the everyday grand for him.

The taxi carries us through the night, and I find myself growing more and more excited about the prospect of spending time alone with Cole. It's thrilling to think that we're stepping out of our usual roles, even if it's just for one night.

"Almost there," Cole says softly, giving my knee a gentle squeeze. The anticipation builds in my chest, making my heart race.

"Good," I whisper back, allowing myself to indulge in the possibilities of what might happen between us.

I've wanted Cole to take me to his bed for so long. I have waited for this moment, hoped it would come about eventually. Now that it's finally happening, I'm in shock.

I'm on the edge of a morass and clinging to Cole for dear life. But he wants to pull me down… and I just might let him.

The night air fills the taxi, cool and refreshing against my warm skin. The tension between us is palpable, and I can't help but bite my lip as he slides his hand up my thigh, inching closer to the hem of my dress.

"Careful," I whisper, trying to keep my voice steady. "We wouldn't want anyone to find out about this little adventure."

"Of course not," he replies, pressing his fingers against the damp fabric of my panties. He begins to rub my clit gently, driving me wild with desire. "Especially not our cab driver."

I turn my head to try and kiss him, but he leans away, whispering into my ear, "No one can know, Savannah. Not a soul."

His words send shivers down my spine, and I nod in agreement, struggling to contain the moans threatening to escape my lips. As he continues to tease me, I grip the edge of the seat, desperately holding onto some semblance of control.

"God, you're so sexy when you're frustrated like this," he murmurs, his breath hot against my neck. "But remember, no noise. We have to keep this our little secret."

I swallow hard, my pulse racing as the pleasure builds. The ache between my legs becomes almost unbearable, and I can barely focus on anything else.

"Almost there," Cole says, his voice low and seductive. He removes his hand from my panties, leaving me aching for more.

"Damn it, Cole," I mutter under my breath, trying to catch my breath. My body feels like it's on fire, and I'm dying for release.

As the taxi pulls up to our destination, I can hardly contain my eagerness. I practically leap from the car. The moment the cab pulls away, I throw myself into his arms.

"Finally," I gasp, pressing my body against his. "Now we can really have some fun."

"Indeed, we can," he says with a grin, pulling me closer.

I suck in a breath and take in our surroundings. The beach-side mansion looms before us, a luxurious retreat from the world outside. The moonlit waves crash against the shore, creating a serene backdrop for what's to come.

"Where are we?" I ask Cole, my voice barely a whisper.

"Rex just bought this place," he explains, sliding his arm around my waist as he leads me toward the front door. "He's not moving in for a while, so I figured it'd be perfect for our little rendezvous."

I can't help but smile at the thought of having this entire mansion all to ourselves. It feels like a dream - one that I never want to wake up from.

"Good thinking," I murmur, pressing myself closer to him as we step inside. The opulent interior takes my breath away, but I can't focus on anything other than the burning desire that courses through my veins.

"Come on," Cole says, tugging me toward one of the many plush couches scattered throughout the living area. We're practically tearing at each other's clothes as we stumble across the room, desperate to feel skin on skin.

Our lips collide in a passionate kiss, and my mind races with thoughts of how turned on I am. My clit throbs with need, begging for attention. But I know that Cole won't give me what I crave so easily - he loves to tease, to make me work for my pleasure.

"God, Savannah," he pants against my mouth, his fingers digging into my hips. "You have no idea how much I've wanted this."

"Show me," I challenge, breathless and eager.

He smirks, his eyes darkening with lust. "Don't worry, sweetheart. I will."

I lean back on the couch, unable to keep from staring at Cole. He's absolutely gorgeous - his chiseled features, smoldering eyes, and toned body are a combination that leaves me weak in the knees.

"God, you're beautiful," I whisper, reaching out to trace one finger down his chest. He catches my hand, bringing it to his lips for a gentle kiss.

"Right back at you, Savannah," he murmurs, his voice low and husky. His eyes roam over me, taking in every inch of my exposed skin with obvious appreciation.

Cole leans in, pressing hot kisses against my neck as his hands explore my body. "I've wanted this for so long," he confesses, his breath warm against my skin. "I've dreamed about having you like this, just the two of us."

"Really?" I ask, my heart swelling with a mix of desire and affection. There's something incredibly intimate about knowing someone has fantasized about you.

"Absolutely," he replies, his eyes locked on mine. "You've been haunting my dreams for too many nights, honey." And with that, he takes my hand and guides it to his cock, already hard and straining for my touch.

My fingers wrap around him, marveling at how good he feels in my grasp. I can't wait to have him stretching me out, filling me up completely. The very thought sends a shiver down my spine, and I can tell by the way Cole watches me that he knows exactly what I'm thinking.

"Be patient, sweetheart," he teases, grinning wickedly. "We've got all night, and I plan on making the most of it."

"Promise?" I ask, biting my lip as I give him a slow, deliberate stroke.

"Of course," he replies, his voice thick with lust. "Now, why don't you show me just how badly you want this too?"

I grin at him, filled with determination as I lean down to capture his lips in a searing kiss.

"Come here," Cole says. His eyes are dark with desire, and I can't help but feel a thrill of excitement. I move toward him, my heart pounding in my chest.

As I straddle his lap, I can feel the heat radiating from his body and the hardness pressing against me. The ache in my clit intensifies, but I know I want to tease him first - payback for driving me wild earlier in the taxi.

"Seems like you enjoyed that little show in the cab, didn't you?" I ask, my voice low and sultry.

"Maybe just a bit," he admits, his hands gripping my hips as he pulls me closer. "But now it's your turn to enjoy."

I lean down and press my lips against his neck, savoring the mix of salt and cologne on his skin. He groans softly, tipping his head back to give me better access. I trail kisses along his collarbone and down his chest, feeling the rise and fall of his breath beneath my lips.

"You have no idea how much I've wanted this," I whisper, looking up at him from where I'm kneeling between his legs. "You're so perfect, Cole. And this...." My fingers wrap around his thick length, giving it an appreciative stroke. "This is absolutely amazing."

"Ah, Savannah," he murmurs, his voice strained. "Don't make me wait too long."

"Patience, darlin'," I admonish gently, echoing his words from earlier. "We've got all night, remember?"

He chuckles, though the sound is more of a groan than anything else. "You're going to be the death of me, darlin'."

"Promise?" I tease, squeezing him just right to elicit another moan.

"God, yes," he breathes, his hands gripping the couch cushions as if to anchor himself. "And I wouldn't have it any other way."

I continue my exploration, my touch light and teasing, delighting in every reaction I can draw from him. At the same time, my mind is filled with thoughts of what's to come - the way he'll fill me up, stretch me out, make me feel whole in a way I've never experienced before. I know Cole's practical nature will eventually collide with my own idealism and be the inevitable end of whatever this unnamed thing between us is. But that feeling is far away right now.

All that matters is this moment and the intoxicating connection between us.

I can't help but smirk as I lean in, my breath ghosting over his throbbing length. I know he's a practical man, always thinking things through with cool logic. But right now, I want to show him how good it feels to let go and just be in the moment.

"Good girl," Cole praises, his voice husky with desire as I run my tongue along the underside of his cock. "You're so incredibly talented, Savannah."

His hands find their way into my hair, gripping tightly as I take him into my mouth. I look up at him, relishing the sight of him fighting to maintain control. It's thrilling to think that I'm the one who's got this practical, logical man entirely at my mercy.

"Fuck," he groans, his fingers tightening in my hair. "You're amazing, sweetheart. Don't stop."

But as much as I enjoy teasing him, I know we both want more. So when Cole pulls me away, his chest heaving as he pants for breath, I don't protest. "Not yet, darlin'," he tells me, his eyes dark with need. "I don't want to cum too soon."

In one swift movement, he lifts me off the floor and throws me over his shoulder. My heart races as he carries me down the back hallway, his muscles flexing beneath my touch. The anticipation builds with every step, making me ache for him even more.

Cole pushes open a door and steps into a luxuriously furnished bedroom. He gently sets me down on the plush bed. Our gazes lock together.

"Are you ready for this?" he asks, his voice low and thick with lust.

"More than anything," I reply, my own breath coming in shallow gasps.

"Trust me, Savannah," he murmurs, his lips brushing against my ear. "I'll make this worth your while."

Cole's eyes darken with determination as he kneels down between my thighs, the warmth of his body radiating onto me. He slips a single finger into my hot pussy, and I gasp at the sudden sensation. My hips instinctively rise to meet him, craving more.

"God, Savannah," he groans, popping his finger into his mouth. "You taste so sweet, just like a good girl should."

Cole's praise is like a drug - intoxicating and addictive. I crave more of it, and more of him.

"Please, Cole," I whimper, desperate for his touch.

But instead of diving in, he smirks and leans back, teasing me with a wicked glint in his eye. He begins kissing around my mons, leaving a trail of heat on my skin as he moves to my inner thighs. His breath is hot against my sensitive flesh, but he avoids the one place I need him the most.

"Patience, beauty," he murmurs, his voice husky. "Lie back and take it."

I obey, resting my head against the plush pillows and spreading my legs wider for him. The anticipation coils tightly within me as I wait for what comes next.

"Be a good girl for me," he says, his gaze locked onto mine. "If you want my cock, you have to earn it."

He dives in, his tongue expertly circling my clit before dipping inside me. My fingers curl into the soft sheets as pleasure courses through me, building steadily with each stroke. But just as I feel myself nearing the edge, he pulls away, leaving me panting and desperate.

"Please, don't stop," I beg, the ache between my legs growing unbearable.

"Ah, but that's the game, isn't it?" Cole grins, his eyes filled with mischief. "I want you begging for me, ready to do anything just to feel my cock inside you."

"Damn you," I gasp, torn between frustration and arousal.

"Is that any way to speak to the man who's about to make you scream with pleasure?" he teases, his fingers dancing over my clit once more.

"Ugh, fine," I relent, knowing that I'm completely at his mercy. "Please, Cole, I need your cock so bad. I'll do anything, just fuck me already."

"That's it, good girl," he praises, his voice thick with desire.

I can't take it anymore. I need him inside me, filling me up completely. With one swift movement, I grab Cole's shoulders and drag him up onto the bed with me.

"Your turn," I say, pushing him down onto his back as I straddle him. His eyes widen with surprise, but the desire I see there is unmistakable.

"Wait," he says suddenly, grabbing my wrist. "Do you want to use a condom?"

"I'm on the pill," I assure him, not wanting anything to come between us in this moment.

"Perfect," he breathes, releasing my wrist and reaching down to guide his hard cock between my legs. The tip of him teases my entrance, and I can't help but shudder at the sensation.

"Kiss me," he commands, pulling my face toward his. Our lips meet in a hungry collision as I slowly lower myself onto him, feeling every glorious inch of his cock stretching me out.

"Take it all, beauty," he urges, his voice a husky whisper against my ear. I do as he asks, letting out a soft moan as I finally take him fully inside me. He's so big, so perfect, it's almost too much to handle.

"Feels so good," I murmur, rocking my hips experimentally as I adjust to his size.

"God, yes," he groans, gripping my hips tightly. "You're incredible."

As we move together, I feel that delicious ache in my clit intensify, the pressure building until I know I won't be able to hold back any longer. But then I remember how he teased me earlier, bringing me to the edge only to deny me release over and over again. A wicked smile crosses my lips.

"Payback time," I whisper, and I can practically see the wheels turning in his head as he realizes what I have planned.

"Please, no," he pleads, but I can tell by the grin on his face that he's just as excited for this game as I am.

"Sorry, darlin'," I say with a devilish smirk, rubbing my clit against his cock. "You're just going to have to suffer for a little while longer."

As I rock my hips atop him, Cole curses under his breath and grits his teeth. The expression on his face is a mix of pleasure and restraint. He grips my waist firmly, his fingers digging into my skin as he tries to maintain control.

"Damn, Savannah," he hisses through clenched teeth, his eyes locked onto mine, filled with lust and admiration. "You're driving me wild."

"Good," I reply with a smirk, enjoying the power I have over him in this moment. But just as I'm reveling in it, Cole surprises me by flipping our positions so that he's on top. My heart races as I find myself pinned beneath him, my legs wrapped around his waist.

He kisses me hard, his tongue exploring my mouth as he begins to thrust into me. Each time he hits home, I see stars, and I can feel my pussy twitching and trembling around his cock. The sensation is overwhelming, and my mind races trying to keep up with the intensity of the moment.

"God, Cole... this feels incredible," I gasp between passionate kisses, desperate to maintain some semblance of composure.

"Tell me about it," he replies, his voice strained from the effort of holding back his own impending release. "I don't know how much longer I can last."

His words ignite a fire within me, and I know I won't be able to hold back any longer. My body tenses, every muscle tightening as I approach the edge of ecstasy. And then, suddenly, I'm there – my orgasm washing over me like a tidal wave, so powerful that I can't even make a sound.

A second later, Cole follows suit, cumming deep inside me and filling me to the brim with his hot seed. As we both ride out the aftershocks of our climaxes, our bodies pressed tightly together, I can hardly believe the intensity of what just transpired between us.

"Wow," Cole breathes, his forehead resting against mine as we struggle to catch our breath. Our lips meet again in a tender, desperate kiss, both of us still reeling from the earth-shattering connection we've just shared.

"Wow indeed," I agree, my voice barely more than a whisper. And as we lay there, entwined and vulnerable, I can't help but wonder if maybe – just maybe – there's something more to this than just raw attraction.

The heat of our bodies melds together, a sensual haze enveloping us as we lay entangled on the bed. Sweat beads on our skin, glistening in the moonlight that streams through the large windows of the beachside mansion. Our breathing slowly returns to normal, but my heart refuses to quiet down, pounding fiercely against my chest.

"Hey, Cole?" I say hesitantly, tracing small circles on his muscular arm wrapped around me.

"Yeah?" His voice is low and rough, making butterflies erupt in my stomach.

"Can I tell you something?" I can't believe I'm about to admit this, but the connection we've just experienced has opened up something within me, removing any barriers that might have held me back before.

"Of course." He props himself up on one elbow, looking at me with those intense blue eyes that seem to see right through me.

"I... I really like you. More than I thought I would," I confess, feeling my cheeks flush with embarrassment. "I thought you were just a thundercloud ready to rain on my day. But that's not true at all."

Cole's face breaks into a wide grin, and he leans down to plant a soft kiss on my lips. "I really like you too, Savannah. You're not like anyone I've ever met before."

My heart swells with happiness, but also a hint of trepidation. We both know that our worlds are miles apart. Him, the cool and collected billionaire that feels nothing, and me, the small-town girl who thrives on human connection and warmth.

"I know things between us aren't exactly... conventional," I begin, searching for the right words.

"Let's just take it one day at a time, okay?" He suggests, his voice gentle and reassuring. "No expectations, no pressure. Just two people exploring what life has in store for them."

"Deal." I nod, feeling a sense of relief wash over me.

He brushes back a strand of hair from my face, seals his lips against mine, and all thoughts and worries vanish while he makes my body sing.

25

COLE

T‍WO DAYS AFTER THE YACHT PARTY, I WAKE UP TO SEVERAL missed calls from Holly. I've ignored her calls for the last few months, aside from whenever Charlie wants to talk to her. But I see that she's sent me a number text messages too. I don't even glance at them before I shower and get dressed.

This is going to be my last quiet morning for a while and I'm determined to treasure it. I've shut myself away since I hooked up with Sav. There are a ton of thoughts filling my head after having unspeakably hot sex. There are so many other things I should be doing with my hands, but they seem useless if they're not busy making Savannah scream my name.

A bit selfishly, I refuse to let Holly crowd in and make herself a nuisance. Not today.

Not before I see Sav, anyway.

I brush my teeth and put on a pair of shoes. But I'm not seeing the laces as I tie them.

Everything is hazy and just a little out of focus for me today. It's almost like I am walking in the clouds and I haven't descended back to earth yet.

After saying goodbye to Charlie, I head to South Shore. My phone chirps yet again. I check it, thinking it might be Sav.

But it's Holly, video calling me.

I sigh and mount the phone on my dash, hitting accept. Holly's face appears. Her long, dark tresses are pulled into a bun and she wears what looks like a matching purple workout outfit. Anger ripples over her expression and she launches right into letting me have it.

"Where have you been?!" she asks. "I've been texting and calling you for nearly a week."

I try not to let on that I'm irked.

"I'm busy. What do you want?"

Her lips thin and she glares at me.

"I thought you might like to know that I'm coming down for a visit."

I accidentally jam on the brake, slowing my car to a stop. "What?"

"I need to see my son, Cole. It's been a while."

If you could call two and a half months a while, sure. I start driving again, keeping my thoughts to myself, but Holly narrows her eyes at my face.

"Don't start." She points a finger at me. "I'm doing my very best."

"I'll just bet you are." My tone is snarky.

She rolls her eyes. "Let me talk to Charlie."

"It's a weekday, Holly. I'm on my way to work already. I know you live in a fantasy realm where everyone is magically wealthy, but try to consider the rest of us who exist on the planet and have these things called jobs that we go to–."

"Very funny!" she snaps. "I'll text you the dates that I'm coming in. Let your parents know to have a room ready for me."

"You're not staying at my parents' house, Holly. We broke up. You can pay for a hotel."

"I've stayed down there several times, Cole. I know that there are no hotels even remotely near the standards of excellence I require. I'm not staying at the Southern Hospitality Inn; they don't even have a spa!"

"I don't care. Figure it out. This is how grown-ups live."

"I can just take you to court, you know. I can ask a judge for full custody."

A bleat of laughter escapes me.

"If I thought you were interested in custody, this would be a different conversation. But be honest. You like living like a childfree woman. It suits you. Don't demand custody changes just to make my life difficult. Think of your kid and what he needs."

Holly glares at me.

"We can talk about this in two weeks. Goodbye, Cole."

She disconnects the call. I clench the wheel in both hands as I pull up outside the South Shore courthouse. Holly has successfully dragged me down out of the clouds and into the muck.

A knock comes on my window, startling me. I look up into Savannah's smiling face. She's wearing the baby pink cape I got her, which makes a hot bloom of pride rise in my chest.

A tiny knot of tension eases within my chest. Not all women are horrible harpies. Here is proof.

I climb out of my car. Sav holds two cups, grinning as she offers one to me.

"You look like someone pissed you off. Hopefully coffee will make it better."

"Will it?"

She holds up her hand. "The largest Americano they had, with a splash of almond milk."

The fact that she remembered my coffee order lightens my terrible mood.

"Thanks. I assume that you're having a big ole hot chocolate?"

"Close!" She winks. "It's a mocha with whipped cream."

"Gross." My lips turn up as I taste my coffee. "Thanks for bringing this for me."

Her smile grows. "Of course. Besides, we have a long day of meetings with potential vendors. I don't want you snapping at them."

"We'll see."

She beams at me. We walk along in silence. Things between us are so effortless and upbeat. The opposite of trying to deal with Holly. How could two people make me feel such diametrically opposite things?

I hold the door for her as we head inside. She flounces into our office, setting her coffee down, and spinning on her heels. She closes the office door behind me and leans against the door.

"Well?"

I set my Americano down and arch a brow.

"What's on your mind?"

Sav looks at me like I asked her what one plus one is. She fidgets.

"Do you want to talk about the night before last? Or is that just something that never happened?"

I take my coat off, smirking.

"It definitely happened."

She looks relieved. "Oh, thank god."

Crooking a finger at her, I lean against the desk. "Come here."

Sav takes her cape off and tosses it on the couch. She's wearing a short black dress with a Peter Pan collar, and black tights. I can't stop looking at those legs, remembering what it felt like to have them wrapped around my naked torso. She gives me an odd little smile as she comes over to stand in front of me.

Sav tosses her blonde hair and bites her lower lip.

And all thought of not touching her flies right out the window.

"I had a good time," she says softly.

"I did too, beautiful." I reach out and pull Sav toward me. Our hips connect first with an electric sensation. I lean forward and kiss her softly.

Sav's hands bunch up the material of my dress shirt. She seems to need to cling to me. I can't say a word, because I sure as hell understand.

I want to cling to this nebulous thing between us, too.

When she pulls away at last, there's a small smile on her face. "I'm sorry about your self-imposed sexile."

"It obviously doesn't mean that much to me if I was willing to throw it away so easily."

Her fingers trace my collarbone.

"Still."

"It was worth it."

She looks at me for a long moment. "Yeah?"

We're pressed together. She's the perfect size in my arms. Just a head shorter than me. My cock stirs and my pulse pounds.

I wonder if locking the door will be enough to keep out any nosy neighbors while I bend Sav over my desk and make her come using just my cock.

Or just my tongue.

No, wait. My fingers are desperate for a piece of Sav.

I can't decide and I know what that means. She's getting everything that comes into my head. Moment by moment.

"Cole?"

"Hm?"

She puts her hands up and pushes herself off, stepping back.

"Do you think it's wise for us to… be close again?"

My lips twitch. I reach out and touch her hand.

"Did you have a good time the other night?"

"Yes."

"Did you come?"

"Yes."

"We're adults. We know what we're getting into. As long as we're both still enjoying ourselves and having fun, I don't see why we would have to stop. Do you?"

She thinks about it, then shakes her head slowly. "I can't think of a reason why we shouldn't."

Looking her up and down, I give her a filthy grin. "Good girl."

She presses the heels of her hands to her cheeks. "I like hearing you say that."

I swat her on the ass lightly. She squeaks.

"Do we have some time before the first vendor meeting?"

She gulps. "Just an hour."

"Then you should get the lock on the door." I pull my shirt free of my dark pants and start to unbutton them. "Get on your knees and suck my cock, beautiful. Then I'll show you how to ride my tongue."

Sav's mouth forms a distinct O.

"Cole!" she says, scandalized.

I swat her ass again, a little harder this time. "You want this. I promise."

Eyes wide, Savannah turns meekly and goes to lock the door.

26

COLE

Phone calls from Holly go unanswered.

Emails from two agents' offices in London sit in my inbox unread.

Dad and Sarah's gentle reminders that I have to figure out where Charlie will go to preschool in the fall are impatiently ignored.

These things are all put on the back burner while I focus on Savannah, the haven from my troubles. Charlie gets most of my time and energy. He has to come first. But every second that's not spent on my kid?

Savannah grabs my attention and shows me, over and over again, why she so profoundly deserves it. I kiss her and touch her whenever I can. At the office, on nights after Charlie has gone to bed, in stolen moments while Charlie is at play practice.

My career suffers, sure. But I can't care about that. Not when Charlie is cared for and Savannah is waiting for me.

Over the next week, I ignore the fact that I'm supposed to be moving toward getting Charlie and myself closer to London. Instead, I work for a few hours and then spend the rest of my time floating in a dreamy haze of Savannah. I go down on her at the office. I fuck her in the elevator of the only half-decent hotel in Cape Simon. She gives me head in my car on the side of the road between the Cape and South Shore.

On this particular Sunday afternoon, we have all but worn each other out. But still, a sizzle of heat fills my veins at the thought of seeing her. I park my car outside the community center and look at my son. He is playing with two toy dinosaurs and making them roar at each other.

"Ready to go see the Stooges?"

He shrugs. "I don't know."

"Remember I told you about the Stooges? They're black and white comedies like Charlie Chaplin used to make. You're going to love them."

"Okay."

"Miss Savannah is going to be here. I know you like seeing her," I say.

"Sav likes the Stoo-biz?"

I grin. "Stooges, with a hard g. And Savannah told me that she picked these movies just for you. She promised that you would like them."

"Wow. I like Sav."

I rush around the car, mindful of the time, and unbuckle him from his booster seat. Charlie squints at me.

"Do you like Sav?"

I hustle him toward the door. "Yep."

"Do you want to kiss her?"

His question freezes my feet to the pavement. My neck practically breaks from how fast I whip my head around.

"What?"

Charlie looks up at me with innocent eyes.

"Do you want to kiss Sav?"

"Why do you ask?" I kneel down and take his hands.

He shrugs a shoulder. "Mimi said you did."

Damn Sarah. I grit my teeth before composing myself and smiling at Charlie.

"Mimi needs to mind her own business. Miss Savannah and I are just friends. Okay?"

Charlie gives me a long look then sighs.

"Okay. I like her, though."

Oh man. Charlie seems to be forming an attachment to Savannah. We're supposed to be leaving the Cape sooner rather than later. I wasn't worried about getting close to Savannah… but I didn't think about how Charlie might start expecting to see her around, too. That tears me up inside.

Not to mention that if Charlie mentions Savannah in passing to Holly, I'm in for it. I will literally never hear the end of her whining and complaints. I just have to hope that he doesn't say anything in front of Holly.

"All right. Want to go inside?"

Charlie nods somberly.

Standing up, I ruffle Charlie's hair and hurry him through the community center's front door and into the auditorium.

The front rows are filled with wriggling kids. Their parents sit further back, chatting casually. There is a projector and screen set up on the stage. But my eyes are already searching for Savannah.

I find her in the middle aisle. She's handing out bags of popcorn from a huge basket. I can't help but notice that she is wearing a short yellow skirt, an off the shoulder white cropped sweater, gray tights, and a pair of dark flats. She looks like an effortless mixture of sexy and cute. Young and innocent, perfect for a day of being with kids.

"Here, pass them down," she says. She doles out ten bags to each row.

Charlie runs toward Savannah, calling her name. She turns just in time to see him before he flings his arms around her legs.

She laughs and pats Charlie on the back.

"Oh hello! How are you doing?"

"Good!" Charlie babbles. "Where should we sit?"

"How about right over there? Dex and Birdie are saving you a seat, I think." She points out an empty seat.

"Okay!" Charlie crows. He practically sprints over to the empty spot and is soon talking animatedly with Savannah's nephew Dexter. Birdie laughs at something Charlie says and helps him into the theater seat.

She turns, raises her eyebrows, and wiggles her fingers at me. "I got them," she mouths.

Birdie's look is knowing and I feel my neck heating. I give her a thumbs up and turn just in time to see Savannah stagger a step. I rush the last couple steps to Savannah and swoop in, relieving her of the basket. She grins and nods toward the front.

"Do you mind passing those out to the other side of the auditorium? I have to start the projector."

Giving her my most discreet smile, I nod. It takes a few minutes of passing popcorn out for Savannah to get the projection on the screen and the sound to play. I make sure Dex and Charlie are comfortable and exchange a few words with Birdie.

But the entire time, I want nothing more than to sneak off to an unused room and bang Sav like a screen door in a hurricane.

She spends the next ten minutes making sure everyone is comfortable, has snacks, and can both hear and see the screen.

It's sweet, and I'm not mad, but once I'm done helping her, I don't know what to do with myself. I can't stand around in the aisle, waiting for her. I don't want to do anything that screams 'I'M SLEEPING WITH SAVANNAH'.

That would blow our cover, generally be uncool, and probably somehow get back to Mrs. Glory Brown.

I finally find a seat at the back of the auditorium, several rows behind most of the other parents. When Sav finishes her checks, she joins me at the back but sits a few seats away from me. I move so that we're only one seat apart and grin at her.

"You look amazing today," I whisper.

She smiles cutely. "Thanks. Anything new going on?"

"Nope."

It's not that I want to hide Holly's upcoming visit. But she has a history of flaking on important travel plans. There's no need to bring something up if there's a chance it won't happen.

Sav drops her voice so low I can barely hear it, and moves her mouth close to my ear.

"Just so you know, I'm thinking about that thing you did to me last night with your fingers."

My cock stirs.

"I told you I could find your g-spot."

The wicked glint in her eyes makes me want to kiss her.

"I thought you just meant with your cock. Which like… duh."

I laugh a little too loudly and a couple of the parents glance back to see me. I ease away from Savannah even though all my senses want me to do the opposite.

"Shh. We're supposed to keep it secret."

"I'm not the one who started this conversation," she whispers. "You used to be Mr. Doom and Gloom, but now you're Mr. Dirty Minded. That's not my doing."

"I beg to disagree," I murmur.

Our eyes meet and for half a minute, we both just stare at each other.

Sav breaks first. She pushes out of her chair and walks over to the popcorn basket. She returns with a bag and plops down, opening the bag. She offers it to me first without missing a beat.

Savannah is too nice to live in this world. People who are as sunny, optimistic, and kind as she is don't stay that way forever.

I take a handful of popcorn and loudly tell her thanks. One of the fathers turns around and frowns at me. I give him an apologetic shrug and he stiffly returns to the movie.

On the screen, one of the Stooges hits the other on the back with a fly swatter and causes his victim to fling himself to the floor. The crowd in the auditorium laughs.

I use the moment as an excuse to move into the seat next to Sav's and stealthily put my hand on her knee. She looks at me with a happy smile and tosses a piece of popcorn at me. Opening my mouth, I try to catch the kernel. But it sails past me and over my shoulder.

"You're terrible at this," I whisper.

Her response is to pepper me with several kernels in quick succession. I miss them all because I apparently lack that kind of coordination.

Taking a piece between my fingers, I throw it at Sav. She moves quicker than lightning, opening her mouth and catching it with ease.

My brows rise. "That's pretty impressive."

"I keep telling you. I'm not a flat surface. I have more facets than you'll probably ever know."

"I take that as a dare." I flash a smirk. "I'll learn everything about you soon enough."

She just gives her head a shake. "I think I'm way more than you can handle."

"That sounds like a challenge. And darlin', I'll take that bet."

She dismisses me with a wave. I grab her hand and lace my fingers through hers, holding it tightly.

The projector screen reflects onto to her face, making her complexion seem pale. But I think I see the bloom of pleasure rising to her cheeks as I hold her hand in the dark.

SAVANNAH

"Where in the frick did I put that diagram?" I mutter. I check through the stack of blueprints on my desk and release a frustrated moan.

Cole turns in his chair and raises an eyebrow.

"What's the fuss?"

"I had a hand-drawn diagram of our proposed changes to downtown South Shore somewhere on my desk…" I riffle through the blueprints again. "I have no idea where it's wandered off to, though."

Cole stands up and scoops a piece of paper off the floor, depositing it in the middle of my desk.

"There you are, my lady." He bows ceremoniously with a smirk on his face. "What's going on? You've been a stress case all week."

"We have to submit the drawings before the planning commission recesses for a month." I lean on my desk and massage my temples. "And CSAT has featured us three times in the last week. When I was at Grandad's open house last week, Maxwell and Maxine Parker came up to me and were pumping me for information about our relationship! Between deadlines and headlines, I feel like my whole life is under scrutiny and past due."

The smile drops from his face.

"I don't know who Maxwell and Maxine Parker are. But if I ever find out who's behind CSAT, I am going to punish them."

"Whoever CSAT is can get bent." I crack my neck and stretch my arms. "I feel like it's their personal mission to get us kicked out of this office. I'm just waiting for Mrs. Brown to stroll in here and tell us to get our stuff out of here."

He raises his hands. "Who knows what she'll do. I say we cross that bridge when we come to it."

Before I can answer, Cole's cell phone starts vibrating on his desk. He frowns and picks it up.

"Sarah? Is everything okay?"

He stiffens and goes still. Worry crosses his face.

"Okay. Just bring him here. I'll take him to the hospital."

Cole hangs up and jumps to his feet. "My Dad and Sarah are bringing Charlie back from visiting Nag's Neck. Sarah says that Charlie ate some boiled peanuts and now his mouth is red and swollen. Good thing my dad was there with them. He said he spotted the same symptoms of an allergic reaction that I had when I was a kid."

"Oh my god." Panic makes my brain a perfect blank. I grab Cole's coat and hand it to him, them grab mine too. "Should I...?"

He opens the office door. "Come if you want. Just don't make Charlie wait."

I put my coat on and hurry past Cole, who follows me out of the building.

His phone rings again and he picks it up immediately. "Hello?" He listens for a moment. "Is it that serious? I would really rather you go to Lighthouse Hospital." He scowls and shakes his head. "I'll be there soon."

"My Dad said that Charlie is having trouble breathing." Cole grabs me by the arm and sprints to his car. "They're taking him to Sisters of Mercy here in South Shore." He looks faintly panicked.

"Sisters of Mercy will treat Charlie very well," I try to soothe as we get into the car.

"Sisters of Mercy is not a very nice hospital. But... I don't seem to have much of a choice."

"I don't need you to tell me what my closest hospital is like. It takes care of South Shore families just fine and it's run on South Shore taxes."

Cole purses his lips. "Can we put this conversation on ice until I see my kid?"

"No need. I'm just saying that I live in this town. I don't need someone that was raised in the Cape to tell me that my local hospital is subpar."

"Okay, okay. I'm sorry. I'm just worried."

He didn't need to say that. He's driving twenty miles over the speed limit as it is. I put my hand on his arm and give him a tense smile.

"Charlie's going to be fine."

Cole is silent as he pulls into the small hospital parking lot. The hospital itself is a white building approximately the size of a big box home improvement store. As we head inside, I make sure to follow Cole closely.

Cole rushes over to the reception desk.

"I got a call about my son Charlie Bennett."

The receptionist looks at us both. "Can I see some ID?"

We both hand over our identification as I text my father, letting him know that I'm here.

"Cole!" Mr. Bennett pops his head out of a set of swinging doors. "He's okay. He's being seen in here."

Cole grabs my arm and moves to the door. I can see his dad narrow his eyes as he looks between us. But he simply steps back and waves us through the doors. As I pass Mr. Bennett, he touches my shoulder.

"Nice to see you again, Savannah."

I smile. "You too. Wish it was under better circumstances."

There are four small examination areas here, each separated with green curtains. Mr. Bennett takes us to the second area, and pulls back the curtains to reveal Charlie lying on a gurney.

Cole gasps. "Jesus."

Charlie's mouth and eyes are swollen almost shut, and his face is an alarming shade of reddish pink. His breathing sounds ragged and harsh, and he is attached to some sensors. I suppose that they are to monitor his heart rate and breathing.

Cole lets go of my hand and flies over to his son. He sits down and brushes back Charlie's matted bangs. Charlie opens his eyes, though they are still so puffy that they are narrowed into slits. "Daddy?"

"Hey kiddo. How are you feeling? Are you okay?"

Charlie shakes his head and closes his eyes.

"I had trouble breathing," he croaks. "They gave me some bad-tasting medicine but now I'm having trouble... um... keeping my eyes open."

"Oh, buddy." Cole's voice is tense with emotion. He pulls up the blankets around Charlie's little body. "Close your eyes. We are going to stay and watch over you, okay? We'll be right here when you wake up."

"Promise?" Charlie whispers.

Cole kisses his knuckles. "I swear."

Charlie turns his head. He is out like a light in the next few seconds.

Sarah sits up and gently releases her grip from Charlie's hand. She stands and folds her arms, shaking her head. "That was the scariest hour of my life. Lord alive."

"Thank you for bringing him here. Even though this isn't the best hospital, it was here when Charlie needed it."

Mr. Bennett nods thoughtfully.

"You know, I knew what it was as soon as he started having an itchy mouth. Savannah, you might not know this, but Cole had the same kind of reaction to peanut butter cookies. Just random, out of the blue like that."

Sarah chimes in with a fond smile. "Except that Cole went for a walk on the beach that day, and only thought to come back when he couldn't see or breathe. He is lucky one of our family friends was over at the house. Jim's a very smart doctor that carries an EpiPen in his bag."

"I had just moved in a week earlier. And I kept thinking that the stress was somehow to blame for the incident." Sarah puts her hand against her heart. "I was so scared."

Cole looks at me and shrugs.

"All I can remember is that I had all the cherry popsicles I wanted while I convalesced."

"Knock." A bright voice calls. "Can I come in?"

Sarah pulls back the curtain. A slim Asian woman in a white lab coat pokes her head into the room. I would know that face anywhere.

"Grace!" I say. "I didn't know you were working down here." I turn to Cole. "Cole, Grace and I went to college together. I had no idea that Grace was working all the way down here! The last thing I heard; you were working at Emory University's hospital in Atlanta."

"I was! I came down here to get away from the hustle-bustle." She touches me on the arm. "If you don't mind, I need to talk to…." She looks down at a medical chart in her arms. "Mr. Bennett?"

"Yes," Cole says. His dad says, "you've got him" at the same time.

Grace smiles at the two men and tucks her straight black hair behind her ear.

"Cole Bennett, I should say," the doctor corrects herself. "Charlie's father."

"That's me." Cole raises his hand. "You can speak freely around everyone here, though."

"It's nice to meet you. I'm Dr. Liu." Grace is flipping through Charlie's chart. "It looks like he had the symptoms of anaphylactic shock after eating some peanuts. Is that right?"

"Yes. I had the same thing when I was twelve."

Sarah speaks up. "When you were thirteen and three quarters, actually."

"It's helpful to know that there is some family history of anaphylaxis," Grace says. She flashes me a quick smile.

"Yes. Thanks." Cole doesn't make a face, but his dry tone tells Sarah to back off. "Back then, the doctor recommended me bed rest for two days and an emergency appointment with an allergist. Is that still the recommended treatment?"

Grace is scribbling in Charlie's file.

"Yes. Until you see the specialist, absolutely no tree nuts of any kind. No homemade snacks. Check the labels of everything he puts in his mouth, including his drinks. Make sure that there is no possibly cross contamination. The nurse will bring by an informational packet."

Cole nods. "Got it. Thanks, Dr…"

"Dr. Liu." She smiles at us all. "I'll need to keep Charlie here for three more hours to monitor his breathing. But after that, you can take him home."

"Dr. Liu, you are a lifesaver. Literally!" Sarah proclaims. "Thank you for saving our grandson."

Grace smiles lightly. "All part of the job. Happy to be able to do it, ma'am."

"We are very grateful," Mr. Bennett rumbles.

Grace turns to me. "Sav, I have to go check on my other patients. But I just moved back to the area. I would love to reconnect."

If Cole's family were not here watching us, I would crush her in a hug. But since we are being watched, I just touch her arm slightly. "My number hasn't changed. Has yours?"

"Yes." She looks troubled for a moment. She fishes a card out of her pocket and holds it out to me. "Here, my cell phone is on there."

"Got it." I take the card and tuck it in my jacket. "It's so good to see you."

Grace pauses and then gives me a quick, hard hug. "Call me!"

She heads off to do rounds and I smile after her. "That's one of the smartest women I've ever met. We went to Agnes Glen College together."

"Wait, you went to Lucy's alma mater?" Sarah asks. "No wonder you're such a smart cookie."

"That's how I found out that Sav needed a job," Cole cuts in. "Lucy is the glue that brings us all together."

"Plus, she's the sweetest person alive," I add.

Sarah looks at me with an approving grin. "The more I learn about you, Savannah, the more I like you."

I blush. "Thanks."

Mr. Bennett looks at his watch. "Cole, do you think that you've got this handled? I think I'm a little bit tired, truth be told."

Cole nods emphatically.

"Thank you both for getting Charlie here. You can go ahead. Sav, you can get a ride home with my folks if you need to."

"No. Nothing better to do. You're stuck with me." The denial is out of my mouth before I can even consider that it may be wiser to accept the ride.

He shoots me a grateful look. "Good. We can talk shop while Charlie sleeps."

Mr. Bennett claps Cole on the shoulder on his way out. "Don't work too hard, you two. You keep him in line, Savannah."

"Yessir." I nod. Mr. Bennett touches my shoulder for a moment and then walks out. Sarah follows him, but not before hugging Cole and me tightly.

"Let us know if you need anything at all, you hear?"

"We will," Cole says, waving her off.

Poor Sarah. She can't catch a break even though she works pretty hard to make Cole's life easier and better. Cole seems unwilling to see her good points. If we were staying together, I would make an effort to repair this relationship, for both their sake, but if we're just scratching an itch, then if doesn't make sense. Still, my heart hurts for the relationship I know they could have.

After they are gone, Cole sighs deeply. He turns to me.

"Thanks for staying with me."

"Of course. I'm ride or die, baby." I mean it as a joke, but Cole gives me a funny look.

"You are, aren't you?"

I duck my head. I certainly never meant for him to read into my jest. Having Cole's back feels as natural as breathing, and letting him lean on me feels right in a way I am not sure I'm ready to examine.

"I'm all right," I say. "Probably a good person to take to the ER."

He sits down beside Charlie with a heavy sigh. "Thanks for coming with me. I know that hospitals can be rough for some people."

"Are you kidding?" I force a smile to my lips and give Cole a thumbs up. "My mom lived here in the last few months of her life. I'm as comfortable with the setup of this hospital as I am with the arrangement of all of my living room furniture. The doctors and nurses at this hospital are freaking angels on earth."

To say that Cole looks stunned would be an understatement.

"I had no idea, Sav. Honestly. When I badmouthed the hospital earlier, that was just stress talking."

I offer him a reassuring smile.

"I didn't take it too personally."

He rubs his temple. "I still shouldn't have said it. I'm sorry."

Cole is sorry? That's something new.

I sidle toward the curtain door. "I am going to try to raid the cafeteria for a fresh cup of coffee. Need anything?"

"I don't think so."

"Well, I'm still gonna bring every snack that the vending machine has. Nothing with peanut allergens, though."

Cole goes for his wallet. "Here, let me give you some cash."

"No way. Just chill out."

He eyes me. "It's not the first time that someone has told me to do that."

I grin at him. "All right. I'll be right back. You won't even know I'm gone.

I head out of the room to give Cole some alone time with his son. My pulse is finally slowing from the initial panic over Charlie, but now it's racing for a different reason.

Could Cole be any more attractive sitting protectively by his son and watching over him as he sleeps?

Something is definitely wrong with me, but a small smile hugs my lips as I head toward the cafeteria.

28

COLE

After a day of bedrest, Charlie was quite literally bouncing off the walls. The specialist appointment was still weeks away, and he seemed to take the new rules about eating in stride, though he moaned a bit about not being allowed to bake cookies with Sarah while I was gone.

A week later, I'll admit to being a little glad to hand my kid to his grandparents and take the weekend off. A few months ago, the idea of leaving in the middle of a project would have sent me into heart palpitations. But we are at a standstill with permits, and nothing I would be able to do over the weekend would change that. So I thought, why not? Why not spoil my girl?

The pale sun hangs in a partially cloudy sky as I race down the road.

Savannah rides beside me. Her window is rolled down and her hair is trying to escape through the opening. She smiles and leans her head out the window. Her pink lip gloss shines in the sunlight, highlighting her lips.

I want to kiss her. I know exactly how inviting and warm her response would be. Just thinking about it makes my cock stir.

Savannah makes me feel like I'm going crazy.

She opens her eyes and rolls her window up halfway. "I hate to be a nag, but where the heck are we going?"

I look at Sav with a sly smile. "On a mini-vacation."

"I know that much. You had me pack a bag, remember?"

"Yep."

"But you can't just leave the Cape. What about Charlie?" She peers at me.

"Even though he is definitely recovered, he's currently being babied by my parents. The specialist told us Charlie's in the clear as long as we carry two EpiPens everywhere we go. Sarah got him a special zippered pouch shaped like a dinosaur for his EpiPens and Charlie is obsessed with it. My parents took him up to our house in Charleston for the weekend to take his mind off his new allergy."

Sav nods and then looks out her window at the beach. We've traveled down the coast a bit, driving the scenic route along a one lane coastal highway. Since Savannah has lived in South Shore for her whole life, I'm pretty sure she has been this way before.

On the horizon, a group of newly constructed homes springs up. Each one is two stories, with reddish wood shingles, large windows, and an expansive wraparound deck with steps that lead down to the beach. I pull up to the first house and cut the engine.

"We're here."

Sav gets out and shades her eyes as she looks at the house. "This house is huge!"

"Bennett-Taylor Real Estate just built all five of them. I'm going a little stir crazy living in my parents' house. I told River that I needed to rent a place of my own for a month or two and he gladly handed over the keys. We're the first ones to stay here."

I trot around to the trunk and retrieve our bags. She looks a little surprised as she walks to the back door. I hand her the keys and she makes quick work of the lock.

"Are we staying here for the weekend?" she asks.

"If you want to stay here, then yes. Otherwise you can visit for the afternoon or the night."

I usher her inside. There is a staircase to my immediate left and a short hallway off to the right. I drop the bags at the door and follow Sav as she walks into the living room and kitchen.

"Oh my god." Her attention is riveted on the view. The front of the house has floor to ceiling windows with glass doors leading out to the deck. Other than a wooden walkway leading down from the wraparound porch, there seems to be nothing between Sav and the beach.

"Holy crap!" Sav looks back at me, her expression stunned. "This view is incredible."

"Just think. You could make coffee and sit outside in the morning. Or have a glass of wine and curl up by the fireplace at night."

She turns to the rest of the house, surveying the off-white kitchen, the teak dining table, and the cozy off-white couches and fuzzy blankets. The entire house is decorated in polished cherry wood and burnished brass. Sav points to the very top of the house where a loft is tucked away with a built-in cherry wood ladder going from this floor to the highest point.

"What is that?"

I give her a smile. "I was thinking that for the weekend, it could be our sex nook. That is, if you wanted to stay the night."

She bursts out laughing.

"A sex nook built into a living room is not a thing."

"It could be."

I take off my coat and beckon for hers. After stowing them on the back of a dining room chair, I take her hand and pull her down onto the couch.

She falls into my lap and kisses me, then heaves a sigh. "This is luxurious."

"You deserve to be spoiled a little."

She wrinkles her nose. "When you leave Cape Simon and I go back to my normal life, I'll miss this." She flushes. "The white glove treatment, I mean."

"You won't miss me when I'm gone. Is that what you're saying?" I tease her. In the back of my throat though, I taste something bitter.

Will she miss me? Will I see her again when I come back to visit?

Sav schools her expression. "I'm trying to very carefully tiptoe around that topic."

"Relax. No one is declaring their undying love right now. We can just sit together and enjoy the view."

"I know. My whole life, I've been looking ahead. Now I'm trying to live in the moment."

My cock stirs. I look her up and down. "You really want to live in the here and now?"

She smirks. "Why do I feel like you're about to seduce me?"

"You must be clairvoyant." I grin at her and then drag her onto my lap so that she's straddling me. "Because you just read my mind."

Sav kisses me and laughs.

"Come on, I have a surprise to show you," I tell Savannah, taking her hand and leading her up the staircase. She looks at me with curiosity sparkling in her eyes, her excitement contagious.

As we reach the top, I open the door to the primary bedroom, revealing a spacious and airy room filled with natural light. The sound of the ocean waves crashing outside creates a serene atmosphere, perfect for relaxation.

"Wow, Cole, this is amazing!" she exclaims, looking around the room in awe.

"Wait until you see this," I say as I usher her into the primary bathroom. I watch her eyes widen as they land on the enormous, jetted bathtub positioned right by the window, overlooking the sea.

"Is that...?" she stammers, her voice full of wonder.

"Yup, a whirlpool tub with a view," I confirm, grinning. "What do you think?"

"Absolutely incredible," she breathes, her face lighting up with delight. "Can we try it out?"

"Of course," I reply, reaching over to start filling the tub with warm water. As it fills, I turn back to Savannah, gently unbuttoning her blouse before sliding it off her shoulders, exposing her delicate skin to the soft glow of the room.

"Your turn," she says, tugging at my shirt, her fingers grazing my chest.

"Fair enough," I chuckle, quickly removing my own clothes before helping her with the rest of hers. Once we're both naked, I climb into the tub first, the hot water soothing my muscles instantly.

"Here, let me help you in," I offer, extending my hand to Savannah. With my assistance, she eases herself into the tub, settling on my lap with her back against my chest. The feel of her body pressed against mine sends a jolt of desire through me, my cock hardening against her.

"Isn't this amazing?" she sighs, eyes closed, clearly enjoying the sensation of the water and my touch. I can't help but agree.

"Absolutely," I reply, kissing her neck and inhaling the intoxicating scent of her skin. She moans softly, causing me to grow even more aroused.

"Does that feel nice?" I whisper into her ear, my voice low and seductive.

"Very," she murmurs, leaning back into me, her body responding eagerly to my touch.

"Good," I say, feeling a sense of pride in giving her pleasure. My mind races with thoughts of the many ways we can explore each other's bodies and desires throughout our time together. I find myself grinning at the possibilities.

"Let me wash you," I suggest, grabbing the soap from the edge of the tub. I lather my hands, the bubbles forming between my fingers. As I start to run my soapy hands over Savannah's body, her skin feels slippery and smooth beneath my touch. She relaxes into me, laying back with her hair cascading over my shoulder. God, she's unbelievably sexy.

"Don't forget to get my back," she teases, a playful smirk on her lips.

"Wouldn't dream of it," I reply, working the soap up her arms and then down the curve of her spine. My fingers trace patterns on her skin as I work my way around her body, enjoying every second of this intimate moment.

"I think you're going to like this," I whisper in her ear. There's a hidden panel on the side of the bathtub. I open it to reveal a nozzle connected to the bath.

"Wow, what's it for?" she asks, genuinely curious.

"Watch and find out." I turn the dial on the panel, sending a powerful spray of water shooting from the nozzle. Her eyes widen as I aim it at her breasts, the force of the water causing her to giggle.

"Whoa, that's intense!" she exclaims, laughing as the water splashes against her skin.

"Isn't it? Let's see how the water feels on the rest of your body." I plunge my hand down between her legs, guiding the jet of water to hit her just right. She groans, shifting her hips slightly to help me find the perfect angle. Her grip tightens on the edge of the tub, her knuckles turning white as she calls out my name, pleading for more.

"Please, Cole, don't stop," she begs, her voice breathy and desperate.

"Not unless you beg me to," I assure her. My cock grows harder, my own arousal ratcheting up as I watch her squirm under the intense sensation.

"God, you're amazing," she gasps, gripping the side of the tub for support.

"Just relax and enjoy this. I'm going to make you cum hard," I reply silkily. As I continue to spray her with the water jet, my other hand roams her slippery, soapy skin. I pluck at her nipples and she bites her lip to hold in a groan.

"Come on, Savannah," I coax her with a cocky grin. "Be loud for me. The sounds you make are so damn sexy."

She laughs, but I fix my gaze on her, letting her know I'm serious.

"Really? You like it?"

"Absolutely. It's a huge turn-on," I tell her. She seems to take my words to heart. She lays her head back beside mine, letting out a throaty groan that sends shivers down my spine.

"That's it, beautiful. You are such a good girl," I murmur into her ear as I guide her hand to her breasts. "Play with your nipples for me."

Her fingers tremble slightly, betraying just how turned on she is by the water jet aimed straight at her clit. It's intoxicating to witness her pleasure, to know that I'm the one pushing her to these heights.

But I want more. I want to explore every inch of her, to find all the spots that make her gasp and moan. So, with a wicked gleam in my eye, I move the jet lower to hit the tight pucker of her asshole.

Savannah yelps in surprise, digging her hand into my arm. "Cole!" she exclaims, clearly taken aback by the new sensation.

"Relax," I hush her gently, my voice firm yet reassuring. "It's just water. Does it feel good?"

She bites her lip, considering my question as her cheeks flush a deep shade of pink. "Yes, actually," she admits, a shy smile playing on her lips. "It feels... mmm... different, but really good."

"See? There's no harm in trying new things," I say, my practicality shining through, even in this heated moment. "Just trust me, okay?"

I continue to tease her with the water jet, watching her body respond with such fervor. Her whole body shudders suddenly and her eyes roll up in her head. She looks like she's having an out-of-body experience, but I think it's actually an orgasm. When the wave finally passes, she opens her eyes again.

"God, Cole," she breathes, her voice filled with desire and wonder, "I don't know how you do it, but you always manage to make me feel so amazing."

"Believe me, Savannah," I reply, my eyes locked on hers. "The feeling is entirely mutual."

"God." She writhes against me. "It's intense."

"Imagine this, Savannah," I murmur against her neck. My lips trace a path along her sensitive skin as I continue to maintain the water jet's steady stream. "I'm deep inside you. Yet at the same time, I'm directing the water just like this. You'd feel so naughty, so full. Wouldn't that feel incredible?"

She moans softly, nodding in agreement as she leans into my touch.

"Turn around and face me," I instruct, letting go of the handle for a moment. As the water ceases its flow, Savannah shifts her position, straddling my lap with her legs on either side of mine. Her eyes lock onto mine, filled with trust and desire.

"Take control, sweetheart," I encourage her, feeling both turned on by her confidence and proud of her willingness to explore new sensations with me. "Show me what you want."

Without any further coaxing, she takes charge, reaching down to position my throbbing cock at her entrance. I can't help but admire her self-assuredness, so different from my own need to analyze and calculate every move. She exudes a passion and spontaneity that make me feel alive in a way I've never experienced before.

Feeling bold, I reach down with my free hand, rubbing my cock teasingly against her clit as I watch her reactions closely. But instead of welcoming my touch, she pushes my hand away with a playful grin.

"Cole," she chastises, her voice sultry and full of promise. "This time, I'm calling the shots."

Her words send a thrill through my body, igniting an even deeper hunger within me.

"Okay, Savannah," I concede, my voice husky with anticipation. "You want it? Show me what you've got."

As she sinks down onto my cock, she groans loudly and throws her head back.

"Fuck, Cole," she gasps. Her breaths come quickly as she works up and down my length, teasingly withdrawing almost completely before slamming back down to take my whole cock once more. "Your big cock feels so good in my tight little pussy.

"Feels amazing, gorgeous." I murmur encouragingly, my own breathing ragged as I struggle to maintain some semblance of control. With one hand gripping the edge of the tub for leverage, I pick up the nozzle with the other, aiming the water jet at her exposed asshole.

"Are you ready for this?" I ask, my voice thick with passion but still seeking her consent.

"Bring it on," she replies with a wicked grin.

The moment the water hits her, I can feel all of her inner muscles tighten around me. I can't help but curse under my breath, the pleasure nearly overwhelming me. Her moans grow louder, more urgent. "Cole, I'm so close," she gasps.

"Go ahead, beautiful," I encourage her, my heart pounding in my chest. "Let go."

"Ah, Cole!" she cries out, her nails digging into my shoulders as she teeters on the edge of ecstasy.

At this moment, I'm struck by the beauty of our connection. The way Savannah reacts to me is so sensitive, and so trusting. I didn't realize what a gift it was until she gave it to me. She was everything I never knew I wanted.

"God, Savannah, you're incredible." I groan, feeling my control slipping away as she takes charge of our movements. My hand grips her hip, urging her to go faster, deeper.

I drop the nozzle, focusing all my attention on the sensation of being inside her. I hold her still, working my hips against her, driving my cock in and out like a piston. She grips my shoulders, moaning my name, her eyes locked onto mine.

We only have so much time together, and I want to spend it all inside of her. With an iron force of will, I tame my desire and focus on her.

"Ready for more?" I tease, picking up the nozzle again as we continue to move together.

"Always," she breathes, her voice barely audible over the sound of our bodies colliding.

With a wicked grin, I aim the water jet back at her sensitive asshole. The sudden pressure sends her over the edge, her scream filling the room as her nails dig into my shoulders.

"Cole!" My name on her lips is the sweetest sound I've ever heard.

Every muscle in her body tenses and spasms, her pussy clenching around me so tightly that I can barely breathe.

"Fuck, Savannah!" I gasp, my eyes rolling back in my head. I struggle to maintain my own composure. It's a battle I know I'm losing, but I don't care. Everything about this woman drives me wild, from her confident touch to the intoxicating scent of her skin.

As her orgasm subsides, she slumps down against my chest, panting and trembling. I hold her close, my heart pounding wildly within my ribcage.

"Are you okay, Cole?" Savannah murmurs. Her eyes are concerned, despite her complete exhaustion.

I find myself smiling at the thoughtfulness behind her question, even as I fight to catch my breath.

"I am trying not to come," I say, joking through my clenched jaw. "I want to give you as much pleasure as possible."

She brushes back a strand of hair that's plastered against my face. "Watching you lose control is a rare treat. Let me see it, baby."

I groan and begin slamming my hips into her. Her pussy grips my cock and I close my eyes, trying to focus.

"Damn. God damn," I mutter.

"Be loud, Cole. Tell me how much you love my pussy. Tell me how hot and wet I am. Tell me that you've never fucked such a dirty girl before."

I swear I feel my brain jerk at the sounds coming from Savannah's lips.

"Savannah!" I growl.

The pressure building inside me is overwhelming. I can't hold back any longer. I start cumming in her, filling her to the brim. My hips pump again and again as my climax takes over.

I'm in freefall and Savannah is the only person in the world who will catch me.

"God, Savannah," I gasp, my voice barely more than a whisper.

A smile spreads across her face as she leans in to kiss me. I'm reminded yet again of how utterly intoxicating she is. She laughs, breathless from our encounter, unable to speak.

"Let's get out of this tub," I suggest, though my legs feel like they might give out any second. But somehow, I find the strength to grab her and stand up. Water streams everywhere as we step out of the tub, our limbs tangled together.

"Here," she says, grabbing a towel and wrapping it around herself. She hands me another one, her eyes meeting mine with a playful glint. "I'll help you."

"Deal," I reply with a grin, taking the towel from her. We work together to dry off, stealing kisses between each swipe of the towel.

I scoop Savannah into my arms, marveling at the contrast of her soft skin against the hard muscle I've built from countless hours in the gym. The water drips from our bodies as I carry her across the room, her laughter filling the space around us like a symphony.

"Are you ready for bed?" I tease, my voice low and sultry.

"Only if you're joining me," she replies, her eyes dancing with mischief.

"Wouldn't miss it for the world," I say as I lower her onto the plush bed, the subtle scent of lavender drifting up from the sheets.

I pull the covers up over Savannah, making sure she's warm and cozy. "There," I say with satisfaction. "Now you won't get cold."

"Thank you," she murmurs, snuggling deeper into the bedding. "You're so thoughtful, Cole."

"Only for you, Savannah," I confess, my heart swelling with an emotion that feels both foreign and familiar at the same time. I slip into bed beside her, wrapping an arm around her waist to pull her closer. She nestles her head on my chest, sighing contentedly.

"God," she says softly. She presses a tender kiss to my chest. "I feel so fucking alive when I'm with you."

Her words claw at my chest.

I am falling in love with this girl, I realize. I feel like a fool, but at the same time falling in love seems inevitable.

I'm terrified of falling in love. Holly always made me feel like I wasn't ever good enough for her love, that I was not really worthy. She made me feel small.

Savannah, though? Savannah makes me feel like a *giant*. Like anything is possible and that her love is a natural consequence of spending so much time with her.

I thought I was in love with Holly… but whatever I felt then is nothing compared to the awesome, frightening, giddy emotions that ride me now. Who could be with Sav and not completely lose their mind?

"You make me feel something deep. More than I ever meant to feel."

Her mouth twists but she doesn't say anything. Maybe nothing is needed at this moment.

LATER, WHEN OUR BREATHING SLOWS, I BRUSH A KISS ACROSS Sav's knuckles. "You're awfully quiet."

Sav makes a face. "Sorry. I was just thinking about my living situation. I think I should move out of my Grandad's house with my next paycheck. It's just nice to have my bank account looking nice and plump for once. But the second I write a check for my apartment deposit; I know that my bank account will be looking malnourished again."

I turn on my side, using one bicep as a pillow. With my free hand, I touch Sav's golden curtain of hair.

"What would you say about moving in here?" I blurt out. "Just for a few weeks. I've rented this place for four months, but you could stay here after I leave."

There's really no genuine thought behind it or anything. I just said the first thing that happened to be one the tip of my tongue.

"I'm sorry, what?" Sav tenses up and looks at me like I'm speaking tongues. "Did you just ask me to move in with you?"

I sit up, nonplussed at her response.

"Not really. I mean, Charlie can't know that we are together. We would have to keep our hookups extremely low key. But if you liked living here, I could see about renting it for a year."

She looks puzzled. "You're staying for a year?"

"No, but you could stay here after Charlie and I go to London. I would pay, of course."

I can see that she's about to say no. Putting a finger to her lips, I silence her.

"Think about it. It would be convenient for both of us."

Sav pushes her cheek out with her tongue.

"Convenient. That's not really the way I wanted my first 'not-boyfriend' to ask me to 'live together'," she says, using air quotes. "I can't just live here and not pay rent. That's not really how the rest of the world works."

I grab her hands and pin her in place with my eyes, "Sorry, gorgeous. It's not very romantic. You should think about it, though. It's a sensible solution to your problem."

"If I promise to think it over, can we change the subject?"

I kiss her bare shoulder and she shivers.

"What would you rather talk about?"

"I don't know. Anything other than you moving away. That thought bums me out."

That gives me pause.

"It does?"

"Well… yeah." She sucks in her full upper lip. "I'm enjoying this… thing between us. I know you'll leave. But I don't need to be reminded of it every second. It's not as if I will forget and you'll just stay here."

I'm not going to lie. It's oddly warming to realize that she cares about my presence.

"Are you saying you like me?" I tease.

"Of course I like you. What kind of question is that? I wouldn't be naked and vulnerable with you if I didn't like you."

I shrug. "It's a nice fact to know. I like you too, if it wasn't obvious enough."

"I can't decide if that makes me happy or if I feel bad for you because your standards are so low."

"Ouch. I'm wounded!" I put my hand over my heart.

Sav smiles and rolls her eyes.

"Terrible pantomime. You really don't know how to talk to a woman."

That makes me smile. I trace my fingers across her clavicle and bend my head to kiss her neck.

"How about we don't talk?" I suggest.

She kisses me on the lips. "What did you have in mind?"

I whisper against her mouth. "Let me show you what else I'm good at."

She smiles and puts her hand on my hip, pulling me toward her body.

2 9

———————

SAVANNAH

A WEEK LATER, I WAKE UP BEFORE THE SUN RISES AT COLE'S house on the beach. I look over at the sleeping man at my side and my heart gives a funny squeeze. It's funny. I wasn't sure somehow that Cole would be here when I woke up. Every time I wake up here, I think maybe I've dreamed him up out of gossamer, feathers, and air. But now I look at him, his brow smooth, his handsome face unlined. No, he is no dream.

He's incredibly, deeply real.

God, he's breathtaking. Even without those azure blue eyes pinning me with his intense gaze, he makes my knees feel weak.

My phone buzzes faintly. I remember now that's why I woke up. Grabbing my phone and slipping on an ultra-soft, borrowed robe, I pad downstairs to check it.

Something must be going on. I have five brand new Cupid's Arrow matches. And the men are the chatty type.

Holding my breath, I sit down at the kitchen counter. My eyes travel up to where Cole is sleeping.

I feel silly about checking my matches. Like I can't do it here because Cole would find out and be mad at me.

But he wouldn't be mad. He can't be.

He's the one that's leaving.

Pushing those dark thoughts aside, I open the app and check my messages. The very first is from what looks like a genuine cowboy.

Happy Valentine's Day, Savannah. Would you like to grab a drink to celebrate with me?

My mouth opens in shock. Is it the fourteenth of February already? I quickly exit the app and see the date emblazoned on my screen. *2/14.*

Oh my god. How did I not know that this weekend was Valentine's Day? I would never have come over to Cole's house if I'd known. Cole and I haven't even defined our relationship. It feels silly to insist on spending Valentine's Day together.

Then again, we did have some really spectacular sex last night.

"Sav?" Cole calls downstairs.

I jump and push my phone across the table, face down. My heart jumps into my throat.

"Yes?" I croak.

I hear Cole's footsteps as he descends the stairs. He has pulled on a pair of boxer briefs but nothing else and his muscular body is almost too much for my eyes. I blink and look away, swallowing.

"Morning," I manage.

Cole smirks as he comes over to kiss me.

"Good morning. You seem tense."

I keep my eyes on the kitchen island before me and shake my head.

"Not more than usual."

He strides over to the kitchen cabinets and starts opening them. "Want coffee?"

I swing my gaze over to him and find myself staring at his ass. God, the man has such toned legs and an ass that just won't quit. I open my mouth to respond, but can't come up with anything appropriate.

"I'm going to take your lack of an answer as a yes." He starts making coffee. I scrunch my face up.

I shouldn't feel embarrassed about ogling Cole. Nor should I feel weird about using Cupid's Arrow. And yet, somehow, I feel both.

Turning in my seat, I stare out as day begins to leak in slowly at the bottom edge of the sky. Fingers of navy infiltrate the black night and start to sluggishly leach the stars from the sky.

"Here you go. Happy Saturday."

I jump as Cole sets down a mug on the counter with a clink. He comes around from the kitchen with a mug in hand, and strides out toward the front windows. I swallow.

"Happy Valentine's Day, you mean."

I'm testing him, perhaps. To see if he knows the date.

Cole looks back at me, a little surprised.

"Today's the fourteenth?"

So he didn't know. My stomach knots.

"Yep."

Cole sips his coffee and nods. His expression is impassive, but I can see him tense. I don't think I'm imagining that there is tension in the air that wasn't there moments before. He stares stonily into the distance and drinks more coffee.

Silence reigns for several long seconds. Then he asks, as if casually, "Was that why your phone was buzzing this morning?"

Blood rushes to my face. I want to lie and tell him no, but I nod.

"Yep."

Cole arches a brow, but he is very carefully not looking at me. "From your one-word answers, I'm guessing that it wasn't your grandfather wishing you a happy holiday."

I grit my teeth, but force myself to answer in a cheerful tone. "Nope."

He rubs his messy hair with one of his big hands. Then he looks straight at me, impaling me with his dark blue eyes.

"Are you going to leave today?"

My eyebrows jump up. "No. I wasn't planning to go anywhere. If you'll have me, that is."

Cole considers me for a moment. Then he walks over to me, setting his coffee cup down on the marble countertop. He draws me into his arms slowly, as if I am a bomb that might go off at any second.

His eyes bore into mine.

"I know I can't give you anything real. But there is nothing that anybody else can offer you that burns hotter and brighter than my hunger for you."

It feels like he's ripped open my chest and exposed my beating heart. I kiss him then, because I have to. It's as dire and precious a need for me as my next breath.

Cole's lips taste sweet with a hint of salt, rich with a unique flavor that is all his own. He opens his mouth to me. Our tongues meet. His hands grip my waist. My breath comes out in short pants.

I can't get enough of Cole Bennett. He's driving me wild. The sheer ferocity and relentless unfairness of this goddamn kiss make tears prick the corners of my eyes.

Cole pulls back, breathing hard. He leans his forehead against mine.

"Will you be my Valentine's date this year?" he asks softly.

His words cut me and leave me bleeding. They make my soul restless.

"Yes," I whisper. "I'd do anything you asked me to, Cole."

"Savannah…." He cups my jaw and kisses my lips. "We should make this date count."

He feels something for me. I can tell by the way he looks at me. Like he's trying to etch my face into his memory. I don't know how to make him say it, though.

All of the words that come to mind are morose and self-pitying. I suck in a breath and lift my chin. I know I'm about to let myself down before I even say a word.

"What should we do?" I ask, my tone chipper.

A fleeting look of surprise bursts over Cole's face and then disappears.

He purses his lips. "How do you feel about horses?"

"Fine?"

Cole squeezes my fuzzy-robe-covered hips.

"After we have coffee, I'll take you horseback riding. You brought a pair of tennis shoes, right?"

It's easy to slide right back into the natural rhythm of banter with Cole. I make a derisive noise.

"Why would I have brought tennis shoes? My instructions were just to pack a bag."

He feigns surprise.

"But what if the activity that I had you packing for was a ten-kilometer race?"

I cackle with laughter. "I would tell you that you accidentally asked the wrong girl out."

"That's too bad." His eyes sparkle. "I'll stick with you anyway."

I kiss him. He deepens the kiss. Our morning is soon occupied with stripping each other's clothes off and fucking in the sex nook rather than any kind of bothersome emotional conversation.

It's not perfect. But damn, it feels good.

Do I wish that I had the temerity to tell Cole that I want him to stay? Yes. But I don't feel like I have the right to tell him what he should be doing with his life. I am starting to feel invisible again, this time to the one person that I thought really sees me.

What am I supposed to do about that?

HOURS LATER, AT SARAH'S RIDING STABLES, I STARE ANXIOUSLY in the eyes of a gorgeous horse.

"Are you sure about this?"

I turn to look back at Cole, who tightens the saddle on a beautiful gray mare. He's dressed more casually than I've ever seen him before in worn jeans and a gray Atlanta Kings' sweatshirt. I'm wearing a snug pair of jeans borrowed from Sarah, one of Cole's oversized black hoodies, and a pair of Sarah's riding boots with extra thick socks.

Cole looks at me teasingly. "Do you trust me?"

"I guess I can trust you." I look at the horse uncertainly. "But I don't know about Beautyberry here."

He takes the mare by the bridle and strokes her neck. "She's the tamest, sweetest horse you'll ever meet. My hand to God."

I touch her cheek with quivering fingers. She lifts her head, and moves forward a step to move my touch to her ears. I scratch her ears, and she snorts and stomps.

"See? You two are already friends."

Cole lets go of Beautyberry's bridle. He makes a wide arc around her back legs as he guides a tall, gleaming chestnut horse to stand five feet away.

"This is Laurel," he says. He ruffles her mane. "She's a good girl too. Aren't you?"

The horse nuzzles his pockets and he laughs.

"Sarah usually keeps apples and carrots in her coat for a treat. I'll have to grab some from the tack room when we finish so we can give them something to munch on."

I look up at Beautyberry speculatively.

"Or we can just feed them and let that be my first horse experience."

Cole grins. "You have to ride on the beach one time in your life. It's an experience like no other. If you hate it, we'll turn around."

"Ugh, okay." I stare at my horse's saddle. "But how am I supposed to sit on her back?"

"With a boost from me." Cole wiggles his eyebrows as he comes over to stand behind me. His big hands grip my hips. "Ready?"

Feeling Cole so near and ready to help is kind of hot, not going to lie. I open my mouth.

"Uhh, I–."

He lifts me up as if I am weightless. My hands scrabble for purchase on the saddle. I swing my leg over the horse and sit down.

No one is more stunned that I sat so easily and gracefully than I am.

Cole is busily puts my feet in the stirrups and adjusts the saddle some more. Then he steps back with a smug smile.

"You look great. I told you that you would learn quickly."

I blush and pick up the reins.

"Easy, Zen master. Let's see how the actual riding goes."

Cole mounts his horse, seemingly without effort, and picks up the reins. He looks confident on horseback, something I never expected. Sarah told me that Cole rides horses, but seeing it in person is something else altogether.

"Okay. We're going to head out the door and right out to the beach. All you have to do is hold the reins in both hands, and gently nudge Beautyberry with your heels. To stop, pull back on the reins gently. She has done this a thousand times so you can relax and let her do most of the work."

Feeling nervous, I let out my words in a squeak. "Okay! Got it!"

"You're going to do great. Let's go."

He clicks his tongue, and squeezes his heels, spurring Laurel into action. I don't even have to do anything, because Beautyberry just trots after Laurel, eager to get outside.

A well-manicured sand path leads out through a scraggly strand of trees to the beach. I wiggle in my saddle as my horse carries me that way without hesitation. Cole pulls up beside me, and eyes me, his gaze roving over my legs.

"Are you feeling all right?" he asks.

I flush and nod.

"I'm just getting used to riding. Thank goodness that Beauty-berry seems totally unbothered by anything I do."

He smiles. "As long as you're having fun."

Cole clicks his tongue, and urges Laurel into a trot. Beauty-berry surges forward, and I grab the pommel of my saddle for dear life. Cole rides through the trees and out onto the beach. I'm close behind, eyes wide, heart rate shooting through the roof.

The swell and wash of the ocean is directly ahead of us. The tide is high right now, but the sky is clear and the waves hit the shore with a steady, soft rhythm. Cole soon slows his horse back to a plodding pace and looks back to me.

Waiting for me. Watching over me.

I catch up to him and then pull the reins back, slowing my horse. Cole grins.

"What do you think so far?"

I exhale a long stream of breath.

"I'm not a total disaster on a horse. So that's nice."

"You're doing great. It might help if you straighten your spine. I know it's counterintuitive, but riding with your back at the right angle will help prevent you from being sore later."

Glancing down at my horse, I nod.

"I can definitely see how you could get sore from riding."

He squints out along the coastline ahead of us. "We won't go very far. I don't think we'll risk any saddle sores."

"Speak for yourself," I joke.

"Yeah, yeah," Cole says with a grin.

"How long have you had horses?" I ask, curious. "I think Sarah said since you had them since you were a kid?"

His smile drops away. "The stables and horses were a wedding present to Sarah from my father."

"Ah. And I gather that you have some beef with Sarah. Possibly involving the horses?"

"I don't have beef. I just remember Sarah moving in right after my mom died." He stares off into the distance. "It felt like I was the only one still mourning Mom."

"That had to hurt. I bet you felt really isolated."

He blinks. "I did. I was already pretty mopey at that age. But then my dad marrying Sarah was like throwing kerosene on a fire."

I can just picture him as a preteen, feeling so mad and sad at the whole world. If I weren't riding a horse, I would hug Cole.

"God. How awful. I'm really sorry that you had to go through that. It really brings new light to the second time I met you."

He raises a brow. "New light?"

"Yeah. When I sat down at your table at Gem's Diner. I remember you saying that your family was blended. And you shared a look with Rex that I didn't understand. Now I think I'm beginning to get it."

He gives me a wry smile. "Yeah. It was a huge deal at the time. And Dad made it worse by dropping all this money on

Sarah and… one day, I just lost my cool. No one in the family has ever let me live it down."

I consider this. "I don't mean to disagree with your story. But… I haven't heard anything about it. And I've spent the last two months all but living with your family."

He rolls his eyes. "We don't introduce ourselves by telling strangers our petty squabbles. Does your family?"

I chuckle. "No, we certainly do not. In fact, no one in my family ever says anything unpleasant to each other."

"No?"

I shake my head vehemently. "No way. My mom was the only exception. My mom would tell anybody anything. Whether it was me or Grandad or a perfect stranger. It didn't matter if June Guthrie felt that you needed her opinion. And if you got your feelings hurt by what she said, she would always claim that she was just telling the truth. It was… mildly infuriating."

"Where did the advice to be sweet and clean come from? Because that's not the woman you're describing to me."

My brows draw down. "I think my mom spent her whole life taking a lot of shit from people for being brash. In her way, I feel like she was trying to protect me. I don't know why my sister didn't ever get the same treatment from her, though. It's a puzzle without an answer."

He pulls back on the reins and brings his horse to a gradual halt.

"It sounds like you still have anger bottled up inside." He tilts his head to the side, looking me up and down. "I don't know if you know this, but I've been told that stuffing anger deep down is not the best way to handle so-called 'emotions.'"

"I'm not angry. Are you crazy?"

His blue eyes pin me in place. "Am I?"

"On this topic? Most definitely. Besides, who would I even be mad at? My mom died. You can't be mad at a ghost."

Cole's lips turn up and I see a sparkle in his eyes. "Well, you could. Not sure how successful that would be, though."

"Blahhh. This mom-talk is bumming me out." I stick my tongue out. "Let's talk about something else."

"How about a race?"

My eyes bug out of my head. "What?"

"Come on. Let's see how fast we can go up to that big cluster of trees." He points down the beach.

"I don't know…. I'm just getting comfortable."

"Maybe you need incentive."

"Incentive?" I ask.

"Yup. How about if I win, I get to blindfold you and tie you up tonight. And if you win…." He gives it some thought.

Without even a moment's pause, I blurt out, "If I win, you have to let me do whatever I want to you without moving or making a sound."

I grin and his eyes twinkle with a challenge.

"Oh, it's on," he says. "I'll even let you–."

Squeezing my horse and getting her going, I take off without even listening to the rest of Cole's words.

30

COLE

"Right here!" Charlie declares. He sets down his tiny folding chair on the beach.

"Good spot!" I tell him.

I drop the ice chest, and whole mess of tarp I'd been carrying, then brush some sand off my shin as I look to our left and our right. Thirty feet away on the right side, Jared Williams and his husband Diego are lighting a fire. Several kids laugh and run around the chairs set up in the area that they have staked out.

Jared looks over, and I raise my hand to him. He waves and then returns to trying to kindle a fire in the pit he has dug out.

To the left is a small family that I don't know. The wife is already sitting in a chair, busy reaching in their cooler, and preparing their oysters. The husband and son are down by the water's edge playing tag.

It's nice that my neighbors seem to be doing well. But where on earth is Sav? I expected her to show up by now. I check my watch and sigh silently.

"Dad!" Charlie says.

Giving myself a shake, I turn to him. "What's up, kiddo?"

He stomps his foot. "Help."

"Yes, sir." I give him a mock salute and spend a couple of minutes securing the tarps. Then I point to an empty spot a few feet behind our camp. "Want to start digging the fire pit?"

"Yeah!" Charlie squeals. "I'm gonna dig."

"Sounds like a worthwhile venture."

I scan the beach, looking for a familiar female figure. I finally spot Sav standing further up the shore. I raise my hand to beckon her over.

She heads toward us, looking vibrant in her baby pink cape and dark jeans. Her hair is pulled back in a ponytail, and two spots of pink seem to have found a permanent home in her cheeks. She's carrying a huge, covered casserole dish, and lugging a large tote bag.

"Happy Charbroiled Oyster Festival," she says when she reaches our camp.

"Sav!" Charlie stops frantically digging, and runs over to hug her. She squats down so that she is eye level with him, then does the Secret Handshake with him.

It's really just a fist bump and finger guns. But I wouldn't dare ever say that to Charlie. He grins like a madman every time he and Sav share one.

"Hang on. I think I have your hat."

Sav sets her casserole dish down on the nearest tarp, and looks in her tote. She fishes his hat out, and hands it to him.

"I found it when I was cleaning up after everyone left play practice yesterday."

Charlie stuffs it on his head.

"Thank you!"

"You're welcome."

It turns out, being secretive and low key is not in my wheelhouse. But keeping my liaisons with Savannah close to my chest proved to be unnecessary. One morning, Charlie caught Savannah in my bed and barely blinked an eye. I know she felt awkward, because she made him blueberry pancakes, and that seemed to be all my son needed to accept her new place in our life.

As for what I needed? That still remained to be seen.

He purses his lips. "Can you stay over again?"

"If you'll have me." Her lips twitch. "I've only stayed at my house for three nights in the last two weeks."

"Can you make pancakes? I like pancakes."

Sav laughs. "You bet I can, Charlie."

I clear my throat. "I hate to break this reunion up, but aren't you supposed to be digging a fire pit for us?"

"Oh yeah." Charlie runs back to the pit and starts wildly flinging sand.

"His energy level is astonishing. Scientifically near impossible," Sav comments.

"He's right about the house when you're not there, though. The house," I lift my brows, "missed you last night."

She smiles. "Oh? Is that right?"

"Yeah, that's right. I would also like to make it clear that the house would very much like to kiss you right now. The house probably would if the house's kid weren't around."

"The house will get plenty of affection later. I wouldn't want the house to worry."

"The house will take you up on that offer." I nod to the casserole dish. "What did you bring?"

She bites her lip. "Black-eyed peas cooked with ham and collards."

"Whoa! I didn't know you cooked."

"Well, I don't really. This is the only dish that I have perfected. But…." She winces. "It's actually for my sister."

"Your sister? Why?"

She shrugs. "Because Birdie asked. And truth be told, I wasn't sure that you would want me to join you today."

Her words echo dully in my mind. What in the world is going on in that head of hers?

"Why wouldn't I want you here?" I ask, my neck growing hot. "You've been staying with me for a week now. What's different about today?"

Sav looks at Charlie, and then out at the sea. She shrugs. "I don't know. The Oyster Festival is usually a family event. I thought you would want to be with your actual family."

I grab her by the hand, and walk out toward the ocean. When we are almost touching the surf break, I turn to her.

"I'm spending the day with the people I care about. Why don't you stop second guessing everything and leave the rest for me to worry about?"

Her expression tightens and she looks away.

"I would really rather not make a scene, Cole. This wasn't a referendum on whether or not we're a couple. I just made black-eyed peas."

"So don't make a scene." I grab her hand and squeeze her fingers. "Come hang out with me and Charlie. If you want, we can share our spot with your family."

She looks at me like I've just sprouted a second mouth.

"I don't really want my family to know that we are… whatever we are. Birdie knows, of course. But I don't feel like my Grandad or nephew need to know."

"They won't have an inkling." I release her hand and take a step back. "At least not from me. Scout's honor. I'm just your friendly boss."

"Uh huh." Savannah appears unconvinced.

I start to walk backward. "Invite your family. That's an order."

She looks slightly frustrated, but she pulls out her phone and starts texting. I make a few more trips to the car, lugging firewood, extra chairs, and a beach cabana out to the sand. As soon as Charlie finishes digging the pit, I lay the firewood in the cavity and set it ablaze.

Savannah's sister Birdie, her nephew Dexter, and her grandad show up with a chest of oysters and a few side dishes. Grandad throws the ice chest down beside ours, while Birdie hugs Sav. Dexter makes a beeline for Charlie.

"Wow! Nice spot. Hey, Cole!" Birdie waves and shades her eyes. "No other Bennetts here, huh?"

I offer her a sly smile.

"I assume that you're talking about Rex. He's down south, playing at the Kings' training camp."

Birdie goes red, and glares at me. "No one said anything about Rex," she mutters.

"Sorry. That's usually what people mean when they ask after the Bennetts. They are really asking when Rex will arrive. The point has really been driven home to me since I arrived for this extended vacation."

"Uh huh." Birdie looks me up and down as if trying to decide my worth. "I just wanted to know if Lucy was coming."

"I have no idea what she's up to. Probably drawing or sculpting, if I know her."

I brush sand from my fingers and shake her grandad's hand.

"Cole Bennett," I say by way of introduction. "It's a real pleasure to meet you, sir. Savannah tells me some wild stories about growing up in your house."

"Does she now?" He casts an eye over Sav, who is approximately the color of a beet. "Call me Karl."

I grin. "Karl, have you got any wisdom for me when it comes to shucking oysters?"

Her grandad lights up like I just told him that Santa is about to visit.

"You asked the right old man, Cole. Let me show you my method."

"Oh god." Sav and Birdie both groan.

"Save yourself!" Birdie cries, pretending to be in mock-agony. "Grandad had a method for everything. The best way to paint a house. The fastest way to drive to the bank. The way to carve a turkey that saves the most meat."

"Don't listen to my granddaughters. No one complains about my methods when they get to eat that final turkey sandwich because I carved the turkey properly."

I raise my brows. "Oh, now I'm even more curious. Let's go."

Learning how to shuck oysters in *just* the right way turns out to be time-consuming. Karl is witty with a dry sense of humor. I find him hilarious. But he is also very particular about everything.

"Ya see, ya grip with the glove, and pry with your knife like so." He pops the shell off the oyster as effortlessly as a button off a blouse. He shucks three more in record time, and grins at my shocked expression. "You'll get it."

But I'm lacking the lifetime spent at sea. So while I do improve by using his suggestions, I'm definitely not going to be as quick a shucker as Karl.

I'm used to being the alpha dog in every transaction. But I find myself laughing at my own amateur efforts, and no one is more surprised about my good attitude than me. I keep waiting for that familiar frustration that comes when I am not the best. But it never does. I would wonder what that's all about, except, when I catch Savannah's eye, and find her smiling at me, I think I already know.

Soon the side dishes are warming on the sides of the fire pit, and the oysters are grilling on the grate I brought just for this purpose.

Sav adds butter and Parmesan to each one. The air fills with the scent of sizzling seafood. Birdie and Karl begin playing spades. The boys race around, fighting with two pieces of driftwood that Dexter anointed as swords.

"This is a great day." Sav watches Dexter and Charlie parry with a grin. "It's almost the perfect day."

"Almost?" I put my hands to my heart, pretending her words hurt me. "Alas, fair maiden."

She swats me on the arm. "Stop. You know what I mean."

"What is it missing?" I ask. "Not oysters. We have those covered."

Sav shrugs. "There could be more people here. Don't get me wrong. I'm glad that this little group is eating together. But what about Lucy? And your parents? And the other Bennetts? River and Rex and Eden? Plus Pearl and her family…?"

"You mean our landlady, Mrs. Brown?" I shake my head. "I'm pretty sure she hates us."

"Uh… excuse you! Speak for yourself!"

"I think I am."

"You're talking crazy." She giggles. "Mrs. Glory is a force to be reckoned with. But she loves me. She's just calling it like she sees it."

"Mrs. Brown is a pain in my ass. She's an agent of bureaucracy." I grab chargrilled oysters with a pair of tongs and start stacking them on a platter.

"She's just making you check every box. I know that you fancy people from the Cape may not be used to it, but that's how everyone else gets things done right in the real world."

I shake my tongs at Sav.

"I'm really starting to think that you have a hang up about rich people from the Cape. I'm not rich. Not really."

"Are you serious?"

"Not entirely. But partially."

Sav puts her hands on her hips. "Have you seen your brand-new beach house lately? Before it was owned by you, it was owned by your family's real estate agency. You're working for your famous, pro-athlete brother, trying to build a multi-billion-dollar sports complex! And… and the rest of you Bennetts all grew up in a mansion with stables!"

By the end of her speech, her voice is squeaky and her hands wave around in the air.

"Whoa." I set the platter and tongs down, and grab Sav's hands. "Easy there, tiger. I'm privileged. I'm aware."

"Are you, though?" She cuts a look at me. "Sometimes I wonder if you know just how lucky your whole life has been."

I want to step closer and tug her into my arms. But Karl and Birdie have noticed our fight. They're both slowly dealing cards, and trying not to make it apparent that they're eavesdropping.

Against my better judgment, I drop her hands and step away. I give her an easy smile. "Let's talk about it later."

She huffs and shoves a hand through her hair.

"No. I should say I'm sorry. I don't know what has gotten into me today."

I shrug. "No sweat off my ass. Consider it forgotten."

Sav offers me a tight smile and claps her hands.

"I think the food is ready!"

My phone buzzes in my pocket. I pull it out, checking the screen. It reads, *Andrew Mayes.*

Shit. He's my contact at the Mayes Agency. Why is he calling now? I end the call quickly and send him a text.

> Can't talk now. Can we schedule a call
> Monday?

He answers immediately.

> Things have shifted. A seat has opened up
> here. Are you ready to sign a contract and
> move?

My mouth goes dry.

> Maybe. Details?

> This is serious, Cole. I'm holding a
> partnership seat open for you. Don't make
> me wait.

> Talk Monday morning. If you have the details,
> I will have an answer for you within 24 hours.

> Fine. Monday. I'll have my assistant forward you details.

I stare down at my phone, paralyzed. The entire time I've been here in the Cape, I've angled for this sort of opportunity. And here it is.

A partnership seat at the Mayes Agency here in our London office. It just arrived earlier than I'd imagined. I've sent over all of my paperwork, and committed to bringing my client roster as well. Managing my athletes from London will mean a lot of flights back to the States, but Charlie and I can manage that without breaking a sweat. On paper, it sounds like the partnership offer I've been wanting my whole life.

"Cole?" I blink and look up. Sav touches my arm gently. "Are you going to eat with the rest of us? Do you want me to fix you a plate?"

I force a smile to my lips. "Nope. I'm coming right now."

She smiles at me. "You'll have to let me know what you think of my black-eyed peas."

"Okay."

I'm not really listening though. Instead, I'm trying to figure out just what the hell I will say in response to the much-sought-after move to London.

31

SAVANNAH

"Can everyone hear me?" I cup my hands over my mouth and shout over a crowd of children dressed as the characters from Wizard of Oz. "If you still need part of your costume, please see Bev. Bev, wave your hand please."

Bev smooths her oversized white cardigan, and stands up straight. "Right here!"

Jess comes up to my right elbow.

"Let's get this dress rehearsal on the road," she suggests. "If you don't mind."

"You and Meg are the ones in charge of what happens on the stage. I'm just… coordinating!"

"And doing it with style," Jess says with a wink. She turns to the crowded stage, and raises her voice. "Let's move everything off the stage, please! Start finding your places, everyone. How is the back of the house doing?"

Jared flashes the auditorium lights, and then the stage lights. "Lights are working!" he confirms.

I hurry to the edge of the stage, and carefully sit down before sliding down to the floor of the auditorium. It's not the most elegant way to climb down from the stage, but it does keep me from flashing everybody my red lace panties. Looking around, I see the few parents that are sprinkled throughout the seats, mostly peering at their phones. Then I spot Cole. As usual, he's in the back of the room. His dark hair looks like it could use a comb. He stares intently at his phone screen, and occasionally types something.

I try to be casual about wandering back toward him. Cole doesn't even look up as I sink into the seat beside his. I have to elbow him to pull him away from his phone.

"Hey. What's so interesting?" I ask. I use a teasing tone, and try to keep it light.

I'm trying to cover the anxiety that has bloomed in my chest about Cole being secretive around his phone. I might be imagining it, but I swear he has been frowning down at it so much the last two days.

Has Cole's ex been in touch? Is she asking to get back together with him?

My mind darts around in a thousand different terribly dark directions.

"Hello?" I prod.

Cole jumps like he's been caught doing something wrong. He gives me a nervous look as he puts his phone in his pocket.

"What's happening?"

"The kids are about to run through the play for the final time. I think my part is done."

He frowns. "Oh."

"Are you all right?" I pat his arms and torso. "Limbs in place, major organs functioning okay?"

Cole tenses his jaw.

"Yes. Do I not seem okay?"

"I don't know. You've been acting oddly since the oyster bake."

He inhales a long breath and then blows it out slowly. "I'm fine."

I squeeze his knee. "You seem really, ultra, extra fine. Most totally fine people need to reassure others that they are fine."

He gives me a look. "You're hilarious."

"I'll be here all week."

Cole crosses his arms and glares off in the distance. I wait a few beats for him to respond, then I push.

"Something is bothering you. I can tell."

"Maybe I just don't like playing twenty questions. Ever think of that?"

I bite my lip. Cole is being weird, whether he wants to admit it or not.

"Let's change the subject."

"Glad to."

"Do you want to be my not-date to put flowers on my mom's grave next week? My Grandad, my sister, and Dex will be there. It's not really a memorial ceremony. More of a walk in the graveyard."

It's been months since I put flowers on Mom's gravestone. Since her birthday in October, at least. I want Cole's companionship to brace me against the torrent of sadness and bitterness that are sure to drift to the surface of my mind.

But Cole looks at me with horror. "I think your family will know that something is going on between us if I turn up and hold your hand at your mother's burial site."

I roll my eyes. "They already know. You made me invite them to charbroil oysters!"

"Grilling oysters is a world apart from a cemetery visit."

I run my tongue over my teeth. I'm annoyed. Cole's hot one minute, cold the next view of our relationship is exhausting. First everything is perfect and we are fucking in his sex nook. Then things are complicated and I need to be more understanding of his plight.

It's hard not to show the anger on my face.

"So that's a no?" I ask.

"Yeah, I would say so."

Grabbing Cole's hand, I lock eyes with him. "There's nothing you want to talk about?"

I don't think I've ever seen Cole blush. But, for the first time since I've known him, two spots of red appear in the apples of his cheeks.

He shakes his head, carefully disengaging from my touch.

"I should go. I have to run an errand."

He stands up and moves past me. I flatten myself against my seat to accommodate him. Then I decide I'm not letting him literally run away from this conversation, and stand up to follow closely behind.

As soon as we are a safe distance from the doors, I turn to Cole, palms upturned.

"What is going on?" I demand.

"Nothing." He scowls at the ground. "I'm just busy."

I hear my mom's voice. *Cleaner than sunshine, sweeter than honey.* My fists bunch, but I try to hide my frustration.

"Are you trying to break things off with me?"

Cole looks like I've just knocked him upside the head with a two-by-four.

"What? No! Not everything revolves around you, Savannah."

I take several seconds before I reply.

"So, there's nothing that I need to know?"

"No!" he shouts.

I reel back. "Why are you yelling at me?"

"I just–." His phone buzzes, and he stops talking to look at it. "Shit. I'm sorry. Can we talk later?"

I take a step back. My heart aches in my chest. I'm confused about what's going on.

If this is Cole seeing me, I don't want it. I thought it was enough, but… something has off about our relationship for the last few days.

Why am I taking on all the risk here?

"I don't know, Cole. Can we?"

"Sav, I just need to take this call. Please."

"You can take all the calls you like." I lift my hands and take a step back. "Don't let me stop you."

Cole slides me a frustrated look. "Don't be like that."

He glances down at his phone. My heart feels like it's bleeding out from a thousand tiny papercuts. Cole glances back up at me, mouths "later", and then turns his back as he picks up the call.

Tears prick the corners of my eyes. I whirl and hurry back through the swinging doors of the auditorium. I slink back to my seat in the last row. The show is about to start, regardless of whether Cole is here or not. I swallow hard.

Cole is going to miss the performance of the play that I put on for his kid. The same play that we've been practicing for months! It's *unacceptable*.

My hands are clenched into tight fists. My heart is pounding.

I can't remember ever having felt so angry and confused. What on earth is Cole's problem?

32

COLE

I TYPE IT OUT QUICKLY. MY FINGER HOVERS OVER THE SEND key. It's a lot of money to demand for a year's salary. But I know I'm worth it.

I know that if Andrew Mayes turns me down, my fall-back plan is to wait right here in Cape Simon until I'm approached by another firm.

And then Savannah won't ever have to know about my indecision over whether to leave.

I hit send. Seeing the three dots appear below, I hold my breath.

I gulp and let my phone drop to the carpeted ground by my feet. I picture how angry Rex is going to be when I tell him that I've accepted the job.

And Sav… I can't imagine the hurt in her eyes were I to admit that I've been negotiating my salary for close to a week.

On top of all this, there is still the question of Holly's visit. She emailed me her flight info, but I am still not telling anyone. I can't disappoint Charlie if his mother flakes out again.

Part of me prays that she'll be a no-show. I have enough muck to wade through without adding Holly's nasally whining to the mix.

I wander out the back door, turmoil filling my chest cavity. I missed the beginning of Charlie's dress rehearsal and when I returned, Sav was nowhere to be found. I texted her… and eventually, she texted back.

Now I'm just sitting on the back deck of the beach house when Sav arrives in a taxi. She steps out of the car as I bound down to the street to press a hundred-dollar bill into the driver's hand. She smiles at me as the taxi leaves.

But it's a hollow, plasticine smile. It lifts her lips but doesn't even attempt to reach the hazel depths of her eyes.

"Hello." Sav clutches a large tote bag, and makes no move to embrace me.

"Thanks for bringing the new proposals from the planning commission to me. I know your car is still in the shop. But Charlie is upstairs lying down. He isn't feeling great, he says."

"Not a problem. That's what personal assistants are for, right?"

Her tone is cold and formal. Her expression is standoffish, like she's a filly that's about to bolt from the training ring.

This is not going at all how I pictured it would. I lick my lips and shove my hand through my short hair.

"Listen, Sav. About the other day…"

She puts up her hand to stop me.

"No need." A determined smile hugs her lips. "I get it. Breaking up with your employee is awkward."

Her words hit me like a bucket of ice water dumped over my head. I'm in utter shock.

"What??" I manage.

"Isn't that what you were about to say?" Sav asks. She seems a bit wobbly.

I surge forward and grab her hands. She seizes up, looking at me with wide eyes.

"What are you doing?" she asks.

"Savannah. The last thing in the world I want is to not see you anymore."

The words come out in a rush. They aren't particularly well thought out or perfectly put. But I have never meant anything more.

She squints at me. "Okay…"

"I'm sorry I was a dick. It's… complicated."

"You ducked out and took a call during Charlie's play. Unless it was his mom, I don't see what could possibly be complicated enough to make that okay?"

I blink. "You're worried about *Holly*?"

She *should* be worried. She *should* feel like I'm being purposefully evasive. She *should* think that I'm an awful partner and dad.

I'm lying to Sav. Or at least not telling her the whole truth. I'm giving her vague answers instead of being honest about going to London. But I just can't bring myself to do what I'll have to do.

I have a choice to make between being with Sav or starting the new life I have planned for myself. One way or the other, I'll have to give up something that I cherish.

Just not *yet*.

I slide my hands to her waist, and pull her flush against my body. She makes a soft sound and peers up at me as if I'm an enigma that she can't quite figure out. Telling her the real reason why I'm being shady would only hurt her more in the long run. And I would deserve it if she decided to never speak to me again. So I'm lying… but it's kind of for a good reason.

…right?

I push out a breath. "I'm sorry that I was a dick to you. I honestly didn't mean to upset you."

Sav licks her teeth. Anyone else would be scowling or maybe shouting at me. But instead, her body just remains stiff in my arms.

"Are you going to tell me what you were so upset about?"

I wince. "Yeah. Uh… it was a few things. Something with work. And my ex called me and said she's coming to visit later this week."

That's a quarter of the truth at best. The fact that Holly called weeks ago was just another thing I was keeping from Sav.

"Wait… your ex as in, Charlie's mom?"

Sav blinks. She seems to latch on to the bit about Holly. She must think Holly's visit is the reason for my behavior, but that's only partially true.

Holly will be here at the end of the week, after all. I allow Sav to be misled. I'm a giant douchebag for letting her believe what she's glommed together from the breadcrumbs I have been feeding her.

It feels a lot like lying. I wince even as I tell Sav the morsel of truth.

"Yes. Holly said she's coming to visit Charlie. Far be it for me to tell her she can't."

She sucks in her lower lip.

"Oh."

I brush back a lock of her hair and cup her jaw. She shivers and I seize on the opportunity.

"Let's go inside and get warm," I insist.

She makes a face.

"I suppose we can talk as well in there as we can out here."

I hustle her into the back door and help her take her coat off. When I offer to hang up her tote bag, she produces Charlie's knit cap.

"It got left in the auditorium again."

Taking it from her, I smile.

"Thanks. This is his favorite hat."

"I know. He wears it all the time. He told me that it has a dinosaur on it, so it's powered by dinos."

"That sounds like Charlie." I smile. "Do you want a glass of wine?"

She gives me a funny look as she sits down on the couch by the front window. "Thanks, but I'd rather have my wits about me today. I'm stomping all over the line between being your personal assistant and being someone you call when you're lonely and want to get laid."

Her words stop me cold.

"Savannah, I have never indicated that you mean so little to me."

She crosses her arms and looks out the window. "No?"

I walk over to the couch and reach out, tipping her head up to look me in the eyes. I don't like the anger and hurt that I see.

Did I put them there?

"I won't be in the Cape forever. You and I both know that." I cup her cheek. "But does that mean we can't enjoy this heat between us while we still have it?"

"I think…." She closes her eyes and nuzzles my hand. "I think I'm starting to feel more for you than a casual hookup should."

Her whisper pierces my heart. I sit on the couch beside her, pulling her into my arms.

"Sav. Look at me."

Her eyelashes flutter open. I'm caught in her sharp hazel gaze.

"I don't know if this is a good idea anymore," she confesses. "I know that you might be able to keep things as they are, but I don't think I can. It… it isn't making me happy."

I inhale sharply. At this moment, I would say anything that she asks of me.

"What is it that you want to hear from me?" I tuck a strand of her blonde hair behind her ear. "Do you really need me to tell you that I think about you constantly? Maybe you want me to admit that I miss you when you leave the room. Or that the thought of you using dating apps makes me insanely jealous?"

She gives me a surprised laugh. "Jealous? Of what?"

"Anyone else getting to touch and kiss you! If you don't know that I'm crazy about you, I'm sorry that I haven't just outright said it out loud. I just… I imagined that you already knew."

Her eyes go wide. "You're crazy about me?"

She repeats my words like they have some kind of hidden meaning.

"Yes, Savannah." I trail my fingers over her upper arms. "I think you'd drive any man to madness. I mean, just look at you."

Sav catches my hand and kisses my palm. "I– I feel the same way. About you."

"Yeah?" I ask. My heart rate ramps up. "I hope you do."

She flushes and looks down at her lap.

"I am crazy about you. But knowing that you're not in the Cape to stay is… hard. You won't be here forever. And I won't leave."

Pulling Sav close, I kiss her. I know that London is only a week or two away. But I can't bring myself to say it plainly. What a piece of work I am.

"What if we admit that we won't solve it today?" I ask.

She sighs and her brows knit. "Then it will be like all the other days we've spent together."

"No." I shake my head. "It'll be great."

God damn it all. Just hearing that Sav feels the same way I do is already throwing everything into turmoil. She schools her expression.

"Aren't you supposed to be the practical one? The same guy who lectured me about how people need to take off their rose-colored glasses?"

I kiss the back of her hand.

"What if I would rather spend time with you than worry about what's practical?"

She pulls a face. "I don't know. How can you be excited over a future that is so… uncertain?"

"I don't know. It must be something in the water down here."

Sav shakes her head, but a hint of amusement touches her features. "It's not like you to be so optimistic."

"I've never been so crazy about anyone before." I take both her hands and lock eyes with her. "I wish I'd met you before I met Holly."

Her lips twitch.

"I hate to break it to you, but I was probably still in high school when you and Holly met. If we ran into each other back then, I would've thought you were hot, but you wouldn't have given me a second glance."

"Then we met each other at the right time, didn't we?"

I can't help but gaze at Savannah, her beauty amplified by the dim light of the room. She sits next to me on the couch, her legs crossed, and a hint of mischief in her eyes.

I pick her up and enjoy the little squeal she makes as I toss her on the couch. Then I kneel and cage her body with both of my arms. God, I can smell her excitement and need. My mouth waters. I lean close and whisper in her ear.

"Is this what you want?" I ask, my voice low and husky with need. I tease the scrap of lace at the front of her panties.

Her breath hitches. She nods, unable to find her voice. It's clear that she wants me just as much as I want her. The thought alone sets my blood on fire.

"Can you handle it?" I challenge her, my fingers brushing against the lace. The heat between us ripples through the air, leaving no room for anything but our hunger for each other.

"Try me," she breathes. The words are barely a whisper.

As I lower my head, dropping tender kisses on her knees, I can't help but marvel at the softness of her skin. With each touch, she trembles ever so slightly under my fingers. It's a silent testament to our electrifying connection. My hand ventures further, exploring the tiny triangle of sheer fabric between her legs, and she whimpers softly.

"Shh," I whisper, pausing for a moment. "Are you going to be my good girl?"

I lock eyes with Sav once more. The intensity of our gaze is palpable, as if we're both teetering on the edge of something life-changing.

Savannah nods quickly, biting her lips in anticipation, and pulls my hand back to the front of her panties. Her eagerness sends a shiver down my spine, making it abundantly clear that our attraction extends far beyond the physical realm.

Honestly? I find her brain as sexy as the rest of her.

"Please." It comes out as a whimper. Her voice is barely audible. "Cole, *please*. I need this."

I press a soft kiss right over her clit, feeling the heat of her arousal through the delicate fabric. Her back arches off the couch, her heels digging into my muscular back as she moans softly. Her fingers tangle in my hair, urging me closer, demanding more.

"God, Savannah," I murmur against her, my voice ragged with need. "You're so fucking sexy."

"Then don't hold back," she implores. Her words fuel my desire even further. "Take me, Cole. Make me yours."

Her plea sends a shiver down my spine, awakening a primal hunger within me that I've never experienced before.

I chuckle softly and oblige, my tongue darting out to lick the lace, savoring the taste of her desire. My fingers deftly tug at the sides of her panties, pulling them tight against her pussy. She surprises me by stifling a groan and tearing the delicate fabric. I take that as my cue to strip the garment off over her head, leaving her completely bare before me.

"Damn, Savannah." I murmur appreciatively into her skin, my eyes drinking in the sight of her glistening folds. "You're something else."

"Shut up and kiss me." Her voice is thick with need. I grin and dive back in, pressing searing kisses to her inner thighs, inching closer and closer to her core.

"Make me feel alive, Cole," she whispers. Her fingers twine in my hair, guiding me to where she needs me most. Her hips buck. The air hums with her desire and need.

I bury my face against her exposed pussy, feeling the heat and wetness radiating from her. As I start to lick her clit, she pushes my head closer with a hand on the back of my neck. Her hips begin to move instinctively. Her pussy grinds against my mouth. The taste of her arousal is intoxicating and it makes it nearly impossible to think straight.

"Fuck, Cole." She gasps. Her voice is strained as she struggles to stay quiet. She reaches for a pillow on the couch and presses it against her mouth to muffle her moans. The fear of being caught only heightens the excitement and danger of the moment.

Her body tenses beneath me as I focus on her clit. I apply just the right amount of pressure and feel her begin to quake.

Her entire body seizes up. I know she's close. I suck harder on her clit as her pussy begins twitching uncontrollably. She rides the intense wave of pleasure. Her moans are cried against the pillow pressed tightly against her lips.

She's so vulnerable and uninhibited that it feels voyeuristic to watch her come apart. God. *Damn.*

As her orgasm subsides, she releases the pillow from her mouth, panting heavily. I can't help but feel a sense of pride at the pleasure I've given her. I allow myself to revel in the moment. It's thrilling to see her lose control like that. And even more exciting knowing that I'm the one who made it happen.

"Thank you, Cole," she breathes. Her eyes shine with a mixture of gratitude and unsated desire. "That was amazing."

"I adore you. So thought I would worship you the way that you ought to be idolized." I'm unable to tear my gaze away from her flushed cheeks and the way her eyes shine like precious gems in the dim light. Carefully, I reach down and tug her skirt back into place, hiding the evidence of our passionate encounter.

"You're going to ruin me, Cole." Her eyes are somber. "How will anyone ever be able to make me feel the way that you can?"

"Come here," I say softly scooting back onto the couch and holding out my arms for her.

Savannah doesn't hesitate for a moment. She practically collapses into my embrace as she cuddles against my side. I can feel the warmth of her skin pressed against mine, even through the thin layers of clothing separating us, and it sends a shiver of delight down my spine.

This woman is unquestionably *all fucking mine*. For now, at least. Tomorrow, I will have to give her up. But not now. Not yet…

33

SAVANNAH

I STAND RIGID, MY KNEES AND ELBOWS LOCKED, AND STARE AT Birdie and Grandad's backs. I'm a couple steps behind them as they lay roses on my mother's grave.

It feels like I'm viewing my family mourning my mother from the bottom of a pool. I blink to try to clear my vision. My chest tightens with the need to breathe. But I am still separated from them by a thick wall of water.

Birdie sniffles, and folds her hands in front of her body. Grandad reaches out and rubs her shoulder in a gesture of comfort. I wish that I could cry and wail and make enough of a racket that Grandad would notice me. That he would come hug *me*. But I can't even begin to express my anguish over my mother's death.

Taking a chink out of the dam that holds in my grief would surely allow the trickle of sadness. But that feeling would swell and unleash a torrent of heartache. It would wash me away in a raging river of misery, drown me in a tidal wave of pain. I can't begin to cry, because it might be the beginning of the end of me.

Every time that I glance at my mom's gravestone, a wave of seething anger engulfs me. I can't figure out why or what's going on.

So I stand still, my gaze averted, until Birdie and Grandad look at me.

"Is there anything you want to say to Mom?" my sister asks.

A flash of dizziness passes through me. I close my eyes and shake my head.

The things I have bottled up inside are not the kind of things you say to a celebrated woman, much less to a grassy patch of ground that is all that's left of her. I want to say things like the fact that she taught me to control my emotions, but not how to safely express them. I can't find a release valve because my mom didn't help me build one into the vault of my emotions.

She never got to see me as a full, healthy adult. In that regard, she let me down.

Instead, Mom left this world with so many things between us unsaid. Perhaps she thought she would have more time. But she didn't, and now I'm standing here, staring at her grave, struggling with loss.

And because I am so flawed, I picked a man to love who can't even stand here beside me while I try to grapple with the emotional fallout. Cole let me down too.

It's not really his fault, though.

No one can carry the burden of my bitter, sour feelings. That's why I stuff them down, deep into the hole where emotions go.

My grandfather startles me by rubbing my shoulder.

"Are you okay?" he asks carefully.

No. I'm drowning. But I can't force my burden onto him.

I force a smile and say the line that everyone expects from me. "I'm fine!"

"Come on." Grandad's touch is gentle as he guides me to his car. "How about we go to Gem's Diner for a slice of pie?"

I bleat an unexpected laugh.

"Mom did love their pie," I say. Tears appear unbidden at the corners of my eyes. If they spring forth, they'll ruin the day by making everyone else sad.

It's my responsibility to carry this weight in silence. I breathe in and out until I am under control again.

Birdie, meanwhile, stares out the window. She seems hollow and fragile right now. Grandad remains stoic. I clear my throat and make conversation, talking about anything, grasping for a distraction. For some reason, I think of taking rides in his car as kids. Birdie would sit in the front seat and jabber about whatever was going on in her life. And me?

I was left in the back seat, looking out the window, and daydreaming. Distantly, I wonder if that girl saw me now, what would she think? Would she recognize me? Or would she still be caught up in her thoughts and unable to express them?

Checking my phone, I see no missed calls or texts. I'm not expecting to hear anything from Cole, but a tiny flicker of hope that still lived in my chest dims. I know it's crazy to imagine him striding up to the gravesite and folding me into his arms, but that's exactly what I was hoping would happen the whole time I stood there. I wanted him to surprise me, to want me in all ways, not just in bed. No, I didn't want to, I needed to. But I can't say it.

I clutch my phone against my chest and stare blankly out the window.

"Sav." At the sound of Birdie's voice, I float back down from orbiting the moon. With a start, I recognize the parking lot at Gem's.

I get out of the car mechanically. Birdie takes me by the hand, squeezes my fingers gently, and gives me a small smile.

"The cemetery was tough, huh?"

For a second, my mind is completely blank. I was focused on where my not-boyfriend is and why Cole hasn't texted me today. My cheeks burn bright red.

"Uh… yeah," I answer lamely. "It was."

Birdie wraps me in her arms and hugs me tight. I bring my hands up to mirror the embrace. One thing I'll say about Birdie is that she gives really wonderful hugs.

Letting her lead me through the front door of Gem's, I look around with a sigh.

The owner, Gem, sticks her head out of the back when we come in. Gem is an older woman of fifty-some years with gorgeous caramel skin, dark eyes, a raven mane of hair. A chef's apron seems permanently attached to her petite body. She spies my Grandad and lights up.

"Karl!" She hustles over and shoos us toward the first open booth. "Good to see you, papi. And you girls! You both look like fashion models."

Birdie and I both notice the way that Gem leans in and pats his arm. Birdie raises a brow at me, and I stifle a smile.

"So glad you are here. Pearl is off today, so it's just me and Diego in the kitchen. Ay me."

Birdie grins and elbows me. "It's nice to see you, Gem. Could we all get coffee?"

"Coming right up. You want a few slices of pie, too?"

"And vanilla ice cream, if you have it," I suggest.

"Mmm, pie à la mode," Grandad says. "I just realized that I'm hungry."

Gem beams at us, and rushes away. Soon, we're all sipping our coffee and listening to Birdie tell a story about Dex's school. Grandad makes eye contact with me, and reaches across the table to pat my hand. I give him a sad smile. He doesn't understand me. But that doesn't mean he's not trying.

The door chime rings as people enter. I hear my name shouted.

"Sav!"

I look up and see Charlie rushing toward me at a million miles an hour. Barely catching him before he crashes against my body, I release a muffled squeak.

"Charlie!" A petite, elegant woman with dark hair, and an expensive pantsuit chides him. "I'm sorry. I don't know what has gotten into him."

"Mommmm! I know Miss Sav! She works for Daddy. Right, Sav?"

My throat is suddenly as dry as sandpaper. I look at the woman, who can only be Charlie's mom. Which makes her Cole's ex. I gulp.

"Right." I force a smile to my lips. "I'm Savannah."

I don't offer her my hand. She sizes me up with a smirk, and tosses her hair.

"I'm Holly." She tugs at Charlie's arm. "Come on, Char-Char."

Two seconds later, Cole bursts into the restaurant. "Hey, I found the–."

He stops abruptly when he sees Charlie trying to escape Holly and climb into my booth. The alarm on his face is almost funny to see.

If I weren't personally in the middle of a cardiac event, that is.

"Hiiiiiiii," I greet him stiffly. "Umm, how's it going?"

He shoots his cuffs and I notice that he is wearing a black suit, a gray tie, and a starched white shirt. Funny, he has been wearing jeans around me for a couple of weeks now. Then his ex appears, and Cole is dressed to the nines.

"Hello, Savannah." He extracts Charlie from my booth and puts him down. He looks distinctly nervous. "Have you met Holly?"

I squint at him. "We were just introducing ourselves."

Holly peers at Cole and me, then offers a bland smile. She curls her hand around his bicep.

"We should get a booth in the back."

She bats her eyelashes at him. Cole looks at her like she is spouting incomprehensible gibberish. He shakes her off, and grabs Charlie.

"Nice to see y'all," he says, reddening. He ushers them both ahead of him, his footsteps hurried.

"Whoa." Birdie puckers her mouth as if tasting something disgusting and spreads her hands down on the table. "That was a surprise for me. Sav, did you know that Cole's ex was going to be in town?"

I shrug a shoulder. "Not really. I think Cole said something about her planning a visit a couple of weeks ago. He's been pretty mum on the topic."

Grandad purses his lips. "She and Cole seemed close."

"Very close," Birdie says. She narrows her eyes. "And here I was, thinking that you and Cole were an item."

"What?" I try to look exasperated.

Grandad slides out of the booth, pointing to the jukebox in the corner. "I'm going to see what they have for tunes."

"Gem has had the same music since the seventies," I mutter.

But he's gone in the next second. Grandad is making himself scarce. Backing away from potential conflict, would be my guess. It makes me sad that I can't even tell Grandad such a small part of my life.

I roll my head and crack my neck. Fidgeting, I'm half-listening to my sister and half all the way in outer space. In spite of my best efforts, I find myself sneaking a peek at Cole. I catch him looking right at me. He jumps and looks away with a guilt-riddled expression.

Just what the hell am I missing here?

"Savannah." Birdie elbows me. "You are hooking up with Cole, aren't you?"

Shame fills me, and I drop my gaze.

"I was. Or maybe I still am? I– I don't really know," I confess. "Did you see his ex? She's so… cosmopolitan."

My sister snorts. "I can tell you this much. You don't know what she is. And when she tried to hang on Cole's arm, he shook her off like she was a big ole tick on a coon hound. There was some weird energy going on there for sure."

It takes every bit of my strength not to look at Cole again. "Why wouldn't he warn me that she was going to be here today? He was so vague when we talked about it earlier. I didn't even know for sure that she was visiting."

"Because men are idiots. Trust me. I'm a single mom for a reason."

Gem swings by with several slices of pie, and two dishes of ice cream. She refills our coffees, makes a little chit chat, and then moves on to another table. Grandad slides back into the booth and nudges a fork at me.

I sigh and pick up a fork, using a tine to nudge at the golden-brown pecan pie. My sister gleefully digs into a piece of banana cream pie, while Grandad pulls a piece of chess pie toward him on the table.

"Hey! You have to share!" Birdie teases.

"Let the man enjoy his favorite pie in peace," I chide. "You know Gem probably saved it just for him. She's beyond sweet on Grandad."

"Don't be ridiculous," he declares. "And if you think that you're getting that entire slice of banana cream pie to yourself, you're in for a world of hurt. That's next on my list."

He punctuates it by pointing his fork at Birdie with mock seriousness.

"You'll take this pie from me when I'm dead," Birdie fires back.

"So much tension over pie." I smile and look up, catching Cole's eyes. He holds my gaze for several seconds, his eyes bulging slightly as if he is trying to communicate something with me through telepathy.

What on earth is that about?

I shrug a shoulder at him and turn back to my food. My sister pulls out her phone and drops her fork.

"Aw, crud." She shows me the screen. An image is splashed across it, something from CSAT.

I'm looking at a recent photo of Cole, taken while he's crossing the street. He's smirking and looking satisfied with himself. But it's the headline that makes my jaw drop.

Cole Bennett Signs Contract To Move To England For Big Bucks.

My eyes widen as I scan the short article for information. Unfortunately, I only see "eight figure salary" and "moving next week" before my eyes fill with tears.

What the hell is going on? Is this true?

Standing up, I grab the phone and wave it at Cole. He frowns and gives his head a tiny shake. Holly turns around, glares at me, and then reaches across the table to grab Cole's hand.

Marking her territory, it seems.

That's it. I have to leave this restaurant right now before I cause a scene.

"Birdie, could you–?"

"I'm coming right on your heels," she says, standing up. "Grandad, I'll text you in a few minutes."

I rush out the door, bypassing Gem. Gem gets a look at my face and blanches. She moves aside and lets my sister exit the restaurant just after I do.

Birdie wraps an arm around me, murmuring that it'll be okay. I fix my eyes on the horizon and speed walk out of the parking lot.

If I break down, I'm certainly not going to do it in front of Cole and his ex.

34

COLE

Holly insisted on staying in my parents' house for the duration of her visit. I've had enough of her for the day, so I plan to drop her and Charlie off and go… well, literally anywhere else. I have had enough of Holly for one day.

On the drive, all I can think of is how sad Savannah looked when she rushed out of Gem's. I want to text her, but Charlie is being clingy and whiny. On top of all that, Holly doesn't give me an ounce of personal space.

She's always leaning in or hogging the armrest between our seats. Other than giving me intense claustrophobia, she makes it impossible to send Savannah a thoughtful text.

Like that would fix anything.

Holly manages to contain herself until we are parked in front of La Villa Coralle. Holly unbuckles his harness and Charlie wiggles out of his seat, flinging his door open and getting out of the car. I climb out and Holly does the same, but her smirking gaze studies me.

"So. It seems like you've kept yourself occupied here in Cape Simon."

I grimace. "Not in front of Charlie."

"I'm just asking questions," Holly says, playing the innocent as usual.

I wince at her whiny tone. It's one of the things that I have definitely not missed at all since she left me at the altar.

Gritting my teeth, I say, "Holly, I think you need to drive yourself around from now on. You left me at the altar. My days of kowtowing to you are behind me. It's bad enough that you insisted on staying at my parents' house."

She crosses her arms. "You're just mad that I caught on to your secret romance."

The urge to slam the car door is strong. "No, Holly. I am not. You are taking advantage of my generosity by poking your nose where it doesn't belong."

Holly rolls her eyes. "Your Dad and Sarah were excited to see me."

"The only reason you are here right now is because I want you to spend time with our kid. If you think my parents were happy to see you after what you did, you're delusional. I had to beg them to let you stay here."

"We all could've just stayed in your new place," she pouts.

I clench my jaw. My eye starts twitching.

"Just keep pushing me, Holly. Find out what happens."

I grab Charlie's new favorite dinosaur toy out of the car, and shut the door hard. Charlie runs up to me, hugging my leg. I offer the toy to him, but he just shakes his head and clings to me.

He is a kid clearly in need of a nap. I pick him up, and he clings to me like a baby koala. Carrying him inside, and talking him into taking a nap are epic feats in themselves.

It's almost half an hour later when I creep out of his bedroom, trying to close the door quietly. Holly is hanging in the doorway opposite Charlie's bedroom and she smirks when I step out.

"So are you going to tell me about your little side piece now?" Her voice is raised, the opposite of what I need right now.

"Shhh!" I head for the main living room, anger flooding my brain. "If you wake Charlie up, I'm going to make you leave."

As expected, Holly is right on my heels.

"Speaking of my son, she seemed awfully chummy with her. I have the sense that they have interacted quite a bit. Tell me, Cole. Were you here playing house with your cheap hooker of an assistant?"

Holly has always had this remarkable way of getting under my skin. I stop short, turning on my heel. She stumbles and gazes up at me.

"Cole! Don't be mad. I'm just trying to get to the truth. If we are going to be moving to London and living together as a family unit, I need to know if you slept with other women while I was gone."

I take a step back, glowering at her.

"What are you talking about? What are you talking about, when we live together? That's gibberish."

"Well?" Holly gives me a sly smile. "Since I will never sign off on you taking Charlie out of the country without me, then you'd better take me too. You don't have much of a choice. And I figure that we have Charlie, so we might as well be a family unit in a new city. I let my parents know about the plans a couple of weeks back, and they have already paid the deposit on one of the best private schools in the UK. Charlie will love it. Plus, I've found a great apartment that we can all live in. Four bedrooms, close to Charlie's school–."

I have no choice but to stop Holly's flow of words. "Jesus. Are you insane?"

She swats my arm.

"Don't you want to be part of a family again?"

I'm horrified and I don't bother to hide my expression.

"With you? I'd rather knowingly skydive without a parachute. Maybe I could be ripped apart by a pack of coyotes instead. Or perhaps–."

"Cole!" She looks pissed. "This was supposed to be a new beginning for us."

"According to who?" My eyebrows rise and I shake my head in disbelief. "I knew that having you here was a terrible idea."

Holly grabs my arm hard and looks me in the eye. "You would give up a chance to provide Charlie with the life he probably dreams about at night?"

"How would you know what Charlie dreams about?" I ask, bewildered. "And as for the other part of your question. You left me at the altar, and then I found out you'd been screwing that guy from the gym. We are not a family, and you made sure of that. When you were fucking that mystery guy while my son watched TV downstairs, *you* killed our family. Our family unit, as you call it, is dead on arrival."

I rip my arm from her grip and walk away. I can't ever remember being so angry before. Holly follows me into the main living room, her tone wheedling.

"That was a mistake."

I march to the large sliding glass doors and head outside. When Holly follows, I round on her.

"We broke up. You left me, standing there waiting for you, in front of everyone we love! I was ready to pledge my life to you, but you rejected me in the most public, and humiliating way possible. The only reason you are here is because you gave birth to Charlie. Notice I didn't call you his mother, because no mother would manipulate a child the way you have! All of that, in addition to the fact that *you* cheated on *me*. You manipulated our son to keep the truth hidden. So I'm at a loss as to why you think I would ever sink so low as to take you back."

A startled laugh leaves her lips.

"Clearly you aren't too upset about the wedding to bang your assistant as soon as possible."

I point at the center of her face.

"That's not the same and you know it. Now do us both a favor. Cancel the apartment in London. Tell your parents that if they want to see their grandchild, that they can request a visit."

Holly huffs and folds her arms across her chest. "I'm not letting you take him."

"Oh, Holly." I chuckle and it sounds like a threat. "I will drag your ass into court and fight you. Not only that, but I'll bury you. If you think that photo evidence of your cheating will not come out, you're wrong. And remember how you lied on your taxes and had to pay big penalties? That will come out, too. Every single thing you have in that huge closet of skeletons will be dragged out and paraded around. I am done with handling you so gently!"

Holly looks like she's sucking on a lemon. "I don't understand why you're being so nasty all of a sudden."

I swear, I'm about to lose my mind. Fixing her with a scowl, I hiss at her.

"I've waited for years, Holly. Years! You know what? I should thank you for not showing up at our wedding. If you had, I might still be trying to make things between us work. It took me coming down here and dating someone who really cares about me to realize what a vile, toxic person you are." I brush my hands off dramatically. "I'm done with you. If you want anything else, including to see my son, you can go through my attorney."

She draws herself up and walks back out of the house, slamming the glass door behind her. I follow her, making sure she leaves the house. An Uber that she called pulls up and she gets in, slamming the door.

A part of me hopes that's the last I ever have to see of her. I know that I shouldn't wish that, for Charlie's sake. But if it's the last time, I'll be glad to see the backside of her.

As much as my encounter left me shaky and drained, I know what I need to do. It's what I've needed to do since I saw her in the diner, but couldn't get the chance. With a sigh on my lips, I call Savannah.

There's no answer. Just her stupid voicemail with her overly bright message.

"Hi, it's Savannah—!"

I hang up and let out a frustrated sound. A hand comes out of nowhere and lands on my arm, making me jump.

Turning, I see the last person I want to talk to when I'm going through a crisis.

Sarah arches a brow at me. "Did you see the post about you on CSAT?"

I groan. "You and Dad are on Instagram?"

"You bet your butt we are. And we read all about how you are going to take off for London."

"That's not decided," I gripe. "Andrew agreed to let me take six weeks to wrap up my affairs stateside, but he wasn't happy about it. I have to talk to Rex about the state of the training camp project we're working on. If I left, he would have to figure out how to replace me."

Sarah folds her arms across her chest.

"And how is Savannah taking the news of your imminent departure?"

Keeping my expression neutral, I mask the cringe I feel deep in my bones.

"I haven't talked to her yet."

"Don't you think you should? If the guy I was over the moon about was about to leave town, I'd certainly be upset."

Her words give me pause. Yes, Savannah told me that she feels something for me. But… it's not love, is it? I guess we left things between us rather murky.

"Why do you think that Savannah is 'over the moon for me,' as you put it?" I ask, trying to read her face.

Sarah touches her temple and looks tired.

"Anybody with eyes can see that you are both in love with each other."

"In love? With *Savannah*?" I blurt out. I shake my head. "Sure, there are feelings there. But it's more complex than that."

She pushes out her cheek with her tongue.

"You're insane. All you and Savannah need is time to figure things out. If you want to go talk to her to convince her to give you another chance, you're more than welcome to go to her. I can watch Charlie."

The back of my ears heat with embarrassment. Sarah is doing me a favor here, even though I am not always very gracious with her.

I can't let Savannah go another second feeling like I lied to her. I really need Sarah to do this for me, so I can fix things. Bobbing my head, I say, "Thanks, Sarah."

"You're very welcome, Cole." She claps her hands and shoos me off. "Good luck. I hope she is willing to hear you out. I would be livid if I was her."

My stomach turns over. I close my eyes for a second. "Shit."

"Yeah, no kidding." She starts to pull me toward the front door, then steps behind me and gives me a push. "Go on."

I pause, catching her gaze.

"Thanks, Sarah. For real."

"That's what family is for, honey. Now get going before Miss Savannah turns into a pumpkin."

35

SAVANNAH

I'M FLOPPED ACROSS MY BED LIKE A LOVESICK TEENAGED GIRL. I'm all out of tears to cry and now my face is just a blotchy, mottled mess. My body is trying to give new meaning to the words 'shapeless' and 'boneless.'

This feeling absolutely blows.

I'm already listening to Taylor Swift, the edgiest and most rebellious music I know. While she sings a catchy pop song about a girl done wrong, I am making faces in the mirror on the back of my door.

Cole's ex is in town. She's pretty and polished and sleek, all the things that I am not. Cole really messed up by not telling me to expect to see her.

And that's not even mentioning the fact that Cole is really moving to London! Not only that, but he lied to me about his plans. Or at the very least, didn't tell me the entire truth. Who does that?

When I think about how hurt I felt when Cole decided not to come to the cemetery, it kind of seals his fate. I fell for Cole, head over heels. But I didn't sign up for being lied to and pushed to the side whenever his ex is available.

I can't believe myself right now. Cole was never my boyfriend, but I went and fell in love anyway. And it hurts to know that he'll never understand how much he hurt me, because I refused to ever let him see it.

My gaze eventually wanders over to my art wall, just to the left of my door. It features a collage I made in junior high for a class project about my inner soul. There are several cut outs from magazines, smiling young celebrities and female gymnasts leaping with ribbons. A smattering of peeling gold stars adorn the cut out letters that form the words that I've always lived by. *Cleaner than sunshine, sweeter than honey.*

I make a face at the collage. Right now, I'm seriously considering ripping that ugly old thing off the wall and tearing it to teeny tiny pieces.

Instead, I whisper to it.

"That's bullshit," I inform it. "You should stop telling people that kind of nonsense."

As if the collage is pushing back, a knock comes on my bedroom door. I startle so hard that I fall to the floor with a yelp.

Birdie opens the door and sizes up the situation. She offers me a hand to help me get up.

"I was going to ask if you're okay. But...," She waves her hand. "Clearly you're not."

My face flames, and I quickly turn off the Bluetooth speaker that's blaring angsty girl rock.

I glance at my watch. "It's after four. Shouldn't you be at work?"

"I'm leaving right now. I just came up to tell you that Cole is here. He's asking for you."

My heart seizes in my chest and my stomach does a backflip. "He's here?"

"Yeah. He's waiting downstairs. Do you want me to tell him to leave?"

"No. No, I'll come down."

"Are you sure you're okay? I can call the restaurant, and let them know I'm going to be late if you're not a thousand percent certain."

I hug my sister hard. "It's really okay. Thanks for looking out for me, though."

Birdie gives me an extra squeeze, then steps back. "I love you, Sav. I always will, no matter how terrible the music you blast might be."

I fake a gasp. "How dare you! Taylor Swift is great."

She rolls her eyes. "Come downstairs now, before Cole's pacing wears a hole in the living room carpet."

Straightening my pink skirt and oversized white sweater, I trot down the stairs after my sister. As Birdie swishes out of the house, I find Cole standing by the mantle in the living room, looking as impossibly handsome as ever. His azure gaze is focused on the family photo that was taken just before my mom passed away.

"Cole," I say simply.

I'm incensed and I am on the very brink of just telling Cole to leave me alone forever. I can't say anything else, because I am so damn mad that it threatens to boil up and bubble out of my mouth.

He clears his throat as he spins on his heel. "Savannah. Hey."

Biting my lip, I fold my arms across my chest. A little part of me wants him to throw himself at my feet and try to apologize. But the bigger part of me is ready to throw down.

This guy has really fucked around with my heart and now I'm ready to let him find out.

"What do you want?"

Cole nods toward the front door. "Why don't we take a walk?"

I don't want to take a walk with him. Instead, I'd like to scream and stomp my feet and cause a ruckus.

But I'm way too well-mannered for that. So I head toward the door, stopping for my warm fleece-lined boots and a coat. I pick up the baby pink cape and pause. Then I think better of it, and choose my long, gray-checked coat instead.

Cole watches warily, but doesn't make a peep. He just follows me out of the house.

"So?" I prompt, once we are outside. I'm tense and covering my anger with a frosty demeanor. "What did you come here to say?"

Cole clears his throat. "So... that CSAT posting."

"Uh huh." I start walking because it seems better to have something to focus on. One foot in front of the other, watching my footing, seems to ease some of the pressure that's building inside my chest and threatening to burst free at any moment.

"First off, who is CSAT? Because their sources are pretty damn good."

My mouth pulls to the side. "I don't know. Is that what you want to talk about?"

Cole looks down, shaking his head.

"No. I want to talk about the post that said I'm moving to London right now. It's not that simple."

"What do you mean?"

"I mean that I have been offered a great job. My dream job, actually. But I haven't said yes yet."

I stop, turn to Cole, and stare him down. "Why not?"

He rubs his neck. "The only thing stopping me is you."

"I don't know why I would be keeping you from doing anything." I purse my lips and then force a smile to my lips. "This was only supposed to be temporary. Either one of us were supposed to be able to pull the rip cord at any moment. Isn't that what we agreed?"

His eyes narrow. "Well, yes, but…." He falls silent for several moments.

I want to cry. But I don't. Years of quietly suppressing my negative thoughts allow me to smile brighter.

"Are you having trouble thinking of leaving?"

"I thought we would have more time."

"More time to what?" I keep beaming at him.

He grimaces. "Will you stop that?"

"That's not an answer to my question."

He squints. "I guess I just needed more time to spend in this bubble that we've created."

"And after the bubble pops? In your mind, do I just get left holding the bag?"

"No." Cole grimaces. "I don't know."

"Huh." I fire another plastic smile at him from my built-up arsenal. It's my way of giving Cole a thousand middle fingers

"Enough with the fake smile!" he says. "Just be real with me for ten minutes."

I tilt my head. "It doesn't work like that."

"Why not?"

"Because I'm not a freaking vending machine. I'm a person."

He grits his teeth. "Sav, I know that. I'm just asking you to let your guard down for a minute. You know you don't feel like smiling right now."

"Don't tell me what I feel." My hands curl into fists and I squeeze them. "I think we're having this entire discussion because of your feelings. Or lack of feelings. Stop trying to have a big blow-up fight with me."

Cole grabs my hand, yanking me close and staring down into my eyes.

"I don't want conflict, Sav."

My breath leaves my mouth in small puffs that are visible in the frosty air.

"No?" I ask.

"No. I just need to know that there is something worth struggling over."

My smile fades a little.

"To be clear, though. You still plan on moving to London for a few years at least."

He hesitates then nods. "Probably, yeah."

"So you want to hear how much I've invested in this relationship. But at the same time, you still have your finger on the panic button. If we have a bad fight, you could just call up your London contacts and vanish in a weeks' time. That's what you want me to live with?"

Cole laces his fingers with mine. His eyes never leave my face.

"You would have to trust me. We could work something out."

I smile at him. "But only until you get tired of me. Right?"

"Not exactly."

My head hurts. I feel like Cole is shredding my heart and leaving little chunks of it in my chest for me to survive off of.

I offer him my brightest smile. He knows what I'm going to say before I even get the words out.

"Maybe this offer is a compelling reason for both of us to bail out."

He pulls me close, lowering his lips to mine. Sealing my mouth to his, he kisses me. I want nothing more than to kiss him back and make this work.

But if Cole still plans to leave, I can't actually see the point of it. I would just be more deeply involved when he hits the eject button and jumps out of the plane.

I can't do it.

Putting up a hand against his chest, I gently push him back. Cole's eyes search my face.

He looks lonely and hungry, just like he did the first time we kissed. There is a newer, darker shimmer in his eyes. But I don't know how to give it a name.

"Cole, this is a terrible idea," I say softly. "If we aren't willing to do this right, we should just walk away. It may hurt now, but imagine how hard it would be if we had to do it a year from now. Or five years. I'm pretty sure it would kill me."

Cole brushes a lock of my hair out of my face. "I think I'm in love with you."

My stomach flip flops and the ache I feel inside my chest hurts so damn bad. Hot tears crowd the corners of my eyes and I can feel a tear slip down my cheek.

Too little, too late. I shake my head.

"I think I love you too."

He looks at me, stunned. "You're crying."

Shaking my head, I laugh and wipe away the tears. "My mom always said that little girls should be cleaner than sunshine and sweeter than honey. I am trying my damnedest to stay clean and sweet for you. You get my drift?"

"Ah, Sav." His voice is choked with emotion. "You don't have to be any kind of way to impress me. You're one of a kind, you know that?"

He cups my cheek. I turn my head and kiss his palm. Then I feel another treacherous tear falling down my cheek.

Sucking in a deep breath for strength, I step away from Cole.

"I think this has to be goodbye." I offer him a shaky smile. "I can't work with you anymore. I know I'll see you at the play, if you and Charlie are still around next week. But I'll ask you to keep your distance."

"Sav—"

"No! You lied. Several times, you lied. About things that would affect me very deeply. I am hurting. And you making overtures to try to keep me for a little bit longer is not going to cut it. You realize that you're treating me like garbage, right?"

Cole looks completely stunned. His cheeks flush and he seems unsure how to respond.

"I'm sorry, Savannah."

"You should be." Tears gather in my eyes. "You hurt me, Cole. Cut me to the quick."

"Is there anything I can say that will change your mind?"

I shake my head slowly. "Not unless you can promise me more than vague maybes and nebulous tomorrows."

Cole looks gut-shot. He eyes me for a minute and I swear I see a sheen of tears in his eyes. "What would you have me do?"

I throw up my hands, aggravated.

"Be an adult. Say goodbye. Promise me you're going to pay me what you owe me."

He chuckles and it's the saddest goddamned sound. "Don't worry. I'll pay you out like I promised. I know you want to move out of your Grandad's place."

I wrinkle my brow and try to play it off like everything is okay. "Good luck in London. Mind the gap, or whatever it is they say."

Cole reaches out to me. Then he thinks better of it, clenches his fist, and shoves his hand in his pocket.

"Bye, Sav."

I turn and walk back home, my tears flowing freely, my heart feeling strangely numb.

3 6

COLE

I GET OUT OF MY CAR, CURSING AS I CATCH MY JACKET ON THE seat belt. Winding myself up, I slam my car door. The day is overcast, but somehow bright, and it's irritating me.

Just decide whether or not to rain, I think furiously. The rest of the world makes much harder decisions every single day.

As I stomp toward the marina entrance, River watches me with a raised eyebrow. He opens his mouth to say something, but I just throw up a hand.

"Save it."

Humor passes over his face, there and gone in a flash. "I was just going to say hi."

Pulling back my sleeve, I check the time.

"Let's just get this over with."

I trudge down the plankway toward the docks. Rex and Dad are waiting about a hundred yards down, and I head toward them, feeling like I'm carrying around a ton of bricks. It was difficult to get out of bed this morning. If Charlie hadn't come to check on me, I might have stayed under my covers all day.

Insulated and safe.

Dad gives me a bear hug. I blink, biting my tongue.

He is way too old to be trying to lift me off my feet.

"Cole! Glad you're here." He smiles at me. "I thought you were still hiding out."

"Hiding out?" I echo. I give him a puzzled look. "From what?"

"You tell me."

"Oh, we'll get into that. Believe me." Rex grins and bumps my shoulder with his own. "But first, we have to check out Dad's new drip."

"My what?" Dad asks.

"Rex is just making sure we all know that he's cooler than us," River adds helpfully. "Good job, Rex."

Rex flexes and brushes imaginary dust from his shoulder.

"Someone has to be the cool one."

As we start down the pier toward the dock, I roll my eyes. "Can you guys just go ahead and give me a condensed version of whatever it is you want to talk about? I have a lot of planning to do."

Rex isn't listening. He whistles as we walk down the dock toward my dad's brand-new boat. It's sixty-five feet of sleek white fiberglass encasing a powerful engine.

"Jesus," River exclaims as he follows a few steps behind me. "You must have dropped a mint on this baby."

Rex hops on board like he climbs onto small yachts all day, every day. He's never been one to feign disinterest in the newest toy, whether it be a car, plane, or a huge mother of a boat like this one. He disappears inside and River rushes around me to catch up with him.

"Dibs on the best seat!" River yells.

I climb on board, shading my eyes from the broad light gray sky overhead. Inside, I'm wondering if I should feel excitement over this boat.

All my feelings are oddly blunted because I'm feeling forlorn and lost ever since Sav kicked me to the curb. Now I'm floating in a cloud of unpleasant numbness and I'm surly about it.

Dad comes up behind me, patting me on the shoulder. "You okay, son?"

I shrug a shoulder. "I'll figure it out."

That's a dirty lie and we both know it. I feel like I've cut the boat's mooring and now I'm floating free in a pool of gloomy muck. But my father just claps a hunter-green bucket hat on his head and gives me an encouraging smile.

"I know this has been a hard year for you. First Holly, now Savannah…"

"Who said anything about Savannah?"

He chuckles. "You've been wandering around town, looking like a puppy that's been kicked. Three times now, I've found you on the beach in front of the house, staring into the ocean. Like you don't have a house of your own to mope around in. And Rex says that Savannah doesn't work for you anymore. I can put two and two together."

I scowl. "The last thing I need is my brothers gossiping about me."

Dad gives me a long look.

"They're just concerned about you, Cole. The whole family just wants you to be happy."

"I am happy," I growl. "Now can we get this show on the road? I'm only here because Rex threatened me with violence if I didn't come and bond."

Dad laughs. "Well, someone had to do something about you mooning around the place and sulking like a shaved cat. Besides, this might be the last time we see you for a while. After you leave, there are no guarantees that we'll see you regularly."

His words just make me shake my head. Dad ducks as he heads down a short set of stairs into the boat's living room. Copying his movement, I trail behind him.

I have to admit, this boat is really luxurious. The floors in the small living room are polished wood, the furniture is white leather, sleek wood, and burnished gold accents adorn the walls and sconces. Rex and River are already sprawled out across the two wall-to-wall banquette couches that span either side of the boat. Dad heads toward the aft where a set of stairs will presumably lead him to the helm and navigation console. I start to follow him, but River jumps up and practically tackles me.

"Not so fast."

He steers me to the couch and pushes me down on it. I land with a whuff and glare up at him.

"What is this? Rex already forced me to come out here. Now I can't even pick where I sit?"

River sits down beside me and grabs my knee with a grin. "We are going to talk about it once we get out onto the open sea."

"When I am isolated and can't leave?" I scowl at him.

"Exactly," Rex says. He winks at me. "See, River? He gets it. We just kidnap him and force him out onto the water to talk some damn sense into him."

I cross my arms and tilt my head back.

"Dad, are you on board with this plan?"

I hear the engine roar to life just before my father pops his head down the stairs.

"Just relax, Cole. Let your brothers try to talk some sense into you."

I grit my teeth as he vanishes and the boat starts to move. Rex has his phone out and is grinning down at the screen. River looks at me with a shrug and leans back, lacing his fingers behind his head.

"This is ridiculous. You both know that, right?" I tell them.

Rex doesn't look up from his phone screen.

"What's ridiculous is you thinking you can go to London and start fresh. I'm telling you right now. This is as good as you're going to get."

"What about my happiness?" I ask, feeling salty.

River's lips twitch. "Are you saying you weren't happy two weeks ago when I dropped by your office? Cause you could've fooled me. You and Savannah were obviously about to rip each other's clothes off when I came in."

Rex chimes in. "And did he look happy, River?"

"Yes, he did!" River smirks at me. "Let's do another one, Rex."

Rex sits up. "That's easy. Three weeks ago, I drove by Cole and Savannah holding hands and walking down the street. Literally anybody could see them, but they were too wrapped up in giving each other googly eyes to think about that."

Their cheerful tones make me grumpier. I scowl at both of them.

"I was happy then."

"And what made you happy?" River asks. "Was it just everything going your way? No, that can't be it. Because you kept telling me that the South Shore planning committee had it out for you and wasn't giving an inch."

"Nope, I'm pretty sure the answer is about five and a half feet tall, blonde, and pretty as the day is long."

My dad cuts in. "Would that be Savannah?"

"It would indeed," River says, nodding. "She's the only reason that Cole has been so cheerful for the last few months."

I cut them all with my gaze.

"It's more complicated than that. For instance, what about my professional ambitions?? Rex, of all people, you should know about sacrificing everything for your career."

Rex laughs. "Oh, you wanna make it about that? What about them? You promised me that you would see this project through. Yet you're supposed to be leaving with it mostly unfinished. You got the committee's ear. They are willing to work with you, or at least they're willing to work with Savannah to figure this whole thing out. You're leaving us all high and dry!"

"You'll find a replacement," I say with a sigh.

"I don't want a replacement! I want my brother to do what he said he was going to do. You might not be aware of it, but everyone else has their own stuff going on. You can't be flimsy when the time comes for one of us to call on you."

My jaw drops. "I… hadn't thought of it that way. I figured you could replace me easily."

"I can't replace you. You're a vital part of the project. Besides, you do realize that I could sue your ass for… something legal-sounding that I don't really know about. But I could text Walker and find out in two shakes of a rabbit's ass."

I give him a warning look.

"Are you planning to sue me, Rex? Is that what I'm hearing?"

"Maybe." Rex smiles devilishly. "If I have to, I will."

"No he won't," River sighs. He eyes Rex. "Remember what we discussed? No threats. We are just pointing out the upsides to staying in the country. Namely, the fact that Cole is obviously completely Looney Tunes for Sav."

"You guys have been talking about me?" I ask. It's not a denial of his words. I don't have the strength to lie to my brothers.

River turns to me. "Sorry, Cole. But it's true. She sent me a text message saying it was nice to work with me, but since then she's been radio silent. So what the hell did you say to her that caused the rift?"

The engine cuts off and I hear Dad clomping down the stairs. He comes into the room, pushes Rex's feet off the couch, and takes the seat beside him.

I focus on River. "Who said that I caused the rift?"

My dad snorts. We all look at him and he waves us off. "No, go ahead. You're doing fine."

I scowl at Dad. "In case none of you actually thought this through, I do not appreciate being kidnapped for this shitty intervention."

I've been a mess all week, but I thought I was holding it together. Having my whole family tell me otherwise is embarrassing and frustrating in equal measure.

Rex splays his fingers.

"No one wants to be here, Cole. But the fact is that you are making yourself unhappy by stubbornly trying to move across the Atlantic Ocean. Even though you've built your life here. Charlie is comfortable here. You met a girl that makes you less of a cranky asshole. You have a billion-dollar business opportunity if you stay here and build this damn sports camp."

River cuts in. "But none of those totally valid reasons, apart or together, are enough to stop you from insisting that you're going to move to England and have a fresh start. Why is that, d'you think?"

I open my mouth to fire back, then pause. I have been so laser-focused on what I could do. I've never really stopped to think if I *should* move to London for business, though. It's the logical next step.

I grate out, "Because I NEED a fresh start! My relationship fell apart, my wedding was called off, my son lost his mom… I don't want to be in the place where it all happened anymore. I want to go somewhere where I am not the guy who failed!"

My brothers' mouths hang open. My father squints at me. You could've heard a pin drop in the silence that followed. It's like a shock wave just rolled through my family.

"Son, I had no idea that you felt that way." My dad leans forward and pins me with a stare. "You are so much more than just the bad things that have happened to you here. You know that, right?"

"Then why does it feel like if I don't escape, I'm doomed to repeat the past?" I ask. Frustrated, I swing my gaze to both my brothers. "Tell me what to do! Tell me how to do things differently than I have done so far. Please, if you think you know better."

River snorts. "Three of the closest men in your life are in front of you, telling you that you're making the wrong choice. The question is, can you listen?"

"And keep your word," Rex says, a sour grimace playing over his face.

My jaw tenses. "I can still plan every single build that I would plan here when I'm in London. It's not as if we don't have the technology."

"But son. You don't have to scramble for any more clients. You can rest on your laurels."

Rex chimes in. "I've just been waiting for you to take the reins here, Cole. Say the word and I will go back to my actual career. Did you know that I am a whole-ass pro athlete?"

"I don't think you can just butt out," I tell him.

"Brother, you don't know how badly I want to give up being the asshole that controls everything. I'd way rather you be that asshole."

I lift my chin. "Let's say I don't leave. I can take charge. But if I stay–."

"Then you have to apologize to Sav for whatever your stupid ass did or said that drove her away," River supplies. "That's literally why we corralled you onto this ship, dude."

"So what did you do, son?" My dad leans forward and squints at me. "Did you tell her something dumb?"

Rex cups his hands around his mouth and calls, "Did you tell Savannah that you're not bonkers in the tonkers for her?"

"No." I push my cheek out with my tongue. "But I might have said that I couldn't promise her anything more than what we had, though."

"Ooof." River screws up his face. "That's brutal."

"Yeah," I tell him. "That's what I'm saying."

Dad gives me a long look. "I think you're running."

"Yeah, I'm trying to escape from all the terrible shit that's happened in this town."

"Cut the bullshit, son. You aren't running from Holly. Or to a job opportunity. You're running because Savannah loves you and you love her. And you are worried that if you have the chance to be happy… you might screw it up." He crosses his arms. "Go on. Tell me I'm wrong."

My mouth goes dry. I feel like I'm stripped and hogtied, awaiting something terrible to happen to me. My knee starts bouncing up and down. "I… am not sure…"

"God, Dad's right." Rex whistles. "Look at Cole squirm."

River smirks and elbows Rex. "I think you've got it."

"You're dicks. All of you." I pull a face.

"I'm just waiting for you to say it," my dad announces. "It'll be easier for you if you just say it aloud, right here."

I know exactly what Dad's trying to get me to say, but I play stupid. "Say what?"

"Stop being as dumb as a bag of hammers and say that you love Savannah!" Rex shouts.

"Err…"

"I. Love. Savannah. Say it with me now…" Dad coaxes.

"I…" I close my eyes. "I do love her, you know."

"We know!" Rex and Dad say at once.

"Say the phrase so we can move on with our lives," River jeers.

I scrunch up my face. "I love Savannah?"

Rex cheers. My dad looks satisfied. River purses his lips.

"Fucking finally," he says.

"What?" I ask, feeling my neck growing hot.

"You're a real dickhole sometimes," Rex announces. "An absolute ass-munch."

"I have no idea what that is, but I agree with the principle," Dad says. "Here is the real question. How are your knees? Because as far as I see it, getting on your knees, groveling, and showing Savannah that you know that you fucked up is your one and only shot at fixing this."

Having her back… I would beg for that, I realize. On my knees, however she needs me.

"I don't know." I shove a hand through my hair. "I told her how I felt already. What if I ask her to be with me, and she still rejects me?"

There is a long spell of silence. Rex and River push back into their seats. I'm guessing that neither of them feels particularly qualified to give me relationship advice.

My dad sighs and locks eyes with me.

He leans back and holds up two fingers.

"In my life, I've had the privilege to have two great loves. Your mother was my high school sweetheart. We fell in love when we were still kids and married straight out of high school. I never had to worry or struggle for anything with your mom. She was just light, and sweet, and good."

He swallows, his voice growing thick with emotion. "When I lost your mother, I never thought I would find love again. I didn't even think it was possible to have two great loves. Especially one right after another like that. I met Sarah at a grief group that she had found when she'd lost her husband Ed. And I tell you, I was as scared as I was in love with her. I… I had to tell Sarah what I felt. But doing it made me feel as fragile as a brand-new baby."

My brothers and I are silent. These are deep, dark waters and they are treacherous for even the bravest man to tread. Eventually my father looks up, his deep blue gaze spearing me where I sit.

"If I hadn't made myself vulnerable all those years ago, I don't know what our lives would be like now. They would definitely not be as full or as rich as they are. And that's because of Sarah stepping up and taking over the household. She knew I was struggling, and she carried the weight for me when I couldn't. And in return, I was able to ease her burdens." He stops and swipes at a tear that rolls down his cheek. "I tell you what. I think that someone up above put Sarah in my path, knowing that she could love me, and I could love her. And we could heal each other."

I blink rapidly, staring at my dad. I've been on this planet for more than thirty years and this is the first time I've ever seen him this emotional about anything. Sav might say no, but I realized that by not being vulnerable, I never even gave her an option to say yes. I always decided for us.

It's time to hear her decision.

Rex, who runs hot-blooded, and is nearly always emotional about everything, is the first of my brothers to hug Dad. They embrace without thinking, as easily as they draw their next breaths.

River jumps up next, briefly wrapping my dad in a tight hug. I run my tongue over my teeth and then clamber to my feet, giving Dad a quick but hard hug. Dad surprises me by not letting go right away.

He whispers in my ear, "Go get your girl, son. I know you can do it."

I feel the beginning of tears pressing the corners of my eyes. Glancing around, I see that everyone is swiping at their eyes and clearing their throats, embarrassed to be showing their feelings.

Rex tosses himself back onto the leather banquette. "So? How about it? Did we do a good job convincing you to stay?"

"Please?" River rubs my back. "Pretty please with black-eyed peas? Rice and everything nice?"

I nod slowly. "You've talked me into it. I'll stay at least until I talk to Sav."

"Thank goodness," Dad says. He gives me a relieved grin. "I'd say that calls for a celebratory beer."

He jumps up and presses on a section of the wall, which opens to reveal chilled bottles of wine, and frosty cans of beer. He pulls several cans of Sweetwater Seasonal Ale out, and passes them around. For a few seconds, there is nothing but the sound of tops being popped over the gentle rhythm of water lapping.

Dad holds his beer up. "To family."

My lips twitch. "And to interventions, I guess."

"Cheers." We all lift our beers and then I take a sip. The ale is foamy and bitter, but it's a familiar and comforting taste. I let the almost-creamy bubbles burst over my tongue.

"So, I have half a plan," Rex says, looking around. "Hear me out."

"A plan to...?" River prompts.

Rex poses, fluttering his eyelashes. "To tell Savannah that Cole is fruity as a toucan over her and wants her to be his one and only. You know. Make a public declaration of love and ask her… I don't know." He looks at me quizzically. "To ask her to marry you?"

"I wouldn't ask that question unless you already know what her answer will be," Dad injects.

"To… be your girlfriend?" River suggests. "At least tell her what you feel."

"You'll have to have a chat with Charlie," my father intones.

"Charlie loves Sav," River muses. "Talk to him, but you can already bet that he's on board."

"Yeah, that sounds right." I make a face. "What am I doing, exactly?"

"Okay," Rex says, spreading his hands. "This is what I'm thinking–."

"Oh god," I groan. "Do I want to hear this plan?"

My father shrugs.

"I heard it on the ride over to the marina. It's half-cocked and has a lot of moving parts," Dad grouses. "Butttt…"

"It's genius," Rex says, shooing away Dad's words. "Now what you'll need is…."

3 7

SAVANNAH

BREATHE. JUST BREATHE.

I straighten my short blue dress, and look toward the door of the Cape Winery, the nicest wine bar on the Georgia coast.

Today, I'm officially moving on from Cole. He was wonderful - interesting and hot, debonair and funny. But he isn't my *dream* guy.

He doesn't have long, flowing hair. If Cole plays guitar, or wanders, shirtless, on the beach, I haven't seen it. And most importantly...

Cole isn't sunny. He is very intelligent, endlessly amusing, and gloriously sexy. But no one would mistake his intense thundercloud of a personality for sunshine.

This guy that I found on Cupid's Arrow... he might hit all the right buttons. Maybe, just maybe, this time I will meet my Prince Charming.

I see Will when he sweeps into the bar. He tosses his chin-length, gorgeous blond hair. He looks around the room, and I can see that he's wearing a well-worn, camel hair sweater over a pair of dark jeans. He spots me, and his face splits into a grin.

God, he is absolutely drool-worthy. Six feet even, handsome like an Abercrombie model, with his sleeves pushed up to show his forearms.

It's funny, but I don't feel the pull that I usually feel when I think about my dream guy. But then again, maybe it's too early to tell.

"Savannah?" he asks.

I stand and paste on a smile. "You must be Will."

"So nice to meet you." He shakes my hand and gestures to the empty seat next to me. "May I?"

"Omigod, please!" I sit down. "Thanks for agreeing to meet me."

"Totally. I was going to throw on my wet suit and surf. But I read your message and like… you're so freaking beautiful. I couldn't believe it."

I blush slightly. My smile falters.

It's not that I don't want him to notice my beauty. I do. I dressed up and came on this date! But coming from anybody but Cole, the words sound hollow.

I force my smile to brighten. "Thanks. I think you are super handsome. Just ten out of ten. I mean, WOW."

Will grins. "Right on. Are you from here?"

"Yup. Born and raised. You?"

"I'm from Charleston, but I have some family down this way. I'm visiting them, and working as a traveling veterinarian. I mostly work with marine wildlife."

"Oh wow! That sounds amazing. Like dolphins, and whales, and stuff?"

He winks. "If it swims, I take care of it."

The bartender comes to the table to get our order.

Will looks at the menu for three seconds and then orders. "Like a... like a Gewürztraminer would be good? Or an Eiswein?" He looks at me. "Do you want to split a bottle?"

I struggle not to make a face. The wine Will wants is white and extremely sweet. I was planning on grabbing something dark and bold.

"I think I'll just grab a glass of cabernet." I smile. "But that's the great thing about this place. We can each get what we like!"

He smiles and hands the menu back to the bartender. "I'll just have a glass of what she is having. I'm easy like Sunday morning."

I offer him a weak smile. "That's good to hear. Cheers."

The bartender brings the wine over to our table and I pick up the glass. Everything that I do feels arduous and mechanical.

Will clinks his wineglass against mine and takes a sip. He considers the wine, then shrugs.

"Is it okay?" I ask.

He waves me off. "More than fine. It tastes like red wine."

Sipping my wine, I look him up and down. I try to think of what I should ask him next. *What should I ask my future soul-mate?* For some reason, my mind is a perfect blank.

"So… do you like the beach?" he asks.

"I love it. You know how it is, being from the coast."

He nods. "Same, obviously. What do you do for work?"

I flush and force my smile to remain steady.

"I'm… in between jobs right now."

His smile falls a little bit. I shake my head. "I know, I know. I just left working for a grumpy boss, and I've taken a few personal days to deal with the aftermath of all that. But I have an interview on Friday."

"Oh yeah?" Will asks. "That sucks that your employment relied on a grumpy guy. I can't stand grumpy people. I am obsessed with trying to cheer them up every time I see them. It's not really the most fun thing."

I tilt my head. "Are you me? I do that."

Will laughs. "Maybe! Are most of your exes upbeat?"

I cackle at that. "No. As a matter of fact, my last ex was super grouchy."

He nods and swirls the wine in his glass.

"I get the attraction. My last ex always rained on everyone's parade. She's the reason I'm specifically trying to date people that are more cheerful and bright."

"Wait, really?"

"Yeah, really!" He grins. "It's like, no one cares about your emo problems. Right?"

My smile tightens as I digest that bit. He's saying all the right things! And yet… they are falling on deaf ears. There's something missing here. A fire, a passion, a push-pull of emotion.

I guess I can't help but compare him to the months and months of time I had with Cole. Do I even want the upbeat kind of guy that I've always longed for? Or has Cole ruined that, too?

"Uhh, I guess?" I say, trying to keep the conversation alive.

I ask Will a question about his family and he happily chats about that for a while. The entire time he's talking, I can't stop thinking that he checks all my major boxes. He is beautiful. He's a doctor. He seems to have a sunny disposition.

And yet…

And yet, I find him a little on the boring side. Actually, it's more like a lot on the boring side.

He's been telling this story for more than five minutes and I stopped listening after… what… thirty seconds?

God, is this what I have to look forward to in the dating pool?

"So anyway," Will concludes, "That's why I don't ride a motorcycle anymore. They are so cool, and you feel so powerful, but they are just too dangerous. Don't you think?"

It suddenly occurs to me that I was looking for something I don't actually want. My dream man is not actually the one who makes my heart flutter. So I decide to stop dreaming once and for all.

Wistfully, I smile at Will. I reach out a hand across the table.

"It's nice meeting you. But I don't feel any chemistry here."

His eyebrows jump up and he laughs.

"Chemistry? That's a myth."

"No." I shake my head softly, smiling. "For me, it's essential."

Fishing a twenty out of my purse, I place it on the table. Then I wish him the best of luck, and leave the restaurant.

The wine bar's door swings shut behind me, muting the clink of glasses and murmur of conversation. I let out a breath, feeling the night air cool my flushed cheeks.

That date was a disaster. Sure, Dr. Dreamy was charming at first. It was all sparkling eyes and bright smiles. But as the date wore on, his sunny outlook felt cloying, like a glass of iced tea that had too much sugar. He was the human equivalent of a motivational poster.

To make things worse, I couldn't stop comparing him to Cole. With his sharp wit and practical outlook, Cole challenges me. He doesn't just smile and nod. Cole engages, debates, and pushes me to think deeper. I never realized how much I craved that until now.

"Savannah!" Lucy waves at me from across the street, her bracelets jangling. I wave back and jog over to meet her.

"Hey! What are you doing here?" I ask.

Lucy shrugs. "Just wandering. I needed some inspiration for my new installation. What about you?" Her eyes dart to the wine bar behind me, a knowing look on her face.

I roll my eyes. "Let's just say that date did not go as planned."

Lucy smothers a laugh. "Not feeling the dreamy vet, huh?"

"More like wishy-washy vet," I mutter.

She puts a hand on my arm. "Maybe you need someone who will challenge you. Who will fight for you...and with you, if need be."

I chew my lip, thoughts of Cole surfacing again. "Maybe," I say softly.

We're quiet for a moment, both of us thinking of him. Then Lucy perks up. "The guys took Cole sailing today. To talk some sense into him." She emphasizes the last part.

I frown, confused. "About moving to London?"

"Mmhmm." Lucy gives me a pointed look. "Not that I think he's actually going anywhere."

Hope and uncertainty war inside me. I want to believe her, but should I?

Lucy links her arm through mine. "Come on. Let's get ice cream and talk about something happier."

I let her pull me down the street, focusing on her bright voice as she describes her latest art project. But part of me still lingers on Cole, wishing things could be different between us. Wishing I was brave enough to fight for this, for him.

I let Lucy's chatter wash over me as we walk, not really listening to her words but soaking in the comfort of her presence. She's always been able to lift my spirits, ever since I met her during a yoga class on our college campus.

My rocky road ice cream sits mostly untouched as we claim a picnic table outside the shop. Lucy dives into her rocky road with gusto, but I just pick at mine, my appetite fled.

"Earth to Sav. Come in Sav." Lucy jokes after a lull in the conversation. "What's going on in that head of yours?"

I shrug, staring down at the table. "Nothing really."

"Oh come on." Lucy nudges me with her elbow. "It's me you're talking to. Let it out."

I hesitate. Part of me wants to unburden myself, but the other part shies away from being so vulnerable. From admitting how lost I feel.

Lucy reaches over and gives my hand a squeeze. "It's okay to not be happy all the time, you know. You don't always have to put on a brave face."

My vision blurs with sudden tears. I blink them back furiously. Lucy's right, of course But if I falter now... what if everything falls apart?

Lucy pulls me into a hug. "Oh Sav."

"It's just..." I start legitimately sobbing and hiccupping in her arms. "Cole left me, and I'll probably never see Charlie again and I tried to make myself feel better by going on a date and it was awful! Just awful. I don't even know what I want or who I want it with anymore. How am I supposed to live like this, Lucy???"

She tsks as she strokes her hand down my back. "Oh, your poor thing. I'm so sorry. My brother is a complete tool. If it's any consolation, Rex says that Cole is an emotional wreck too."

I cry for a minute, unable to help myself. "I'm sad because I really fell in love with Charlie, too. He's so bright and imaginative and sweet. And now all my casual mentions of events coming up this year have turned into lies, because I can't go to any events with him. Cole made me a liar!"

"It's okay," she murmurs. "You're not alone. I'm here for you, no matter what."

"I'm a wreck. It's just been an emotional week for me."

Lucy pulls out a packet of tissues and hands them to me. "I didn't know that thing between you had gotten so serious. Cole is a complete idiot, for what it's worth."

I take a shuddering breath as I pull back from Lucy's embrace. She keeps one arm wrapped around my shoulders, a comforting presence.

"I'm sorry," I say, wiping at my eyes. "I didn't mean to just break down on you like that."

"Don't apologize." Lucy gives me a little shake. "That's what friends are for. And clearly you needed to get some things off your chest."

I nod, taking a sip of water to steady myself.

"I guess I have been bottling things up lately. Ever since...." I trail off, but Lucy knows what I mean.

Ever since things ended with Cole. Ever since he said he was leaving town and didn't want to hold me back. Ever since I walked away from him because loving him was too hard.

Lucy sighs, stirring her melted ice cream with her spoon. "My brother can be an idiot sometimes. He thinks he's doing the right thing by moving to London."

Despite everything, I feel a glimmer of amusement. "He didn't even ask if I would consider a long distance relationship."

"That's because he's an idiot. You don't just get attraction and empathy with every single rock you look under. It's a rare find."

I dip my head. "When Cole and I were together, it was like... like nothing I've ever felt before. There was this spark between us. We had this chemistry that just felt so right."

Lucy nods, a knowing look in her eyes. "I could see that, whenever you two were in the same room. You lit each other up."

"Exactly," I say. I feeling almost elated to finally say the words out loud. "And it killed me when we ended things. I know he was trying to be practical, thinking about the future and all that. But as it turns out, my heart doesn't care about any of that."

"Oh, Savannah." Lucy reaches over and gives my hand a comforting squeeze. "I'm sorry. I know how painful this must be for you."

I blink back the tears that are threatening to spill over again. "I just miss him so much, Luce. And I hate feeling like this. I feel like my heart's been ripped out of my chest, torn to pieces, and stomped on. I don't know how to get over him."

Lucy looks at me intently. "Then maybe you shouldn't get over him. Maybe you should fight for him instead."

I stare at Lucy, caught off guard by her suggestion. Fight for Cole? The thought both thrills and terrifies me.

"What do you mean?" I ask hesitantly.

Lucy grins, a mischievous twinkle in her eye. "I mean, don't give up on my brother so easily! He's being an idiot if he thinks moving to London is the right choice. His heart is here, with you."

"We need to make you look irresistible when Cole gets back," Lucy says around a mouthful of ice cream. "I'm thinking we give you a whole new look. Maybe some highlights in your hair, a spray tan, new outfits...."

I laugh, shaking my head. "Lucy, Cole likes me for me. I don't need a makeover."

Lucy waves her spoon dismissively. "Of course he does. But it doesn't hurt to enhance your assets a little." She wiggles her eyebrows suggestively.

I roll my eyes, but I can't help smiling. It feels good to have someone in my corner. Ever since my parents died, I've been so focused on taking care of myself that I haven't let many people get close. But Lucy has long since barreled her way into my heart and refused to budge. I'm grateful for her years of friendship.

As we finish up our ice cream, the conversation turns more serious. "I know you're scared to put yourself out there again with Cole," Lucy says. "But you have to be willing to take emotional risks if you really want to find love."

I nod, knowing she's right. "I'll try. It's just hard. I feel so vulnerable. What if he still leaves?"

"Then at least you'll know you gave it your all." Lucy squeezes my hand.

38

SAVANNAH

I'M RUNNING LATE TO THE COMMUNITY CENTER. THE WIZARD of Oz is supposed to have its debut in less than three hours and there are still plenty of last-minute tasks to take on. I rush into the building, but it's perfectly empty. The lights are off, and it is eerily silent in here.

Where is the heck is everybody?

"Hello?" I call out. "Is anybody here?"

A shape coalesces out of the darkness. It's my sister Birdie, and she has the biggest grin on her face.

"Hey, Savannah. How's it going?"

I look left and right, throwing my hands up in bewilderment.

"Where is everybody?"

She just keeps grinning like a goon. My stomach is in knots.

Why is my sister being so weird right now? She looks like the cat that ate the canary.

"I have some news. You're not going to like the first half. But you're going to be happy in the end. Okay? Remember that I said that."

Uh oh. A gathering storm of anxiety begins to well up inside me. First the break up with Cole, now whatever this is? Birdie honestly couldn't have worse timing.

"What news? Birdie, I swear, if you don't tell me what's going on, I'm gonna scream."

Birdie comes over to me and takes my arm, gently ushering me out of the front doors of the community center. She turns around, and glances up the building's crumbling facade. Her words are gentle.

"On Monday, the community center will be condemned. It's been purchased by the Bennett-Taylor Real Estate group for the purposes of being demolished to make room for a new hotel. A place for visiting players to stay while they play at the new training camp. Yada yada, you know the rest."

I gape at her. Betrayal claws at my chest. If Birdie is telling me the truth, then after shredding my heart into smithereens, Cole did the exact thing I begged him not to do. That complete bastard!

"Cole pushed ahead with his plan even though I warned him not to?" I ask carefully.

Birdie gives me a sympathetic look. "I know. It's not what you wanted to hear. But there is more. A big huge silver lining inside that thundercloud."

My sister gives me an even smile and strokes my arm.

I tug my arm from her grasp, pinning her with my gaze. How Cole managed to get Birdie mixed up in all of this, I don't know. But it's apparent from her words that he has turned my sister and confidante against me. My heart aches.

That fast-talking idiot. Only two hours ago, I was thinking that tonight would be the night I told him how I really felt. But now I could honestly strangle him.

"What an inconsiderate... dick!" I cry. "First Cole took that job in England. Now this? You're in on it, too, whatever it is. What's next, I'm kicked out of Grandad's house, effective immediately?"

"Now just hold on." She starts pulling me away from the center and down the street. "I'm going to ask you to reserve judgment until you've heard all the facts."

Tears press at the corners of my eyes. I promise myself that I am not going to fall apart, but damn if I don't want to break down right now. I promised Lucy that I would make myself vulnerable to Cole. But this feels dangerously close to being a pushover. Sniffling, I brush away a tear before it falls onto my cheek.

"Are there facts that could possibly make Cole not look like a prick? Because if so, I'd love to see them."

"I don't want to ruin the surprise." She smiles at me, but doesn't answer my actual question. "Come on. It's not much longer. When you understand everything, you'll feel better. I just need you to come with me to see something."

She drags me down the sidewalk.

Another figure materializes out of the shadows and steps into the middle of the path.

Cole.

He's wearing his dark suit, and looking at me with a very grave expression. His puffs of breath in the wintry night air rise against the dark gray backdrop of the street.

He's the last person I want to see right now. My tender feelings haven't had a chance to breathe, let alone bounce back from the emotional effects of our break up. I'm not strong enough to see him.

Not yet. Maybe not ever.

I know this sounds stupid. I know that I promised Lucy that I would try to fight for her brother. But seeing him now feels like I'm being vivisected in front of Birdie, flayed and cut open, left with my heart beating too fast, for the entire world to see. It's a vulnerable feeling and I'm afraid that Cole will just trample over me again. I'm not ready for it.

For *him*.

What is Cole thinking?

When I lock eyes with him, my heart plummets to the floor and smashes to pieces like a fragile piece of glass.

"He promised to leave me alone," I murmur to Birdie.

"I think you'll want to hear what he has to say," my sister whispers.

"You're a traitor for doing this."

"If you're still mad in an hour, you can give me a wet willy like we would do as kids." She grins. "An enticing offer, I bet."

It's the first time I can ever recall wanting to punch my sister directly in her mouth.

Why is she betraying me? And why is Cole backtracking on our agreement to butt out of each other's lives?

I trudge toward him, my face set in a grimace. He's standing next to the darkened, two-story building that once housed Peterson's Grocery. I stop a few feet away, my heart racing like I've just run a marathon. My soul feels like it's made of lead.

Why does just being in Cole's presence turn my legs to jelly? My body still yearns for him, and against my will, my lips ache for his kisses.

"Hello, Sav," he greets me.

"Cut the crap. You promised me that you were going to leave me alone. And you were supposed to take that stupid job in England. What's this I'm hearing about you having the community center condemned?" I twist up my mouth, but I can't stop the words from bleeding out. "I'm disappointed in you, Cole."

He winces. "Ouch." He spreads his fingers out over his heart. "I guess I deserve that."

"Well, my words wouldn't hurt if they weren't true."

He seems to consider me for a moment. Then he saunters closer to me.

"I want to start this off on the right note." He presses his lips into a thin line and frowns. "I'm sorry, Sav. I have done and said some things in the past week that I don't know how to fix."

I lift my chin. "You've been a total bastard."

"Well… I won't make excuses for myself. I handled everything wrong. I wasn't open or vulnerable. I saw you, and saw the amazing love you offered me. And I got scared. Scared of being hurt again. Scared of maybe not being able to give you what you deserve. Or of not deserving such a wonderful, brilliant ray of sunshine in my life. I made excuses about my career and moving to London. But really, I was running away from you."

My mouth opens and closes several times. I stare at him, bewildered. My heart beats so loud and fast that I am sure everyone in the county can hear it.

Cole's saying all the right things. Everything that my battered heart could want. But can I believe them?

Do I dare take a chance on this man when he has already ruined me once?

"This is… not what I expected you to say," I blurt out at last.

"I'm sorry. I don't deserve your forgiveness, but I'm going to beg you for it anyway." He comes close enough to touch me and picks up my hand. He turns it over and kisses my palm as he kneels down. "Please, Savannah. Please forgive me. I love you. And I think you love me. Give me a chance to make things right."

I swallow around the lump of emotions that has settled in my throat.

"I'm not sure I can," I rasp. "I think you shattered my heart into too many pieces to ever make it whole again."

"Give me the next hour to convince you. All I'm asking is for your time. If you won't forgive me after that, I will leave you alone."

"You said that before!"

"I know." Cole looks pained. "My brothers told me that I was being a fool to let you go. They were right, of course. But they also helped me realize that I was about to go down a path I couldn't come back from, when all I really wanted is to be here with you. Please, Sav. Please, let me at least explain what is happening with the community center."

He looks at me with this desperation in his dark blue eyes. I'm scared. Of him, of myself, of opening myself to be hurt again.

But I think of the conversation I had with Lucy. Will I be able to say that I gave it my all if I walk away now? No, I don't think so.

"Okay," I whisper. "I'll give you an hour."

Cole kisses my wrist. "Thank you, darling."

His words make me want to fling myself into his arms and satisfy myself with a kiss. But I won't do that. I refuse to be a stupid, wishy-washy person. I give him a stern look and pull my hand from his grasp.

"Your time already started, Cole. Get moving."

"Right." Cole gets up, and then raises his arm to indicate the shuttered grocery store next to us. "Starting tomorrow, this is going to be the new temporary community center for the next year until a new one can be constructed a block away."

"What?" My eyebrows jump up and I look to the darkened store windows. "You… this… I don't understand!"

Tears of confusion well up. He moves closer and touches my hand, but I rip it away. He grimaces and then bows his head.

"My family's company has leased this property to renovate it for the community's use while the new community center is built."

I shake my head. "This building doesn't have a stage. Your own damn kid is in the play that… I guess just won't go on now?"

He holds up a finger. "Bear with me for a few more minutes. Okay? Then you can really let me have it if you still want to."

"I hate this," I tell him. "And I hate that you're doing it. I want you to just come out with it already."

He winces. "That's fair, but I'm still going to ask you to do it. It'll be worth it, I promise."

"I'm hearing a lot of promises and not a lot of follow-throughs."

"You'll know everything in fifteen minutes."

Cole grabs my hand and leads me into the alley between the buildings. His hand covering my own feels warm and real. I just have to keep reminding myself that I am looking for something real *and* lasting. That's where this whole relationship faltered.

I want Cole to want to stay here forever. Him offering me a relationship for a week or a month or a year is *just not enough anymore!*

The whole thing makes me heartsick.

The alley behind the buildings is just wide enough for us to walk through without contorting our bodies, or pressing against each other. I keep sneaking glances at him through the corner of my eye.

He has not gotten any less handsome since the last time I saw him. If he had any sense of decency, he would be covered with giant boils or something. But he's as dreamy and good-looking as ever. *Damn him.*

We get to the back alley that runs along the gap between the end of this row of buildings and the back of the buildings on the other side. It's especially dark in the shadows. But Cole waves his free hand, and two pale lights blink to life over the dumpsters pushed against each building.

I look at him, wrinkling my nose. But he just holds up his hand.

"See these back entrances?" He points to two battered sets of aluminum doors.

"Yeah." I shrug. "Is this what I'm supposed to see?"

"God, you're so impatient." Cole grins like an idiot. "Just remember that these doors are here. They allow easy and free access to each building."

"Okay…?" What I am supposed to get from that, I have no idea. My brain is leaping from one fact to another, but it's unable to make any connections.

He tows me toward the back door of the opposing building. I try to figure out which building it is from where we are in space, but I have no idea.

Until he opens the door.

There is a decommissioned movie theater seat leaning against the wall, stained and with its guts busting out in places. The air is redolent with the familiar scent of stale buttered popcorn.

"Is this the movie theater?" I ask Cole.

"That's what it has been for years. But before that, it was an actual theater for live plays. In fact, it has apparently been poorly retrofitted with a screen–."

"That's too small for the theater," I say. "Right?"

He smirks. "This is the other half of my plan. I've made a deal with the theater to pay for a complete renovation. Part of the deal will be a screen that can be moved off the stage more easily. Because the community center must have somewhere to put on plays for the next year. We start renovations tomorrow, after tonight's performance."

My mouth is an O of surprise. It takes me a moment to catch up.

"Wait, you're planning to put the Wizard of Oz on here?"

"Yes."

"And you're going to renovate this theater to be able to accommodate movies and live stage plays"

He rocks back and forth on his heels, a vague smile on his face. "That's the idea."

My whole world tilts on its side. I struggle to remain upright.

Is this real? Did Cole give the community center a rebirth?

Moreover, did he do it for *me?*

I tug on his hand and ask, "You planned this?"

Cole flip-flops his free hand. "Sort of. I came up with the ideas, but I had a lot of help."

"This is... a really good compromise," I whisper. "I'm floored."

"That's what I told Mrs. Brown and the rest of the planning board to get them to rubber stamp this plan."

My throat needs clearing before I can speak again. "I'm glad that you decided to go this route. It's really well thought out. The community will really appreciate this."

"Look, Sav. If I'm honest, I don't care about the community center. I don't even care about South Shore or Cape Simon. But you do. I'm not doing this to finish my project for Rex. I'm doing it for *you*. It's basically what you were suggesting the entire time. I was just too stubborn to listen."

My hand flies to my heart. My gaze connects with his.

"You're doing it for me?" I repeat.

"Yes, Savannah. If you said that the Appalachian Mountains were too damned jagged, I would do my best to smooth them all out, even if it took the rest of my life. Don't you see? There's nothing that I wouldn't do for you. I love you."

My heart is in my throat. I feel the first tear break free and run down my face.

"Really?"

"Really," he assures me. "If I thought that you would say yes, baby, I would drop to my knees and ask you to marry me."

My eyes bug out. "What?"

"I'm serious. I'm trying to show you that I'm all in."

"That's not… I don't want a proposal. Don't do that. *Please*." I tug at my hand, but he doesn't release me.

"Not yet. Maybe in time." He squeezes my hand. "There's more, if you want to see it."

I'm far too emotional to speak without crying like a baby. I just nod my head and brush away a tear that hits my cheek.

Cole places a hand on my back, and guides me up a skinny corridor that I now realize is probably the fire exit. When he opens a second set of doors, I see the dingy red theater seats. I step in and look around. The theater lights are dimmed, and the big room is empty. The projector is on, but nothing is playing on the big screen. It's just white.

Cole ushers me to the front row, sits me down, and offers me a huge bowl of popcorn. I accept it, stunned.

Did Cole go through with all this planning for me? I know it benefits his family in the long run, but it sure feels personal right now.

"Are you ready to see a show I put together?"

I gaze at him like he's an alien descending from a UFO, and I've wanted to believe for my whole damn life. *Is he for real?* Sniffling, I nod.

"Uh… yeah?" is all I can think to say.

Cole sits down and looks to the back. "Cue the show!"

On stage, two volunteers lift the projection screen and awkwardly carry it off stage. The projector flicks on, and a wobbly light washes over the stage.

A group of children run out. One boy is dressed as a thundercloud and carrying a lightning bolt. Another girl is dressed in a bright yellow outfit, and carrying a large rainbow. Charlie comes out dressed normally, beaming so hard it looks like it hurts his cheeks.

My heart squeezes painfully. I love Charlie. I love his energy, his imagination, and his big toothy grin. Losing Charlie is one of the things I've struggled with the most ever since I found out his dad was really moving away.

Giving a little gasp, I put my hand over my mouth. Cole grabs my other hand and gives it a squeeze.

"Thundercloud and sunshine fell in love," Charlie announces. "Thundercloud was grumpy. He was mad and sad."

The little thunderstorm runs around in circles, waving his arms and yelling.

Charlie laughs. "Sunshine was lonely. She thought no one saw her."

The little girl skips around the stage, making sure that everyone sees her grinning. I give a startled huff of laughter.

Is this supposed to be about Cole and me? If so… they are doing a really good job.

"Sunshine and Thunderstorm…." Charlie starts, then stops. "Daddy? I don't remember."

Cole pats my hand and rises, jumping up to sit on the stage. "Let me help. Come here, Charlie."

Charlie runs to him and Cole catches him in his arms.

"Sunshine and Thunderstorm worked together," Cole continues the story. "At first, Thunderstorm would try to rain all over Sunshine's day."

The little girl representing the sun bolts across the stage with a shriek. The thunderstorm runs after her, screeching at the top of his lungs. For the next bit, Cole has to yell to make himself heard over the noise of the actors.

"But eventually, Thunderstorm realized that he actually really liked Sunshine. He secretly wished that he could be more like her. She made people happy wherever she went."

The kids stop screaming and take each other's hands, swinging them as they walk around the stage.

"Sunshine was really nice to everyone, but she paid special attention to Thunderstorm. She made him feel special. She remembered things he said. She brought him coffee. And Thunderstorm realized that he was falling in love with Sunshine. That even though they bickered sometimes, she made every aspect of his life better."

Tears slip down my face as I watch Sunshine and Thunderstorm embrace. I can't help but smile.

"When Thunderstorm got a job offer overseas, he and Sunshine fought. She felt sad, like even Thunderstorm wouldn't like her anymore if she showed him who she truly was. He was scared too, afraid to tell Sunshine how he really felt. So they decided not to see each other anymore."

The sun and the thunderstorm run to opposite sides of the stage, each crossing their arms and looking angry.

"Thunderstorm realized that Sunshine probably had a lot of emotions she hid under her rainbow. And he decided to make a last-ditch effort to woo her back," Cole says. He looks down at Charlie, bouncing his son on his lap. "Can you remember the last line?"

Charlie shakes his head. Cole leans down and whispers in his ear. Charlie grins and belts out, "Forgive me!"

"Good job. Thanks for helping me tell my story." Cole kisses Charlie on the head and sets him down. Then Cole wriggles off the stage and walks back to me. He kneels down before me and looks me deep in the eye.

"This is me groveling. I'm sorry I was such a stubborn bastard."

I give my head a shake. "I don't understand. Are you turning down the job in London?"

"It's already done." He grabs my hand and places a gentle kiss against the inside of my wrist. "I don't have to have a fancy job. But I need you, Savannah. I'm afraid I can't live without you."

My jaw drops. I don't know if I heard him right.

"Cole...," I struggle to piece sentences together. "I don't understand. What changed your mind?"

He looks circumspect. "Honestly? It was my brothers and my father telling me to knock it off, wise up, quit being a scaredy cat, and ask you to marry me."

I shake my head. "Honestly Cole? You fucked up."

His smile slips away. "I know. I know I did. I deserve the blame."

I grind my teeth. A part of me is willing to cave and accept his apology. But another part of me wants to hold him off just a while longer. I can't be so forgiving that Cole thinks he can just walk all over me again and apologize later.

"I'm not marrying you, Cole. I haven't even decided if I forgive you yet!" I yelp.

"Please forgive me. Please, Sav." He kisses my knuckles. "You don't have to agree to marry me. But I need you in my life. I need to know that you are by my side."

I shake my head. "What if I say no?"

"Then I'll lose the love of my life."

I pinch my lips together and stare at him. I press my knuckles against my mouth, and try to hold in the tears that are overwhelming me. Cole hesitates for a second and turns his head to look at the stage.

"Could y'all give us a moment in private? Not you, Charlie. Just everyone else."

A keening sound escapes my chest. I bow my head and struggle to keep it in.

Cole pulls me out of my seat and down onto the floor with him. He wraps his arms around me tightly. Vaguely, I think I can feel his fingers in my hair, pushing it back.

"Savannah, it's okay to cry."

A jagged sob bursts free, and I double over in agony. All the times I held my tongue. Every moment my mother told me to stay sweet when I wanted to scream. Each moment that I stuffed my feelings deep down inside since I was a freaking child.

All of that comes up right now, publicly spewing out, my wails loud and ragged. Cole stays and holds me, rocking gently from side to side. He's not put off when my crying lasts a minute, three minutes, five minutes.

He just makes soft, encouraging sounds and lets me feel all my feelings. I feel torn up inside… but also, strangely liberated. When my sobs finally fade away, he's still holding me. I feel limp, as see-through as a jellyfish, and completely wrung out.

"I'm sorry," I whisper. "My old saying is–."

"Girls should be cleaner than sunshine and sweeter than honey. I know." He tips my face back and searches my expression with solemn eyes. "That old saying doesn't mention not crying or expressing perfectly ordinary negative emotions. I think you are clean and sweet. But you're a human, too."

I offer him a paltry smile. "I feel like a dirty dishrag right now."

"Well, you're not." He shrugs. "Facts are facts."

Cole stands up and helps me to my feet.

"You didn't answer my question," he tells me. "Will you forgive me? Will you move in with me and Charlie? Will you help my family's company transition the community center?"

I don't want to cry anymore, so I just nod.

"I will," I whisper.

"I love you, Savannah. With all my heart, all my soul, and all my bossy attitude. Thank you for reminding me that I can love again."

"Oh god. I love you too. So much I don't think I can hold it all inside my head."

He kisses me, tender and sweet. There is an undercurrent of spiciness in it. But Charlie is watching us the whole time. I make it a point to pull back from Cole's kiss. I walk over to Charlie and start to ask him a question. Maybe offer him a hug.

But Charlie doesn't really do normal hugs. He climbs up and takes a flying leap at me. My eyes bug out as I try to catch him. My arms fasten around his waist and my heart ends up in my throat.

"Oh god," I squawk. I hug him against my body. "Charlie! You could've fallen, you crazy kid."

Charlie beams at me. "You caught me!"

I wipe away a tear and bounce him on my hip.

"That's right, Charlie. I always will."

Cole comes up behind me and gently pries his son from my arms, taking on Charlie's weight.

"Just the three musketeers, living together on the beach. How does that sound?"

"I love that plan!" Charlie shouts.

I wince, reaching out to tickle him.

"That's the kind of enthusiasm I like to see."

Charlie grins. Before he can respond though, Meg creeps out onto the stage.

"Hey guys? We still have a play to put on. The audience is queued up outside, waiting to be let in."

"Oh my god." I blush. "Sorry, Meg!"

"It's not a big deal. Glad you got your happy ever after fairy-tale thing. But we have a bunch of seriously antsy kids back here."

"Thanks for helping me out, Meg," Cole calls. "We're sending Charlie back to get dressed. The Wizard of Oz waits for no man!"

After he helps his son climb onstage, he turns back to me. I go to him, my body snapping to his like a magnet. Our lips find each other as if we've been kissing like this forever. It feels so god damn good.

It feels like home.

At the back of the theater, the doors open, and people start to crowd in. The babble doesn't even reach my ears, though.

"I love you, Sav. So damn much."

I touch his face. "God, Cole. I love you so much that it hurts."

His kiss is magical and healing, and like gulping in fresh air after being under the water for much too long.

I'm lost in Cole, drowning in his love. And in this moment, nothing else matters.

39

———

COLE

THE MORNING SUN GLINTS OFF THE MOVING TRUCK AS I HEAVE another box inside. I wipe sweat from my brow and glance over at Savannah. She's laughing with my dad and stepmom while they carry a dresser towards the house. Her smile makes my heart skip a beat.

I never pictured myself with someone so vibrant and warm. Somehow it works between us. She challenges me to loosen up, and I keep her grounded.

"Daydreaming over there?" Savannah teases. She walks over with two glasses of sweet tea.

I grin and take a glass. "Just thinking about how happy I am."

She smiles and brushes a kiss over my lips. "Me too."

I pull her close, deepening the kiss. Her body melts against mine.

A throat loudly clears behind us. We break apart to see Mrs. Brown smirking with a gift basket. The older woman is not someone that I feel comfortable around, but Sav seems to like her a lot. And I'll cede all opinions on people to Sav for now.

I'm still eating humble pie this week.

"Well, well, no more hiding I see!" Mrs. Brown thrusts the basket at us. "A little housewarming gift for the happy couple. But don't forget, your new project proposal is due soon."

"Thank you so much!" Savannah gushes. Mrs. Brown waves and hustles down the driveway.

I snake an arm around Savannah's waist. "I guess the secret's out."

She nuzzles my cheek. "I want to tell the whole world."

"That's good. Because we're on CSAT every damn day now." I pause, squinting at Sav. I accuse her mockingly. "You swear you're not CSAT?"

"No!" She swats my arm. "We've talked about this. I already said that I'm not CSAT and I don't know who it is."

I grunt. "Just checking. Whoever it is, they get the most embarrassing photos. I want them to move on to fresher meat."

Savannah notices the look on my face and comes over. "Everything okay?"

I smile and pull her into my arms. "Couldn't be better. My future is right here."

She kisses me softly, joy shimmering in her eyes. "You know just what to say to soften me up."

"I like you like this, all soft and willing."

She grins and moves away. "Just wait till you see me tonight, when I'm so very grateful to you for your help moving my boxes. I'll be extra amenable to any advances."

She wiggles her eyebrows.

"*Ooh.* I can't fucking wait. Just give me a taste."

Her lips twitch. "No dessert until you've cleaned your plate, Cole. Do the heavy lifting and just know that you'll be *rewarded.*"

She sashays over to pack another box and I bite my lower lip. Damn, the woman knows just how to get me to do what she wants. She's already got me wrapped around her pinky finger and I know it. I heave a sigh.

"I could've hired some movers to help with all this," I say as I pick up the next box.

Savannah shakes her head. Her ponytail swishes. "Nope, I want to do this the old-fashioned way. It's a ritual, like the changing of the seasons. It's the beginning of a new chapter."

I chuckle. She's always been the poetic one. Me, I just see a mountain of boxes that I'd rather pay someone else to deal with. But this is important to her, so I'll happily go along. Happy not-quite-wife, happy life, I guess.

"Dino smashes monster trucks!" Charlie howls. I manage to move out of the way in time for him to come crashing down the hall.

"Nuh uh! Monster truck wins every TIME!" Dexter screams.

Savannah's grandad wanders over and puts his arms around the boys' shoulders.

"How about you two come with me, and I'll teach you my secret fishing trick for baiting the perfect lure?" He winks conspiratorially.

"What's a lure?" Charlie asks.

"It's a cricket! Or a worm!" Dex shouts.

Grandad grins. "I've got both. Why don't you come and see my set up in the garage?"

The boys' faces light up and they eagerly follow Grandad towards the garage, chattering excitedly about what the secret to baiting lures could be. I smile as I watch them go, glad to see our families coming together so seamlessly.

Just then Rex and River arrive. My stepmom and dad huddle around them, glad for any chance to see their family. I greet my brothers and then immediately put them to work moving boxes. There's laughter, and lively conversation as we work together loading up the truck.

Savannah compliments my brother Rex's muscles as he easily hefts a heavy box. He flexes and she laughs. I move over to put my arm around her waist.

"This one?" I point to her. "She's off the menu."

"Oh, Cole," Sav grins. "Please be reasonable."

I smirk. "Nope. I licked you. Now you're all mine."

She dies laughing and I can't help but pull her close and kiss her. Her lips are addictive, warm and sweet and made for my lips alone. Her charm and sincerity delight me constantly. I feel a rush of warmth when I watch her interact so naturally with my family.

I've never experienced this before. Having a partner who fits in effortlessly with my loved ones is completely new. It's a good feeling, this pride and contentment. Sure, it comes with the occasional rash of insane jealousy that I strive to keep in check. But Savannah never gives me a reason to doubt her. Unlike my relationship with my ex, I never have a reason to second guess the fact that she loves me.

I heave another box into the back of the moving truck, muscles straining. This one is heavier than it looks. As I set it down with a thud, I glance over and see Savannah and her grandad speaking in hushed tones near the porch.

She's holding out an envelope insistently while he waves it away, shaking his head. After a moment, he sighs and takes it from her hands, enveloping her in a tight hug.

Curious, I make my way over. "Everything okay?"

Savannah smiles. "Yeah, I just gave Grandad some of my savings to help with expenses now that I'm moving out. With the money you gave me, I think that we might be able to figure out a way to keep the house in the family."

I nod, impressed by her selflessness. Her grandad has been like a father to her since she lost her parents. She would do anything for him.

I don't mention the fact that I've already approached River and asked him to figure out the nuances of buying her grandad's house. I want to make sure that Birdie can stay in the home while Grandad can use the money as he wishes.

My own father claps me on the shoulder then, jolting me from my thoughts. "Ready to head over to the new place?"

I nod, and we climb into the truck's cab, letting the roar of the engine fill the silence between us at first.

After a few moments, Dad clears his throat awkwardly. "Listen, son. I know we've had our rough patches. But I want you to know I'm sorry for not being there for you more after your mom passed."

I grip the steering wheel tightly, shocked. We've never really discussed this.

"It's… okay…," I say, not quite knowing how to answer. This isn't really the time or place for such a conversation.

"No, it's not okay. I was distracted," he continues. "By grief at first. And then I fell in love with Sarah. It's no excuse, though. I should've made more time for you all. I'm sorry about that."

"It's really all right. You don't have to apologize."

He looks at me. "I just don't want to leave things between us unsaid. You know?"

I pat his knee. "I appreciate that."

At length, we pull up the drive to the new house. I cut the engine and turn to face him. Hearing my dad actually acknowledge the problem is refreshing. I suck in a deep breath, and stare at him for a long beat.

My dad is asking forgiveness, as I did last week. If I got a blank page and a fresh start, he deserves one too. I swallow against the tangle of feelings in my throat.

"I forgive you, Dad," I say simply.

We embrace roughly, clapping each other on the back.

"Love you, son," he rasps. "Don't you ever forget that."

"I love you too."

As we get out of the truck, I feel lighter. Like a weight has been lifted between us.

I nod to my dad as my brothers' trucks pull up the drive, parking behind my convertible. Sarah's sleek SUV turns down the street. Savannah waves from the passenger seat.

As soon as she hops out, I sweep her into my arms and kiss her deeply. She giggles against my lips.

"What was that for?" she asks.

"Just because I can," I say with a grin.

My family looks on, smiling and joking about young love. For the first time, their teasing doesn't bother me.

I take Savannah's hand as we walk inside our new home together.

"I love you," I tell her sincerely.

She squeezes my hand, her eyes shining. "I love you too."

THIS FEELS RIGHT. LIKE COMING HOME.

It's been a long road and a hard-fought love. But my soul has found its resting place right by Savannah's side.

THE END

4 0

SAVANNAH

ONE MONTH LATER

THE METALLIC SCREECH OF THE BULLDOZER'S BLADE SCRAPING against concrete makes me wince. I squeeze Cole's hand tighter as we watch the community center's west wall crumble into a pile of rubble.

"It's bittersweet, isn't it?" Cole says. "I'm sure it's hard to see the community center torn down. But we have set up a pretty good system to get us through the year between now and the opening of the new one."

I nod, blinking back tears. As a kid, I spent countless afternoons in that rec room with Mom, playing board games and listening to her laugh.

Cole wraps his arm around me. "Hey, it'll be okay. And we have the hotel design to look forward to."

I blow out a stream of breath. "I know."

He squeezes me.

"I had a thought. We could build something beautiful here to honor our moms. A memorial garden with a fountain, benches, trees…. Anything we want. We'll have it on the ground floor of the hotel, in the center. Maybe it'll have a reflection pond."

"And rose bushes!" I add. "Pink ones for your mom, yellow for mine."

Cole smiles. "I love that idea. We'll plant them side by side. Then you and I can come by anytime we're missing our moms. And there will be a quiet spot to contemplate."

I can picture it now. The yellow and pink roses intertwining as they bloom every spring. A thoughtful tribute.

"Well, my mom would hate the quiet spot bit. But she'd like a rose garden that was named after her," I say.

For some reason, that makes me laugh. Which in turn brings me to tears.

Cole notices my tears and pulls me close.

"It's okay to feel sad and miss her," he says. "And it's also okay to admit that you don't love everything about someone even if they are dead. Your mom was great, except this huge chip she built on your shoulder about showing your real feelings. You can feel any way you want to about that. It doesn't make you any less warm and bright."

I cling to him, beyond grateful for his steadying presence.

"I want to photos of your mom. I know they are at La Villa Coralle. But you have to promise that you'll bring them home next time you're there." I ask. "I want to know the woman who raised such an incredible son."

Cole chuckles. "All right. It's a promise." He hesitates, then adds, "I have to give Sarah some credit too. Without her, I think my whole family would've toppled like dominos."

I smile up at him, touching his face.

"We should do something nice for Sarah soon."

His lips twitch. "I didn't agree to all that."

"You just wait. I'll have you two confessing your love for each other soon enough. It's practically my whole life's goal at this point."

He snorts. "Let's just get through the building of the hotel first. Then we can talk about family shit."

Cole's phone buzzes, interrupting our moment. He checks it and sighs heavily.

"Let me guess. Is it Holly again?" I ask.

"Yep. She's texting me now. Hold on."

Two seconds later, he scowls at his phone and hisses.

"What the hell? She's backing out of taking Charlie to Atlanta this weekend." He shoves a hand through his hair, frustrated. "I'm so tired of her disappointing him like this."

I rub Cole's back. I wish I could make it better. But Holly is still an uncomfortable subject for me. I haven't figured out how to act around her. And any attention Cole pays her makes me crazy with jealousy.

Still, I say, "I'm sorry. I know how hard this is on both of you. That completely sucks."

Cole's jaw clenches, old hurts rising to the surface. "She always does this. Gets his hopes up and then bails. It kills me to see how much it hurts him."

"You're a wonderful father," I assure him. "We'll figure something out for Charlie. He knows how much you love him."

Cole manages a small smile, covering my hand with his. But as we drive on, his anger simmers just below the surface. I wish I could ease his pain, but all I can do is listen.

"I just hate that I'm the one with custody, so I have to break the bad news to my kid. I really hate her for this."

I nod emphatically and murmur comforting things in Cole's ear. Inside, I'm quietly happy that I don't have to deal with seeing her in person again.

I'm not perfect, okay?

We pull into the driveway and head inside. Meg greets us at the doorway, putting her shoes on. "Charlie was great! I'm super late to my study group, though."

Cole pulls cash from his wallet and gives it to Meg as she flees. He raises his eyebrows at me.

"Think Charlie is still alive?" he asks me, his eyes sparkling.

"Let's see." I cup my hands around my mouth and shout up the stairs. "Charlie! We're back!"

Charlie comes bounding down the stairs, happy to see us. But his grin fades when he sees the look on his dad's face.

"What? Is it Mom?" he asks.

That slays me. I press a hand over my heart.

Cole sits Charlie down to break the news. The poor kid's lip quivers and his eyes fill with tears.

"Mommy isn't coming?"

My heart shatters. If I could take back my envious thoughts and trade them for Charlie's happiness, I would. Charlie is the most lovable kid I've ever met, for god's sake.

My heart breaks seeing Charlie so distraught. I kneel down next to him.

"Of course your mom loves you, Charlie. She wanted to see you so much. But sometimes grownup stuff gets in the way, even when we don't want it to."

Charlie's cries grow louder. He looks completely crushed. "But we were gonna see the dinosaurs and sharks at the museum! Now I can't go!"

"I tell you what," I say gently. "How about if your dad and I take you to the museum this weekend instead? I'd love to check out those dinosaurs with you."

Charlie looks up hopefully. "You would?"

"Absolutely," I say, ruffling his hair. "We'll have a great time, just the three of us."

Charlie manages a small smile, though his sadness still lingers. Cole mouths "thank you" over his dark head. I nod, heart aching for this sweet boy and his complicated family. For now, all we can do is be there for him.

Charlie's sadness lingers for an hour. I suggest that we all take a walk along the beach to keep our spirits up. The afternoon sun is bright as we walk, but it is doing little to cheer Charlie up. He kicks half-heartedly at the sand, hands shoved in his pockets.

Cole and I exchange a worried glance. We both hate seeing Charlie so down.

"Hey, look!" I say, pointing. "I think I see a sand dollar over there."

Charlie glances over without much interest. But as we get closer, his eyes widen. Nestled in the wet sand is a large, perfect sand dollar, pearly white and smooth.

"Whoa, cool!" Charlie kneels down to pick it up, turning it over in his hands. For the first time since we left the house, I see a real smile spread across his face.

"Good find, kiddo," Cole says, ruffling his hair.

We continue down the beach, Charlie eagerly scanning for more treasures. After a few minutes, he lets out an excited yell.

"Dad, Savannah, look! A shark tooth!" Charlie holds up a small, triangular fossil, his grin huge.

"Awesome!" I say. "That must be from a really old shark that lived here millions of years ago."

Charlie's eyes shine with wonder. For now, thoughts of his mom are forgotten as childlike curiosity takes over. Cole playfully nudges my shoulder, relief washing over his face.

As long as we're here for him, Charlie will be okay. At least that's what I tell myself.

"Sharks are like living dinosaurs, you know," I tell Charlie. "The species has been around for hundreds of millions of years. I read an article recently that said that there are a few sharks alive today that are probably over five hundred years old."

"Really?" Charlie examines the tooth in awe.

"Yep, sharks are ancient. Some of the earliest shark fossils are from hundreds of millions of years ago. That's before the dinosaurs even existed. I went through a shark phase as a kid where I couldn't stop learning cool stuff about sharks. If I'm honest, I might still be in that phase."

My eyes crinkle. I catch Cole looking at me with such warmth and admiration that it makes me flush.

"What?" I ask.

"I just never pictured finding someone who fit in to my family so well. It's like we are a puzzle, and you're the missing piece."

His words hit me in the soft, gooey center that is my heart. I'm so happy I feel like I'm glowing with positivity and light.

"Dad!" Charlie tugs on my hand. "Stop being kissy-kissy. Sav's trying to tell me about sharks!"

"Thanks right. Stop being so distracting." I arch a brow and point at Cole with faux sternness.

As I chat with Charlie about sharks, he hangs on my every word, completely enthralled. We walk slowly down the beach. We make sure to stop periodically so Charlie can dig through the sand for more prehistoric treasures.

After finding a few more shark teeth, Charlie takes off running down the shoreline, stopping to dig excitedly whenever he spots a potential fossil.

Cole slips his hand in mine as we follow several paces behind, keeping a watchful eye on the bobbing mop of dark hair up ahead.

"Well, I think you just sparked a new obsession," Cole says with a chuckle. "Forget dinosaurs. Looks like Charlie's moved on to sharks."

"Hey, sharks are just as cool as dinos," I reply with a grin. "Maybe I can take him to the aquarium sometime to see the shark exhibit. I bet he'd love that."

Cole smiles, giving my hand a grateful squeeze. "You're a natural with him. I have no idea how you do it. But god, thank you. You are exactly what he needs right now."

My heart swells. I squeeze Cole's hand back. "Charlie is a wonderful kid. I just want him to succeed and be happy."

"I think everyone wants that for their kids."

I shoot him a smile and give him a quick peck on the cheek.

We arrive back at the house. Charlie's pockets bulge with shark teeth and seashells. As we come up the front walk, I spot Grandad sitting in one of the rocking chairs on the porch.

Cole notices him too. "Hey Charlie, why don't you take your treasures inside and get washed up for dinner? Savannah and I will be right in."

Charlie doesn't need to be told twice, bounding up the steps with an enthusiastic "Hi Grandad!" before disappearing into the house.

"Karl." Cole sticks out his hand to Grandad. Grandad takes it, offering him a soft smile.

"Hello, Cole. Thought I would try to get a few minutes alone with my granddaughter."

"Of course. We're making DIY pizzas for dinner if you're free after."

Cole touches Grandad on the shoulder and follows Charlie inside, leaving me alone with Grandad on the porch. I sink down in the rocking chair beside him. I sense that this might be a serious conversation.

"Evening, sunshine," Grandad says, his wrinkled face creasing into a smile. "Have a nice walk on the beach?"

"We did," I reply. "Charlie found some shark teeth and got really excited about prehistoric sea life. I think Cole and I might take him to the natural history museum or the aquarium this weekend."

Grandad nods, rocking slowly in his chair. "That boy sure loves learning new things. Gets that from his daddy, no doubt about it."

He falls silent. Grandad has a faraway look in his eye that usually means he has more to say. I wait patiently for him to gather his thoughts.

"Listen, Savannah." He smiles a little sadly. "I know I wasn't always the best at reading your feelings when you were younger. Your mama had some weird ideas she picked up from God knows where. About what girls should and shouldn't do. And lord knows that she never followed it herself, but she let you think you couldn't show your true feelings. And since she was the mama, I deferred to her. All I want is for you to be happy now. I mean truly happy. You deserve that, sunshine. Don't ever let anyone make you feel you need to be anything but yourself."

My eyes fill with sudden tears. I reach over and squeeze Grandad's weathered hand.

"I am happy, Grandad. Happier than I've been in a very long time."

He smiles, patting my hand gently. "Well, that's all this old man needs to hear."

I can't stop the tears from spilling down my cheeks. Grandad's words touch something deep inside me that I've kept locked away for so long.

"I'm sorry," I choke out. "I don't mean to get so emotional."

"No apologies needed," Grandad says kindly. "Let it out, sunshine. I should have encouraged you years ago to say what you feel."

I lean over and wrap my arms around his frail shoulders. He smells of Old Spice and sea salt, just like he did when I was a little girl.

"I love you," I whisper.

"Love you too, sweet pea," he replies, patting my back. "Now dry those eyes. I believe someone mentioned pizza?"

I let out a watery laugh as I sit back, dabbing at my eyes with my sleeve.

"Personal pizzas and cookies. Obviously, it's Charlie's night to plan dinner. So there are chocolate chip cookies coming right up."

Charlie sticks his head outside. "Grandad! You know about sharks?"

"Do I?" A grin splits Grandad's face. "I've got stories that will chill you right down to the bone."

"Nothing too graphic or gory, I hope." I give him a look.

Grandad laughs. "We'll keep it G-rated."

Charlie excitedly leads Grandad inside to show him his shark teeth. My heart fills watching them. Cole slips his arm around me and I lean into him contentedly. I smile as I watch Charlie pepper Grandad with questions about sharks, barely letting the old man get a word in edgewise.

My heart is so full when I look at them. Grandad looks a bit overwhelmed but his eyes crinkle with warmth.

Cole's arm is solid and comforting around my waist. "Think your grandad's gonna be okay over there?" he murmurs.

"Grandad is thrilled anytime anybody asks about fish. Charlie just made his day." I lean my head on his shoulder. "Your kid has that effect on people. His enthusiasm is infectious."

Cole presses a kiss to my hair. "I better start prepping the pizza and cookies, so the little shark expert has something to snack on."

I give him a playful salute. "Aye aye, captain."

As Cole heads to the kitchen, I make my way over to Charlie and Grandad.

"Mind if I steal Grandad for a minute, kiddo?" I ask. "Those cookies won't bake themselves."

Charlie nods absently, already engrossed in his shark teeth again. Grandad pats his shoulder and stands.

"Quite the imagination on that boy," he remarks as we walk to the kitchen.

"He's one of a kind," I reply fondly.

We chat and laugh as we mix up the dough. A feeling of complete contentment washes over me.

This kitchen. These people. This is home.

And I'm glad to have found my place in their world.

41

COLE

ALMOST EXACTLY EIGHT MONTHS LATER

THE JACKHAMMERS POUND AWAY ALMOST GLEEFULLY AS I PULL into the parking lot. Our newest hotel, all steel beams and scaffolding, is nothing but noise at this point. For the moment, it's just an eyesore that we'll have to pretty up for the tourists.

Savannah's perched on my desk when I enter the office, legs crossed, skirt riding high on her thighs. Before I can say good morning, she pounces, kissing me hard.

I slide my hands under her knees and lift her up. She wraps herself around me like a koala clinging to a eucalyptus tree.

"Missed you," she murmurs against my neck. Her floral perfume fills my nose.

"Missed you more." I carry her to the couch and sink down, keeping her on my lap. She plays with my tie, loosening the knot.

"How's the construction coming along?"

"Loud." I brush a strand of hair behind her ear. "But we'll have another five-star hotel on the coast soon enough."

"My hero." She kisses the tip of my nose. "Building up the family empire one giant baseball training camp and concierge hotel at a time."

I chuckle. Savannah nuzzles against my neck, her breath warm on my skin. I run my hands slowly up and down her back, content to hold her close.

"So where've you been all morning?" I ask.

She sits up, an impish grin on her face. "Wouldn't you like to know?"

I raise an eyebrow. "I would, actually. Spill."

"Okay, okay." She takes a dramatic pause. "I had a doctor's appointment."

The way she says the words makes them sound important. My pulse quickens. A doctor's appointment could mean...

No. I shouldn't assume. But the possibility takes root in my mind.

Could Savannah be pregnant? We've talked about having kids someday. But are we ready for that step?

I search her face, looking for any hint, any sign. But she just smiles innocently back at me.

"Everything okay?" I ask, trying to keep my voice casual.

"Yup, all good." She hops off my lap and heads to the Keurig. "Want some coffee?"

I nod absently, my thoughts racing ahead. Savannah pregnant. A little boy with her eyes, a little girl with my smile. Our own family. The idea fills me with a warmth I didn't expect.

I want that. I want that with her.

But I don't press for more details. If there's news, she'll share when she's ready.

Savannah hands me a mug of coffee, then settles next to me on the couch again. She's quiet, staring down into her own mug, and I wonder if she's working up the nerve to tell me something.

Finally she looks up, a blush spreading across her cheeks.

"It was a false alarm," she says softly. "I was a few weeks late, so I thought… you know, why not. But I'm not pregnant."

"Oh." I try not to let my disappointment show.

She bites her lip. "But it got me thinking. I know we said we would have kids someday, but... why not now?"

I feel like someone socked me in the gut.

"Now?" I say. It comes out as a pretty undignified squeak.

"I was just thinking, you know. We love each other. We both want more kids eventually. So why wait?"

Her words catch me off guard. She's ready for this? The idea that she may be ready to start a family with me shakes me. The realization fills me with a sudden swell of uncertainty and a tinge of hope.

But am I ready?

"I just feel like something's missing, you know?" she continues when I don't immediately respond. "Our lives are great as a threesome. But they could be even better with a fourth member. Our own little squad."

I reach over and squeeze her hand, finally finding my voice again.

"I didn't realize you had been thinking about this."

She shrugs a shoulder. "I tried to keep it to myself. Before you say anything, I was not because I didn't want to share, or I didn't think my opinion mattered. I was just trying to sort out whether I was just going through a baby crazy period or if this was something that I really wanted. And then when my period was late…." She screws up her face. "I really wanted to be pregnant. I hope I don't sound completely bonkers."

Staring deeply into her eyes, I put a finger to her lips. Her words stir something deep in my chest.

"If you're ready for that step, then I am too. I want that with you, Savannah."

She breaks into a dazzling smile. "Yeah?"

I grin and pull her into my arms. "Let's make a baby."

She laughs, smacking my chest playfully, then beams at me, her eyes shining with joy. "I'm so glad you feel the same way! I was worried you might think it's too soon."

I shake my head, cupping her face in my hands. "With you, nothing ever feels rushed. I know we're ready for this."

She nuzzles against my palm. "You really are the perfect man, you know that?"

"Only for you," I say with a wink, eliciting another laugh from her. I gaze into Savannah's eyes, seeing the same awe and joy reflected there. "I love you," I whisper.

"I love you too," she breathes.

In the next few minutes, words are lost as we rip at each other's clothes and urge each other on. I have her bent over the desk, naked and quivering, as fast as I can help it. Savannah presses up against me, gasping my name over and over. I feel her body start to tense and I know she is close.

I drive my cock home with a single spasming thrust. With a cry of ecstasy, she shudders against me. I follow right after, burying my face in her hair.

We lie still for several moments, just holding each other. I run my fingers lazily through her blonde tresses.

"Do you think that worked?" Savannah asks softly.

I smile. "I guess we'll find out in a few weeks. But either way, we'll keep trying. We've got all the time in the world."

She sighs contentedly. "Just think, this time next year, we could be bringing a new life into this world."

The thought thrills me to my core. Kissing the top of her head, I say, "I can't wait until you're pregnant with my baby. Did I just find a new kink?"

She laughs. "I should be grossed out by that, but I'm not."

"What? Wanting to impregnate you feels pretty natural."

"Ew. Stop saying impregnate. It sounds like a medical procedure."

"It kind of is," I offer. When I shrug, she swats my shoulder. "Hold that thought. I have a surprise."

She perks up. "I love surprises."

Smirking, I offer her a hand and pull her off the couch.

"What's going on, Cole?" she asks with a smile. "You're being so mysterious."

I grin, savoring the anticipation. "I got something for you. I was going to sit on this until next month, which is the one-year anniversary of you starting to work for me. But...."

I guide her over to my desk. She raises her eyebrow until I pull a drawer open. A distinctive robin's egg blue box sits in the bottom. I fish it out and wave it in front of her face. When she sees the Tiffany & Co logo, her eyes go wide.

"Cole!" she gasps.

I pick up the box and get down on one knee before her. Her hands fly to her mouth in surprise.

"Wait!"

"What?"

"Are you going to propose while you're buck ass naked?"

"Seems like as good a time as any. Would you prefer that I wait?"

She narrows her eyes on my face for a second. Then she grins and shakes her head. "You're crazy. But that's why I love you."

I grab her hand and stare dramatically into her eyes.

"My darling Savannah," I say, opening the box to reveal not an engagement ring but a Ring Pop nestled in the dark blue velvet folds. "You are the sunshine in my life. You're smart. You're hot. You're wickedly funny. You make my life better in every way. Would you do me the honor of becoming Mrs. Bennett?"

Savannah lets out a little shriek of delight. "Yes! Of course I'll marry you!"

She hugs me so tightly that I actually struggle to breathe for a second. When she pulls back, I slide the candy ring onto her finger and stand to pull her into a passionate kiss. She throws her arms around my neck, nearly knocking me over in her enthusiasm.

When we finally come up for air, I say with a chuckle, "We can go pick out your real engagement ring together. I want you to have exactly what you want."

"Oh, Cole," she says, admiring her temporary Ring Pop bling. "You know I don't need anything fancy. All I need is you."

She kisses me again, and I feel like the luckiest man in the world.

Savannah pulls back from the kiss, her eyes shining. "I can't believe we're getting married!" she exclaims.

I take her hands in mine. "You're my soulmate, Savannah."

She smiles. "I feel the same way. I've never been surer of anything in my life."

I caress her cheek. "Just think, soon we'll be husband and wife. And maybe...." I raise my eyebrows suggestively.

Savannah blushes but her grin grows wider. "And maybe baby makes four," she says cheerfully.

Unable to resist, I sweep her up into my arms bridal-style. She lets out a delighted shriek.

"Practicing already?" she teases.

"We've got to start preparing for our future," I say with a wink. I carry her over to the couch and lay her down gently before stretching out beside her.

She snuggles into my arms. "I'm so happy, Cole. This is a dream come true."

I kiss the top of her head, breathing in the sweet scent of her shampoo. "For me too, my love. For me too."

Savannah gazes up at me adoringly as we lay together on the couch. "I can't wait to go ring shopping," she says. "But only if you come too. I want us to pick it out together."

I smile and brush a strand of hair from her face. "Of course, sweetheart. We'll go to Tiffany's and choose whichever ring speaks to you."

Savannah's nose crinkles. "Tiffany's? That's too fancy for me. I'd rather go somewhere more low-key."

"Anywhere you want," I assure her. "I just want you to have the perfect ring."

"As long as it comes from you, it'll be perfect," Savannah says. She kisses me softly.

When we break apart, I take her left hand and run my thumb over her candy ring. "I know this isn't much, but it symbolizes my promise to you."

Savannah beams. "It's the most romantic gesture ever."

She wraps her arms around my neck and pulls herself up to kiss me again, more passionately this time. I respond eagerly, tangling my hands in her hair.

After a few heated moments, Savannah draws back, slightly breathless. "Maybe we should start practicing for that family now," she suggests coyly.

I grin and roll her beneath me. "I like the way you think, future Mrs. Bennett."

Savannah giggles as I trail kisses down her neck. This is only the beginning of our new life together.

And I can't wait to see what the future brings.

THANK YOU SO MUCH FOR BEING A PART OF COLE AND SAV'S romance! I'm so grateful to have a romance reader like you! As a special token of my gratitude, I've written a bonus epilogue with your favorite characters – Cole & Savannah. Read it here.

I must admit, I have really enjoyed writing this series. Billionaire romance is my number one love, but forbidden is a close second. I'm over the moon to write some tropes and stories that I've been longing to write for years. Get ready for me to weave a web about baby bargains, fake fiancés, best friend's little sisters, and more!

The Bennett-Taylor siblings each deserve a happily ever after... and River and Pearl will be the next to get a spicy, swoony love story! You can turn the page to get a taste of what is in store for them in The Fake Fiancée Proposition!

42

RIVER

The sky is unexpectedly blue and beautiful over Cape Simon today. The warm sun spills a golden hue over the Cape Winery and Bistro. The sunlight illuminates the white satin drapes that cascade from the rafters like waterfalls of light.

I take it all in with a jaundiced eye. The soft rustle of elegantly dressed guests mingling among tables adorned with crystal glassware and silver cutlery makes me feel restless. Blush pink silk ribbons dance on the gentle breeze. The scent of fragrant pink flowers infuses the air with the kind of romance you read about in fairytales.

I'm here at Cole and Savannah's engagement party, gritting my teeth. These parties are not exactly to my taste.

"Beautiful, isn't it?" Savannah sidles up beside me. Her voice is a melody that matches the clingy blush pink silk dress hugging her curves. The fabric catches the sunlight and casts a glow on her skin that makes her look ethereal.

She seems like the perfect woman to pair with Cole. Together, they are a replica of the bride and groom you'd find atop a wedding cake. It's nice, if you can stand how sugary sweet their whole deal is.

"Sure," I reply, adjusting my suit jacket. "If you're into this sort of thing."

She's a vision. I'm glad that I talked Cole into kissing her feet and begging her to take him back.

"River, don't be such a cynic. It's a party. Lighten up," she chides gently. She flicks at my blush pink silk tie. Her fingers graze my chest briefly.

Lightening up isn't exactly my forte.

I'm more the guy who stands back and observes. I make mental notes of the dynamics at play in every situation. And the dynamics in play here are patriarchal enough to make anyone gag.

Cole strides through the crowd, his suit tailored to perfection, a physical embodiment of coolness. That blush pink tie of his isn't just an accessory. It's a statement.

He's saying he's a man who can blend sentimental gestures with a businesslike demeanor.

"River, come join us," Cole calls out, waving a hand in my direction. His smile is practiced, but it's genuine enough to draw a few happy glances from the surrounding guests.

"Be right there," I respond, watching as he turns back to a cluster of well-wishers, doling out firm handshakes and charming smiles.

I move through the throng of people, each step measured and precise. I can't help but feel like a wolf in a field of sheep.

I'm different than most of these people. I don't want their cheesy good tidings or need their sentimental happily-ever-afters. Having a blushing bride on my arm has simply never been a part of my plan.

"Congratulations," I tell Cole as I approach. The words feel foreign on my tongue. "You two seem... happy."

"Thanks, River," he replies, clapping a hand on my shoulder. "It means a lot coming from you."

"No problem. You asked, I answered. So I'm here with bells on."

"I appreciate it. I know that all this wedding mumbo jumbo isn't really your scene. I promise, there are only six thousand more bridal events before the actual wedding. Then you can relax," Cole says, grinning and ribbing me.

I lift a shoulder in a casual shrug. "You and Savannah admittedly make a pretty cute couple. Just promise me there will be no funny business about setting me up with a bridesmaid or anything. It's the last thing I want."

"Relax, will you? Everybody who knows you knows that you're against marriage."

I give Cole a look. "It's a sham. No offense. It's the old world desperately trying to reach into modern day relationships, just to fuck with them. Why should any of us have to do the whole swoony proposal schtick and promise our partners forever? *Blech*. Not for me."

Cole squeezes my shoulder and offers me a wan smile.

"No one expects that from you. You've made your views clear."

Wrinkling up my face, I sigh. "Today's about you, though. And I know that all the hearts and flowers and diamond rings are your idea of happily ever after. So... congratulations."

He shakes his head with a wry smile. "Thanks, I think."

When Cole gets distracted, I take a leisurely stroll through the sea of pastel-clad guests. Each one seemingly more enamored with the spectacle than the last. My eyes skim over smiling faces, all drunk on love. Or maybe that's just the open bar.

Either way, their blissful ignorance grates on me. But I hide it well. After all, I'm River.

The man of steel nerves, icy heart, and an endless hunger for dollar signs.

All I care about is where my next million is going to be earned.

Lost in thought, I round a table adorned with more pink petals than a florist's shop and nearly collide with a vision in...

Well, would you look at that, more blush pink silk. Pearl Brown nearly topples over, and I grab her, trying to right her.

She's all soft curves wrapped in that peasant blouse, and her light brown skirt sways gently, a stark contrast to the rigid structure of the party around us. With her dark hair in neat braids, her sable skin looking dewy and perfect, and her flawless cheekbones, she's a freaking knockout.

"Sorry, didn't see you there," I say, steadying Pearl by her shoulders.

Pearl is a waitress at Gem's Diner. She happens to be very close friends with Savannah. Which I suppose is why she's here. And did I happen to mention that she's absolutely stunning?

She makes my withered, frozen husk of a heart constrict in my chest.

"River," she breathes out, a hint of surprise in her voice that suggests she wasn't expecting to be swept up in my orbit today. "This place is crowded enough to lose your own shadow."

"Seems like it," I agree. I take a step back, but I'm not able to peel my gaze away from Pearl's face quite yet. Or the hint of cleavage that she's showing off. I murmur, "You look like you're about to bolt for the nearest exit."

She offers a small laugh, her fingers nervously smoothing down her skirt. "Is it that obvious? I guess these kinds of parties aren't really my scene."

"Join the club." I lift my glass in a mock toast. "But hey, at least we're dressed for the occasion. Your blouse matches the decor to a T."

"Ugh," Pearl rolls her eyes but there's mirth dancing in them. "I swear, Savannah must have sent a memo to the whole town about the dress code."

"It was a thousand percent my mom's doing. She's been on cloud nine ever since Cole and Savannah announced that they were getting married," I reply. "She's been trying to convince them to get married at La Ville Coralle."

"Hah! I think Savannah is nice enough that she would just let Sarah bulldoze her way into planning the entire wedding without her input."

I smirk. "That sounds like my mom's dream come true. I'm glad that someone in the family is going to give her what her grandmotherly heart so desires. The rest of the family is definitely not on the same track and Cole and Savannah."

Her lips twitch. "So, you're not interested in the whole for better or for worse thing?"

I laugh. "Not even vaguely interested. At this rate, even Rex will be married before I go down. And Rex hasn't spent two consecutive nights with the same woman… well, ever."

"Honestly? Same." She wrinkles her nose and sighs. "I should probably try to mingle."

Her reluctance is as clear as the day is long.

"Or," I suggest, leaning in with a conspiratorial whisper. "You could hide out with me. I'm thinking about sneaking out onto the patio with a bottle of whiskey."

"Is that so?" She quirks an eyebrow, amusement flickering across her features. "You know I love whiskey. How would you feel about making that a bottle of cinnamon whiskey?"

"Gross," I say, feeling a smirk tugging at my lips. "Cinnamon whiskey tastes like chugging those little heart-shaped candies. Bleh."

"I can just find somebody else to talk to," she fires back.

"You're awfully quick to leave me! Listen, if cinnamon whiskey is a requirement, I can procure the supplies. I think I saw a bottle behind the bar."

"Oh, it's on." Pearl flashes me a naughty grin.

That grin goes down as smooth as a shot of real, un-cinnamon-flavored whiskey. I could get used to this kind of flirtation between the two of us.

I grin at her. "Who knew dodging forced social interactions could lead to a secret whiskey mission?"

"As Sava says, I'm hearing a lot of talking but I'm not seeing a lot of follow-through. Get your ass in gear." Pearl gestures with a flourish. Together we navigate through the throng of guests, side-stepping the occasional overzealous dancer.

We reach the fully stocked bar, an oasis in a desert of social niceties. In addition to having every wine under the sun, the Cape Winery allows guests to choose from an assortment of varied alcohols. The bottles are lined up in precise lines and the bottle of cinnamon whiskey is very close to the door.

"Looks like we found the treasure," I whisper to Pearl. I wait until the bartender turns away, then filch the bottle I want. But I also make sure to leave fifty dollars in the spot where the bottle was.

"Definitely worth the expedition," she agrees, following me out of the overcrowded bar and onto the patio.

It's the end of March here and still quite crisp outside despite the sun shining down on us. I sweep my jacket off and offer it to her.

We make eye contact. You know, I've never noticed before, but her darkened amber colored eyes are just the color of a very expensive shot of whiskey.

Pearl blushes and accepts the coat, pulling it on. "Thanks."

I open the bottle of cinnamon whiskey, and take a couple of gulps. It burns as it goes down my gullet and I wince. It's so sweet that I'm pretty sure my gut is going to rot out on contact.

I make a disgusted sound. Pearl eyes me but I just raise my hands.

"It was an honest reaction."

"Uh huh," she says. Pearl takes the bottle and sips from it, wiping daintily at her lips when she's done.

"So, Pearl," I say, my tone curious. "How's life treating you?"

She hesitates, taking another sip from the bottle before passing it back. "Actually, things are terrible." Her voice trails off. She glances away, toward the beach in the distance.

"Sounds serious." I take a shot of the whiskey and prod her, nudging her gently with my shoulder. She takes the bottle back but doesn't make any move to drink more just yet.

"My great aunt Delta's land," she finally says. Her whiskey-colored gaze returns to mine and I find it tinged with worry. "The property tax bill came. Land assessors were just out, and they assessed an amount for the property taxes that's astronomical. We could lose everything if we don't figure something out."

"Damn, that's rough." My brow furrows as I process her predicament.

Aunt Delta's estate is one of those intricately woven pieces of the town's tapestry. Located just south of South Shore, it's almost priceless. The land has fifty miles of shoreline and it is in pristine condition. I would be lying if I said the real estate lawyer in me didn't perk up at the mere mention of the land becoming *distressed*.

By distressed, I mean possibly underwater on property taxes.

And Pearl... she doesn't deserve this stress.

"Have you considered any options?" I ask, trying to sound helpful rather than like the vulture I am.

"Not yet. I just don't want to have to sell any of it." She sighs, the fight seemingly draining from her. "I'm at my wit's end, honestly."

I lean back against the linen-covered table, watching the light play across her face, casting shadows that shouldn't be there on such a bright day. A plan begins to form in my mind.

A solution that could solve both our problems.

"Maybe…" I venture, drawing her attention. "I might have a way to help."

"Really?" Surprise lights up her features like the sun breaking through clouds. "What kind of help are we talking about?"

"Let's just say," I pause, the thrill of the gamble running through my veins, "it's a mutually beneficial arrangement."

Her eyes narrow slightly, intrigued and cautious all at once. But behind that caution, I see it.

The spark of hope. That this might just work after all.

The possibility of a deal hangs in the air between us like the heady scent of the vineyard's blooms. Pearl's gaze, now a perfect blend of hope and skepticism, pins me in place.

Until the whirlwind that is Savannah sweeps in, her satin dress fluttering behind her like a superhero's cape. She bangs open the patio door and looks between us with some surprise.

"Oh, there you are!"

Pearl hands me the bottle of whiskey, grinning sheepishly.

"Please don't tell anyone that we decided to sneak off for a tipple. I don't really understand why anyone drinks wine."

"Well, I'm sorry to interrupt," Savannah chirps. She loops an arm through Pearl's. "But I need you to come settle an argument. You don't mind, do you?"

The attention slides to me. I shake my head and raise the bottle at them.

I hate to lose my only friend at this function, but I'm not the type to make a fuss. The bride asks for Pearl, so the bride gets to pull her attention away.

"Of course not," I say. "Pearl is quite popular today."

"Thanks, River," Sav says. "Don't stay out here too long. It's frigging cold!"

Pearl throws me an apologetic look over her shoulder. She starts to take off my jacket, but I shake my head.

"Keep it. It looks better on you."

"You're ridiculous."

I cup my hand to my ear. "What's that? Ridiculously handsome, you said?"

"You're awful. We'll talk later, though?"

Oh, you can bet on that.

Savannah starts pulling her through the patio door.

"Definitely." I flash her a reassuring smile, already plotting how I can turn our potential deal into something concrete.

As Pearl is whisked away inside to the sea of well-dressed guests, a seed of anticipation takes root within me. I straighten my jacket and weave through the crowd, searching for Sam amidst the rich laughter and clinking glasses.

I've been planning to approach my stepdad when the moment was right to talk about buying Pearl's great aunt Delta's property. And time has just become a pressing factor. If another realty company gets wind of the distressed nature of the Brown property first, I might miss out on a land development deal that's a once-in-a-lifetime opportunity.

"River!" Sam greets me with a handshake that feels more like a business transaction than a familial greeting. He looks every inch the tycoon in his tailored suit. His presence is commanding even in this celebratory setting.

"Sam, I have a proposition for you." I lean in, aware of the curious glances from surrounding partygoers. My pulse quickens.

Not from nerves. No, it's the thrill of the chase provided by the game of business.

"Let's hear it," he says, raising an eyebrow.

"The Brown property that's about ten miles south of here. You know the one?"

Sam nods and sips his champagne. "Miss Delta's got a bunch of little bungalows on the beach down there."

"Right. It's prime real estate, especially with the training camp being built just north of the Cape. When the training camp starts boosting the economy, people will start flocking here. There won't be anywhere for them to stay. Except if we get in while we can… and build a resort."

"A resort?" Sam arches a brow. "Are you gambling that you can make South Shore a beach destination?"

"I think if we don't do it, someone else will. We could develop an upscale, exclusive destination. We would be tapping into a market that we build and would be just waiting to be served."

"Interesting," Sam murmurs, though his eyes remain as impenetrable as ever. "It's worth talking about. But Cole's engagement is the focus right now. Everyone loves a good love story."

"True, but business doesn't wait around for love stories to unfold. This opportunity is ripe for the picking."

"Is it now?" Sam's tone is noncommittal, yet I see a flicker of interest that tells me I've planted the seed just where I want it. The challenge now is to make it grow.

"Absolutely." I nod, confident. "I just had a chat with Pearl about the fact that her family is struggling to pay their property taxes. She basically threw up a white flag. The land is teetering on the edge of becoming a distressed property."

Sam scratches his chin. "Does Pearl know you're over here repeating her family news that she probably told you in confidence?"

I feel my neck heat. Sam doesn't pull any punches in telling me that I've misbehaved. It's always been that way, ever since he married my mom and my family moved into his house.

I keep my face perfectly straight. "No, she doesn't know that I'm telling you. But that doesn't mean it's not happening anyway."

"An idea that preys on someone's hardship isn't an opportunity. It's exploitation," he states firmly. His eyes scan mine for a flicker of understanding.

How did Sam get a reputation for being such a shark in business? He's definitely acting like a helpless little guppy right now.

I press my lips into a thin line, keeping my retort at bay.

"I see your point." It's all I can do not to scream in frustration.

"Besides," Sam continues, smoothing out the front of his impeccably tailored suit, "you know how things work around here. I've agreed to help fund the hotel to the tune of a few million dollars. And I did it as an engagement present to Cole and Savannah. They are the ones getting special treatment because they are engaged."

He gestures toward Cole. At the moment, Cole stands beside Savannah, her hand delicately resting on his arm. She smiles at him and he drops a kiss onto her head without interrupting the flow of conversation around them. Both of them are the poster children for pre-marital bliss.

"And his engagement buys five million dollars of investment?" My eyebrow quirks up, the cogs in my mind whirring with possibilities.

"I wish you didn't see it that way, River."

"But in essence, I'm right. Right?"

Sam sighs and starts explaining to me as one would talk to a teenager who has been bad. Like he's trying not to shout at me, though he very much wants to.

"Commitment is valued, River. It shows stability and foresight. It speaks of the good qualities of a man. It says that a man wants to be taken seriously and can be relied upon," Sam explains.

But I see the words for what they are. My stepdad is showing me the mark and asking me to meet it.

I nod slowly, letting the implication settle over me like the evening shadow creeping across the vineyard outside. Commitment, huh?

The word leaves a bitter taste. A binding contract to something or someone… forever. Yet the rewards of matrimony are tempting.

The path to what I want is suddenly pristine and clear as glass.

My gaze shifts back to Pearl. She's animatedly talking to another guest, her hands expressing more than words ever could.

There's a natural elegance about her. A simplicity that's refreshing in a world where everything comes with strings attached.

A dark thought begins to take shape in my mind.

A thought that has shapely legs, a perfect ass, and looks an awful lot like Pearl.

What if I just pretend to be engaged? Sam would never have to know. And Pearl would get money or something out of the bargain. Whatever she wants, I'll give.

In exchange for playing my fiancée for a few months while I get this project off the ground….

"Perhaps I should consider it," I muse aloud. I'm talking half to Sam, and half to myself, while the idea takes root.

"Consider what?" Sam asks, leaning in with renewed interest.

"Nothing important." I deflect with an easy smile, brushing off the question like I would the lint on my sleeve. "I'll just enjoy the party for now."

"Good, man." Sam nods, clapping me on the shoulder before turning to mingle with other guests. He leaves me with a simmering mixture of relief and anticipation bubbling away in my chest.

As I watch Sam disappear into the crowd, the smile fades from my lips.

Engagement as currency. It's a game I hadn't considered playing. But desperation? It's a cunning game master.

And at this moment, I know I'm ready to make a move that could change everything.

~

Intrigued? Snag The Fake Fiancée Proposition right now!

ABOUT VIVIAN WOOD

Vivian likes to write about troubled, deeply flawed alpha males and the fiery, kick-ass women who bring them to their knees.

Vivian's lasting motto in romance is a quote from a favorite song: "Soulmates never die."

Be sure to join her email list to keep up with all the awesome giveaways, author videos, ARC opportunities, and more!

Vivian's Works

Cape Simon Billionaires
Small Town Billionaire Romance
The Grumpy Boss Agreement
The Fake Fiancée Proposition
The Playboy Rival Arrangement

Hush Hush Club
Forbidden Billionaire Romantic Suspense
Such A Good Girl
Such A Bad Girl

Married At Midnight
Forbidden Billionaire Romance
Deal With The Devil
Wed to the Devil
Vow to the Devil

Ruined Castle Trilogy
Forbidden Billionaire Romance
The Single Dad
The Nanny
The Caress

Broken Slipper Trilogy
Forbidden Billionaire Romance
The Patron
The Dancer
The Embrace
Possessive

Dirty Royals
Forbidden Royal Romance
Cruel Heir
Sinful Princess
Pretend Princess

King's Capture Duet
Dark Billionaire Romance
King's Capture
Queen's Sacrifice

Sinfully Rich
Steamy Billionaire Romance
Sinful Fling
Sinful Enemy
Sinful Boss
Sinful Chance

Billionaires Ever After
Steamy Bad Boy Romance
His Best Friend's Little Sister
Claiming Her Innocence
His Fiancé To Keep
His Lovely Virgin

Addiction Duet
Angsty Dark Romance
Addiction
Obsession

Other books
Wild Hearts

For more information....
vivian-wood.com
info@vivian-wood.com